THE LOST VOICES - LIBER 1

COLIN C. MURPHY

CYGNIA
PUBLISHING

FIND OUT MORE...

To discover more about Colin C. Murphy
and his books, and news of forthcoming projects,
visit his website, which you'll find at the end of
The Lost Voices - Liber i.

In memory of the lost voices
of my ancestors.

Pompeii West

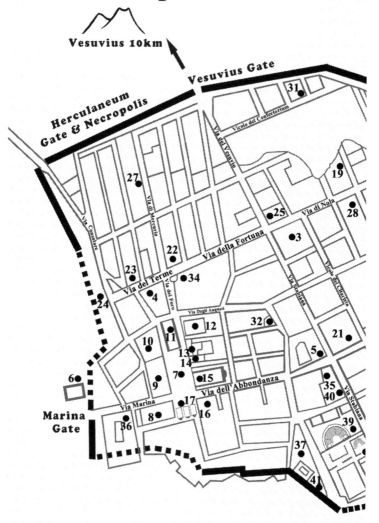

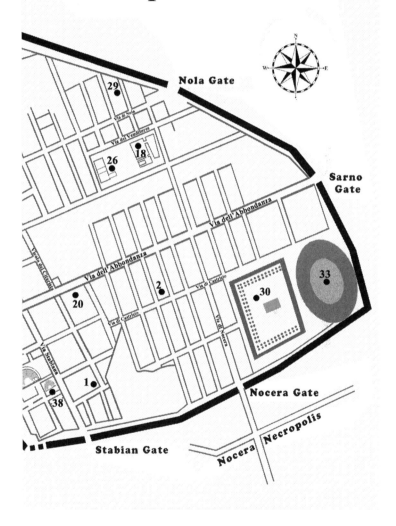

MAP KEY

- 1 Bar of Verecundus
- 2 Bar of Euxinus
- 3 Baths - Central
- 4 Baths - Forum
- 5 Baths - Stabian
- 6 Baths - Suburban
- 7 Forum
- 8 Forum - Basilica
- 9 Forum - Temple of Apollo
- 10 Forum – Granary
- 12 Forum - Macellum (Market)
- 13 Forum - Sanctuary of the City Lares
- 14 Forum - Temple of Vespasian
- 15 Forum - Eumachia Building
- 16 Forum – Comitium (Political Assembly)
- 17 Forum - Municipal Offices
- 18 House and Inn of Cominia
- 19 House of Cosmus & Epidia
- 20 House of the Cryptoporticus

- 21 Home of Epidius Sabinus
- 22 Home of Gnaeus Alleius Maius
- 24 Home of the Golden Bracelet
- 25 Home of Caecilius Jucundus
- 26 Home & Bakery of Publius
- 27 Home of Restitutus
- 28 Home of Tiberius Verus
- 29 Inn of Mariona
- 30 Large Palaestra
- 31 Home of Staphylus & Romula
- 32 Lupanare (Brothel)
- 33 Spectacula (Amphitheatre)
- 34 Temple of Fortuna Augusta
- 35 Temple of Isis
- 36 Temple of Venus
- 37 Temple of Hercules & Minerva
- 38 Theatre (Small) (Odeon)
- 39 Theatre (Large)
- 40 The Gladiator Barracks
- 41 Triangular Forum

PREFACE

All of the characters who feature in this book were real people, from the wealthy politicians to the bakers to the slaves to the prostitutes, although, with a few exceptions, their lives as depicted, relationships, professions etc. are fictional. Gnaeus Alleius Nigidus Maius for example, was a politician, wealthy property owner and sponsor of games and his chief slave was called Primus. Celadus was a champion gladiator, as was Albanus. Urbana and Restituta were prostitutes who worked for a bar owner called Verecundus. Many others are also represented in the roles they actually played in Pompeiian society. But to a large extent, the personalities, lives and loves of all the character are invention. I pray to the ancient gods that I have not done any of them too great a disservice.

All of the graffiti and inscriptions are similarly real and the vast majority are from Pompeii, although I have used a small number from Herculaneum, Rome itself and a few other provincial Roman towns. I have also taken a great deal of licence with the graffiti in that some pre-date the period of this book's story by decades or even longer, although I present them as though all are contemporary to the events described. Most of the graffiti appear exactly as they were written, although in a small number of cases I have used only part of a particular graffito to better suit the narrative. Handwritten graffiti, adverts and notices appear as *italics* and formal inscriptions on monuments, gravestones or objects etc. appear as BLOCK CAPITALS. A list of the locations of each graffito and inscription or its source is provided at the back, along with a glossary of most of the ancient Roman terms used in this book, a brief note on Roman coinage (quadran, as, sesterce, denarius) and a list of the deities referenced.

I have also taken a great deal of licence with Roman naming conventions, which generally had a structure of praenomen (first or personal name, of which there were a very limited number of choices), nomen (clan name) and cognomen (an extra personal name or nickname). Different forms of address were used depending on the situation, e.g. a family member would probably use the praenomen when addressing someone, but the nomen might be used in more formal settings, or a combination of nomen and cognomen, or all three. Some people even had an extra cognomen. The cognomen might also be used in informal situations or when signing documents. Women were generally known by the female version of their father's nomen. Many of these conventions changed over time or were more loosely observed. I have adhered to the convention to some extent, but to avoid confusion (e.g. because of the limited number of praenomen available), I have been selective with the part of the name that I have used to avoid characters' names clashing. I hope purists won't get too worked up about it.

The usual date for the eruption of Vesuvius is 24 August, AD79. This is a much disputed date for many reasons, such as the type of agricultural produce that was found in the shops, which was more typical of October, the warmer clothing that many of the victims were wearing, coins recovered that were minted in September of that year, and the normal prevailing wind direction, which was also more typical of October. For these reasons I have chosen an unspecified day in late October as the date of the eruption. But to be perfectly honest, it doesn't really matter one way or the other, especially to the victims of the eruption.

Streets in Pompeii did not have signs naming them, although the main streets might have been known by the gates to which they led. I have taken the liberty of using the street names that were assigned by modern excavators, principally as a means of giving events and characters a firm location relative to each other. I have also cheated by locating Publius's bakery and Cominia's inn, along with a couple of other homes, in the large part of Pompeii that is as yet unexcavated, and whose treasures – artistic, architectural, cultural, human – and graffiti have yet to be unearthed.

O gentle Ilithyia, who has the power to produce a timely birth, protect the matrons in labour; whether you choose the title of Lucina or Genitalis. O goddess, multiply our offspring.

– Roman prayer in Horace's Epodes 17

PRAEFATIO

I'm almost forgotten now. My name almost unknown.

Only a handful of the teeming billions could speak of me with some small understanding. And even those lack any real insight. They only speak of me, not to me. And to some, I – and my kind – are even objects of humour. The ancient delusion of a naïve race.

Oh, how my star has fallen.

But there was a time my name was spoken with reverence. When men and women cried my name aloud. Clutched at the heavens in supplication. They made sacrifices, of blood even, in the hope that I would stir from my ethereal slumber and grant them a morsel of divine favour, so that the fruit of their sweaty copulations might safely make the journey into sentience and long life.

My name is Lucina, by the way, the goddess who brings the unborn from the darkness of the womb into the light, and then I am, or try to be, their guiding light as they grow to adolescence. Whereupon our ways part, and I surrender their keeping to other gods.

This talk of how things once were has brought many tales

and images of long forgotten souls back to my mind. Because, you know, I felt I was sleeping, buried even, for a long time. Then something awoke me.

Yes, I remember. It was the sound of digging. Men digging. All across the lands where we gods once reigned supreme. But most especially in one place whose rediscovery has excited them greatly.

They dig with immense care, brushing tiny specks of dust away, revealing things of great beauty and value. No, not jewels and gold and priceless arts, although they have found many of these things. I speak of the scratchings of men and women on the walls of that inconsequential, doomed town. All too pithy reminders that this was a place where the hearts of thousands once beat. Where many small lives were lived out. Look at those badly formed words. Brief sentences hurriedly scratched with the tip of a blade. And behind each, a life. A small life, yes, perhaps not worthy of a statue or a verse in a book, yet priceless in its own way. Each tiny message conceals a tale of envy or love or lust or ambition or hope. Look at them...

Celadus the pride of the girls

Marcus loves Spendusa

Actius says a big hello to his mother Cossinia

Can't you hear them speak? In the market. By the temple. Beside the bathhouse. They're everywhere. Listen. Listen to them calling out across time.

I hear every nuance of sound. I can even smell the air, sweet or foul, that swirled about that moment in time. And most of all, I feel the emotion, also sweet or foul, that swelled within the breasts of those long forgotten souls. I can even see inside their little heads. All I have to do is close my eyes. And there they are.

Cominia, Chrestus, Publius, Gnaeus, Urbana, Restitutus and all the others.

Forget your mighty kings and politicians and great artists and men of learning and look down now upon these little beings who seem to be of no consequence to the greater world.

I can take you there, you know? You would like that?

Well, then, come, take my hand. Let us step back into their world and...

Oh wait.

Just as our visit begins, Vulcan must have his fun.

SCAENA 1

AD62

Mortem

Take hold of your slave girl whenever
you want; it's your right! [1]

Look down there. Look down at that little backwater, that inconsequential little hamlet known as Pompeii. A dot on the vast map of the Roman world. It has never produced a person of real note in the span of its existence. None of its politicians have ever even attained the rank of senator. None of its writers have ever produced a work worthy of debate. The murals and frescoes in some its grander homes have all been produced by men from other places. Its architecture has all been copied from elsewhere. And so on. A few notables have kept a holiday villa here, such as Cicero, and it is a popular place to visit if drinking, gambling and whores are to your taste. The area does produce a nice wine, Falernian, though even that is said to leave the drinker with a throbbing head. Oh, there is one slight thing for which this petty little place holds a reputation: garum, a sauce made from rotting fish. Hmmh. Better than nothing, isn't it?

But let us look closer.

Down there. Right below us. You see that man scurrying along the Via Dell'Abbondanza, that's Rufus Junius Caesennius Paetus. See how he weaves a little from side to side? He's been in the tavern of Amaranthus, and before that meeting a man called Aulus Umbricius Scaurus in the basilica, a local maker of garum. He'd been in another tavern near the forum before his meeting, which was not a wise thing to do, as the smart Umbricius Scaurus insists on keeping business and drinking apart. Scaurus whirled away telling Rufus not to waste his time and the poor persecuted wretch sought solace by hastening into another bar before heading back to his lodgings to face his wife. And now look at him, miserable as can be, dreading the thought of listening to her caustic tongue berating him again for his weaknesses, of which he has many.

THE FLOWER OF GARUM, MADE OF THE MACKEREL, A PRODUCT OF SCAURUS, FROM THE SHOP OF SCAURUS [2]

The Roman world is dominated by men, and and all Roman husbands, Rufus included, have complete legal and moral authority over their wives and can beat them with impunity, or even kill them in some circumstances. But the laws recorded on scrolls and the reality are so much different in practice. And Rufus in effect has no more power over his wife than a man has over the shape of the moon.

There she is now, Severina, coming along a side street,

making her way towards the Stabian Baths, layered with clothing against the February wind.

He is fortunate on this occasion, for his wife's face is burrowed so deeply inside her palla that she doesn't notice him as she crosses the street not ten paces from her drunken spouse. But he recognises her. That manner she has of carrying herself, proud and haughty, the deliberate haste of her step.

What a bitch, he thinks, as relieved, he watches her disappear along an alleyway. He's full of bitterness, our Rufus. Hates his wife. Hates this town. Hates his family. Hates his life. What he hates most of all of course, although he hasn't come to admitting this, is himself. But soon, none of that will matter to him.

Now a brightness has appeared in his eyes. He's smiling. Because he guesses his wife is making her way to the baths, as she often does in the afternoon. And she is without her slave, Cygnia, who was the creature that occupied his thoughts as he sat alone in the bar.

With images of Cygnia in his eyes, he doesn't see the young man running towards him, he too blinded by his own, more noble visions, and they collide, Rufus's drunken feet unable to maintain him upright and he crashes to the ground, landing in a mess of filthy water and urine.

The youth, Publius, mutters an embarrassed apology and hurries away.

Rufus gathers himself, cursing, and hurries on until he reaches his lodgings near the Nola Gate. It is an inn run by a fat woman called Mariona. Rufus and Severina haven't managed to buy a house yet, although they've looked at several, but none matched her lofty requirements, much to Rufus' disgust. So they stay at Mariona's lodgings, occupying the entire second floor, six rooms in all. What a waste of money, Rufus thinks each time he climbs the stair. After all there are just the two of them, and the slave girl. My snob of a wife has no sense of thrift, he thinks while neglecting to include the money he has squandered in bars and in playing tali until his pockets were empty.

I'm going to fuck her, he thinks. I'm going to fuck Cygnia. I own her after all. I can do whatever I want with her. And I'll threaten to cut her throat if she breathes a word to Severina.

He opens the door to Cygnia's sleeping chamber. Empty. Rufus has found his lodgings deserted. He curses several times and kicks out at a stool, which crashes against a wall. He stands looking down at her empty cot with its solitary blanket, erotic thoughts filling his mind. He senses an erection below and frowns. It must remain just that: an erection with no place to go.

That noise downstairs is probably Mariona, stomping about with her fat feet. He returns to his own room, which is separate from Severina's, and has been since his fall from grace, washes his face and drinks water from a jug. He curses again that Cygnia is absent, then goes downstairs and follows the sound of Mariona's singing, locating her in the kitchen with her slave, a tall Kushite with skin as black as the night.

– Rufus Junius!

Good fortune to Mariona ₃

The size of her disgusts him. Does the woman ever stop eating? And all of Pompeii must know that she only purchased the Kushite for her own sexual pleasure. It's not like she's ever going to get a proper man to fuck her. He considers all of these things behind the mask of a smile.

– Mariona. Do you know the whereabouts of my wife and her slave?

Mariona is much liked in the town. She has a jolly demeanour and always has a bright smile for everyone. But she is terribly sad much of the time, because her young husband was summoned away to fight in Emperor Claudius' conquest of

Britain almost twenty years ago and he'd never returned. And so she'd taken to eating as a poor means of solace. Yet she never troubled the world with her pain. And she never indulged in sexual relations with her Kushite, called Chrestus, despite what the tittering classes might suppose. People, when they meet her, can't help but like her.

– The mistress has gone to the baths, I believe. And she asked me to prepare some food for her return. She sent Cygnia to the market.

– I see.

Rufus mulls this over. He reaches out an arm to a wall to steady himself, misjudges the distance and almost falls sideways. It is comical, but Mariona spares his blushes by looking down at some vegetables she is chopping, a task she has no need to do, but enjoys nonetheless. The Kushite, busy dissecting a chicken, grins and turns his head away quickly.

– Would you perhaps, like food yourself?

She is thinking that food might sober the drunken lout a little.

– Please. You're most kind.

– Oh, no trouble. I'll serve it in the triclinium if you like. Would you like to recline there while the food is prepared? Chrestus will bring you some water.

– I will. I'm rather tired. But if I could have some wine also to slake my thirst.

Mariona gives him a thin smile. The last thing he needs is wine, she is thinking. What a fool the man is. She nods to Chrestus as Rufus departs for the triclinium and the slave fills a jug of wine then waters it more than necessary. He delivers the wine, but finds Rufus has already fallen asleep on the couch and is snoring heavily. He frowns. Were a man to behave as this one does in his homeland, he would be thrashed and exiled, or worse.

Look at Chrestus. Now there is a man. Whatever African goddess ushered him into the world must have been proud of her day's work. His black skin glistens in the soft light. Muscle strains against the stitching of his tunic. He stands tall and erect, his eyes subtly investigating all they survey. It is nine years now since he enjoyed his freedom and no matter how many moons pass he yearns for the days that he could ride his horse in chase of a boar, make love to his beautiful wife Amina, teach his son to ride and make an arrow strike a small piece of fruit on a tree. Yet he accepts his lot. He knows that he will never see them again. He was taken when his tribe, allied to others, attacked a Roman frontier settlement, not through greed for power or wealth, but as a response to countless brutalities the Romans had been inflicting on them for years. Chrestus, then just a young man of twenty, led his people from the front, his powerful legs bracing him to the horse's sides as his bow unleashed arrow after arrow, felling at least ten of the enemy before his animal was brought down and he was overwhelmed. After their defeat, a Roman centurion had ordered the prisoners to be butchered, but as heads rolled one after the other, Chrestus had been spared the undignified death when the Roman commander intervened. He'd realised that such men would bring a high price on the market and over two hundred of them were spared. And so he'd gone from warrior to being sold as one would a pig.

Still, he accepts that he was defeated by a superior force, and he respects the Romans for that, if little else. And he could have done worse. He could have been sent to the mines or to the daily filth of the fullery or some such awful den. Mariona's purchase of him was a surprise. He was still young then, she a plump, matronly lady. Like others, he suspected there was a sexual motive. But she had never made a single demand of him in this regard. And so he came here, to this house, to live a life of relative comfort. He no longer hunts boar, but accompanies

Mariona to the shops and the market to buy cuts of meat and sacks of flour. He doesn't drink water from a river, but from a fountain that springs from the stone wall outside the house. He carts amphorae of wine about. He cleans the latrine. He plants flowers in the peristyle garden.

Oh such a waste of a man.

But you know, it could be worse. And all things change.

They hear the sound of Rufus awaking and Mariona tells him to bring their guest his meal. On the way to the triclinium, out of sight of the others, Chrestus spits on the food.

SCAENA 2

Beautiful angel ₄

But let us leap forward a little, unless you want to observe Rufus' sloppy eating habits. Yes, let us go and meet Cygnia. There she is, leaving the market that is held on the Palaestra each Friday, clutching a sack containing four lamps, as ordered by Severina, who is always complaining that Mariona's lodging house is as dark as a tomb at night.

Look at the eyes of the men following her progress as she departs, their imaginations alight with the possibilities that lie beneath the curve of the thin stola about her hips. Oh, to own a slave like her, they think. But even if they could afford her, their wives would never allow it of course. Hahaha, did you see the little woman by the olive oil seller's stall, pulling her man's hair as punishment for giving such a lascivious stare? But Cygnia has that effect. Fair hair that hangs about her shoulders. Celtic skin without blemish, but for the birthmark that resulted in her slave name. The soft curve of her cheeks either side of delicate, pink lips and a slim nose. And what eyes. Of a blue that is an image of the summer sky, yet which shyly evade the gaze of others, and conceal a controlled wildness and a sharp mind. And empathy. Yes. There is more to Cygnia than mere flesh. Her beauty runs deeper than that evident to her fellow mortals. What a joy it must have been for some Celtic goddess to guide her from infancy. And see how the men's eyes stray below her face to that figure, breasts firm and full enough to defy any tunic to conceal them completely, her rear a delight of curve and crevice and her legs slim and long, gracing her with an elegant stride. As for the rest... well, that is for her knowledge alone, and perhaps the man who might win her heart. Cygnia is eighteen.

Oh I almost forgot. She bears a second blemish besides her birthmark, this the work of man. There is a stamp about the size of a coin just at the top of her arm where it disappears beneath her tunic. It is a brand, made with a hot iron when she was first captured. It rarely comes into her sight, and yet its presence reminds her each day of her lowly place in the world.

And for all that, she does not flaunt herself? Look at her hurrying along the Via di Porta Nocera, her head repeatedly dropping from the stares, her shoulders curved in a slump as she tries to make herself smaller, so hasty to be gone from this busy, dirty street that she tramps into pools and splashes muddy water against the bare skin of her shins.

– Hey Venus! Take your time!

A brutish man attempts to block her path. He grins to his friend for approval. Cygnia tries to walk around them, but the sidewalk is too narrow. Now he is clutching his crotch obscenely.

– Yeah. Take your time with this!

Both men laugh uproariously as Cygnia pushes past them without having to drop down into the street, which resembles a shallow stream. Yet she has to endure her backside being groped. No real matter. Although Cygnia does not know it, within the hour both of these brutes will be dead and forgotten.

Despite her discomfort at such encounters, Cygnia is actually glad to be out of the lodging house, where she had been a virtual prisoner since her master and mistress had arrived in Pompeii almost a month earlier. She knows she is beautiful, but often curses it. Isn't that hard to fathom? She was given to Severina because she was deemed too much of a distraction for the male slaves in Rufus's father's home in Rome. And how she hates her mistress, who hates her in return. Poor Cygnia believes this is simply because Severina is of a nasty disposition, but I can tell you, being privy to Severina's thoughts, that it is jealousy. She comforts herself that Cygnia is a mere slave, a worthless thing to be bought or sold at the market, her inferior in every way that matters. And yet she cannot shake herself free of her intense jealously of Cygnia's looks and intelligence. And her resentment at the way her husband's eyes follow her about a room.

This part of the town is quieter. Fewer bars and taverns. She is looking up now, craning her head back to stare at the bright blue winter sky. She is smiling at the vastness of it all, wishing she could take off like a bird and soar up and then float to wherever she wished in the wide world. Somewhere she would not be bound by slavery. But the slave Cygnia will never leave this place.

There is the lodging house ahead and trepidation fills her heart again. She hopes she has purchased the correct lamps. Well, it doesn't matter much anyway, she thinks, as Severina will always find a cause to fault them. Her heart fills with gloom at the idea of entering the building again and once more being confined with nothing more than the voice of her mistress berating her endlessly. But at least there is Mariona, where she can find some comfort. The lady took a shine to her from the day they arrived. When the mistress is absent Mariona speaks to her as though an equal, chattering about clothing and her garden and other silly matters. She knows Mariona's heart is heavy, despite her outward lightness. She also likes Chrestus. He treats her with respect and he seems to her to be a man of great pride.

As she exits the vestibulum into the atrium she can hear shallow voices from the back of the house. She turns and up the stair she goes. She shivers, glad to be in out of the cold. There seems to be no one about. She is unpacking the lamps now, each one in the shape of a reclining Venus, placing them neatly on a small table in her mistress's room. She fills each of them carefully with olive oil, not spilling a drop. This miniscule task complete, she is unsure what other work she should do. She exits the room and goes to her own tiny sleeping chamber. And there she sits and waits.

SCAENA 3

I am furious! 4a

But where have I taken you now? What is this bustling street? It is the Via Dell Abbondanza, the busiest thoroughfare in town. And there, see. Severina returns cleansed from the baths. Yet she could not wash away the grit that clogs her thoughts. Cygnia is among those things that occupy her. She must stop beating the girl, she thinks. But she does not consider this through any newly found compassion. The beatings leave marks and marks may devalue her greatly. She would fetch a fine price at the slave market, and one such auction is to be held at the Hall of Eumachia in a week. She is pretty, thinks Severina grudgingly, and a virgin, and would be keenly sought by one of the rich old bastards who have retired to this town. With the money she would fetch, Severina could purchase two, perhaps three slaves. An older woman as her maidservant and a male to replace her husband's manservant, who had run off during the night as they'd journeyed to this cursed place from Rome.

Rome. She recalls it with a curious mixture of loss and loathing. Her happy memories of her strutting about with the other ladies of her class amid the clothing and jewellery shops, or wasting away afternoons as she entertained them, sipping wine and nibbling grapes and biscuits under a warm sun in the peristyle, while repeatedly dropping boastful crumbs from her lips about her husband's great success and the honeyed life that lay ahead for her, and her many children, when they came along.

But where is it all now?

When she landed Rufus Caesennius Paetus, second son of Lucius Junius Caesennius Paetus, an extremely wealthy and rising politician at the time, three years ago, all her dreams of a life of idle wealth seemed set to follow. But then that weak, dim-witted husband of hers had to go and fuck it all up. After his father had served as Consul Ordinarius, he'd been granted the governorship of Cappodacia in the east, where Rome was engaged in a war with the Parthians. Rufus was sent to serve at his father's side and when out on patrol one afternoon, the centuriae he commanded had been attacked by a couple of hundred Parthians. In the midst of the skirmish, which the Romans easily won, Rufus had fled and hidden behind a boulder, only emerging when he knew that victory was secured. He was branded a coward, a crime that would warrant being clubbed to death for most soldiers, and sent back to Rome where his father hired an expensive lawyer to defend him against the allegations, and the man was skilled enough to clear Rufus's name. But Severina had watched the proceedings and seen the officers of his century testify to his bravery in battle. But she could see in their eyes that they despised the man whose name they defended, that comrades of theirs had fallen while he cowered behind a rock, and only promises of well-filled money sacks had bought their tongues. Everyone else could see it as well. Her husband became the butt of jokes. Rufus Lepus, they called him behind his back. Rufus the Rabbit. For he burrowed under rocks to hide from his enemy. Having assigned him a suitable animal sobriquet, hers inevitably followed. She soon learned that among the fine ladies she had once named as friends she was known as Severina Parvulas Mus. The Little Mouse.

Worse follows. Rufus's father knew the truth all too well. And while his legal rescue of his son had also saved a great deal of the family honour, he would have nothing more to do with him. He banished Rufus from Rome for as long as he, the father, was alive, and ordered him not to settle anywhere within one hundred leagues from the city boundary. Pompeii was just ten leagues outside that limit and the nearest thing they could find to civilisation.

She couldn't divorce him? Her family had no real wealth to speak of, and to remain in Rome, even as a divorcee, would have been too humiliating. So she had gone with him. His father had given him a sum of money, enough to make a start, no more, and a solitary slave each, one of whom absconded because Rufus had forgotten to shackle him at night. What a fool. And it seemed her husband didn't even have seed enough to provide her with a child.

Jupiter help him if he's not spoken to that garum-maker, Umbricius Scaurus, she is thinking. She has heard mention of him in several quarters, a bright star in the garum trade. And while businessmen, no matter how rich, were beneath her social strata, they desperately needed to secure a future source of wealth, so that one day they could return to Rome in style. This is her plan.

These three, Rufus, Cygnia and Severina have all converged now on the Lodging House of Mariona and her slave Chrestus. Follow me inside and watch what happens next.

SCAENA 4

Gods give me safety from the tormentor ₅

The light from the tiny window high above her head is fading now as the afternoon moves along, and her room grows darker still when the figure appears in her open doorway. She jumps to her feet at the sight of Rufus.

– Dominus. Did you require me?

– Yes I require you.

He slurs this. Says it with a nasty grin. Rufus is a man of many weaknesses. No self-control, poor fool. It is why his fear overcame him in Parthia, why he succumbed to the temptation to drink his nerves away before meeting Umbricius Scaurus earlier, and it is why, despite the warnings he has received from his wife, including threats of castration, that he has decided to rape his slave.

His desire blinds him to his wife's threats. And this is so easy to justify. Severina has denied him her bed and her body for months. He is a man of flesh and blood. He has needs. Why should he waste money on whores when he has a ready-made whore in his home? And besides all that, compared to Cygnia, he thinks that Severina has the face of a pig and the body of an old hag.

– Remove your tunic.

Cygnia blurts a response. – Dominus...but the Domina...

The poor girl. She cannot refuse an order from her master. Yet she knows that her mistress will be enraged beyond measure, and not just with her husband.

– That bitch. Don't mention her to me. Do as I say!

His voice is raised. His breaths shallow. His eyes empty.

Cygnia is backing up against the wall, terrified. He grasps out at her tunic, seizing her shoulder and ripping. Cygnia is torn between resisting – in which case he will beat her into submission – and submitting – in which case Severina will beat her. She offers token resistance as her mind searches for an escape. Her breasts are bared now and he is groping them and slobbering at her face. He disgusts her. The smells of wine and digesting food pour from his open mouth. She feels tears stream from her eyes. His hand drops to her crotch.

Oh I apologise for taking you here. Turn away if you wish.

But now look again. The drama moves to its second act and a new player enters.

– You bastard! Let her go!

Rufus feels a tremendous weight against his back and fingers digging into his shoulder blades. The bulge of his erection beneath his tunic is already shrivelling as he turns to face his attacker. The control, the sense of power is also abandoning him with equal rapidity. But it is being replaced with rage and not fear. For he knows that voice, and it is not his wife's.

– Get off me you fat bitch, he roars.

Mariona ignores the insult and throws him against the wall. Cygnia scurries to her bed and tries to cover herself. Rufus lashes out and his fist connects with the side of the landlady's head. She staggers backwards through the door into the narrow corridor. Rufus too is startled almost to sobriety. He glances at the girl on the bed and then turns his burning eyes on the woman.

He screams. – How dare you! She's my property and I can do what I like with her. She's a fucking slave!

– What sort of a Roman are you? You act like an animal! My Marcus would have taken a whip to you! Mariona responds.

Her very honourable and abstemious lost love is never far from her thoughts.

– Who the fuck is Marcus you fat old whore?

Newly enraged he lunges at the woman, coming through the door and reaching for her throat. She turns towards the stairs and is relieved to see the towering bulk of Chrestus appear before her.

He pushes his body in front of his domina and stands fully erect. His beautiful face is a picture of defiance, pride and honour. He could be put to the sword for striking a Roman citizen, and yet that is just what he does, planting a fist into Rufus's face, and them man collapses in a heap. He rubs his jaw and struggles to stand up, using the wall for support. He stares up at the Kushite, the control he felt earlier has drained from him like water from a shattered jug. Once again he is Rufus Lepus, cowering in fear behind a rock.

'You're fucking dead, slave, he says. They'll hack you into little bits before you die. Your head will on a spike this time tomorr...

– What is this? What's going on here?

Ah the lovely Severina has joined us. Rufus is saved. But leaps from the boiling pot into the fire beneath. His situation is little improved, he thinks. Maybe even worsened.

Mariona gives a brief run through of events, but is surprised by Severina's response. I give her some credit. She holds her expression of calm with skill.

– Remove yourself from our lodgings, for which we have paid. What passes up here is none of your business.

Mariona is left speechless. She casts a sympathetic glance along the corridor towards Cygnia's room, but the girl is not to be seen. Then she beckons to Chrestus and they depart.

Now her face changes. A man might think her suddenly possessed by a demon of the underworld. – Get out of my sight you infernal maggot.

She whispers this. There is no need to raise her voice as every word drips with loathing. Rufus considers a response. An excuse perhaps. A denial. An effort at boldness. But his consideration of all these things takes no longer than a solitary second. Then he turns away and removes himself to his sleeping quarters further along the corridor.

She stands there for a few moments. She looks up to the ceiling, imploring the gods to grant her some respite. Her head drops and her gaze turns to the open door of her own chamber. Within, she can see the four lamps she ordered Cygnia to purchase. All neatly lined up on a little table in the centre of the room. She walks in, picks one up and examines it. It is precisely what she wanted. The reclining Venus, the hole at the top of her head from where the flame would spout, the larger hole at her navel for pouring in the oil. She flings the lamp across the room at the wall where it shatters in an unseemly mess. The others follow. She looks about, grasps a stick she keeps and stomps from the room. Behind her, a hundred tiny rivulets of olive oil stream towards the floor.

– No Domina, please! I did nothing wrong!

– You stupid whore! Those lamps are useless! You're good for nothing!

There is no need to watch this scene. But hear it, we must. Besides, it will be brief. Severina's earlier resolution not to beat Cygnia, lest she lower her value, is forgotten. The girl's screams are piercing as the first of the blows land. Cygnia attempts to escape, but there is nowhere she can run, she knows, where Severina will not find her. But yet she runs on some instinct. One sent by the gods perhaps? By a particular goddess even? Perhaps. All you need to observe is Cygnia running along the corridor towards the stair. And here comes Severina behind her, one thought on her mind: To beat the girl to within an inch of her life.

She is not to know it, but at that instant she is within an inch of her own life. Or death, I should say. And she is drawing closer and closer.

Listen. That low rumbling noise. What is that? It grows louder with each heartbeat. The floor shifts beneath their feet and for a moment Severina seems to mimic her husband's earlier drunken state. Both women are thrown to one side against the wall. A look of terror is passing over Severina's face. Cygnia's too. She looks over her shoulder at her mistress.

And from somewhere beneath them, or from beyond the walls, a scream is heard.

But I'm going to take you to another place now. Yes, I know you wish to see how events unfold here, in this lodging house. But the lives of others concern us too. Do not fret. I will carry you back to this place and to his moment in time. But for now, we must look back almost to the start of our tale. I can do that you know? Flit across time at a whim. It is a useful gift to possess.

You do recall, do you not, Rufus's earlier, brief encounter with a young man in the street, when he'd been knocked off his feet? That young man was Publius. Let us return to that moment. Come with me.

SCAENA 5

*Pyrrhus to his colleague Chius I grieve because
I hear you have died, and so farewell* ₆

Chius Caelius Bassus is dead. But at sixteen, Publius Comicius Restitutus cares little of such things. Death is the business of a far away future, one indeed that seems so far away, it might never come. This is what he is thinking. Did you not deceive yourself so at sixteen? Publius feels he possesses the potential to knead the world around him into the shape he desires. His strong bones, supple muscle, pounding heart and sharp mind grant the belief that anything is possible. Do you remember that illusion? Oh never mind.

One thing that our Publius does know with some certainty is that this Chius Caelius had a lot of friends, for they almost entirely block the narrow street that leads to the Via Stabiae, to which he wishes to proceed with some urgency.

He hears a wail pitched high above all the other sniffles and murmurs of grief and he negotiates a tight path though the crowd to catch a better view, fetid water, inch deep, tickling the soles of his feet as he moves towards the centre of the street. Let us linger here a moment by Publius's side, it might be interesting.

Up ahead the funerary procession awaits, led by six or so women dressed in dark, hooded robes, each of whom claw at their own breast. Hear how their shrill voices beseech the gods for relief from the torment of their grief? They suffer no real grief, of course, as they are professional mourners. Those people coming behind them with the curving brass horns slung across their shoulders are the cornu players, playing the death march. The four torch-bearers behind these seem a particularly unnecessary extravagance, considering it is daylight. It is as though the scale of one's funeral is a reflection of one's importance in life. As if it is of matter now. As if the gods cared. Ah you should see some of the departing shows that the very wealthy put on. We gather as gods and watch these together, you know, howling with laughter.

Now here at least comes some genuine grief. The pallbearers emerge through the narrow door and there is the unfortunate Chius, all done up in his best toga, a coin fixed steadily upon his lips as payment for Charon to ferry him to the world of the dead. Publius is thinking two things; what clever contrivance prevents the coin from falling; and those poor slaves carrying the body, for Chius in life had been a gentleman of great girth. One of the slaves at the front weeps openly as he turns into the street, and Publius is wondering whether from the pain of supporting his master's body or at the possibility of being sold to some brutal master, or through love.

He feels frustration now at his lack of progress. He will have to find another route. Go back the way he came. He curses Chius Caelius Bassus silently for in an hour he will be but a few handfuls of dust residing in a metal urn outside the town walls. Whereas he, Publius Comicius Restitutus, has important matters of the living to attend to. He has an appointment at the theatre that, he believes, will chart the course of his own life. If he is to die at some infinitely distant time, he thinks, nobody will pay mourners to chant his name. The whole world will chant it in genuine loss. Oh the dreams of youth.

But stall your flight, young Publius, and learn a little. The theatre is not going anywhere. Well, at least not for a little while.

About to leave, he pauses as a black-robed woman whom he rightly guesses to be the wife of Chius, emerges from the doorway, three younger women clutching at her arms as they seek to offer support. She is perhaps fifty or even sixty; it was difficult for him to tell such are the contortions grief has wrought on her features, and her cries are markedly different from those of the professionals, in that they seem to him to come from some dark well deep in her being. The younger women too, most likely her daughters, are gripped in a feverish grief, tears blinding their eyes as they step into the street, heads shaking slowly from side to side in denial of the reality of their father's passing. They are followed by about ten men – the extended family, bearing wax masks held aloft on sticks in front of their faces; the images of ancestors who had already made the journey to the afterlife.

All might take comfort from the manner and timing of Chius' passing, which happened as he slept. There are many worse ways to go.

Publius is troubled now by his earlier cynicism. How casually he has dismissed Chius' passing as a mere inconvenience to him. He turns to a middle-aged man at his shoulder.

– Who was Chius Caelius?

The man appears momentarily puzzled.

– Who was he?

Publius nods. The man stares away at nothing for a few moments then returns a doleful gaze back to the proceedings.

– He was just a kind man. That's all. At least he was to me.

Publius stands unmoving for a moment then bows his head

towards the departing procession. As the crowd begin to walk slowly after the train of masked relations he finds himself almost alone in the street, a vague sadness having clouded the excited purpose of earlier.

He heaves a sigh and turns on his heels, trotting back the way he's come, then dodging down narrow streets and through laneways behind shops and houses until finally he emerges into the Via Stabiae. Far back to the north end of the street he can see the tail-end of the funeral procession crossing and disappearing towards the north eastern side of town, bound for the necropolis outside the Porta Ercolano, or Herculanean Gate. Beyond them on the horizon he can see the snow-capped Vesuvius, and a chill February wind whistles down from its slopes, slicing through his tunic, making him turn away and hasten his step even more. He collides with a semi-drunken man outside a thermopolium, and is rewarded for his clumsiness with a collection of epithets that seem to pursue him along the Via Stabiae for fifty paces. That was Rufus, you'll recall. And we already know much of what the day holds in store for him.

The street is hectic on this day when the townspeople prepare to celebrate a sacrifice in honour of the town's guardian spirits. But I must restrain myself from commenting on the irony of that. An approaching crowd of men bearing urns of wine force him to take three quick hops across the raised stepping stones, which this time of year often just stay clear of the stream of rainwater, replete with human and animal waste and the general detritus that is discarded each day. The theatre is in sight above the rooftops now and he grins. He ducks from the bustle of the street into the welcoming calm of a narrow laneway. Here Publius pauses to catch his breath.

The colourful frescoes on either wall draw him along the lane, haunting his eyes with their depictions of theatrical scenes that had been played out to weeping and laughter and cheers almost since antiquity, or so he'd been told by his tutor, Mulus Antonius. The fact that the original theatre had been built in the time of the first Punic War is a source of awe to him. Mortals do love old things, though, do they not? They offer reassurance of some level of continuance, even to young Publius, whom, as I said, believes he might live forever.

He moves along and past the entrance to the smaller Theatre of Apollo from where he can hear male voices raised in song. The airs accompany him, echoing along the narrow alley and then through an open doorway into the dark, vaulted passage that cuts under the tiered seating of the town's main theatre. He emerges into the bright light and blinks, and when his eyes have settled themselves, they are filled with the spectacle of the magnificent scaenae frons, towering above the stage to his left. He has been here many times, of course. But then the place was filled with chattering hordes and he was just a dot lost among them, high above the stage and far back among the common people. Look at his face – it is a strange mix of reverence and fear. As he climbs up on to the stage his eyes never leave the columns of stone that support the balconies where appear many of the performers. He is intimidated and suddenly unsure of himself. How might one so young as he hope to ever write a play worthy of such a place? But he has come this far. He turns at the sound of voices. But it is just a few workmen high above at the rear of the theatre, hammering at something. He stands there a moment, in the centre of the empty stage and gazes out at the thousands of spectators he imagines are staring back at him. He has quite an imagination, this one, and his dream is filled with amusing detail. The crowd rise as one to hail the greatest play-wright in the Roman world. The young Nero himself has come to Pompeii specially to applaud the work of Publicius Comicius Restitutus. The Emperor rises from a throne set up in the orchestra, his hands clapping enthusiastically, a hearty smile stretched across his face. Pretty girls hurry to the front and toss up bouquets of flowers that rain down about Publius's feet. The roar of the crowd is thunderous, deafening –

A voice snaps behind him. – Who are you?

The Emperor, the crowd, the pretty girls, the flowers, all disappear. Publius swings about in fright. The man coming through the central stage entrance is dressed in a long tunic of lurid green.

– Publius Comicius Restitutus, sir.

– I don't care what your name is. What are you doing up here?

His voice trembles. – I'm here...I'm here to see the director. I have an appointment.

– Who do you think you are? Pylades? In future enter through the side gate to the back of the stage.

– Yes sir, I'm sorry.

The man makes a face of distaste then ushers Publius through to the rear, where a few groups of men and women are gathered, some dressed in costume, some strutting about reading from scrolls, others tending to the hair and make-up of performers. There was a time when this place would have been devoid of women, or certainly of female actors. It was forbidden to a woman to act in any of the classics, as it was believed that their inferior nature made them incapable of grasping the meaning of the roles. Although they were eventually allowed to perform non-speaking roles. Tch. Women do however perform in mimes, which are among the most popular plays with Roman audiences. And you might be shocked to hear that when the mime was of a bawdy, comic nature, sex might even be performed live on stage, which might prove problematic were all the actors men. But I digress.

Look. Publius walks among them as though a man landed on an island populated by people with several heads. It is so removed from the daily tedium of this small town, or anywhere else for that matter.

– Saenecio. This boy says he has an appointment with you.

The man says this in a mocking tone, pitching high the word 'appointment'.

The tall, bearded man is Saenecio Fortunatus. He cuts an imposing figure, especially to Publius, who is a full hand shorter. But Saenecio also possesses charisma. He has bright green eyes shaded by bushy brows and his crown of black hair seems wind-blown, although there is not a gust of wind in here. He wears a full-length white robe, which swishes against the stone floor as he turns. He tilts his chin high and looks down at the youth along the length of his nose. Publius is not to know this, but it is an image that Saenecio has worked hard to manufacture over the thirty-eight years of his life. Strip him bare and you will find a lonely, wifeless, self-doubting individual. Still, he is not the worst, Saenecio.

Mulus taught his pupils here ₇

– And who are you?

Publius repeats his name in full.

– Ah …yes. Mulus Antoninus mentioned you. Says you're very bright. Are you bright, Publius Comicius Restitutus?

– I don't know, I suppose…

– One thing you'll have to learn about the theatre, young Publius, is that modesty does not become us. You must proclaim your greatness to the world. Shout it! Yell it from the rooftops! Scream it from the mountains….

He becomes theatrical as he says this, lifting his voice and sweeping his arm in a wide arc towards the sky. Publius is taken aback and stares at Saenecio open-mouthed. Then the man glances about at the actors and stagehands, who after a moment's pause, explode with laughter.

Poor Publius doesn't know if he is being mocked or not. He has gone a little red, as you can see. Saenecio chuckles briefly to himself.

– I trust Mulus, young man. If he says you are bright, you are bright. And he showed me some of your scribblings. Of course, if I did agree to hire you...

Saenecio stops himself, noticing that Publius's face has dropped. He realises that he has offended the youth.

– Oh don't mind me. I've called far greater writers than you 'scribblers'. Now, as I was saying. If I hire you, it will be as a stagehand. No, I lie. It will be as a stagehand's assistant. You will spend most of your time fetching water, carrying messages, arranging wardrobes.

Saenecio is guiding Publius about the area, pointing at this and that. Some of the others spare them a glance, most ignore them.

– You will spend a great deal of your time fetching food from the thermopolium down the street. And when you're not doing that, you'll probably be cleaning the latrines. That Fabia leaves them in a terrible state.

Saenecio says this as he passes a short woman who is being fitted for a pleated blue dress studded with countless silver buttons by a slave girl. The woman turns to the director and makes a good-humoured snarl, allowing the shoulder of the dress to fall loosely down. Publius's eyes are instinctively drawn to the bare skin of her shoulder. The woman spots this, reaches up and pulls at the fabric, baring a breast for a moment. Publius gapes, and the woman, slave and the others around chuckle.

– Ignore them, lad, Saenecio says, leading him away. – Actors. Tch. No wonder they are seen as no better than whores. Come out here.

They have emerged through one of the smaller entrances in the scaenae frons and Publius finds himself back on the empty stage.

– Do you understand what I have told you? There is no glamour in the position you seek. But I can promise you that you will learn everything there is to know about the art of theatre.

– I understand, sir. I knew that. Mulus explained it to me. I don't care. I'll do anything you require of me. But this is what I want. Well, to write plays of my own is what I want. To have them performed. But he says I need to learn about their craft and how the actors interpret them and how they are staged before…

– Slow down, young man. Do you know how little money you would be paid? The terrible hours you'd have to work? When others are finishing their work, you'd be just starting. And you would have to work on holidays, when everyone else is celebrating and drunk and all your friends are out chasing girls. Are you sure you're prepared to make those sacrifices?

– I am, sir. And more.

Saenecio is looking into Publius's face. He sees there a reflection of himself over two decades ago. The boy has the will, certainly. And indeed, he may have the talent also.

Publius's voice interrupts his thoughts. – Sir, what play are they performing? Publius nods back towards the changing area.

– Oh, nothing. Just a pantomime. The Slave Girl's Ghost.

– Oh, I don't know that one.

– Tch. Piece of rubbish. Written for the masses. Jokes, fucking, more jokes, more fucking. It is rare I get to stage anything of worth these days. It's the only way I can meet the expense. That sort of trash is the only thing that will put enough arses on those seats out there. And who inspires you, young Publius?

– I've always liked Platus. And Terentius especially. And the writings of Lucius Seneca of course.

Saenecio' substantial eyebrows lift. – Hm. I must warn Seneca he has a fan, and perhaps even a rival, the next time I see him. Well, young Publius. You seem adequate to the task. You may start tomorrow. Be here by the sixth hour.

Look at Publius's expression. Such is the joy contained behind his face it resembles a wine skin filled to bursting.

– Thank you, sir. I'll be…

But Saenecio has already whirled away, clapping his hands with authority as he strides back behind the stage shouting. – Right. Full dress rehearsal. Let's get a move on, you pack of illiterate whores!

As he listens to the good-humoured groans emanating from the dressing area, a small rain of dust descends upon Publius's head. He looks up at the stone columns and balconies that form the scaenae frons. A second larger shower of dust descends and he has to cover his eyes. He dismisses it as the result of a gust of wind, then hears the clink of metal, and when he looks down there is a small coin near his feet, which he picks up and dusts off. It is very old, at least to him, a sesterce minted to celebrate Julius Caesar's victory over Vercingetorix over a century beforehand, which he'd learned about in his history lessons. He looks up but there is nobody on the structure.

The coin was dropped by a bricklayer when the theatre was being built and has lain undisturbed until this moment. Until something disturbed it.

Publius takes it as a good sign, of his job in the theatre and of his destiny as to be a writer. The coin does commemorate success after all, if you were Caesar, that is. And not the Gaul…

Before he knows it he is almost back to his home on the Via Livia. All the way his head bubbled with joyous thoughts of the career he was about to commence. Such is his excitement he must restrain himself on occasion from skipping along like a small girl.

That's his home there. The one with the bread shop at the front. That short, fat man selling the last of the loaves is Epaphroditus. It's almost closing time and he's anxious to be away to his new wife, Thalia. He's recently a freedman who is now employed by Publius's father, who runs this bakery. Publius senior used to be a soldier, long ago. Saved the life of a Legatus Legionis, no less.

– Evening Epaphroditus.

– Young Dominus. You look happy with yourself.

Publius only replies with a grin. He enters the dark vestibulum and his mood is dampened a little. He is unsure how his father will take his news. Yes there had been discussions about his future, but all had been inconclusive. Never has he brought up the possibility of the theatre. Now he sees the folly of that. He takes a deep breath and opens the door to his father's tablinum, but it is empty. A handful of papers lie scattered on the table. His father is a disorderly man. It is a wonder, Publius sometimes thinks, how he manages to run a business, small though it may be.

He continues along the narrow corridor towards the peri-style and triclinium. Their home is modest by the standards of the wealthy. There is no fancy atrium. There is little adornment to the walls, no wondrous vistas of frolicking gods or elysian landscapes, merely a few birds and flowers painted on dull red walls. Their peristyle and garden, which you can see directly ahead, has just a single colonnade along one side and features little attempt at ornamentation, except for a few flowers in pots in the summer. Almost all the space is given over to growing cabbages, turnips, onions, garlic and the like. Although at this time of year it is a dreary, muddy patch enlivened only by a few splashes of green. He passes an open door to the kitchen on the left, where Vivia, their middle-aged house slave is at work cleaning pots, her back to him. She's a Celt, part of the reward his father was granted when his military service had ended. She was over forty two decades ago. Still, beggars couldn't be choosers. They have another slave, a man called Servulus, but we'll get to him.

Servulus was here ₉

On the right is the closed door of the triclinium, and he can hear voices from within. Look how nervous he has suddenly become! His hand rests on the handle, but he doesn't press it open. He takes a very deep breath. He has adopted his most resolute face. He closes his eyes, opens them a moment later and enters.

The family are gathered around a table. There are no elegant couches. Publius senior has no illusions that he is one of the Roman elite, who choose to dine while reclining. He'd gotten rid of the original couches the day he'd leased the house from the businessman Lucius Caecilius Jucundus. A decade in the army had hardened Publius senior's backside – along with his attitude to such excesses. When you ate on campaign, the best seating arrangement you might hope for was a rock by the side of the road.

Everyone turns and looks.

Let me introduce Publius's family to you.

Prima, the mistress (*of this house*) ₁₀

The dark-haired woman on the left is his mother, Prima. She's almost forty now, although still attractive. She used to be quite the Venus, and her husband was proud to receive the envious looks of others when he ventured out with her. At the far end of the table is

Publius, the paterfamilias. He was never a physically attractive man, his face angular, with a pointed chin, prominent ears, not to mention a cheek scarred from battle. He's short also, but his shoulders are still broad. He works hard, and he likes to consider himself an honourable man. But he did something many years before which tainted that honour badly and he's been trying to suppress the guilt of it ever since, or to find a suitable penance. The two children facing us are Cornelia Quieta, she's eleven and quite a chubby child, as you can see. Unfortunately she inherited her father's looks. Yet she possesses a lovable bubbliness, a disarming directness and a good heart. The brown-haired boy is Restitutus. He's twelve and adores his father, and has listened with attentive ears to the man's tales of battles in far-off places. He dreams of killing barbarians by the dozen and joining the Iuvenalia army corps later in the year. He and his brother look more like their mother, don't you think? But they're very different creatures.

– Publius! Where have you been? You're dinner's nearly cold, his mother scolds.

– It's pork stew, says Cornelia with a grin.

– But why does Vivia always put in onions?

Restitutus hates onions.

His father chips in. – Leave him alone, Prima. You can't expect a young man of his age to be running home on time to his mother every day. I'm sure he had business to attend to.

Cornelia giggles. – What's your business's name? Poppaea or Marcia?

Publius playfully smacks his sister's head. – Shut up you little squirt.

His mother eyes him suspiciously as he fills his bowl from the serving dish in the centre of the table and tears off a piece of bread. He catches her look and shakes his head.

– I wasn't with a girl.

Publius senior looks at him. – Maybe it's time you were. You've your head in books or in the clouds half the time. You should be spending your free time doing the things other lads your age are doing.

– Father. Can you help me with my shooting later? They're having an archery contest in three day...

– No he can't, Restitutus.

– But why, Mother?

– Because you were beaten again by your tutor today, were you not? You've been neglecting your studies. There's too much playing at soldiers going on. You'll learn that Greek passage after dinner or I'll beat you myself.

– But Mother, it's a waste of time.

Cornelia giggles again. – Yes, we don't even know any Greeks.

Her mother scolds. – You be careful, young woman.

– Leave Restitutus be, Prima. Anyway, maybe the boy is right. What good is Greek to...

Prima fixes him with a rigid stare and he lowers his eyes and falls silent. When the notion takes her, she can command him as easily as a centurion can a legionnaire.

Have you been watching Publius while this little family squabble continued? He has his head down, his nose almost lost in the bowl of stew. He is trying desperately to contrive a way to raise the matter of his new job. But he looks up now at the sudden silence. He knows something has passed between his mother and father, something beyond a mere marital tiff, but he can't identify what it is. He's seen it before between them. It seems to leave the room colder.

– Where were you anyway, Publius?

He meets his mother's eye. Then he turns and meets his father's.

– I've been to the theatre. I've been given a job there. I start tomorrow.

He has blurted it out almost without knowing.

His father drops his spoon into his bowl.

– What job?

– Assistant stagehand.

– Assistant stage....

That's all his father manages. The others are staring at Publius, who picks up a cup and drinks some water, trying to appear nonchalant.

– How did this come about, Publius?

His mother's tone is a little surprised, but not rebuking.

– Mulus mentioned me to the theatre director. He said that if I want to be a playwright I'll have to learn all there is to know about the theatre. And the best way to do that is...

– Is to be a fucking assistant stagehand?

His father's voice is suddenly loud and angry.

– Publius. Don't use your army tongue in my home!

– Never mind that, woman. Do you mean to say that I've spent a fortune having you educated so that you can become a theatre shithouse cleaner? Well, you can forget it. You can go back tomorrow and tell them you're forbidden to take the job. By Jupiter, I'll not have you spending your life cavorting with people no better than thieves and prostitutes! Especially after all the money I...

Publius blurts, his own anger rising. – Yes, we know, after all the money you spent.

– How dare speak to me like that, boy!

Publius senior stands now, his arm readied to strike his son. But he restrains himself.

– Publius! If you'd calm down we might hear more of this.

Prima shouts at her husband, and everyone falls silent for a time. His father throws himself back into his seat. If he were a pot, steam would issue from his head. Cornelia and Restitutus cower in their chairs, not knowing where to fix their eyes.

– Publius, why didn't you discuss this with us?

– Because he knew I'd forbid it.

– I'm sorry, Mother. I thought you'd be pleased. You know I've always wanted to write plays and poetry.

Publius senior snorts. – Tch. What sort of a living is that for a man?

Publius is indignant. – Annaeus Seneca is advisor to the Emperor himself!

– *Ohhhh.* Excuse me. You've a job with the Emperor in Rome. And I thought you were going to be a latrine cleaner at the theatre.

– Publius, your sarcasm isn't helping.

His father's face suddenly becomes conciliatory. He leans across the table towards his son.

– Publius. I'm glad you got your schooling. And Cornelia and Restitutus too. And it was what your mother wanted. And I didn't expect you to work as a baker either. But I thought you'd go into business. Or become an advocate. Or an architect. Something you can earn a living from. I mean, if I died, who's going to provide for our family?

– You're not going to die. You're as healthy as an ox.

His father slams his fist down on the table with such force that all the crockery leaps and the others jump in unison.

– That's not the point! It doesn't matter anyway, because you're not working in the theatre.

It is Publius's turn to stand. – You can't stop me! I'm sixteen! It's my life and...

There is a loud crash. In the kitchen, a cascade of pots and crockery has rained down on Vivia. She screams.

The table is trembling. Publius senior grasps it as though to steady it. But finds his arms are trembling in harmony. The surface of the wine in his cup ripples as though a wind is passing over it. He feels a shuddering beneath his feet that journeys up his limbs. And now the legs of his chair are shimmying across the floor.

Restitutus screams. – Father, what is it?

– Everyone out to the garden!

Cornelia is screaming now as she rises. The serving dish has danced to the edge of the table. Publius instinctively catches it as it falls, then realises the futility of what he has done and drops it.

– Quickly!

They are scrambling over the chairs towards the open doorway that leads directly from the triclinium to the peristyle colonnade. Once they reach the garden beyond they should be safe. Before the first of them can pass through the door, three of the colonnade columns collapse as though they were tinder wood and the entire roof crumples to the ground, blocking their exit.

They are trapped.

SCAENA 6

1, 567 sesterces – the sum due for payment, as contracted with
Lucius Caecilius Iucundus, by 13 August, for the auction of
Nimphius, slave of Lucius Iunius Aquila, less commission.
Lucius Iunius Aquila declared that he has received this sum, in cash,
from Lucius Caecilius Iucundus.
Transacted at Pompeii on 29 May, in the consulship of Manoius
Acilius and Marcus Asinius. ₁₁

Let us remove ourselves from this moment and inspect another earlier happening. Let us even leave Pompeii to its own business and take a journey. Come along! Up here, above the houses and temples and beyond the walls. That's the Porta Vesuvio, or Vesuvian Gate below us, and look, the farms and vineyards that thrive off the so-rich soil that coats the mountain and provides all those nice things Pompeiians like to eat and drink. But what the gods gift with one hand, they may just as easily take with another. We're almost there now. See? The great mountain rises in front of us. How vast its bulk seems. At least I'm sure it does to you. But really, it's like a speck of dust in the nostril of Vulcan. Who might sneeze at any moment.

Now, look down towards the lower slopes, where the green starts to fade and the red earth is littered with jagged lumps of black rock. You see that track snaking its way up the mountainside? Where the dust rises? That's two men on horseback I want to introduce you to.

This is close enough. Sometimes the horses can sense my presence and may disturb them. But look, the older bald one in the front is Caecilius Jucundus. He's a wealthy moneylender from Pompeii. You've heard his name before – he leases the bakery to Publius's father. Yes our Lucius has his fingers in lots of pies. He earned his wealth through shrewd investments, some legal, most not. But few are aware of that. He's a careful man, doesn't trust anyone really. And that's how he's survived this long. He's quite ruthless also, and somewhat dictatorial. But he keeps a few close loyal men, their loyalty purchased of course.

All of which lessons have not been lost on his younger subordinate, Marcus Epidius Sabinus. He's the other one, obviously, riding behind his employer and pulling a heavily laden mule in his wake. I remember his arrival into the world some twenty five years ago. His head emerged elongated, as many babies do. But his remained so as he grew, giving him a sharp, angular look. By the time he was ten he was lost to whatever guidance I could provide. Well, his parents never honoured me, so what do you expect? But that hook nose of his is not of my doing, nor the squinty eyes. Nor his bony frame. They were simply the work of Fortuna. And as to his character? I think that bears the mark of Laverna, goddess of cheats, thieves and the like. Anyway, judge for yourself as we go. Shhhh. Listen.

– Jucundus. What are we doing up here, dragging this fucking mule?

– You're being paid, are you not? Stop whining for Jupiter's sake. We're almost there.

Marcus Epidius mutters. – Not paid enough for this shit.

– What was that?

– Nothing. Is that the track?

– Yes.

They turn off on to a narrow, dusty track that can only accommodate them in single file. The vegetation is sparse up here, although it wasn't always this way. Up to the time of the consul Marius this place was covered with vineyards, and then over the course of a single year, everything simply withered and died. There are still streams here and there, so the vines didn't die of thirst. They simply died and no one knows why. Such are the whims of the mountain. And it seems to be having another of its whims at the moment.

– Jupiter's balls! What is this?

– I don't know.

Jucundus is staring wide-eyed at the field of dead sheep into which they have wandered. None appear to have been savaged by wolves and the birds have not plucked at their eyes yet, so they know this is a recent event.

– What's that smell?

– Let's get out of here, Jucundus.

His employer turns on him. – Are you willing to give up on a large profit so easily? I thought you more greedy, and courageous, than that.

– Fine. But whatever we're doing, can we do it quickly and be gone?

Jucundus's assessment is correct, as it happens. Marcus Epidius Sabinus is exceptionally greedy, and not without courage. He's also ambitious, immoral and two-faced, though not in the liking of Janus. Would you believe his family is one of the most respected in Pompeii? Of patrician status, Augustus himself sent them here decades ago so that they could promulgate his values regarding family and children. It all sounds so noble. And so at odds with the creature that is Marcus Epidius

Sabinus, who is despised by his father and cut off from their wealth. And so he works for the moneylender, and is well paid for it too.

– Here we are. Keep your knife concealed and at the ready. Just in case. Jucundus says as they approach the ruin of a building. Two rough looking men stand outside, likely ex-gladiators or soldiers, Epidius thinks. Two horses are tethered nearby. A small stream trickles down the mountain just beyond. Jucundus dismounts.

Perari is a thief 12

– Perari.

– Jucundus.

– Everything go as planned?

– We brought them here two nights ago. Twenty-eight in all.

– Excellent. What shape are they in?

Perari, he's the one on the left, coughs pointedly.

Jucundus smiles. – Oh don't worry. I have your payment. One thousand for each, Jucundus nods back towards the mule. Marcus Epidius glances with some surprise at the heavy saddle bags which he has just realised are filled with secesterces.

– Some are worth much more than a thousand. An educated Greek. A German who could pull your arms out of their sockets. A couple of beautiful little bitches as well. You could sell them for ten thousand.

There is a moment of stillness. No one speaks. Marcus Epidius, still mounted, tightens his grip on the knife beneath the folds of his tunic. Then Jucundus laughs lightly. – We've done good business before Perari. I'll look over the merchandise and make you an offer I think worthy.

Perari nods to his accomplice, who unlocks a door into the structure. Most of the building is in ruins. It is the remnants of a vintner's storage hall from long ago, abandoned soon after the vines died out.

– I'll stay with the mule, Marcus Epidius says.

– The mule will be safe. There isn't anyone within two miles of here. Tie it up. I need you inside.

Jucundus follows the other two into the structure.

Perari's accomplice bends and pulls up a hatch, revealing steps disappearing into darkness. Two torches are lit and the whole party descends.

Epidius is first conscious of the breaths of many people, a cough, a girl whimpering, the clank of a chain, and as his eyes adjust to the light, he sees a large, vaulted room filled with people. There is an odour of shit and sweat. The room is dank, damp, cold and filled with slaves. Men, women, children. They sit against the walls or lie curled together for warmth.

– Where did these slaves come from, Jucundus?

Perari answers. – Mostly from Brutium, Calabria. One or two from Apulia. All far enough from here that nobody's ever going to spot them.

Jucundus nods. – Did you bring them by sea?

– Of course. Safest.

– Do you mean these slaves are all stolen from other Romans?

Jucundus shrugs. – They should take more care of their possessions.

He laughs and the other two join him. Epidius looks worried.

– Of don't fret. We'll remove any markings with an iron if they have them. Then we'll sell them in the slave market through a go-between to different owners. The chances of the original owner ever finding them are almost nil. And even if they do, they'll never connect the sale back to us. I'll bury their origins in paperwork.

Epidius grits his teeth and shakes his head as though they are missing the obvious. – But what if the slaves themselves tell their new owners?

Perari laughs loudly, his chuckles reverberating around the room.

– First of all, they'll know that if they ever talk, I'll cut their throats. And second, you think a pig cares who owns it? To a slave, one owner is much the same as the rest. What do they care?

– Anyway, we've done this many times and nothing's ever come back to us.

Epidius sighs. It's not that he's afraid. It's just that he doesn't want to be caught doing anything so illegal. He has plans for the future that he doesn't want tainted by the scandal of the courts.

– So what now? How do we move them?

– When I've finished my business with Perari here, I want you to lead them down the eastern track as far as Neptune's rock. A man will meet you there just before sunset. He'll take them from there. He doesn't know about my involvement or about this place, and I don't want him to.

– I'm to take them alone?

Perari replies. – Don't worry, they're all well shackled.

– And it's less than a mile. And you'll be on horseback. Couldn't be simpler. By the way Perari, when were they last fed?

The slave thief shrugs.

– And watered?

Another shrug. Jucundus frowns, the creases in his forehead heightened by the flicker of the torchlight. – They're not worth much dead.

He turns again to Epidius. – Go up to the stream and fill a couple of skins and let them drink while I value them.

He of patrician class is not impressed.

– It's bad enough having to drag a bunch of stinking slaves

halfway down a mountain, but I'm supposed to run for water for them too? This is not what you promised when you hired me, Jucundus.

Jucundus shakes his head a little, nods to Perari to give them some privacy and puts a consoling arm around Epidius's shoulders.

– Listen, things will not always be as they are today. I appreciate your talents, Marcus Epidius, but those particular skills are not required of you today, simply to do as I ask. You have to grasp every opportunity when it comes along.

Epidius makes a dissatisfied grunt and shrugs his employer's hand off. – Fine. But I expect to be well rewarded from all this.

– I'll tell you what. Take your pick.

Jucundus nods towards the room full of slaves, where Perari and his colleague are shouting at them to stand, kicking them into life.

– What?

– Take your pick. Any one you want. As your own personal slave. Girl, boy, man. Whatever takes your fancy. One of these slaves alone is worth over four thousand sesterces. Is this not a generous reward for so small a task? You can take your slave outside right now and have some fun while I conclude the sale.

You can probably tell from Epidius's expression that he's still aggrieved, still feels he is being asked to do work that is beneath him. But Jucundus is correct. It is a generous reward. He stomps forward and grasps the torch from the hand of Perari's accomplice, then walks around the edge of the room inspecting the slaves in turn. Each bears an expression of abject misery, weariness or fear. He passes a dark-skinned north African male, a fairhaired Celtic female, a male child of no more than eight, two young girls clinging to each other in terror, a giant of a man – probably the German Perari had spoken of. Each one keeps their eyes fixed on the ground, their shoulders sagging, manacled arms hanging limply in front of them. He stops at a tall, dark-haired female. She alone has some spark in her eyes, a fact of which he can tell as she has the impudence to meet his. She is attractive. But there's also something venomous in that look. Although he senses the venom is not directed at him. Instead she is flaunting it, like it is an asset she possesses. He grasps her face by the chin and cheeks and forces open her mouth so he can inspect her teeth.

– What do they call you?

– Faustilla, Dominus.

Epidius turns to Jucundus. – Her.

Jucundus nods, smiles and indicates to Perari to unshackle her from the wall. Epidius grips the girl's arm and yanks her forward towards the steps. She stumbles several times, the shackles preventing proper strides. But he pulls her along anyway, indifferent to her inability to stay erect. He casts a glance back at Jucundus as he begins his inspections and has a sense once again of being dismissed from the important work. His anger rises. He emerges into the light and drags the girl, stumbling and crawling across the earth. It is a cold February day, even more so up here on Vesuvius' slopes. She is shivering by the time he reaches the small stream, a rag of a tunic her only item of clothing.

– The fucking stink of you.

He pushes her and she falls on her rump into the stream. She sits there, shaking, looking up at him.

– Wash yourself you stupid bitch, while I fill these damn skins.

As he pulls free the waterskins from the mule's back, he is suddenly aware that the stream behind him has fallen silent. He swings about to see Faustilla sitting mystified amid the smooth, wet volcanic stones. The stream is no more. It has vanished, as simply as the water in a fountain will cease when one cuts off the supply.

The girl looks up at him. Ridiculous as it seems to you and I, she is terrified that he will think it is her doing, and indeed, for a moment he does entertain the idea that he has chosen a witch and a shiver of fear runs down his spine. But that thought is abruptly severed when the ground beneath his feet heaves and throws him on his back. He sits there in shock staring at the spot where he had been standing a moment ago, now a mound of red earth that has risen from nowhere to half the height of a man, the event accompanied by a smell that is fouler than a hundred blocked latrines. The noise that has chaperoned the heaving of the earth is equally terrifying, a roar befitting of Mars, which continues unabated as the whole fabric of the world seems to tremble. Rocks and clouds of dust tumble from the mountain and as he looks down towards Pompeii he sees nothing but a blur, either through the fact that he is shaking or the entire town is shaking, or both.

Screams come next. Lots of them. He turns towards the abandoned building and watches as it collapses in on itself. Even the strong vaulted roof of the basement which has stood for two hundred years cannot withstand the mountain's power. Huge chunks of masonry crash down on the slaves and the men who seek to trade them as beasts, crushing them like insects.

– Jucundus! Epidius roars. He manages to get to his feet but appears to walk like a man who has spent his entire day in one of Pompeii's bars. Yet he staggers towards the rapidly disappearing structure and rounds a corner to where the entrance once stood. And somehow, within that chaos, he can hear a single voice screeching through the thunderous roar.

That of Lucius Caecilius Jucundus.

SCAENA 7

The city block of the Arrii Pollii in the possession of Gnaeus Alleius Nigidius Maius is available to rent from July first. There are shops on the first floor, upper stories, high-class rooms and a house. A person interested in renting this property should contact Primus, the slave of Gnaeus Alleius Nigidius Maius ₁₃

Forgive me, but other dramas await us and so I must hasten us from the mountain for now. It becomes smaller as we soar away, yet even though we are now passing above the town walls again, many miles from Epidius, Jucundus and the others, you can still feel its mighty presence, ever looming like a fearsome gorgon, watching the land about in search of prey.

Look down there. All those people milling about in that long, open space. That's the forum, ringed by beautiful temples dedicated to the gods, though none to me, I might add. I'm not important enough to merit my own temple. But yes, the forum. Impressive. Well, the mortals who built it consider it so. And it is because they are mortal that they have built such things of stone and metal, which they believe *are* immortal. We shall see.

But we're not going there. Not to the forum. Not today at least.

Down there you can see the roof of the baths just to the north of the forum itself. And almost directly opposite the baths is a house that is among the finest in the town.

Here we are, back on terra firma, and back to the moment when, in a different part of town Publius Comicius Restitutus is departing the theatre with great excitement in his heart, and in yet another place Rufus Caesennius Paetus is slopping down another goblet of wine as he tries to build the courage go upstairs and rape Cygnia. See the man who approaches? He is of a genial disposition, at least on the outside, and is greeted heartily by every soul who passes him.

You see that large house opposite the baths entrance? Yes, the one with the towering stone doorway with the shops on either side and the floors above with the washing hanging from their windows. That's his home. It is ten times the size of most of the homes in this town. Not that any of the citizens begrudge the man his very fine domus. The fact is that he is widely loved by the people, most of them anyway. Take a good look at him. His name is Gnaeus Alleius Nigidius Maius. He's thirty-nine and a handsome thirty-nine at that. Tall, athletic, charismatic, blue-eyed, dark-haired, intelligent and extremely wealthy. His wife's name is Traebia Fortunata, a pretty thing ten years his junior. He doesn't know it of course, but a tiny growth has taken root in Traebia's lung that will kill her within a year.

TRAEBIA FORTUNATA LIVED TWENTY-NINE YEARS [14]

But back to Alleius Maius. You know, fifteen years ago, when he was just twenty-four, he was elected to the political office of aedile. Two years later he went one step higher and was elected as one of the two duumviri. They're the leaders of the council, in case you're wondering, arguably the most powerful men in the town. And then he was elected again the following year. And the year after. And then he took a break for a year or two to pursue his business interests, and how well he pursued them. And then he was elected duumvir again. But the town hadn't had enough of him. Because every five years they must elect two quinquennial duumviri. And these are the really big movers. Because they could enrol new members to the council, update the list of citizens, award state contracts, and a lot of other important matters. And so once again they turned to Alleius Maius. And that was seven years ago, when he was just thirty-two. That's impressive, I'd say, especially for a man whose mother was a slave.

But you know, he is not loved because he is a politician. Huh, most are despised for the same. Nor is he loved for his charm, although he is not without that either. He is loved because he is Pompeii's greatest benefactor when it comes to entertainment. So essentially, he's a showman, an impresario. He loves to play to the crowd. Gladiatorial games, parades, athletic contests, public works, theatre troupes, all paid for from his very deep purse. And how they adore him for it.

Truly, Gnaeus is a man of the people. Let us accompany him inside his home.

Have you ever seen such an atrium? Look at that magnificent high ceiling, inlaid with carved wooden panels, and the compluvium bordered by twenty gold-painted nymphs. The frescoes on the walls showing the exotic birds were painted by a renowned artist he had brought specially from Capua. And those magnificent full-scale statues that line either side of the atrium like an honour guard to welcome him home are his beloved ancestors, each one beautifully recreated by a master sculptor from Rome itself.

That little girl running from the care of her slave tutor is

Alleia, his beloved daughter. See how she embraces him as though she hasn't laid eyes on him in a month. He also has two sons, fine youths, one studying to be an advocate in Athens and the other being schooled in philosophy in Rome. He picks up the giggling child, the last of his brood and walks toward the rear of house in search of his wife, Traebia. He finds her with his mother, Pomponia, standing under the portico discussing their plans to remodel the peristyle garden for the spring with the addition of a statue of the huntress, the goddess Diana, some hanging plants and a small fountain in the centre. He is surprised by his mother's presence, though not displeased at her visit. But his first thought upon seeing them standing there in the evening light is how blessed they are that they can while away their hours in idle recreation and reflection. It pleases him that he has provided such a life and that they rely on him for its continuance. Well, especially his wife, as his mother is married into the wealthy Alleii family. Looking at her now in all her finery it is hard to fathom that she was once a slave, then made a freedwoman, and then taken as a bride. At which point her young son, Gnaeus Nigidius Maius was formally adopted into the family. And although he benefitted enormously from that fortuitous adoption in terms of education and as the beneficiary of a will, it was really only a leg up, as almost all of his riches have been a result of his own efforts. He truly is a self-made man, a fact of which he is immensely proud.

Pomponia Decharcis, wife of Alleius Nobilis,
mother of Alleius Maius 15

– Traebia, Mother.

He greets them with a beaming smile, embraces them in turn, the child still held aloft. – I found this little sprite in the atrium. Doesn't want to learn any more numerals. Wants to have a bath and play with her dolls.

The women laugh. – Fine, enough learning for today. Go and tell Lucia to bathe you. Then you may play a while before bedtime.

The child is lowered to the ground and scoots away.

– Are you staying for dinner, Mother?

– No, we're attending the Odeon this evening. A performance of that choir from Stabiae that everyone is talking about.

Another slave approaches (the household has seven in all, you know), a man, he bows his head and waits respectfully until Gnaeus turns his gaze upon him. – Yes, Primus?

– Dominus, the Falernian you ordered has just arrived. Euxinus wishes to know if you would like to sample it.

Gnaeus's face lights up. The ladies chuckle. He looks like a little boy who's just found a silver denarius in the street.

– Perfect timing. I've been waiting for this delivery for months and it arrives just before dinner. Have him bring an amphora into the tablinum.

He excuses himself from his wife and mother and hurries to meet Euxinus, who runs a well-known bar in the town and also has a nice sideline in importing speciality wines for the wealthier citizens. Gnaeus greets him in the large tablinum with a handshake as a grunting slave manoeuvres the heavy amphora onto the table. He studies the stamp, which reads:

> *Wine from the farm of Fabius of Cales.*
> *From the year of the consulship of*
> *Claudius Caesar Augustus Germanicus*
> *and Gaius Caecina Largus*

– Twenty years old, Alleius Maius.

– Perfect.

Euxinus is a short stocky man with a genial face. His bar is a favourite among the locals as he always has a welcoming smile, doesn't over-water his wine, sells decent food and keeps a couple of good-value prostitutes at the ready on an upper floor of his premises.

The slave decants some white wine into a jug, which he then dilutes with the same amount of water, Falernian being so strong it will explode into a ball of flame when thrown on a fire. He now carefully pours some into a goblet. Alleius Maius picks it up as though it is a sacred vessel from the Temple of Apollo, eyes it with reverence, swirls it, sniffs it, closes his eyes and sips. Euxinus watches intently. Ten amphorae of Falernian in one sale will bring him a healthy profit.

His eyes open. He smiles, sighs contentedly. – Wonderful. The gods themselves surely don't possess a finer wine.

Wine was received by the master
seven days before the Ides 16

Euxinus laughs and Gnaeus joins him. Even the slave smiles faintly. Look at him. He has more wealth than most men will ever dream of. He has a beautiful wife, two fine sons and a daughter. He has a home fit for an emperor. He sups on the finest wine in the civilised world. And he has the affection of almost all who know him. Gnaeus Alleius Nigidius Maius has everything a man could dream of.

But no, he doesn't. Because no matter how much he possesses, a man like Gnaeus can't be content until he has more. More wealth. More adoration. More power. But will Fortuna smile upon his desire for more in the minutes to come?

The men's laughter fades slowly as they feel the first tremble beneath their feet. Within moments the entire room is shaking.

– What is it, by the gods?

– It's an earthquake! My family!

He bursts though the door into the atrium, Euxinus and slave close behind. Things are crashing to the ground now. The gold painted nymphs come loose from the compluvium above and rain down around them. A huge bronze candelabrum topples and crashes to the floor, spilling burning oil across the atrium. A fresco showing a naked Venus bathing in a sea pool splits into three sections as though torn apart by giant hands pulling in different directions. A large piece comes completely free of the wall and shatters in a million fragments.

Euxinus and his slave are running for the main exit to the street. Gnaeus sees his wife and mother run into the atrium and is maddened that they have stupidly run into the building rather than into the open space of the peristyle.

His wife screams. – Where's Alleia?

But they are fortunate. The slave girl emerges from one of the many cubicula that line the sides of the atrium. She is clutching the terrified child in her arms. He quickly grabs his daughter.

Gnaeus yells. – Everyone to the street.

As they run though the atrium the life-sized statues of his adoptive ancestors topple almost one after the other and they are forced to weave a terrifying path to avoid being crushed. His mother is old and her reflexes and her legs fail her, and the statue of her husband's grandfather tumbles upon her calf. She falls, but is blessed by the arrival of the young slave, Primus, who stoops to grasp her and pull her free of the debris. Gnaeus, almost at the vestibulum, turns and sees them, pushes the child into his wife's arms and returns to assist. The noise is deafening. Chaos surrounds them. Screams pierce the terrifying rumble from every direction. They half lift and half drag his mother backwards along the vestibulum towards the relative safety of the street, lumps of plaster beating on their heads.

As they emerge into the light the first sight he sees startles him. There are a group of eight completely naked women screaming and clutching at each other in terror. They are young and old, thin and fat, smooth-skinned and wrinkled. He wonders for a moment if he is delirious, what strange vision the gods have concocted to bewilder him. Then it dawns. They have been forced to flee the baths without even enough time to return to the changing room and make themselves decent. He pulls his mother to the centre of the narrow street and looks about. Traebia is quickly beside him with their daughter. He embraces them. Besides Primus, he sees three more of his slaves. He doesn't know it, but one of the others is already dead, crushed by one of Euxinus's amphorae when the shelf upon which he had stacked them collapsed.

Pieces of plaster and dust continue to tumble from the buildings above. A woman appears at one of the apartment windows he rents above his home. She climbs to the outside of the window, hesitates a moment then jumps. He hears the snap of a bone as she lands, and the inevitable piercing scream that follows.

The trembling is easing. He falls to the still shaking ground beside his mother. She is in shock, crying, a large gash on her calf, perhaps a broken bone, but she is alive. He stands again. The roar has subsided to a distant rumble and yet it seems the entire world is yelling out in pain, for all across Pompeii he can hear the agonised voices of a thousand souls imploring the gods for help. He sees a washing line that had come loose and fallen to the ground and he takes whatever items of clothing it contains and walks across to the unfortunate women bathers, who wail incessantly through their terror and their indignity. Most still glisten with the water from their bath. They huddle on the ground, trembling from the shock and the cold. He throws the items of clothing to them and eager hands grasp them from the air.

He looks around. His home and the apartments above are still standing. He has built them well, the finest materials, the thickest walls. He walks back towards the entrance.

Traebia calls anxiously. – Where in the gods' names are you going, Gnaeus? It's dangerous!

– It's fine. I'll be back shortly.

He ignores her further entreaties and walks into the house. He negotiates a path though the rubble until he comes to the stairs. He climbs to the first floor. One of his tenants lies dead in the narrow corridor, a bloodied piece of masonry by his crushed skull. He finds the maintenance hatch that leads to the roof and clambers up into the evening light. His home is situated in the higher part of town, which gently slopes away from Vesuvius. From here he can see the extent of the destruction. Several large plumes of smoke rise from the direction of the forum and even though his view is partially blocked, he can see that the Temple of Apollo has been badly damaged. When he looks to his right towards the Marine Gate he can see that the Temple of Venus has virtually disappeared, and where he could previously see its roof there was now merely a hovering cloud of dust. He swings his gaze across towards the theatre district. It is hard to tell the damage, as the giant semi-oval of the seating area seemed intact, but obscures his view of the interior. The giant shape of the amphitheatre at the far end of town also seems unharmed, but in between chaos reigns. Countless homes, large and small, have simply collapsed in upon themselves. Fires rage, smoke billows, roofs have caved in, entire streets are blocked where buildings have toppled, water pours from broken mains pipes, sewers have risen through the ground and spilled their contents onto the streets.

He sweeps his gaze in a wide field across the sea of destruction. Not a single insula has been spared. And then Gnaeus Alleius Nigidius Maius smiles faintly and nods to himself, almost unaware he is doing it.

Did I mention how he acquired his wealth, by the way? No? He owns a building company.

SCAENA 8

Once I've got an opportunity, I never let it go ₁₇

We are back once more on the mountainside, and there is Marcus Epidius Sabinus staring into the rubble of the collapsed vintner's storehouse. The trembling has not subsided yet. It is as though the whole earth had been cursed with a fever. Yet Epidius senses it is weakening. He stays well clear of what remains of the building's walls, as entire stone blocks are still falling in cascades of debris and dust. He is nauseous from the rolling motion that causes him to almost dance to the earth's tune to stay on his feet. Finally it fizzles out and is gone and the only quivering now is in his gut. He holds up his hands and observes that they are shaking and he feels powerless to calm them. His eyes are drawn to Pompeii in the distance. It being a bright winter's day, no haze dulls his view. And he can see with crisp clarity that the town is in ruins.

– Marcus Epidius!

The voice again. He had thought it his imagination. A creation borne of his shock. But it is very real. He staggers into the rubble and locates the place where once had been a hatch leading into the cellar. It is barely discernible now as much of the floor has vanished, collapsed on the unfortunate heads of all below. He lifts a few heavy pieces of masonry away and there, half-in and half out of the floor, lies Lucius Caecilius Jucundus. His lower half lies beneath ten stone blocks and his upper body spouts blood from a dozen wounds. He had abandoned his interest in the slaves and fled for the steps. But not quickly enough. A younger man might have made it. He, Epidius, might have made it. But not poor Caecilius, the fool. He didn't know it, but he was just an old man playing a young man's game. Yes, this is what he is thinking, not how to extract his employer from the rubble, not how to save his life. He is thinking that Caecilius' life has run its useful course. It is time for a new generation to enter the fray.

With the one hand that is free of the rubble, the money-lender reaches out to the younger man and calls his name again in a pitiful voice. Epidius just stares at him. After a while, he turns his head and looks about the mountainside. He can see the mule and a couple of the other horses some distance away. They obviously wrenched themselves free in panic earlier and fled, but now they have calmed again and are happily munching on something. The mule couldn't run very fast anyway, weighed down as it is with bags of sesterces. Epidius wonders exactly how much the bags contain. It must be a great deal, if it was required to purchase almost thirty slaves, even if they are contraband. His thoughts are interrupted by an agonised howl.

– Help me.

Epidius squats down.

– It was fortunate you sent me to do the menial work, Caecilius Jucundus, otherwise I'd be dead now.

The moneylender's hand claws out again, pleading.

– Please.

– You must see the hand of the gods at work, do you not?

They have decided, that among all the death they have doled out, I was to be spared.

A rivulet of blood runs down Caecelius's forehead and drips into his right eye. He tries unsuccessfully to blink it away.

– What was it you said to me, remember, just before you sent me out? 'You have to grasp every opportunity that comes along.' Wasn't that it?

He looks about. He picks up a chunk of concrete. – Thanks for the advice.

There is a moment of disbelief in Caecelius's eyes before the stone crashes into his skull.

But let us look away. It never pleases me to observe mortals murdering one another. The giving and taking of life is the prerogative of the gods.

Here he comes now from amid the ruins, his tunic spattered with the blood of his employer. His face is filled with feverish excitement. There is a satisfied grin touching the corners of his mouth. His hands are clenched into fists at his sides and blood gushes through his veins.

He walks back around the ruin, the dust still settling on what has now become a tomb to thirty-one souls. The slave girl, Faustilla, lies curled in a ball on the dusty earth, her arms enshrouding her head. She is whimpering.

Epidius's grin becomes a smile. His long shadow causes her to look up. Her mouth opens but she does not speak. She has seen that look in the eyes of men before, and she knows what it means. Her whimpering ceases. She rolls on to her front and lies there silently. He falls upon her and takes her.

SCAENA 9

Tears cannot put out the flames
They spread across your face
and darkness comes into the spirit [18]

We are back in the dimly lit corridor in the lodging house of Mariona. The earthquake will last not much more than one lonely minute. But so much may transpire in such a short time. So many lives altered forever, so many ended, so much pain. But also so much courage. And so much revelation. For in these moments the true colour of men's and women's souls are opened for inspection. Cygnia and Severina stand startled and frozen at the sudden turn of events, staring at each other, mouths agape, the noise deafening, the entire building shuddering itself to pieces. One moment Severina is standing at eye level with her slave, and then next she has vanished. The floor beneath her has collapsed and she is swallowed whole by the crumbling edifice, a brief screech her only valediction. Cygnia swings about and darts for the stairs. She emerges into the atrium and looks up. The entire second floor is crumbling, toppling piece by piece all around her. She is close to the vestibulum door, but to her horror it refuses to open despite her panicked wrenching. She sees that the building has lurched so much that the shape of the doorway has altered and the door is jammed solidly. She begins to cry desperately, but her wits do not desert her. She turns as a section of the upper wall collapses into the atrium, and there behind it stands Rufus, trapped on the upper floor, his face a picture of abject fear.

– Cygnia!

He screams from the depths of his being, as if she could somehow intervene, or as if she might even be disposed to. Well, in truth, she would help him, despite what he is. I should say *was*. Because a ceiling beam as thick as a peristyle column swings down and swats him against a wall like a fly. He is no more.

Cygnia runs towards the centre and jumps into the impluvium, which is filled with water no more than a hand deep, but at least it is beneath a small piece of open sky. Yet it offers little protection, as pieces of the ceiling continue to rain upon her. She falls to her knees. A lump of plaster strikes her perfect face and she feels blood pump from an open gash, that perfection that was so admired now tarnished beyond repair. She utters a prayer not to me, or any of the other gods, but to her mother and father, who are dead now, slain when she was taken as a slave. She begs them to hear her, to save her now and ease the pain she knows they felt when they could not save her then. But the remnants of the ceiling beams can no longer support the thousand roof tiles above and a section hurtles down upon her.

And there she lies, the impluvium awash with her blood as the shaking diminishes, just those few seconds too late.

There is Chrestus, struggling to clamber through a world of madness, frantically heaving bricks and beams aside, staggering and falling as he approaches from what remains of the rear of the house of Mariona. He is unhurt but for a few bruises. He alone in this building has emerged unscathed. He sees Cygnia's legs protruding from beneath broken tiles and in a frantic state he casts the weighty shards aside as if they are made of wool. He lifts her face from the pinkish water.

– Cygnia. Little one.

She opens her eyes. – Chrestus.

Her voice is weak. He lifts her and cradles her bleeding head in his lap.

– Mariona?

He shakes his head and she utters a small cry. They remain in silence for some time, if silence you can call it, the din of the fractured town penetrating what is left of the walls.

– Chrestus... she says with an agonised moan.

He tries to comfort her. – You will be well again. I will leave and get help...

She tightens her grip on his wrist. – Who is going to help a slave?

She is silent again. After some time a light brightens her eyes, as though a thought has struck her.

– You must run, Chrestus. Escape. Leave me.

He laughs, shakes his head. – How far you think I get with my black skin? No, I stay with you.

– Then...then I want you to help me...to end this. There's a way.

He looks away, pretending not to hear.

– Listen to me. You don't understand. A knife. Please, please. I beg you.

She whispers into his ear, words only they and the gods will know.

He relents, because of his love for her. He returns some

minutes later, clutching a long kitchen knife. He kneels beside her in the water.

She whispers. – Do it.

She closes her eyes. Chrestus lifts the knife and sinks the tip into her flesh.

SCAENA 10

Live your life,
death is already on its way for you [19]

One last stop. The home of Publius. Remember? The writer-to-be. Well, all such dreams have departed his head at this moment. His only thought is to get out of the collapsing house as quickly as possible, along with the rest of his family. Their path to the garden blocked, his father swings to his left towards a narrow door that leads into the adjoining bakery. The door comes open only after several hefty pulls.

– This way! Hurry!

Prima grips her husband on the forearm.

– What about Vivia?

There is a door leading from this passage directly into the kitchen, but it refuses to budge. Publius senior calls Vivia's name over and over as pieces of plaster come loose above their heads and shower down upon them. He abandons his attempt to open the door.

– Go! We can't wait.

He lets all the others pass before following, ushering them

past the huge oven, which is thankfully unlit at this time of day, as its metal door has warped and been dislodged. The bakery staff is absent and the only other person normally in here now is Servulus, their other slave who works as their stablelman. Publius hears the panicked screeching of their two mules, which are housed in an internal, lightless stable room.

As they move towards the front of the building, the wall of Servulus's cubiculum collapses across their path, but nobody is hurt and they can easily clamber over the debris. Yet there is no sign of the slave. Perhaps he has already fled, Publius is hoping.

His father pauses and yells at the top of his lungs as they pass the entrance to the stable.

– Servulus! Leave them man! Get out!

The slave has entered the stable room and is trying desperately to harness one of the bucking mules so he can lead it to safety. But the animals have no sight in their eyes. They turn this way and that, they kick wildly, they run blindly against the walls, they seem to move in every direction except towards the open doorway.

– Servulus! You fool. Leave them!

Servulus, who is aged thirty-four and not too bright (he only cost six hundred sesterces), loves the animals dearly. Publius senior turns to his son.

– Get out, get the others out!

Publius hesitates for an instant then turns and pushes against the bodies of his mother, brother and sisters. Restitutus struggles against him, calling out his father's name. But Publius forces him on, assisted by his mother. They pass through the mill hall, which houses four stone mills. Publius sees one of the huge hollow grinding stones split apart like a cracked egg and tumble on to the ground. A large lump of plaster lands on his sister's head and she is floored, blood spurting from her scalp.

Publius has to let go of Restitutus who immediately runs back towards the stableroom.

His mother screams. – No!

Publius lifts Cornelia and thrusts the girl at her mother.

– Get her out! Go!

He turns and runs after Restitutus, but the boy has been felled by a piece of stone that shot across the room as though propelled by a sling.

– Restitutus!

The boy is merely stunned, he is relieved to see. He realises that the weight of the collapsing walls is causing the softer bricks to disintegrate, propelling pieces in every direction, and he has to duck and dodge to avoid them. He looks up and sees his father manhandling Servulus, trying to wrest the slave from the stable. A moment later one of the beasts whirls about and its hind legs lash out wildly, connecting with the slave's head and snapping his neck. He falls dead in his master's arms.

– Father! Get out!

Publius senior turns and sees his two sons, one standing, one lying bloodied on the floor. He moves towards the door as a beam gives way above and comes hurtling down on the mules. One is struck across the centre of its back and it produces a high-pitched wail and falls on its side against the retreating man. Publius senior collapses, the beast landing on top of him, pinning him to the floor. Publius yells and falls to his knees. He grabs his father's arms and tries to wrench him free. He feels his father's body shift. If he can just wrench it a few more times.

His father lifts his face, streaked with blood and dust, then grasps his son's hand. – Go, son, get your brother out!

– No! I can't!

– You must!

There are tears coursing from Publius's eyes, his voice cracked and pitiful.

– Please. Save Restitutus. Tell your mother I...

Another beam collapses behind Publius, barely missing his brother.

– Go! Before it's too late!

– I...

– Go!

Two more pulls and he may be free, he thinks. But terror is grasping at him. Quickly taking hold. It overwhelms him. He bends, kisses his father on the head and turns to lift his brother. He staggers backwards, half-tripping over falling plaster and timbers, dragging Restitutus behind him. He reaches the door to the shop and looks back to see his father's face one final time. Publius senior smiles as he realises they are almost to safety. The roof collapses completely just as Publius pulls his brother across the open shop hatchway and into the chaos of street.

Their mother almost falls upon them in her joy at seeing them alive. But her joy lasts no longer than the blink of an eye. The realisation dawns that no one is following them. She grasps her son's tunic at his chest and looks into his face and sees the unspoken horror there that tells her that her husband is dead.

Restitutus awakens and looks about for his father. He leaps up from the ground, panic on his face, and tries to re-enter the building, but Publius seizes him and holds him fast as he thrashes like a skewered fish.

– Father! Let me go you bastard! Let me go! Father!

Prima collapses almost in harmony with the final crumbling of the front of the house, and cries at the sky and wails until her voice runs hoarse. Their house slave, Vivia, is suddenly there beside her, somehow having found a way out, arms enveloping her mistress, she also in agonised mourning at the loss of the man who brought her in shackles from Britain.

So, look at poor Publius. His father dead. His family broken and bloodied. His wailing brother's eyes filled with a rage directed at him. His family's home and business destroyed.

His hand unconsciously slips into the pocket at the waist of his tunic and falls upon the solitary sesterce he found on the theatre stage. For all his ambition, this, he thinks, is the only payment he will ever receive. And now he is laden with guilt. As despite the tragedy that engulfs him, the thing that crushes him most, is that the life that was there for him just minutes before, with all its boundless potential, has crumbled and fallen to pieces as if it too had been a flimsy building sitting upon the skin of the restless earth.

SCAENA 11

MERCURIALIS LIVED 11 YEARS
VESONIA URBANA LIVED 20 YEARS
SALVIUS LIVED 6 YEARS
LUCIUS MANILIUS LIVED 24 YEARS
CAIUS MUNATIUS LIVED 57 YEARS
AULUS VEIUS NYMPHIUS LIVED 28 YEARS
HELPIS LIVED 3 YEARS
LUCIUS E. APRILIS LIVED 20 YEARS
TITUS M. PROCULUS LIVED 25 YEARS
MYTHUS E. FLACCI LIVED 85 YEARS [20]

So, some have lived, some have died. Some perished in infancy, some the flourish of youth, some of advanced age. Others are the victims of horrible injury and wish they had died. Some cannot bear the weight of the grief they carry.

A few are happy.

Some survivors will become bitter, rail against the Gods, curse them to Hades, as if such bitterness might give us cause to fear.

Others don't. They look to us in search of answers as to why we would inflict such a dreadful wrath upon their little heads. What terrible wrong have we done, they cry. How can we make amends? Show us the way so this thing will never happen again.

Many lose their faith. They renounce all belief in the Gods. They reason and ruminate and debate. If the Gods existed, what purpose could such an act serve? Others simply don't care. Their minds are numb to all such deliberation.

But ponder it as you would the farmer ploughing his field. How many tiny lives does he crush without a moment's thought, what chaos does he bring to the world of the insect? Should he cease his farming because of such considerations? You laugh at the very thought. Yet you are less even to the Gods than the ant is to the farmer. But in spring the farmer's greater purpose is revealed in the emergence of an abundance of green shoots from the soil.

Now I must leave you awhile. But we shall meet again soon, I hope. For I am keen to show you how the lives of those that have survived this terrible day have progressed, or regressed, as the case may be.

But for now I must bear the blustering and strutting of Vulcan as he wallows in his handiwork and the thousands of voices that will beg him to spare them further rage.

He will be insufferable for months.

SCAENA 12

AD 72

Vita

～

Hello again. It has been a while, has it not, at least in your terms?

So. Where are we now? Oh yes. We're on the Via Livia, the busy little street that cuts between the Via di Nola and the Via Dell'Abbondanza. It's been some time since Vulcan's little romp, but you can still see much of the damage. Come along. Walk with me.

Look, you see the empty space there on the corner? The entire building collapsed killing twelve people. The land is owned by Marcus Epidius now, but he has no plans to build, at least for a while. And you can still see the cracks in the stonework of some of the other buildings. In fact a few of them look ready to fall with just a strong gust of wind. And people are going about their business as if nothing happened. That's the fuller's slave along there, collecting the pots of urine and pouring them into the big jars on his handcart for use in the bleaching of clothing. Those two ladies at the jeweller's shop are trying to pick some new earrings for an upcoming wedding.

Harpocras had a good fuck with Drauca for a denarius [21]

The big man coming towards us whistling is called Harpocras. He's just been paid and is on his way to Pompeii's lupanare at the other end of town. That's the brothel to you. No wonder he looks happy. But he is of no consequence to us. That other handcart that just passed us laden down with loaves was bound for a delivery to a number of taverns. The lad pushing it was Staphylus, who's fourteen and a slave. All in all, considering what happened in the earthquake, things seem fairly normal, do they not?

More than ten years have drifted by. Some who dwell here have become wiser in those years, some more stupid, some greedier and a handful have become richer, at least in terms of possessions. A few have become embittered.

Now, here's what I wanted to show you. You see the baker's shop on the right? Does the man behind the counter look familiar? Oh his face has changed somewhat from when you last saw him. It looks weary and is marked by near permanent worry lines. And his eyes seem a little vacant. His hair is somewhat wilder and there is stubble on his face, because he doesn't make much of an effort with his appearance. And yet he manages to force a smile for each of the customers as he passes the bread over the counter. Yes, that's Publius Comicius Restitutus. Would-be playwright. But all of that is so long in the past now. So much time has passed since that terrible day when the earth quivered, and Publius has grown to manhood. So much has happened since the roof of this very building collapsed and crushed to death his father and their slave Servulus. But as you can see, it is by now almost as if nothing happened to the bakery. He has worked hard to restore it, and in the early years he came near to giving up several times. But really, he had no choice but to continue. Because from the moment those heavy timbers ended his father's life, Publius, at the age of sixteen, in effect became the paterfamilias. The weight on his shoulders seemed to him almost as heavy as the beams that came tumbling down. But he was strong enough to bear that weight, a fact that surprised even him. And there is more. Much more. But let us listen to him now, hear how the youth's voice has grown into a man's.

Victoria was here [22]

– You ask the same thing every day, Victoria.

He's dealing with a customer, a slave woman from the home of Marcus Cerrinnius Vatia. He smiles at her. Victoria likes to let the shopkeepers she deals with know that she won't be taken for a fool. The infant in the sling at her breast whimpers and she hushes it before resuming her deliberations.

– And so I should. My master would beat me black and blue if I returned home with stale bread.

Her voice is in search of sympathy, but the grin she can't conceal betrays her, as usual.

– And those loaves have been sitting there in the sun all day. Give me four from the the back. Serve that rubbish to the house of Holconius, not me.

– Victoria, Vatia would no more beat you than jump off a roof. And that bread is just fresh from the oven. But if you insist.

Publius passes the loaves over the counter. –That's eight as, Victoria.

– Eight? Polybius's bakery gives a discount of an as when you buy four loaves.

Publius leans over to her. – Yes, but Polybius's bread tastes like wood. Victoria shakes her head good-humouredly and hands over the cash. She grins and says her farewells to Publius just as his plump sister Cornelia emerges through the bakery door. She is twenty-two now and still without a husband. She immediately begins to pick at the corner of a loaf and Publius slaps her hand away.

– Don't do that. Where did Restitutus say he was going, in the name of Jupiter? He was supposed to do this while I went to the grain market.

– He just said he had business to attend to.

– Gods! I'll kill him when he gets back. I have to talk to Narcissus.

Narcissus wrote this [23]

Publius disappears inside to speak to his baker, Narcissus, who used to bake bread for the imperial household in Rome. Narcissus's favourite joke, which everyone is sick of hearing, is that he served as baker to no less than five imperial households; Nero, Galba, Otho, Vitellius and Vespasian. Of course this was because four of them reigned in the same year. But when Vespasian arrived he was understandably wary of all around him, considering the chaos of the previous year, and this even extended to those who supplied his food. And so Narcissus's services were dispensed with and he has ended up here. Publius is grateful to Vespasian, who did him a favour by providing him with the best baker in the region. If his bread was good enough for emperors, it is certainly good enough for Pompeiian mouths. And Publius is not shy about reminding everyone that he employs an 'imperial baker'.

Let's move inside, have a look around.

Now, here we are. If you've never been in a Roman bakery you're probably wondering what's going on. Well, those two big hourglass-shaped stone machines being rotated by the mules are the mills, but you probably guessed that. The young man pouring grain into the top is Hermeros, who replaced the slave Servulus when he was killed in the earthquake. He was actually given to Publius out of the fund that the emperor Nero arranged to help the survivors, as was Staphylus, the young lad you saw in the street earlier. Which is just as well, as otherwise he would have been far too expensive. He looks after the mills and the mules and he's not much smarter than Servulus was. He has attached a bunch of carrots to a rod and fixed it to the mules to lure them forward. That big concrete cone there was also a mill once, but you might recall that the rest of it shattered during the earthquake. Their construction requires a particular stone made in faraway Umbria and so Publius has been unable to afford to replace it.

Let's carry on, and watch you don't step in the piles of dung around the mills. Hermeros isn't great at cleaning up after his beasts. That room on the right, the dark one that also smells of mule shit, that's the stable where Publius's father and Servulus met their end. Now, down this little dark corridor. Those little rooms to the left and right are the sleeping quarters for Staphylus and Hermeros. Can you feel the heat as we enter this wide room? Yes, that large structure on the left is the oven. The other room beyond, by the way, is where a dough maker plies his trade. Oh and look, there's Vivia, the kitchen slave who survived the disaster, coming down the stairs. Gone old, hasn't she? Well, she is seventy-three now, although even she isn't aware of that fact. Publius offered the woman her freedom some years ago, even though he knew he would have to replace her. But she declined, which you might find odd. She said she wouldn't know what to do with such a thing as her freedom. She wanted to remain loyal to the family and the memory of Publius senior. Anyway, Publius has rewarded her with a room of her own upstairs where the rest of the family sleep, and other small tokens.

– We're making as many loaves in a day as we can, Publius. I'm a baker, not a conjurer.

Narcissus is shaking his head as he replaces the cooked loaves with a fresh batch. He's a broad shouldered man of thirty-four.

– But what about firing up the oven earlier, so we have a longer day?

Narcissus nods and then shakes his head almost as one movement. – Yeah, we could do that, but the real problem is the flour. We'd really need the third mill working. Unless you want to buy flour directly from the big mill across town. But you know how expensive ready ground flour is.

Publius sighs and now it is his turn to shake his head. His bakery is small, producing only four hundred loaves a day. The business could make a decent profit if it weren't for all the money he owes Epidius, the man you might remember murdered Jucundus (and then took over his banking concern). It is a struggle to make ends meet, which sees him fretting alone in his bed late into the night. And here comes more trouble.

Cornelia bursts through the door from the living area. – Publius! Quickly! Something's happened to Staphylus!

Publius follows his sister into the peristyle colonnade, which is still only half-repaired as you can see, and through the door in the triclinium. There he finds his mother tending to their young delivery lad who they have seated on the table, and whose face, arms and legs are bloodied. The unfortunate boy clutches at his ribs and groin, almost doubled over in pain, as the others try to examine his wounds.

– What happened?

Prima looks at her daughter. – Cornelia. Fetch some water in a bowl, cloth and bandages. Tell Vivia to come in. Hurry, girl.

She nods at the slave. – He was babbling, Publius. Came staggering along the street without the cart. Said two men had attacked him.

– What men? Staphylus, who attacked you?

– I don't know, Dominus.

Prima is divesting him of his bloodied tunic and he grunts in pain as she pulls it free. He sits there untroubled by his nakedness, his thoughts on other matters. His body is bruised and scratched all over. Through heaving breaths and little grunts of pain, he struggles to speak.

– They just came up and started hitting me. Then one of them turned over the cart and pissed on the bread. All the loaves are ruined, Dominus. I'm sorry.

Publius shakes his head. – Forget the loaves.

– Then they pushed me on the street and started kicking me.

– What did they want? Did they rob any bread?

– No. They just pissed on it then ran off.

Cornelia and Vivia have arrived with the bowl and cloths and Prima starts to bathe the boy's wounds. Publius doesn't voice his suspicions that Epidius was behind this. He summons Hermeros. – See if you can find the cart. I don't want the expense of buying another.

– What about the shop? There's nobody serving now. Half the bread is probably stolen by urchins.

He looks around. – Cornelia. You'll have to run the shop until Hermeros gets back. Where the fuck is Restitutus?

– Me? I have to meet Matrona. We're going to buy a dress for the festival.

She's a flighty one, Cornelia, her head forever filled with dresses and bangles and young men. Has delusions of meeting a wealthy merchant and living a life of luxury in a country villa, and such. Publius rounds angrily on her. – If we don't sell bread we don't make money and you will not be able to afford a dress or anything else for that matter. Now do as I say!

– Obey your brother, girl.

Prima says this as she wraps a bandage around Staphylus's head.

Cornelia stomps towards the shop like a child in a tantrum.

– And don't pick at the loaves. Your arse is big enough as it is.

As she leaves, she bends over and hoists her skirts, wiggling her bare backside at her brother behind his back. Her mother conceals a grin.

Publius is about to return to the bakery when a voice interrupts proceedings. Everyone looks up to see the figure of Marcus Epidius Sabinus in the doorframe.

I beg you to elect Marcus Epidius Sabinus aedile in charge of streets, sacred and public buildings; He is worthy.
Onesimus was the whitewasher [24]

– Oh, I am sorry to intrude. I do hope there hasn't been an accident? Is your young slave injured?

Prima looks away from the man in distaste. But then Epidius has that effect on many people. Publius is thinking that his earlier suspicions have just been confirmed.

– Epidius Sabinus.

– Hello Publius. I was passing and thought we might discuss business matters. But I see you're busy. Poor lad. What befell him?

Publius looks him in the eye. – I'm not certain, but I believe some cowardly cunt hired a couple of thugs to beat him up.

Epidius shakes his head in mock outrage and compassion. – Terrible what goes on. Men such as that should be burnt with hot irons. Still, these are the misfortunes a businessman must face. I know only too well myself. They never end, you know. Ever.

Publius feels like striking him, but he can't do that to one of the town's most prominent citizens. – You wanted to discuss business?

– Oh, yes. Is it convenient?

– Come with me.

Publius turns to leave.

Epidius addresses Prima as he departs.

– Always a pleasure, Prima.

She looks away.

Publius leads him into the tablinum, which served his father for so many years. And he seems to have inherited his father's disorderliness, scrolls and wax tablets scattered about his table in an unseemly mess. He sits behind the table and Epidius takes one of the stools facing him.

– What do you want?

– Well, I wish to remind you that your repayment for your loan falls due on the Kalends of June.

– I know th...

– And you were late with last month's payment.

– Yes, but...

– And also of course that the rent for this fine premises is due tomorrow.

– You'll have your rent.

– And also that due to increased costs, I am reluctantly forced to increase your rent from next month, by ten percent.

– What? You can't do that!

– My hand is forced, dear Publius. And besides, I assure you I can. Your lease agreement specifically states that in the event of you neglecting to operate this business in an efficient manner and to ensure its upkeep, I may impose penalties as I see fit. And

I've been informed that you have recently failed to make deliveries to several households, bars, thermopolia and so on. Your customers are going to desert you Publius, if this keeps up. Furthermore, you have failed to repair the third mill, which has been idle a decade. Its redundancy is a serious impediment to efficiency.

Publius is fuming now. How he would like to reach across the table and throttle the man. But he keeps his calm.

– We've missed some deliveries because of acts of vandalism, theft and assault, as happened today. They're out of my control. And how can I afford to repair the mill if you keep turning the screw?

Epidius exhales a long, ponderous sigh.

– Such are the caprices of the business world.

They stare at each other in silence across the table. Epidius's face betrays nothing of the fact that he is behind all of the misfortunes that have beset the bakery. But why would he hamper the repayment of his own investment? Perhaps he will reveal something of his scheming to us.

He suddenly brightens and asks cheekily – May I have some wine?

Publius slowly turns his head towards the open door and roars. – Vivia! Bring us wine.

They wait in silence. Vivia brings a tray with wine and water and prepares two cupfuls. When she leaves Epidius sits forward. – I am told that you once aspired to greatness as a writer of plays, Publius.

Publius is taken aback. – Who told you that?

Epidius waves his hand absently. – Oh, you know, one hears these things. I am told that you have produced some works for those...bawdy productions...that Saenecio Fortunatus puts on in the forum. Anyway, I ask myself, why does a man who wishes to spend his life in the great world of the arts trouble himself with the burden of running a very difficult business?

Publius laughs. – Even if I had time to write proper plays, which I don't, both theatres are still rubble. What benefactor would purchase my plays? And even if someone did, do you know how little a play earns? I have a family to support. But what is the point of all this?

– The point? Oh, yes. Well, here it is. I wish to divest myself of some of my longer-term lease agreements and sell some premises. I need to raise some capital. And as it happens I have a buyer interested in these premises. There, I've been honest with you. Revealed my motives.

Publius is thinking that an honest word has never passed Epidius's lips. He is aware that Epidius owns multiple properties in the town and beyond. In fact it is well known around Pompeii that he and Gnaeus Alleius Maius are the town's two biggest landlords, and that they would cut each other's throats, possibly literally as well as metaphorically, if it meant outbidding one another for a piece of land the size of a doormat. But this is more than just an ordinary property speculation. He is convinced Epidius has some other scheme in mind, and he is curious.

– What does the buyer want with a bakery?

Epidius shrugs. – It is not my concern. I simply know he wants the place. And this could well serve your interests too.

– How?

Epidius smiles. – I am prepared to write off all remaining payments on your rebuilding loan. Four thousand, four hundred, seventy-six sesterces and three as, if I remember correctly. A lot of money.

Publius is taken aback. He has known Epidius has wanted him out of the lease for months now for some reason, but he never expected him to make such an offer. He merely expected that the man would continue to try and intimidate him out of the place.

– That's very generous. But it still leaves me with a problem. I'd have no income and nowhere to live.

– Ah but you would. Because I'm also prepared to lease you a house on very generous terms and as I'm the party wishing to break the lease on the bakery, compensate you to the tune of a further five thousand sesterces. That should be more than adequate to cater for your needs while you resume your writing career. And really Publius, when you think about it, your brother is a healthy young man now. He will soon be earning his own crust. Your sister we can easily, with my influence, marry off to a suitable individual. Which means you will only have to look after your dear mother, Prima. And you have your slaves, more than you would need in a small household. You could sell one to further provide for your future. Think of it. All those long free days to ponder over your plots and craft your words. Rather than spending them now sweating in that shithole next door. Who knows, perhaps some day you'll even write a play about me.

He laughs heartily at his own joke. Publius is somewhat stunned, as you can probably tell from his expression. Five thousand sesterces? More than five times what a legionary earns in a year. And no more business headaches. No more arguing the price of grain in the market. No more worries about mules dying, equipment breaking, Narcissus leaving to join another bakery. No more monthly struggle to pay the rent and the loan. And of course, although he's long since dispensed with the notion of being a successful playwright, the seed of it briefly stirs to life again in his mind. Much as he despises this man, he is sorely tempted.

And Epidius sees this in his face. He leans in and moves to clinch Publius's decision. – And you're a young man, Publius.

What? Twenty-five? Twenty-six? This place leaves you no time for the important things in life. A wife. A family. And it was such a terrible tragedy when poor Curtia passed away so suddenly in December. But now at last you have the chance to move on, find a new wife.

CURTIA PHYLE
LIVED THIRTY-FIVE YEARS ₂₅

Oh yes, since we last met him, Publius has been married and is now a widower. I'll fill you in on the details later.

The pensive look disappears from Publius's face. He is wrenched back sharply from the imaginings of a different life. There was something in Epidius's tone when he spoke of Curtia's death. Is it possible, he is thinking, that Epidius had something to do with it? A part of his tactic of intimidation? Curtia died when a man on a galloping horse struck her while she walked through Porta Nocera necropolis. Poor Curtia was flung against the tomb of Eumachia, who was a successful woman of great wealth and even has a building bearing her name in the forum. All of which was of no consequence to Curtia, whose neck snapped when it stuck the wall fronting the colossal tomb. Publius is partially correct, for Epidius did order his hired thug, called Albanus, to frighten the woman, and the ex-gladiator had intended to knock her unconscious with the butt of his sword, but she happened to step directly into his path as he approached, and that was that. Epidius hadn't intended to have her killed, but when she was, he merely saw it as a possible complication to his plans.

Publius stares at the man as though his vision might bore into Epidius's mind and reveal the truth, but the businessman has a practiced coolness that betrays little. If there is a remote possibility that he was responsible for Curtia's death, it goes against the very nature of Roman manhood to submit to Epidius. Yet he cannot be certain.

What he can be certain of is the man's character. Curtia's death aside, if he accepts this Epidius's money he will have failed his father and mother. The business Publius senior laboured long to create will have turned to dust at the hands of a man his father despised. He also suspects his mother's contempt of Epidius springs from some past event of which he has no knowledge and he can imagine the look in her eyes if he submits to such a vile creature. Not mention what his brother will have to say.

He stands up abruptly and Epidius's somewhat surprised eyes follow him as he leaves the room abruptly. Publius returns with a money pouch clutched in his fist. It jangles as he places it on the table.

– What's that?

– Next month's rent and loan repayment in advance.

– What about my offer?

Publius just looks at him in silence. Epidius has his answer. He picks up the money and rises. He is almost snarling as he speaks. – You're a fool.

– Well, at least I stopped myself before I became an even bigger one.

After a moment or two, Epidius starts to laugh, laughs all the way to the door.

– You're nothing. *Nothing.*

Look at poor Publius staring at the open doorway through which Epidius exited. His face is a picture of misery.

He whispers. – You're right.

Perhaps misery is the wrong word. What I should have said is self-pity.

SCAENA 13

When I came here, I fucked, then I went home [26]

The sun has set, but some light lingers, clinging to this small part of the world. There is yet enough for you to see where we are. This is the Via Stabiana and just ahead is the Stabian gate itself. See how the streets grow quiet as dark approaches? Many Pompeiians retreat behind their walls and cede the streets to those in search of entertainment; wine, whores and gambling. But this is also the time of lovers and of secret liaisons, and it is one such we shall observe now as we pass beyond the gate.

What are these dark shapes that line the road, you wonder? Well, we now walk the road of the dead. Oh, sorry, that sounds so melodramatic. They are the tombs of people who once lived on the other side of Pompeii's wall. Many mortals believe that after dark their spirits still wander this road, and seek to regain entry into the city, but cannot pass beyond its walls. Look, some of the tombs date to the time of Sulla, others as far back as the Punic Wars. They must have been wealthy, you're thinking, some of these people. Many tombs are as big as houses now occupied by the living, albeit the poorer ones. And for all that, within their stone chambers there remain but a few bones and a handful of dust. These monuments are their last desperate grasp at immortality in this world.

Many Pompeiians would not visit such a place once the sun has set. They fear they will be cursed, or their body possessed by a spirit. But it is also a place where young lovers often venture. Love knows no fear, you see. Or should I say, lust knows no fear.

We're almost there. Shhh. Listen. Over there in the deep shadows behind that tall, square tomb sits a smaller one, and yet a fine one. Gaius Caelius Secundus. Look at the decoration carved in the stone. The shield, the sword, the barbarian entwined in palm leaves. Bet that cost a small fortune. But all of that was almost two centuries ago.

GAIUS CAELIUS SECUNDUS, SOLDIER OF THE EIGHTH COHORT, LIVED TWENTY-EIGHT YEARS, SERVED FOURTEEN [27]

Are you listening?

No, of course you're not. It is not the tomb that interests you but what is taking place on top of it. Hmm. This pair show little respect for the great battlefield deeds of the man who rests beneath them. His tomb is nothing more than a convenient, smooth, yet cold surface upon which to conduct their deed. Listen to the grunts. Almost savage, are they not? They remind me of the frenzied growls of beasts as they tear their prey to pieces. You were granted this rapaciousness for one reason alone, of course, which should be evident. Yet at this moment, such long term implications are far from the mind of the youth whose bare behind rises and falls with such rapidity before your eyes. His name is Atimetus, the adopted son of a well-off former politician called Tiberius Verus. He is twenty-two and quite spoiled and spends as much of his time as possible engaging in the act you now observe. Except the target of his lust changes with as much frequency as he can manage, or purchase. Yet few of the girls he seduces are aware of this, or if they are they are simply happy to part their legs for the pleasures Atimetus's well-filled pockets can offer.

This young rascal, the natural son of his adopted father's former slave, does not concern us much at this juncture. But the girl with her plump, bare legs in the air does. You can barely see her, I know, blanketed as she is beneath Atimetus's jerking body and the dishevelled tangle of his expensive tunic. Let us move in for a closer look. Slowly, come around here, around the side, so that we may look directly down on her face.

Now you recognise her? I know the light is dim, but still you can surely identify the face of Cornelia, sister of Publius. Sweat bathes her forehead and cheeks, and her features are distorted through her exertions. The pair of them almost seem to be in pain, do they not? It is funny, I think. Funny ironic, I mean, that an act of such apparent pleasure for mortals produces such seemingly agonised expressions. It nears its end now, as you can hear and see. At least for Atimetus it does. The thrusts intensify, the grunts pitch upwards, his head lifts to the darkening sky. In five seconds he will cry out with intense gratification as his seed is spilled into the welcoming body of Cornelia. There.

Cornelia's pleasure has been nowhere near as intense, Atimetus not having troubled himself with such a consideration. And yet she bears a look of satisfaction. A grin touches her lips as she embraces the now limp body of her lover. Cornelia, you see, foolish girl that she is, believes she has snared a fine rabbit by giving herself to him. Listen to her foolishness deepen.

She whispers. – Atimetus. Do you really love me?

He lifts his head from her shoulder and stares down at her. He is thinking that her face is as plain as the side of a house, but that she was a really good fuck, but he must not let wine entice such a lowering of standards again.

He mumbles. – Of course.

He climbs down and tidies his attire.

– Will, we meet again soon?

In that pause of silence alone you can read his intentions.

– Sure. Soon.

– When? Where?

– Eh, I'm going to Nuceria on my father's business for a while. After that. As soon as I return I will come see you.

Cornelia climbs down now, straightens her stola about her legs, wipes her brow. She reaches to embrace him once more, but he shrugs her away, trying to conceal it in a smile.

– Cornelia. My lovely. We must go. Your family will be fretting for you. Come, I will see you safely to your street.

He takes her hand and hurries away, pulling her along behind. He is anxious to be rid of the discomfort of her questions.

There they go, through the gate, disappearing into the darkening streets. All that remains of their presence are the stains of their coupling that defile the tomb of Gaius Popidius Rufus. In his battles with the barbarians he witnessed more honour than what passed here tonight, in his place of final rest.

SCAENA 14

At the dedication of the opus tabularum of Gnaeus Alleius Nigidius
Maius, at Pompeii on June Thirteenth, there will be a procession,
hunt, athletics and awnings. Greetings to Nigra [28]

They call this place where we stand the Porta Vesuvio, for
obvious reasons. The mountain rising to the north seems so
harmless. So passive. Pretty even. But it casts a very long shadow,
you know. Come, I wanted to show you something else I think
you may, if not enjoy, at least find interesting.

This point is the highest in the town. That's why that large
rectangular structure over on your right has been built here. It's
the termination of a branch of the Aqua Augusta, which is one
hundred Roman miles long, and supplies Pompeii's citizens and
slaves with a seemingly unending supply of fresh water. Impressive engineering. But there are structures even more impressive
in this place. Look, over there to your right you can see the tops
of some of the forum temples, and beyond those the main
theatre. But there is another one that interests us today. Let's
take a closer look.

Where is everyone? Oh, yes, strange isn't it? A visitor walking through that gate might believe the place has been visited by a plague that stole the lives of every inhabitant. Or perhaps they have all fled in fear of a barbarian invasion? Unlikely, as Rome sits between us and the barbarian hordes. But it is strangely silent on this fine summer's day.

That's the former home of Caecilius Jucundus on your left, by the way. Remember the banker that Epidius murdered on the side of Vesuvius? One of his sons lives there now. The entrance looks a bit tatty, doesn't it? The weeds, the broken flowerpot. But don't pay it too much attention, we'll make a brief return to this house in the dead of night sometime soon.

See that large building site on the left at the crossroads? That's a project of Gnaeus Alleius Nigidus Maius. You know there's only one public baths still in working order since the earthquake? It was a situation that Gnaeus decided to exploit a couple of years back, and that site will soon host the Central Baths, the largest in the town. Romans, rich and poor alike, find the world quite intolerable without their baths, and Gnaeus envisages that the project will yield him a near-eternal source of income. He's also breaking new ground with regard to the old rules about mixed bathing, as he told his architect only to construct one set of facilities. Oh this is a debate that has gone on almost as long as Rome itself. Various emperors, like Augustus, often take moralistic turns and ban the practice. But the famously immodest Romans dislike the inconvenience it causes them and would prefer its return. Gnaeus is planning to exploit that to make his bathing complex the most modern, luxurious and most successful outside Rome itself. Construction will not be complete for many years yet. And to be honest, it will never be complete. You would almost feel like calling out to the handful of slaves toiling away in there today to cease work and rest their weary bones, as not a single drop of water will ever cleanse the skin of any Pompeiian within its walls.

Turn here onto the Via Nola. Where are we going? You'll see.

Still no sign of a Pompeiian citizen. Oh wait. There. That mother sitting in the shade of the doorway nursing her baby. And there's someone else, down that laneway. A slave by the look of him, beating a rug against a wall. So the place has not been abandoned. Although many doorways remain closed, and the few shops in this street are shuttered. One more turn. Here on the right. Ah yes, you recognise the street we recently visited, the Via Livia. There's the bakery of Publius, also shuttered. Not something he would do lightly, given his business's difficult position.

Yes, I hear that. Music in the distance. Trumpets, cornus, flutes and drums, I believe. A triumphal sound. Turn and look south along the street. You can glimpse the crowds lining the Via Dell'Abbondanza. Let us join them.

What's going on? Perhaps a visit by a famous dignitary. The Emperor perhaps? Or a triumphal march? No. No famous generals hail from this backwater. Yes, it is hard to see anything, the people seem to be six deep, all looking to their right in anticipation of whatever is coming. At least you have solved the mystery of the whereabouts of the population. But I think you'll need a better viewing point.

There.

This balcony above the street is perfect. This is Pompeii's main thoroughfare, you know. Its widest street. It kind of puts Pompeii's scale in context, as it would be quite possible to toss an apple to that girl on the balcony opposite.

Anyway, look to you're right, towards the forum. You can just see the head of the procession, but it is still some way off. Those in the balcony across the street clutch a basket filled with rose petals, ready to shower down on the approaching spectacle. The very poor throw leaves, by the way.

But cast your eyes down. This is what I wished to show you.

See who approaches at the head of the procession, mounted on a beautiful white horse, dressed in all his finery. Yes, Gnaeus Alleius Nigidius Maius, regarded by many as Pompeii's leading citizen. Well, certainly its richest. For the moment. He waves and smiles as his horse trots along, happy to accept the plaudits, revelling in the cheering, the rain of petals that showers down upon him. How they love him. Yes, wealth can indeed purchase love of a sort.

Behind him come four slaves carrying a wooden platform on their shoulders. That wood and plaster effigy on the top is supposed to be Apollo, god of many things: music, intellectual pursuits, prophecy, healing. Officially today's events are in his honour, although Gnaeus likes the idea that Pompeiians will subconsciously associate him with the great god.

Now come some cornu and flute players, accompanied by pretty girls in colourful tunics who twirl and swirl in and out of the musicians. The men whistle and make lewd suggestions whenever a girl comes within earshot, and are rewarded with bright smiles.

Two further carts trundle by, each laden with loaves of bread, which more girls toss to the crowd. Another gift from the generous Gnaeus. Publius was only too pleased to be asked to exclusively supply the loaves. It was extra business he hadn't counted on. Of course Gnaeus has his reasons for choosing Publius's bakery. He rarely does anything that doesn't benefit him in some way.

There is lots more to see, drummers, caged beasts, flag bearers, more musicians, but we have lingered here long enough. Let us rush ahead in time and place to the procession's destination.

~

CAIUS QUINCTIUS VALGUS,

SON OF GAIUS, AND MARCUS PORCIUS, SON OF
MARCUS,
QUINQUENNIAL DUUMVIRS,
FOR THE HONOUR OF THE COLONY,
SAW TO THE CONSTRUCTION OF THE
AMPHITHEATRE AT THEIR OWN
EXPENSE AND GAVE IT TO THE COLONISTS IN
PERPETUITY [29]

Here we are. That's quite striking, don't you think? It is the largest structure in the town and it has been here for a century and half. They call it the Spectacula, although you probably call it an amphitheatre. You know they don't even have one in Rome to match this? Or at least not yet, but they've recently started building one. The Pompeiians love their games almost as much as they love their theatre. And look at the crowds! This is a special occasion as Gnaeus has not only financed a hunt in the arena today, but has done so to celebrate the completion of what the council have named the Opus Tabularum. Gnaeus paid a small army of artists to decorate the entire inner wall surrounding the arena with scenes of former gladiatorial games, hunts and athletic contests. Is there no end to the man's generosity? Almost all of Pompeii is here along with thousands of visitors from the surrounding towns and countryside. And everyone is keen to be a part of the action. Come. Let us stroll through the crowds towards that large tent in front of the central arches.

Tables have been set up everywhere. That one is selling trinkets, souvenirs of the great occasion. Tiny, crudely carved wooden gladiators with swords drawn. The children pester their parents to buy them. Next to him is a man selling corn, freshly roasted over a burning brazier. The aroma is attractive, and it draws many customers. And the people sate their thirst from one of the many bar owners who are here selling wine from jugs at higher than usual prices. Oh and look, under the arch over there. It is Restitutus and the slave Hermeros, doing a roaring trade in quarter loaves. Sales are so good that Publius has returned to the bakery with Staphylus to fetch more supplies. Publius's younger brother is a handsome young man now. His dark eyes, sturdy jaw-line and shiny brown hair catches the attention of many a girl. But Restitutus does not appear to be very happy today. He reserves his smiles only for the pretty female customers, but he feels frustrated to be stuck behind the table selling bread when there is so much fun to be had.

Restitutus has deceived many girls [30]

His eyes catch another girl's, but he lowers them immediately and turns to place more bread on the table. The girl turns away. Her name is Urbana and she is a prostitute and a tender soul. She is actually his favourite, and he has spent many a happy hour in her arms telling her how much he adores her. But he shames himself now by denying her in public. Urbana is used to such treatment and the next time Restitutus visits her she will forget his unwillingness to meet her eyes, welcome him with a warm embrace and provide him with whatever gratification he can afford to pay for. Now Urbana has spotted two fairly well-dressed men, visitors, by the look of them, and moves towards them.

And there is another young man you have met. Atimetus. He has already consumed too much wine as you can probably guess, judging by the slight weave of his steps. Follow him for a moment. Now watch. Look ahead at that stall in the open, the one with the canopy selling cheap jewellery. She has her back to us, but that's Cornelia, sister of Restitutus and Publius with a couple of her friends tittering over earrings and bracelets. And now Atimetus has spotted her. Ah. The merriness vanishes from his face. He turns sharply and ducks behind another stall before she can spot him. Let him go. We'll catch up with him eventually.

That man standing on the wooden box and carrying the colourful banner above his head is Daphnicus, and the girl with the scarred face hovering behind him is Felicia. They are both slaves. Let's listen to him for a moment.

– ...the finest inn in Pompeii. The Inn of Cominia Lucilla! Excellent rooms for people of quality. Feathered beds. Two private bath suites! First class food and wine! Stay at the Inn of Cominia Lucilla on the Via del Venditores. Just a short walk from the Spectacula.

He will repeat that a thousand times this day. And at some point we shall take up his suggestion and pay a visit to this Cominia Lucilla's fine establishment. That, I promise, shall provide you with some interest.

But here we are at the tent. It has been specially erected to entertain Pompeii's leading citizenry, another benefaction of Gnaeus's. Let's see what the more moneyed men and women of this little town are up to.

Very pleasant in here, I think you'll agree, out from under the hot sun. Slaves wave huge fans to further ensure the comfort of the guests. Other slaves provide wine, water, fruit drinks and trays of snacks. Men and women alike are adorned with their finest garments, and there is enough silk in here to dress twenty elephants.

Look around. There are a number of people here you'll meet again. That short man there for example, with the red complexion and the big nose, he's Titus Suedius Clemens and that's dark-haired woman beside him is Fabia, his wife. He's been sent to Pompeii by Emperor Vespasian to retrieve lands that have been illegally appropriated from the state. Half the people here are guilty to some level, and they curse his presence.

Yet you can see how they fawn over him as if he is their greatest friend in the world? Oh and there's Saenecio Fortunatus, the theatre director. Although he is by no means a wealthy man, he is a friend and guest of Gnaeus who used to sponsor many of the theatre events. He is forever pestering Gnaeus to finance the re-building of the theatre. And at the back there, you can just glimpse through the crowd the figure of the man himself. Let's move closer. Gnaeus is chatting to one of the current duumvirs, Marcus Lucretius Fronto who's likely to be re-elected this year. I see the surprise in your eyes at the woman who stands by his side. Yes, that is Prima, mother of Publius the baker. What in the name of Venus is she doing at such a gathering? Well, the simple answer is that Gnaeus has been courting her for some time now. His first wife, Traebia died just months after the earthquake and Gnaeus threw himself into his business for many years until a chance meeting with Prima reignited the spark of a relationship that had briefly flourished during their youth. But it's a long story and we'll return to it at a more suitable time.

But doesn't Prima look a little uncomfortable trying to make small talk to all these dignitaries? Secretly she is cursing Gnaeus for inviting her here and cursing herself for accepting. But he was so insistent. She cannot wait for the reception to end so everyone will move into the arena and she can breathe fresh air again.

I beg you to elect Epidius Sabinus duumvir
with judicial power 31

Now, this should be entertaining. Epidius approaches Gnaeus. The two men despise each other. Lucretius Fronto, not a fan of Epidius either, makes his excuses and sidles off. Let's eavesdrop.

– Gnaeus!

– Epidius. I'm so glad you could come.

They smile like old friends reunited and shake hands. Secretly Epidius is here to gloat over a business success. They had both been bidding on the ruin of a property on the Via Consolare, one with a splendid view over the sea to the hills east of Surrentum, which held excellent development potential. The bids were supposedly sealed and secret, but Epidius's bid was successful, thanks to his having his ex-gladiator thug Albanus threaten to cut off the auctioneer's balls and feed them to the poor man's own dogs before his very eyes. Not surprisingly, he informed his client that Epidius's offer was the better, and kept his testicles between his legs.

– And Prima. You are looking as beautiful as ever.

– Thank you.

Prima says this without warmth and averts her eyes.

– Your generosity, Gnaeus, truly knows no bounds. You are the peoples' god today.

A modest shrug. – I do what I can to lighten life's burden.

– Well, you have certainly lightened my financial burden. That property on the Via Consolare will certainly fetch a generous sum when developed. But I imagine that being on the losing side in that transaction will be but the loss of small change to a man of your wealth.

Gnaeus grins at him. – Indeed, but I congratulate you on scooping up the crumbs from my table.

Epidius's smile falters as an ex-aedile and fullery owner called Lucius Popidius approaches and claps Gnaeus on the shoulder.

Lucius Popidius, aedile, Fuller 32

– Alleius Maius. I have heard today's games are to be splendid indeed. One hundred animals in the hunt. Awnings.

Celadus himself to fight. The fullers' guild wish to express their gratitude.

– Oh, consider it my gift to Pompeii, Lucius, in return for all she has given to me.

Epidius briefly wounded, has by now recovered his smugness.

– Oh you are too modest, Gnaeus Alleius Maius. And you not only lift the people's spirits, but all of the council's also. But I'm sure they will continue to repay your generosity in whatever small ways they can.

This comment, Gnaeus knows, is a less than subtle reference to the council's awarding of lucrative public contracts to persons held in high favour. Epidius is correct, of course, as Gnaeus has benefitted hugely from these down the years. Mind you, Epidius would dearly love to be so adored among the council himself for not dissimilar reasons. He shakes his head and smiles. They both know precisely where they stand on the matter.

– As ever Epidius, I ask nothing in return, merely to contribute to the prosperity of my home town.

Epidius takes a goblet of wine from a passing slave and sips. – Of course, if I am honoured enough to be elected duumvir this summer, I shall endeavour to impress your wishes upon the council.

– My wishes?

– Yes. As you just said yourself. You wish nothing in return. I will try my best to see your wishes fulfilled. Enjoy the festivities. Gnaeus. Lucius. Prima, my dear.

He smirks, raises his drink to Gnaeus and walks away. Gnaeus maintains his composure until Lucius Popidius also makes his goodbyes and departs.

Prima whispers. – I despise that man.

Gnaeus's smile evaporates and is replaced with a snarl. –

Epidius? There are few who don't. But I've dealt with others like him before, and...

Prima interrupts him. – And where are they now?

Gnaeus raises his eyebrows at the hint of sharpness in her tone. – Indeed.

Prima looks directly at him. – You know, Gnaeus, sometimes I suspect you might be just as ruthless as Epidius when it comes to business matters.

– Please don't offend me with such a comparison.

A thin smile alights on her face, and then the moment is interrupted by a praeco, or what you might call a crier.

– My fellow Romans. I ask you to take your seats in the Spectacula. The festivities are about to begin!

SCAENA 15

Thirty pairs of gladiators of Gnaeus Alleius Maius, quinquennial, and their substitutes will fight at Pompeii. There will be a hunt. Good fortune to Maius, quinquennial. (Paris Martialis wishes good fortune to Maius) [33]

See the crowd teeming up the stair, crushing each other in the fight to gain the best seats. In a short time this space will be almost vacant, except for a handful of traders like Publius, who will keep their stalls open because the festivities will go on for hours and hours, and many will emerge for more food, wine or water, or simply to relieve themselves.

But let us follow Gnaeus and company through that tunnel in the centre.

Mmmm. Smelly in here. This tunnel is also used as a toilet on occasion. Rich people need to pee just as much the poor. But forget that if you can and focus on the patch of light ahead. And listen to the roar that echoes down this narrow chamber.

Oh, how you are dazzled by the light as we emerge. It is well past noon and the sun strikes you directly in the face. The huge awnings they have extended above the entire arena will provide little shade for those at the front. But you will become accustomed to the brightness and warmth, as the Pompeiians do, and your discomfort will soon be forgotten.

Now, look about. These broad, cushioned stone seats just above us are reserved for the élite. They like their space and do not like their genteel bottoms pressed against stone for hours. In this area the women are permitted to sit with their men, although back in Augustus's day this would have caused outrage. Yet times move on. But up there, high above in the last handful of rows at the back of the arena, you will see exclusively plebeian women, where the old rules still prevail to some degree. Yet many of the younger girls these days are happy to venture into the lower, mostly wooden seats to spend the day with their boyfriends and husbands, or even in search of one such. It is unlikely anyone will complain.

Gnaeus has again been generous in providing publicly owned slaves to sprinkle the crowds with cooling water, and to toss free handouts of bread and fruit. But it is his benefaction of the work in the arena that is the reason for this great event today. You see that high wall surrounding the arena? Six months ago it was a dull concrete grey, its former ornamentation weathered away during the past century. Now look at it. Depicting the glory of countless previous games and hunts: the famous gladiators who have fought and won here, the great venatores who slayed a hundred beasts, the magnificent athletes who ran and threw and wrestled their way to greatness. All those heroic moments are recorded and a little piece of immortality is granted them in return.

It's gaudy, if you ask me. But it is designed to please the masses, and it certainly seems to be achieving its goal.

I see your eye is drawn to the arena itself. Those little hills are wooden underneath, then covered with hard packed soil. The giant boulders are also wooden platforms covered in painted cloths. And the tall poles clustered over to the right are the organisers' attempt to re-create a forest. A hundred shrubs and bushes have been temporarily planted in the ground and there is even a pond there near the centre. They have created their own wilderness in which to stage their hunt, although you do have to use a little imagination.

Proceedings are about to get under way. A crier appears close to us. The duumviri rarely speak personally. Duumvir Fronto's elderly croak can barely be heard across a dining table, never mind an arena. The other duumvir is that little fat middle-aged man with the red face, yes, the one with the beautiful dark-haired seventeen-year-old wife, Sabina. His name is Lucius Statius Receptus, and he's got quite a high-pitched little voice that has earned him the nickname Lucius Puella, or Lucius the little girl. It was decided, diplomatically, at the last council meeting that it would be best if he didn't make any public speeches for the remainder of his term. Anyway, it doesn't bother him too much as his mind is occupied with other thoughts since his recent marriage to pretty little Sabina, as you can imagine. But we shall see more of that ill-matched pair in the future, Sabina in particular.

Sabina, wife 34

The praeco will send his booming voice across the arena in a moment, and lesser praecōnēs throughout the crowd will convey his words to the most distant seats. The crowd has fallen to complete silence. And I shall too for the moment.

– My fellow Romans. We gather today to celebrate the Opus Tabularum, this wonderful work of art which you see adorning the wall surrounding the entire arena. On it you can see the great victories of Phileros the Spaniard, undefeated champion of Pompeii for eight years in the days of Emperor Augustus. You can see Marcius of Capua, famed venator who slew a thousand beasts before your eyes. And you can witness again the triumphs of Hilarus, the retarius who brought down thirty men. And not just these, but countless others, all immortalised in our great Spectacula, the finest in the empire!

A roar of Pompeiian pride echoes back and forth throughout the great structure. The man continues.

– And today we honour he who has bestowed us with this generous gift, and who has many times before given freely from his own purse to allow us to enjoy our traditional games. You know him well, my friends, he is the greatest giver of games, the defender of the colony, the great benefactor to the entire city of Pompeii and its people. He is Gnaeus ...Alleius... Nigidius .. Maius!

Each name is punctuated with an ever higher pitch of tone. By the time he reaches the end, 'Maius' is almost lost in the thunderous applause and cheering. And there is the great man. Observe. He rises, his arms spread wide as though he could embrace every person present. He is good at milking this. See how he raises his arms high to salute even those high up in the arena, and then turns to accept the applause of those at his back. You would swear he knew every one in the arena personally. And look over there at the expression on Epidius's face. He looks like he's bitten into a lemon, yet he must applaud with the rest or appear to be at odds with the people. It must be killing him. Poor thing.

Finally Gnaeus sits and the applause fades, but an excited murmur now fills the Spectacula. People can see the giant wooden cages being wheeled into the arena through the tunnels at both ends. No hunters appear yet. They won't be out for a while. Before the main feast of killing, there are usually a couple of aperitifs for the crowds to enjoy.

You see that small herd of goats they've led into the arena?

Their shepherd now flees as though his tunic is on fire and conceals himself safely behind the cages. The crowd begin to chant. They count. Can you hear it?

– Unus, duo, tres, quattuor, quinque, sex, septem, octo, novem, *decem!*

Five of the smaller cages at either end of the arena are thrown open and from each emerges a starving hound. They snap at each other and snarl, saliva drips from their bared gums. One runs towards the high wall and attempts to hurl himself up its height so he can feast on the people above it. The dog slithers back down to the sand, leaving two dirty streaks on Gnaeus's newly painted walls and the moment brings howls of laughter from the audience. But now the other dogs have scented a prey other than people. The goats too have sensed it and their bleating can even be heard above the crowd. The hounds wander among the fake hillocks and around the bushes, snouts almost to the ground, haunches raised, ready to leap. The poor goats think there will be safety in numbers and cluster together near the pond at the centre. But soon they are surrounded by a host of snarling faces. One dog lunges and the goats scatter, sending the others in pursuit about the arena. The chaos of human voices lifts in joy as the first goat is downed beside the pond. Its bleats turn to screams as the dog tears pieces from its flesh. Blood runs into the sand and spills over into the water, which begins to turn red. The goat's kicking and thrashing is in vain, and finally its screams are silenced as the dog tears at its throat.

Another has been seized to the north end. And another one that tries to conceal itself in the 'forest'. And so it will continue until each goat has been torn to pieces and the dogs', and the people's, appetite has been sated.

And when this is done, the venatores will venture forth, some on foot, some on horseback, and during the hours to come they will pursue and butcher fifty beasts; wolves, bears, boar, bulls.

Such is entertainment in the Roman world. This and worse.

But let's not linger as I would like you to meet someone else. He waits now in one of the dim corridors beneath our feet. He is a gladiator readying himself for battle. Because of the special nature of the event, Gnaeus has also commissioned a unique bonus – perhaps the most famed gladiator in the region will fight the young, rising star, thrilling the crowds with their skills and courage. Come.

Yes it is dark after the brightness above. The torches struggle to illuminate the corridor. But wait a moment.

Girls' heart throb,
Thracian gladiator, Celadus [35]

There. Look at the gladiator who thrusts and parries against an invisible opponent. He is yet to don his helmet, but is other-wise readied for battle. You see his short sword with the top of the blade curved? It is a Thracian weapon that allows the bearer to strike around an opponent's shield, slashing at his back and sides. His name is Celadus the Thracian. Tall, with dark short hair, not exactly handsome, but he has a noble face, I would say. His broad shoulders were ever thus, and brought his mother great pain when she tried to push him free of her body. I was required to answer her screeched prayers to bring him safely into this world. He is a man beloved of Pompeiians, especially young Pompeiian girls of plebeian class. The men too admire him for his skill and his courage, and even for his merciful nature.

The gladiatorial troupe of
Pomponius Faustinus [36]

The two young lads waiting in attendance are slaves, property of Pomponius Faustinus, who owns a respected ludus, or gladiator school, in the town. Ah, he approaches. He doesn't look much like the sort of person you'd associate with gladiators, does he? Skinny, not very tall, shuffling gait, bald, hollow cheeks, thinning, greying hair. Looks like a breeze would knock him over. Yet he has no need for muscle or weapons skills as he is merely a businessman, and Celadus and a hundred like him in Pomponius's ludus are his business. He is all smiles.

– Celadus. I think you've practised enough.

Celadus bows his head to his master.

– Dominus, a gladiator can never have enough practice.

Pomponius smiles and claps Celadus on the bare shoulder.

– A true professional. But I would ask you to stop for a short time. Someone is anxious to speak with you.

– Who, Dominus?

– I, Celadus.

You'll probably recognise the voice that has echoed along the corridor from behind us.

Celadus turns, instinctively lifting his sword then lowering it immediately. He bows his head and passes the weapon to one of the attending boys. The shield on his left arm is also unstrapped as he stands there.

Gnaeus has slipped away on some pretext from the crowd. He smiles.

– Look up, gladiator.

– Dominus. It is the greatest honour to meet you. How may I be of service to you?

– Well, firstly by winning today. And winning well.

– You have wagered on me, Dominus?

Gnaeus laughs, shakes his head. – No, but I am wagering that I can be of service to you as much as you to me.

Celadus is puzzled. Pomponius steps behind Gnaeus.

– Gnaeus has a proposal for you, Celadus.

Gnaeus regards the man with irritation.

– Thank you, Pomponius, I believe I was about to communicate that myself.

– I'm sorry, sir.

– Celadus. You were a free man, were you not?

– It is three years since I enjoyed my freedom, Dominus.

– And you voluntarily joined the ludus to pay off gambling debts?

– To my shame, sir.

– Your shame is well behind you. It has been replaced by glory.

– Thank you, sir.

– Yet you would have to win many more battles to completely clear your debt?

– I think perhaps ten more victories would release me from debt.

– Well, what would you say if you merely had to win one more battle? Today's.

Celadus looks directly at Gnaeus, then to Pomponius, then back again, his face a picture of incomprehension.

– I am a businessman, as you know. And in business a man acquires enemies. The more successful he is, the more enemies, and the more desperate his enemies. I require a bodyguard. But not just some ex-legionnaire. I require a bodyguard whose name will strike fear into anyone who hears it. And who better than the greatest gladiator in Campania? If you accept, your remaining debt will be paid, you will be given an apartment, and I will pay you three thousand sesterces a year, plus bonuses. And you will receive a share of the today's prize money – if the result is to my complete satisfaction.

Poor Celadus is lost for words. He stammers and looks to

Pomponius as if for confirmation this is not a dream. The man nods and grins.

– What do you know of today's opponent?

– Pugnax, sir? I have not fought him before, but I know him. We have met many times in town. He is an honourable young man. And very skilled. He is of the Neronian school. A murmillo. It is a challenge I look forward to.

Pugnax, Neronian, victorius three times 37

– He's a good deal younger than you then?

– I don't know my age, sir, it is perhaps twenty-eight, but yes, he is younger by some years.

– Hmm. Well, I hope my offer will provide the incentive to defeat this younger man, this Pugnax. Do you accept?

Celadus nods feverishly. – Yes, sir, thank you.

– Just don't get killed, or the offer will no longer stand.

Celadus smiles thinly. – Yes, sir.

Gnaeus and Pomponius laugh. Gnaeus turns away, pauses, and turns back again. – One other thing.

– Yes, sir?

He pauses, glances at Pomponius briefly.

– I want you to kill him.

Celadus's eyes widen. – But sir, what if he fights well?

– If you are to be my bodyguard, I want a clear message left in the minds of all those watching. That this will be their fate too if they cross me. And I will also expect you to obey me without question. Is that clear?

Celadus hesitates. Now he understands what Gnaeus meant when he said he expected complete satisfaction. He sees his freedom from debt and from the confines of the ludus, he sees his own apartment, he sees money in his pouch, good food, women, wine. And then he sees the dishonour he must bring upon himself to earn all those things. He has little time to think. He actually likes Pugnax. They have met many times in bars or whorehouses and shared tales of battles and beautiful girls. In another world they might have been good friends.

He briefly considers that the match might result in Pugnax's death anyway, an honourable death. It is a rare thing indeed, but it is sufficient a straw for his conscience to grasp.

– It is clear, sir.

– Good. I hope to see you shortly and hold your hand aloft in victory.

Gnaeus grins at Celadus and whirls away.

I should let you in on a small secret. The gladiator called Pugnax belongs to a ludus in which Epidius has a small financial interest. He won't lose any money of consequence if his man is killed, but Gnaeus knows that Epidius will most definitely be cheering the murmillo. Should Pugnax perish, it will merely be so Gnaeus can enjoy another infinitesimally small victory over the man. He can be quite ruthless when the mood takes him.

Listen. The roaring above has dimmed. Thirty-two beasts lie dead. New hunters prepare their bows and swords and spears outside the Spectacula, ready to enter the arena for a fresh bout of killing. More beasts' cages are wheeled into position. But the crier orders a break in proceedings, with the promise of something special when the festivities resume. Many of the crowd stream out, to relieve themselves, to purchase wine, fruit, bread. Others remain in their seats, fearful of losing their spot.

Prima thanks Gnaeus but says she is feeling unwell. He assigns two slaves to accompany her home. She is unwell in a manner of speaking. She is sick of the sight of blood, but even more sick of the company she has been forced to endure. She finds the pretentions of many of Pompeii's noble folk too much to bear, and although a strong woman, cannot help but be upset at the thinly disguised allusion to her background in the form of questions about her being the widow of a mere baker. She is also angry at Gnaeus for leaving her alone for so long, although she knows that certain functions are expected of him during occasions such a this. There she goes across off through the stalls, not even pausing when she passes her own son's bread stall. She cannot wait to get home and rest in the shade of their small peristyle.

But listen, the special treat that the praeco announced is about to commence. See? In the centre, near the pond, where the whole arena has a clear view. There stand Celadus and Pugnax, swords at their sides, shields held before them, as though standing to attention. The plumage on their helmets is a splash of colour under the bleaching bright of the afternoon sun. Their battle has just been announced and they were greeted with deafening cheers as they emerged from the tunnel. The praeco now lists their victories, each one greeted with a small cheer. And now at last they turn and face each other to do battle.

They have disappeared from sight behind one of those fake hills, but you can still hear the swords clash above the whoops of the crowd. You can even hear the grunts and gasps of the gladiators as they hack at each other. There now, they have returned to our line of vision. Pugnax's youth serves him well early on, and he almost downs Celadus several times. But the Thracian has the greater experience, and by not overly exerting himself with bursts of rage has conserved his energy.

Yet after almost a quarter of an hour's battle the legs of both are weary. It is clear that each is ready to crumple. But now Celadus feints, retreats and allows his knees to buckle a little. Pugnax sees his chance and attacks, but too late realises he has been deceived. Celadus draws blood from his side and shoulders the murmillo to the ground sending a small cloud of dust skywards. Pugnax yells out in pain. The wound is not fatal, but is sufficiently bad to signal the end of the contest. The crowd stand in unison and scream their adoration for the local champion.

Come. I will take you closer. It is necessary. But let us just observe Celadus and nothing more in these next moments.

Here we are. The centre of the arena. All around us the crowd scream their delight. Celadus stands with his sword tip pressed against Pugnax's heart. His face is shielded by his helmet, but I suspect you can see beyond the metal even without my help. The man on the ground has submitted. His sword and shield relinquished. His arm is raised in surrender. He has fought well, Celadus is thinking. He was one of the finest opponents he has ever done battle with and but for the mercy of the gods, he knows the positions could easily be reversed. Many times he has come to this, and each time he allowed the defeated to fight another day. He cannot hear the crowd. His own breathing sounds like a storm inside his helmet. And his own mind is whipping up a storm of its own. His head turns to his left and through the slits he catches a glimpse of Pompeii's élite, standing as are the rest, waiting for the conclusion. At the centre stands Gnaeus, his saviour from slavery...but only if he thrusts the sword. A single word comes into his head and screams itself at him. It blinds him to all other thoughts.

Freedom.

He looks down upon Puxnax again.

– Forgive me, my friend. May the gods be kind to you.

He catches a glimpse of the man's eyes through his visor as he drives the sword through Pugnax's heart. They were filled with disbelief. And now the man is dead, his final cry muffled inside his helmet.

He casts aside the bloodied sword and pulls his helmet free. And now the sounds of the arena come to him. It is a curious mix. Some roar adulation, blind loyalty, hero-worship. But many other voices are filled with disquiet. Does he hear boos scattered throughout the roar? He knows they know that Pugnax fought well, that he had submitted to Pompeii's champion. And yet Celadus chose to run him through when he lay helpless. He stands there unsure of his feelings.

– Freedom.

He says the word aloud. Perhaps it will soothe his own disquiet. It does not.

The cheering lifts again and he turns to see Gnaeus descending a wooden stairway that has been wheeled into place to give him access to the arena itself. He strides across the bloody sand, one arm raised to the crowd, then the other. He comes to Celadus, faces him. The crowd fall silent.

– Congratulations, Celadus. You fought well and will soon be a free man.

He does not reply. He cannot form any words.

Gnaeus lifts a laurel wreath from his side and places it upon the gladiator's head. He then clasps Celadus's arm and thrusts it high above his head. The crowd acclaim him with roars of support, but there is some derision also from those unhappy with the outcome. Gnaeus turns him in a full circle, pausing a moment longer as he stares up at Epidius.

This night Celadus will be feted in the barracks. He will be granted a feast, wine and whores. And tomorrow he will walk though the gates a free man. He is not among Pompeii's greatest thinkers, and so cannot figure out why he feels that this is not the commencement of his freedom, but the end of it.

SCAENA 16

We have wet the bed, host, I confess we have done wrong. If you want to know why, there was no chamber pot ₃₈

We have not strayed too far from the arena, but somewhat further in time, for several weeks have passed and we now stand...oh, I see you are becoming familiar with the street. Yes, that's Publius's bakery, and there he is, loading freshly baked loaves on to the handcart with his young helper, Staphylus. Publius will accompany the young lad on his delivery rounds today, and will keep a large wooden club concealed beneath the cart. He, Restitutus and the others have been taking turns to make sure Staphylus isn't accosted these past weeks. It's just another burden on his shoulders, he is thinking. But you don't need me to read his thoughts for you. Just look at his expression.

But we're not stopping here. Publius doesn't concern us at this moment. His home just happened to be on our way, and it serves the purpose of my tale to show you his home in relation to that of another, as they are very close together, perhaps in more ways than one. Around the next corner to the right. Yes that narrow street. It is a fine little street, is it not? Cleaner than most. Look at the rainbow of colours; the bright pinks, creams and rusty reds of the buildings, the red and green canopies providing welcome shade for those shopping, and some buildings even decorated with hanging baskets, all alive with jasmine, violets, irises, geraniums, lavender. You can smell the scents from here. A pretty scene, is it not? Let us stroll along among the early morning shoppers.

They call it Via del Venditores and it is a favourite street for the wealthier shopper, those in search of jewellery and ornamental silverware and fine lacy cloths to beautify their bodies. Those who occupy these shops were quick to restore their street after the earthquake and they kept the town's painters and plasterers and roofers in pocket for many months. You won't find any seedy bars or brothels along here. And there isn't even a thermopolium to sate your appetite. Although there's a spice seller over there, as expensive as jewellery, you know? And talking of jewels, look on the left there, the jewellery shop of Campanus, the finest craftsman in the Campania region.

CAMPANUS, GEMCUTTER [39]

Campanus will carve you a bracelet of gold in the form of a snake, complete with scales, or fashion for you a small ring inlaid with a hundred tiny precious stones, so intricate you will wonder if it is the work of the gods themselves. He will even immortalise your face on a ring or a pendant, as some do to stretch their existence. But you better have deep pockets, as great skill demands handsome rewards. He intends to be very wealthy before his eyesight begins to betray him, as inevitably it will, he being of flesh and blood, and not cast in metal.

Now let's see. Ah yes there on the right, across the street. Not all the buildings on this street are the shops of silversmiths and silk sellers. That wide building with the wicker hanging baskets and potted shrubs is a lodging house and inn. And a popular one. It has been in the hands of one Cominia Lucilla these last six months and we shall be afforded a glimpse of her momentarily.

The door opens and a girl of seventeen emerges carrying a cloth sack over each shoulder. Her face is a little bent out of shape as you can see, the result of countless beatings from her former master. That is not Cominia of course, but one of her slaves, Felicia, who you saw briefly outside the arena. A voice follows the girl out on to the street.

– Felicia!
– Yes, Domina?

Her face appears briefly at the half-open doorway, although it is mostly lost in the darkness of the vestibulum.

Mustius the fuller did the whitewashing 40

– While you're at the fullers, collect the three tunics we left there four days ago. And I need those sheets returned tomorrow, no later. Tell Mustius that Cominia ordered this. And they'd better be perfect.

– Yes Domina.

What is our business with this lady, you're wondering?

Come. Let us proceed directly to the large room off to the left of the atrium. Cominia Lucilla uses this as her tablinum, which differs somewhat from most other Roman homes. She has adapted this building to better serve as a large hostel and it at variance in many respects. The slave quarters, for example, are not a couple of poky spaces in a hidden corner, but five rooms at the rear of the building, each as large as her own bedroom, although her own bed is unshared. And none of the outer rooms are rented out to retailers, but serve as bedrooms for guests. But let us learn more of Cominia herself.

There she sits behind a table in that dimly lit room. The surface is covered in wax tablets and scrolls, and another of her slaves, a young man named Daphnicus, stands by her side. Cominia has three slaves in all, as well as three paid servants. The Inn of Cominia Lucilla has twenty bedrooms to offer. She is a very successful inn-keeper and businesswoman. Although some of her guests are less welcome than others.

Sollemnes was here 41

– That drunken lout Sollemnes shit and pissed the bed last night. I've had to send Felicia to the fullers with the bedclothes.

There is an irony in this. Felicia takes the piss-soaked sheets to the fullers who will trample them in piss to cleanse them.

– Perhaps I should have turned Sollemnes away when I saw the state of him Domina. I apologise. But Satura insists there *was* a chamber pot. He was probably too drunk to find it.

Daphnicus is a short, wiry man of twenty-seven purchased in Herculaneum. He can read, write, add and subtract, and he and Felicia, the girl you met outside, are a couple.

Daphnicus was here with his Felicia 42

– It's not your fault, Daphnicus. We don't want to get a reputation for turning people away, even if they're drunk. Otherwise we'd be turning away half our custom during the games. At least he didn't shit all over the walls.

Daphnicus laughs. – Also Domina, the man in seven, Dionysios Polybius. I believe he had a whore in his room last night.

– Was she seen?

– Satura assures me it was not necessary to see her in person. There was – Daphnicus coughs – evidence of her presence.

Cominia sighs. – Personally I don't care if he had ten whores in his room. But if he does he must pay for their accommodation. That should discourage bringing whores into my inn. I don't want to earn a reputation as a high-class brothel. Charge Dionysios double for last night. If he complains, send him to me. I'm sure he won't want a fuss in case his wife hears of it.

Dionysios fucks whenever he wants to 43

– As you wish, Domina. One other matter. The baker has been insistent these recent days that we settle his bill. We owe him for three weeks' supply.

Cominia picks up the relevant tablet and studies it for a few moments. You can tell she is irritated.

– Didn't you tell him we would settle his account on the ides of each month like everyone else?

– Yes, but he says he prefers weekly payment. He is a grumpy bastard.

– Yet his bread is very good. The guests appreciate it.

The grumpy bastard, Publius being he, arrives at the rear entrance to the property at that fortunate moment.

Cominia is informed and rises. – It's time I met the baker and set him straight on a few matters.

Now, as I promised you, things will become interesting. Let's follow Cominia as she walks with a slight but noticeable limp through the dimness of the house, along the narrow passage that leads to the street bordering the rear of her property. She steps through the open door. The sun has risen sufficiently to spear a thin shaft of light along this narrow laneway and her face now comes to rest directly in its path. Look closely. She is different. Yet the same. Changed, yet unchanged.

You don't recognise this woman even under the bright summer sun? Hmm. Perhaps I should have said nothing then, secreted her identity within my breast until the last. Kept her as a little twist in my tale. Well, too late now. I might as well show you.

But we must take a brief trip back in time before we resume.

Take my hand.

SCAENA 17

The lucky ones 44

There is a tale from our history of the phoenix, who when destroyed by fire magically reincarnates itself from the ashes. You've probably heard it, or some version of it. Although I've personally never seen a phoenix do such a thing. Well, no matter, let us behold one now, cradled in the arms of another as the world falls apart about her head. Yes, we have returned to the moments after the earthquake and there below us lies Pompeii in ruins. Ignore all the rest, the crumbling temples, the gaping rooftops and the screams of the dying and the bereaved. We will hasten straight down into the atrium of the inn of the recently deceased Mariona.

There Cygnia lies in the impluvium, its waters stained with blood, enclosed in the arms of Chrestus, her body broken and bent. But she is not dead. Far from it. Pains scream from every limb, every muscle, and she can barely move a finger. Yet her mind dances with thoughts, and she makes them dance to her tune.

The huge African lifts the knife and tears at the side of her tunic, revealing the small, coin-sized brand on her upper arm, put there when she was a child. He digs the point of the knife into her flesh. She screeches briefly. He eyes roll and she is thankfully spared any further pain as she slips into the realm of unconsciousness. He continues to cut skilfully, gently gliding the tip of the blade in a circular fashion and then slicing beneath the mark and simply flicking the offending coin of flesh away across the debris. It lands with a splat upon the leg of an upturned stool. Quickly he cups water from the impluvium and splashes it against the bleeding flesh, then reaches and tears a long strip of fabric from her tunic. He binds her newest wound – among the smallest she possesses – carries her to a table he has righted and lies her down, then sets about ripping away most of the remainder of her clothing, with which he binds the terrible gash on her leg, and the smaller one on her ribs.

His hardest task by far concerns her other leg, which is broken halfway along the shinbone. But he has splinted and repaired many such in his homeland and he is equal to the task. He counts her lucky that the bone does not protrude through the flesh, and he resets it as best he can, given the circumstances and the haste with which he must work, then uses the last of her tunic to bind the leg in three places to a flat piece of wood. She never awakens, which is a blessing of the gods, myself included. And she lies there finally, naked but for a small loincloth. Her perfect outer beauty has been tarnished. That within her remains.

Nobody disturbs his work. The citizens of Pompeii have their own concerns. He will spend the next hours, as darkness veils the weeping town, clambering through the ruins of the house in search of the possessions of Cygnia's former owners. He dresses her in a long woolen tunic of Severina's, and this he covers with one of silk, hemmed with blue lace, and then a fine stola, all of which are bloodstained by the end. She stirs at the necessary lifting and twisting, despite his gentleness, yet she remains beyond sense. When all of this is complete, he takes everything of value he can locate and carry, as Cygnia instructed him to do, and he lifts the girl and steals from the house. In the large sack on his back he carries almost twenty thousand sesterces; the money that Cygnia's master would have squandered. She will invest it with wisdom. Rufus Caesennius Paetus has no further need for it, after all. There is nothing one can purchase in the realm of Hades.

There are many still on the streets, of course, fires burn all around them and people frantically flit about clutching oil lamps, clawing through the rubble of fallen homes, crying out names, beseeching the gods for help. Few even cast an eye at the tall, dark-skinned slave as he passes, the small figure in his arms. They leave the town in the starlit night through one of the many breaches in the walls, and he carries her almost a Roman mile – that's a thousand paces – before pausing for rest. In the hours ahead she will stir and cry out in agony many times and he will soothe her, and wet her lips from a skin. An he will then resume, her fingers digging into the flesh of his arms and his back as she tries to resist the demons of pain that have possessed her. The road is broken and churned in parts as though a giant worm has crashed through its surface and then slithered off into the night, and Chrestus stumbles many times, but never falls. The girl fades beyond sense once more as dawn approaches and he hurries his pace. Soldiers pass them on horseback, their clopping hooves warning of their approach, but the small group barely look at them and ride as hard as the road will allow towards Pompeii.

By the time Apollo hurls his first arrow of sunlight across the horizon Chrestus has carried her ten miles to the north along the coastal road to the town of Herculaneum. He enters along a seafront street. Here too Vulcan has left his mark and similar scenes greet Chrestus as those he witnessed in Pompeii. Some houses stand firm, others have crumbled, people still dig with their bare hands among the ruins, although with dwindling energy and hope. If he expected to find help from these people, he soon abandons the thought. He turns into a long, narrow street at the end of which he can see the slopes of Vesuvius. A man sits against a wall, head tilted back, his throat cut, his tunic the colour of cherries, and still glistening. Above his head in the cracked plaster, the word 'Expilator' has been carved with the bloody knife that saw his end. Looter.

A group of soldiers appear from a side street. They are lightly armed, coated in dust and speckled with dried blood. They are Immunes, the class of Roman soldier who excel at certain duties; engineers, field medicine, carpenters. As the earthquake struck its tremors were felt all the way to Naples, which was fortunate as Emperor Nero happened to be performing on stage at that precise moment. It was fortunate not only for his audience that his acting was interrupted, but that he was on hand to command half a legion south to assist those who lived in Vesuvius's shadow. These Immunes are merely an advance team, the rest will not arrive for hours. But for now, for Chrestus, they will suffice, as even the mighty warrior's legs weaken after his night of burden.

– Help me? My mistress has been crushed, but she lives.

The one who appears to be the leader – his name is Primigenius Gellianus – wanders over and pulls back the cloth that partially covers Cygnia's head. His eyes travel to her clothing, and he realises, or thinks he does, that she is a woman of import, perhaps a noble or the daughter of wealthy parents.

Greetings to Primigenius 45

Very wealthy, Primigenius is thinking, considering she owns

a slave as fine as the exotic, muscled figure that stands before him. His orders are to prioritize the nobles and the wealthy before the lower classes. He swirls about and clicks his fingers twice and commands stretcher-bearers to his side.

Chrestus has difficulty keeping pace with the trotting soldiers as they hurry Cygnia's body along towards the north western edge of the town, skirting fallen columns and walls and people. He sees where they are taking her now, and hears the wail of hundreds of voices, and he follows them into Herculaneum's theatre. It is considerably smaller than the one in Pompeii, but sufficient for the needs of this town. But it has never witnessed such scenes of tragedy on its stage. Fifty blazing braziers struggle to warm the cold winter's morning, Scattered about the terrace of stone steps lie the broken bodies of hundreds, their surviving families weep around them as army medics struggle to pull them from the arms of death. Saws hack at limbs, bone levers struggle to re-align legs and arms, glowing tile cauteries are slapped, hissing, against bleeding wounds, forceps are plunged deep as they search out splinters of shattered bone, thick needles plunge through flesh, bandages are overwhelmed by the flow of blood. And all to a chorus of agonized screeching.

The stretcher-bearers carry Cygnia through the crowds of plebeians to the orchestra, the open space in front of the stage. This and the lower tiers of seats are reserved for the privileged, and the poorer you are, the further up you must be placed, and the further from the care of the medics. A man is summoned. He carries no armour and his soldier's tunic is a mess of blood. He is wiping his hands on a cloth as he exchanges words with the stretcher-bearer.

She is placed on the ground and a woman attends her. She is once more stripped of her clothes and dignity, but in this place, no such concept exists. Her bandages are cut away as Chrestus watches and the medic and woman wash and sew her gashes. Her leg is judged to be well set, and the man even takes a moment to congratulate the black slave who watches every move. With her flesh cleansed of blood for the most part, for the first time the African notices the birthmark that sits beneath her left breast. It is a full finger in length and height and is shaped like a swan. When the Romans slave traders took her they named her for the mark, and gave her the Latin name for swan, Cygnia.

When the medic and woman are done, Chrestus reaches down and touches the mark with his finger. He traces its shape and draws some comfort from it, for it is surely a mark of the gods, a sign of a destiny as yet unfulfilled. Well, he may be over-doing it in his interpretation. Cygnia will never become a princess or rule a kingdom or anything of the sort. But he is correct in one respect. It is a mark of the gods. And which god is there at the moment of birth? Yes, that would be me. And I am happy that this fine man finds solace in my work.

He sits now and covers her as best he can with the tattered dress and stola. He carries a brazier to her side to keep the chill away, and faces down the threats of those who protest at its removal.

And finally he sits at her side and rests. His eyes grow weary as he stares up at the scaenae frons. It is remarkable that this one has withstood the earthquake, while the one in Pompeii toppled in half.

She will waken in a few hours and wail with the rest. In the days ahead pus will burst from her wounds and a fever will rise deep inside her and take her within a finger's length of the after-life. Her leg will turn the colour of beet and swell to the thickness of Chrestus's. And through it all he will sit by her side, as he has the rare gift among mortals of seeing beyond her skin, of glimpsing the nature of her soul. And he judges it worthy of his sacrifice.

Her body is young and strong. As is her will. Days will pass. And weeks. And she will recover.

And she will be reborn as the lady traveller from Rome who was caught in the streets as the buildings crumbled, pulled from the debris by her loyal slave. Cygnia will take the name Cominia Lucilla, a name she knows from Rome. No one will question her, or doubt her credibility. Why should they? She speaks with the accent of a fine Roman woman, having spent years in the company of nobles. She knows their dress and she knows their customs. She wears her hair as they do. She eats as they do.

This place will be her home for almost a decade. She has money now, but she will in the years to come acquire a great deal more. At first she will open a small inn here, which like a child, will quickly outgrow its garments, and she will take a larger premises, and acquire slaves of her own, although with quite different motives than the normal buyer of human stock. She will earn the respect of the townspeople and will host a regular clientele, a true sign of appreciation. The Romans value a good businesswoman as much as a good businessman. Until the day will come when an opportunity will fall to acquire a premises in Pompeii befitting her greater ambitions. And she will return to that town with confidence, her head held high.

But we will learn more as we go.

Take another look at the fine theatre of Herculaneum. Today it is a place of endings for so many. But for Cygnia, it is a place of beginnings. And in more ways than one.

SCAENA 18

No young buck is complete
until he has fallen in love ₄₆

Cominia recognises him almost immediately although she has never spoken to him. She has seen him many times in the theatre in Herculaneum. Daphnicus handles most of her arrangements with tradesmen and she only becomes involved when she feels her personal attention is required. It is a rare thing anyway that the baker visits her inn in person.

Publius Comicius Restitutus stands with two loaves in his hands, frozen in the act of passing them into the sack that young Staphylus holds open. Each day for the four months since the woman opened her inn, his bakery has supplied her with forty loaves of bread. She is a good customer. A regular trade. Cash in his pocket. That is all she has meant to him until this moment. Oh, don't worry, I'm not going to tell you that his heart is pounding and his eyes instantly burn with passion for this woman. And neither does Cominia Lucilla swoon and clutch her hand to her breast as she realises she has stumbled upon her one true love. It is not love at first sight, if there ever was such a thing. Lust at first sight, perhaps, but not love.

But she too is given pause. It is the pause of ruffled expectations. Her mind's eye had constructed a fat, bald man of middle age and little intelligence, although not without some craft. He would be unshaven and sweaty, a singed apron stained with flour and dried-in dough wrapped about his bulging waist. The man before his fails to meet a solitary preconception. He is in his mid-twenties, she guesses, no Adonis, but not bad-looking. Dark hair, a little wild. Sharp, blue eyes peer from an intelligent face. He is average height, fit looking. And she knows him to be educated, or at least suspects this strongly from his visits to Herculaneum's theatre.

Publius's writing output these days may be limited, but his love of theatre has never faded. He travels whenever his work will allow it. He has never abandoned his dreams of theatre that filled his young head a decade ago, you know, but with each passing day he feels like a man trying to grasp hold of a cloud. It is this that etches that near-permanent frown on his face and causes him to snap and rage against the world.

Cominia herself is a lover of theatre. Although such a statement reveals little as almost every soul in the Roman Empire is a lover of theatre. But she and Publius share similar tastes. Not bawdy comedies beloved of the masses, but the more intellectual fare offered by the likes of Publius Terentius Afer, Euripides and Plautus. She observed him many times from the high seating at the theatre's rear to which women are confined. Herculaneum's theatre is small, and he usually sits in the rows just beneath the women's section, an area popular with young men keen to exchange flirtations with the young ladies behind their heads. But this man rarely averted his gaze from the actors on stage, and the intensity never left his face. He wasn't there to be entertained, but to study.

But back to the here and now. Watch as Publius's harried frown disappears when he looks up. He doesn't smile, but his face, well, softens.

Daphnicus addresses him. – My Domina wishes to discuss your demand for payment. Cominia studies him.

– You are Publius? The baker?

– No. I'm Publius, the ladies hairdresser.

He gestures with the two loaves for emphasis, although none is necessary. Staphylus appreciates his sarcasm and titters at the notion. And if you glance over Cominia's shoulder you will see a smile poorly suppressed on Daphnicus's lips. But, as is evident by the look on her face, Publius's humour rankles with the innkeeper. She takes a step towards him.

– Do you seek to cease dealings with the inn of Cominia Lucilla?

– No.

– Then I suggest you treat me with more respect. I can just as easily have my bread supplied by Trophimus's bakery. And at ten per cent less cost.

Publius tosses the two loaves into the waiting sack and takes a step closer, trying not to be distracted by her evident beauty. He glances at the wall that defines the rear of her large property.

– I have heard that your inn is the finest in Pompeii. The rooms decorated with country and ocean scenes. Private bath suites. Two latrine rooms. Food prepared in a fine kitchen. It must cost a great deal to stay here.

– How does that concern you?

– I imagine your guests are used to the best. That's all. If you wish to serve them bread baked with coarse flour that is littered with sawdust, yes, you should purchase from Trophimus. He's an honest man. I know him. He's just a lousy baker.

She smiles at him. – You're very confident.

Yes, Cominia, but only in matters of baking. He knows his

baker Narcissus's reputation is without equal. Poke poor Publius with a stick in any other vital area and he will collapse like an empty sack.

Good quality bread ₄₇

– This matter of your payment. We have never been late settling your bill. Every ides you are paid in full without question.

– I have no complaint about that. But I require payment for the last two weeks nonetheless. I cannot wait until the next ides.

– That arrangement will throw our accounts into turmoil. If we pay you whenever you demand then everyone else....

– But Epidius demands his rent each week and...

Staphylus doesn't know when to keep his mouth shut.

– Shut up, Staphylus.

Publius is angry, as you can tell. He's a private man, you see. And he has pride. He doesn't want the world to know he is being crushed under another man's thumb.

– Marcus Epidius Sabinus is your landlord?

Publius is smarting now. – My business is my business.

Cominia has of course had dealings with the redoubtable Epidius. She earned his rancour almost from the first moment they encountered one another when she outbid him for the property now occupied by her inn.

– Considering the quality of your bread, I suppose some exceptions can be made.

She glances at Daphnicus. – Pay him what we owe him.

Publius stands there in silence for a moment. Then he grasps the sack from Staphylus and thrusts it at Daphnicus. – Here's today's bread. Keep your money. Pay me on the ides.

Cominia is frowning. She feels a little sorry for him, despite the fact that he seems a disagreeable bastard. His pride is evident. And she is thinking that such a thing is a foolishness of men. But part of her is also thinking that she sometimes admires such foolishness.

SCAENA 19

Restituta will dance for you 48

Now, where have I taken you? Oh yes. As it says on the sign there beside the door, the one with the winged phallus and the snake, Welcome to the Tavern of Verecundus. We are to the south of town, near the Porta Stabiae, in case you're wondering. Spitting distance from the Odeon. It is considered a good bar by many Pompeiian males, females having no opinions on such matters, as the only girls you'll find in here are serving drinks or providing entertainment of a more intimate nature. No, no, I don't mean to imply that it's a brothel. And neither does that phallus on the sign suggest the same. In fact you'll find big phallusses all over this place; painted in signs, frescoes, mosaics, carved in stone. The Romans see it as a sign of fertility and luck, so everyone here is accustomed to seeing the erect male organ from the time they are babes in arms. As I may have mentioned earlier, Romans are quite immodest.

Oh, and on the subject of brothels, there are a couple of those in town if you're interested, establishments dedicated exclusively to the supply of sex. But they hardly cater for the demands of the town, it being a port and having a regular turnover of sex-deprived sailors. So lots of bars (and even a couple of shops) do a little trade on the side in the form of renting out a slave or two to cater to the lusts of their customers. And Verecundus has long known that the more wine a customer drinks, the more he will be filled with the desire to copulate, which holds a certain irony – as their desire increases, their ability inevitably diminishes. But that's of no concern to Verecundus, as his strictly enforced rule is 'pay first, fuck later'.

Let us enter before darkness falls. Don't be disturbed by the rowdiness you hear from within. They cannot see you any more than they can see a puff of wind. Come along.

Right. Eleven men, mostly drunk, and a solitary woman, who feeds their drunkenness from a jug. Look, there is a table free by the wall at the back. It will provide a good spot from which we can observe proceedings.

You'll see why we're here in a few moments.

At Nuceria, I won 855 denarii at dice without cheating [49]

Those four men seated around the table on the right, they're playing tesserae, a simple game of dice. The stakes aren't high – a couple of as a throw, enough to buy you precisely one of Publius's loaves of bread. Yet see how heated they've become? They yell aloud at each throw and curse the gods for eternity when they continue to lose. See the player nearest the door, with the long hair tied back? That's Aemilius Celer, professional sign-writer, usually hired by politicians to promote their names at election time. He's playing a more dangerous game. He's cheating. When it comes his turn to shake the dice he employs rapid slight of hand to switch one of the three tesserae to one that is weighted, then removes it when he goes to pass on the cup. Men have had their throats slit for less. But you will not witness such a thing today, you will probably be glad to hear. Aemilius will depart shortly with his immoral profits, as he has another small income to earn this evening, also of a somewhat risky nature, as you shall witness.

It is much better to fuck a hairy cunt than a smooth one: It retains the warmth and stimulates the cock [50]

The others standing by the bar eating and drinking are engaged in a heated debate about which women are the best at fucking. Some argue that it is the native Romans. Others counter that Gallic slaves are by far the best, as Roman women have become too genteel. One particularly likes dark-skinned girls from Africa and his friend by contrast, prefers the fair haired barbarians from the north. They even debate whether women with pubic hair are better to fuck that those that are shaved. They shout and yell and bang their tankards on the bar to stress the cogency of their arguments. You would think they were senators engaged in a vital discussion about the defence of Rome.

You've probably noticed the large fresco behind the bar depicting a naked woman engaged in fellatio. It's been there so long that regular patrons never even notice it, and new arrivals usually give it a glance while ordering a bowl of salted soya beans, but will spare it little more than that. Verecundus had it painted there years ago. He thought it amusing at the time but by now he hates it, and can't afford to replace it.

Oh yes, the reason I brought you here. He comes now through that door at the back, returning from the latrine. He sits at the table next to us and resumes drinking his cup of wine alone. Restitutus, younger brother of Publius the baker. He's twenty-two now and still works in the bakery, although Publius would tell you that he doesn't work half hard enough. He would also tell you and everyone else that his brother, Restitutus, is a loutish, immature wastrel who spends the little he earns on wine and women. And in certain respects he wouldn't be wrong. Of course Publius sees only what he wants to see, only the things that serve to reinforce his view.

But admittedly he is a heavy drinker. Look at him. He's only been in the bar less than an hour and already he has swilled back half a jug of watered wine. He's not drunk yet, but he intends to be. He is good-looking, more so than his brother. He crops his hair short like Publius senior did, the way soldiers often do to discourage lice. He wears a medallion of his father's around his neck that depicts a legionnaire defeating a barbarian, and he carries his father's dagger always, secreted inside his tunic – Verecundus doesn't permit weapons in his bar. And when he has had enough to drink he will happily tell anyone who will listen of his father's glorious deeds, his service under Emperor Claudius in the The Battle of Caer Caradoc, how he saved the life of a legatus legionis, how he was awarded a golden armilla armband for bravery, although he will neglect to mention that Publius senior lost his armband in a coin tossing game. Yes he does treasure the memory of his dead father. Almost as much as he treasures his conviction that his brother abandoned his father as their house collapsed during the earthquake and let him perish so he could save his own skin. And that is what drives his wasteful self-conduct. He carries on in this manner because that is precisely the opposite of what his brother wants and expects of him.

Restitutus also believes that he is the more deserving of the role of paterfamilias, despite being several years younger than Publius. He resents the fact that Publius orders him about, because he believes his brother weak and indecisive. And he has come to hate working in the bakery: the heat, the smells of bread and sweat and shit, the rising before dawn, the bad pay. He is deserving of so much more, he believes. And so he funnels all his frustration into antagonism against his brother.

But like many a young man or woman of his age, he is a jumble of contradictions. His mind, for example, refuses to reconcile the fact that Publius senior would not be impressed in the least at his current behaviour were he alive. To his credit though, somewhere at the back of his mind he recognises that his practiced wildness is not taking him along a course that can have any decent ending, and that indeed it may lead him over a cliff. Restitutus is full of rage, although you would normally not be aware of the fact, as he smiles and laughs a lot and charms the girls with whistles as he strolls the streets. But in his reflective moments, like the one you're witnessing now, he curses the world.

Everything is everyone's fault but his.

His head lifts at the arrival in the bar of a couple of legionnaires. They're veterans, called Evocati, having served their twenty-five years and chosen to re-enlist. Look how he has fixed his eyes on them as they address the girl serving behind the stone counter. He imagines his father proudly standing there in his red tunic and metal curiass and considers how wonderful it would be to stand and greet him and observe the respectful looks of the others in the bar, to enjoy the plaudits of being associated with a Primi Ordines of the Ninth Spanish Legion.

Now he is dreaming of what it would be like to be a soldier. To experience the glory of conquest. He knows the pay is lousy when you start out, but if you're bright and courageous you could eventually become a centurion, or even rise to be a Primi Ordines, like his father. Or perhaps higher. He is a bit old at this stage to join up, but not too old. And after he'd done his twenty-five years he'd still be only in his forties. His thoughts gallop at the possibilities of slaying barbarians and winning honours and hauling himself a couple of pretty slave girls back home to tend to his every need in later years. An unwelcome image of him lying headless in a pool of faraway mud interrupts his stampeding imagination. Yet his own father was released from service after a decade as a reward for his courage. Grim determination fills him as the wine further distorts his thinking. The army, he decides, is where his destiny lies. Publius senior will look at him from Elysium and point him out to his fellow spirits and tell them proudly that there marches his son. Yes, that is it. That is the course he has been looking for.

He's thinking now of engaging the soldiers in conversation. Perhaps they're of the same legion as Publius. Given that they are veterans it is possible they even knew his father, he thinks fancifully. But in the time it takes to consider this they have gulped down a bowl of chickpeas and wine and are already exiting the bar.

No matter, Restitutus thinks. His mind is made up. His course is set.

Of course, it is anything but set, but this caprice is a pleasant diversion from the turmoil of his young life.

Now he is calling to the barmaid for more wine to celebrate his momentous decision.

– Restituta!

Restituta with the pretty face 51

The girl wanders over. She is Verecundus's own veteran, having been a slave here since she was fifteen, which was almost as many years ago. She is no relation, by the way, of our Restitutus, despite her name. As Verecundus's longest serving slave girl she is put in charge of the bar when he is absent, and she is well able to handle the place, even in its rowdiest moments. She naturally doubles as a prostitute when it is demanded of her, but that happens less and less these days as Verecundus entrusts her more and more with the running of his tavern.

She's still pretty, despite the fact that she has had sex with more than three thousand men in her life, and bore and disposed of thirty inconvenient babies before I had the chance to help them into the light. I see you're a little shocked. But she's had it easy compared to some. And the babies, well, pregnant prostitutes are not to very many men's taste, so a woman called Gavia Severa supplied her with a potion of apium and rue to drink and a poultice of apium sap and fennel to press up between her legs, and sometime the babies were no more, although when that didn't work the woman painfully yanked the baby from her womb piece by piece. That is the way of things here. You'll get used to it.

Restituta keeps her hair tied behind her head and wears a bright yellow tunic that reveals plenty of her ample cleavage and comes just below her knees. Not something you'd see on the streets, but Verecundus supplies these alluring clothes to the girls to draw in the men. Her face is thin, angular, her hair chestnut brown, tied back, her eyes hazel. Her work keeps her fit as she is on her feet (or her back) fourteen hours a day, every day. And with all that life has thrown at her, she maintains a professional smile and a general cheery demeanour. You'd have to admire her.

I should be quiet, you'll want to hear the next bit.

Restitutus proffers his cup and the girl fills it from her jug.

– Hey Restituta. Let me have a look.

He pulls playfully at the hem of her tunic, lifting it a few inches.

She slaps him on the side of the head.

– Hands off, Restitutus, I'm working.

– Oh come on, my flower, just a peek. Soon I'll be gone from

Pompeii forever and I won't get to see a nice cunt from one end of the year to the other.

She laughs. – Where are you going? An island of eunuchs?

– I'm going to join the army.

She is sceptical. Restituta has seen many of Restitutus's plans come and go these past couple of years. – Really? Be careful you don't have your cock chopped off in battle.

Restitutus flinches briefly at the notion and the girl laughs. He realises she is mocking him.

– I am. In a year I'll be a legionnaire in a foreign land, conquering the world for Rome.

He gestures theatrically with a broad sweep of his arm and gives her his most charming smile, then grabs at her tunic again, this time lifting it well above her knees before another smack on his ear interrupts him.

– Come on, my blossom. You know you've always been my favourite. I'm celebrating and I'm horny.

– Favourite? Urbana is your favourite. Then Euplia. And then half the whores in Pompeii and then maybe me. I know all your tastes Mr. Baker.

– Don't call me that!

She ignores him. – Urbana told me that you're in love with her. Are you?

– Where is Urbana? Is she here?

Restituta gestures to the upper floor with her eyes. – Working. Two visiting fisherman. She's going to be a while. Do you want her next?

He considers this a moment. – How much?

– The same as it always is. Don't try to bargain with me. Sixteen as.

He pulls a small pouch from his tunic pocket, empties it into his cupped hand and counts it secretly. He looks up at Restituta, who waits patiently at his side. – I have enough for Urbana, but I won't have enough for more wine. Will you give me a little credit?

Give a drop of cold! 52

She shakes her head cynically. – Oh sure, and after you've shot your lot into Urbana I'm sure you'll still be as keen to pay. Forget it. Now make your mind up. Wine or woman?

Other customers are calling for her service. She yells at them to be patient and places a hand on her hip while she awaits Restitutus's response. He sighs heavily and holds up the cup he has already drained. As she fills it he slides his hand around behind her and gently lifts the back of her tunic. Restituta knows what he is at and without blinking an eye she moves the jug above his head and tilts it a little.

– It would be a shame to waste so much good wine, Restitutus, but if you don't take your hand down I will send you home dripping with it from head to toe. And besides, from what I hear, it is not my cunt that you should be thinking about, but your sister's.

Ah. That has captured his attention. His erection fades like a thing shot through with an arrow and the offending hand drops to his side.

– What are you talking about?

Restituta turns and hurries behind the counter to serve other customers.

He calls out loudly. – Restituta! Restituta!

She ignores him until her task is finished but reluctantly returns to the table in an attempt to quieten him. – I'm working, Restitutus. There are other customers. Stop pestering me or leave!

– What about my sister? What could *you* know of Cornelia?

She laughs mirthlessly. – You mean what could a filthy

whore know about a virtuous Roman citizen? I'm good enough for you when it suits you.

Restitutus grasps her wrist. – Fuck it, Restituta. Answer me!

She regrets saying anything now. She's afraid of what lies behind the door she has unlocked.

She shrugs. – I've never met your sister. But it's a small town and we get all sorts in here. Rich and poor. If they can pay for wine they're welcome. They get drunk, they talk. Especially to the girls when they're trying to impress them.

– What did you hear about my sister?

– I heard some young buck, rich bastard, decided to get himself some free cunt. Ow! Let go of my wrist!

– Are you talking about my sister?

– But he doesn't want to know about it, of course. He's telling jokes about it. Saying he'd marry a eunuch before Cornelia. Restitutus, listen, I know a woman called Gavia Severa. If your sister needs it, she can give her a poultice. It only costs…

Restitutus ignores her. – What's his name?

– I don't know. Arbius or Etiumus or something. Let me go.

Look at the rage on Restitutus's face. His family's honour is affronted. You know what his next thought is? Not of Cornelia, or how he will deal with this, but of Publius. This is all Publius's fault. If his useless brother was a proper paterfamilias he would have found a suitable husband for Cornelia when she was fourteen. And now it has come to this.

He stands so sharply that he strikes the table and topples his untouched cup of wine, and he storms from the bar. Restituta opens her mouth to shout after him that he owes her eight as, but thinks better of it. Then she looks down at the red wine spreading across the table and dripping through the slats like a pool of blood.

– Fucking mess.

Indeed, dear girl. And the night is young yet.

SCAENA 20

Vote Isidorus for aedile -
he's the best at licking cunt! ₅₃

Don't be concerned. We shall catch up with Restitutus soon enough. But while we're waiting for his evening to unfold, I thought you might be interested to witness a couple of other incidents in the dark streets of Pompeii. Think of it as a means of proper introduction to another of those characters you met earlier.

I see you're impressed with our location, even in the darkness with only a few of the buildings lit by torchlight. You're standing in the centre of the forum, Pompeii's pumping heart. Although it barely registers a beat after dark. A couple of men stroll through on the way to bars. A few girls lurk in the shadows awaiting the opportunity to sell themselves for an as or two – that's the price of one of Publius's loaves. Those are the desperate ones, getting older, not too pretty to begin with, maybe diseased, no cubiculum to offer their clients, who are also desperate, and so the deed will be done in the open, behind a wall or in a shop doorway. If they show their faces around here by daylight, by the way, they'll find themselves flogged or worse. But after dark, the authorities adopt an attitude of out of sight, out of mind.

So, really I should have taken you here in daylight, when the place is teeming with the life of Roman society, business, politics and religion. You could have more appreciated the fine architecture of the temples and places of industry. And it perhaps would have helped you grasp the power of the gods over Pompeiians. That looming structure behind you to the north is the Temple of Jupiter. Even in the moonlight you can probably tell that's it's leaning over to one side. It's still waiting for repair after the earthquake. There's also the Temple of Apollo over there, the Temple of Venus used to be beside it, but is a mere pile of stones now. There is none to me of course. I'm not important enough. In terms of the gods, a nobody.

Although there are no political machinations afoot in the forum this night, there is some related mischief happening in a street off the northern end. Follow me. I will explain as we walk. This is where they vote, the people of Pompeii. Over there in that building they call the Comitium. I should say that Roman elections are not exactly a perfect example of democracy at work. It's a complicated system that groups citizens according to their wealth or status, and then these groups are sub-divided according to, for example, profession or age. If the majority in the group give Candidate A fifty-one votes and Candidate B forty-nine votes, then it counts as one vote for candidate A and so on. So it's not exactly representative. And the other problem is that it is not anonymous either, so intimidation is often rife.

No women are allowed to vote. And no slaves of course. There are lots of other rules, but that's a simple version in a nutshell.

And an election looms in July, just a month hence. Given that this place is but a speck of dust on the face of the world, you would be surprised how much value some men place in ascending its political ladder. There are four posts on their little council up for grabs, two aediles and two duumvirs. The aediles are the lesser posts. These men supervise the markets and are supposed to look after the temples and streets, making sure the temples are cleaned, the altars are properly decorated, arranging workers to repair a blocked sewer, settling rights of way, that sort of thing. It's not exactly the power of the gods they seek. Still, it can be a useful stepping stone to the other position that will be on offer next month, that of duumvir. There are two of those as well, reflecting the system of electing two consuls as leaders of the Roman Senate that dates to the earliest days the state, (although, since the republic came crashing down, these are subordinate to the emperor.) The duumviri are the top of this small political ladder, almost. They wield a considerable degree of power, at least in terms of this backwater. The duumviri administer justice and preside over town council meetings, which of course allow then them lord it over their friends and neighbours, and lets their wives strut about with their noses in the air. The other thing the duumviri do is administer public money, which is a useful weapon to have in your armoury if you want to influence the decisions of others and surreptitiously line your own pockets. Having said that the duumviri are expected to provide games and spectacles at their own expense to entertain the masses. But the cost of such things is but a pittance compared to the money they can make through using their influence for certain business parties' benefit. So men will expend great energy and wealth in the pursuit of this position.

Some will even kill. But when all is said and done, it is about power. It may be just a small provincial town in the back of beyond, but it still all boils down to that. Isn't it always with mortals? In some form or another. Power, you see, equates with fame, and fame is a rung on that other ladder of immortality, or the illusion of such.

This way, under the Arch of Tiberius and around to our right. Many of the voters will file into the forum via that street ahead, where you can see the lights of several torches dancing in the blackness. Three men are at work, even at this time of night. Let us see what they're up to.

Listen as we approach. Their idle talk may tell us something.

– Hold the ladder Florus, for the love of fucking Jupiter, or I'll break my neck.

You can't see them very well in this light, but the man on the ladder with the bucket of paint and the brush is Fructus. His colleague, the one holding the ladder with one hand and the torch with the other, is Florus, as you may have guessed.

– Will you both keep your mouths shut? I don't want any of Vatia's friends finding out about this or I'll end up with my legs broken.

Aemilius Celer painted this sign by the moonlight 55

Ah yes, the man at the back, you've met him briefly very recently. That is Aemilius Celer, signwriter, frequent patron of the Bar of Verecundus, cheater at dice and cheater at his business. As I mentioned, he is Pompeii's most skilled sign writer, and business is brisk each year around election times, when the candidates seek him out to record their names and virtues upon the town's walls in an effort to secure votes. Although it is not evident from the sign his workers are painting at the moment, his current employer is our friend Marcus Epidius Sabinus, who is standing for the position of duumvir, having served as aedile previously. Epidius also supports the election of a young man of his acquaintance called Gnaeus Helvius Sabinus, a distant relation, for the position of aedileship, who if successful alongside Epidius, will underpin the strength of his position as joint head of the council. One of Gnaeus Helvius Sabinus's principal opponents is a man called Marcus Cerrinius Vatia, so Epidius has hired Aemelius Celer to do a little electioneering on Vatia's behalf. Are you confused? Well, take a look at the sign young Fructus has just painted:

All the deadbeats and Macerius
ask for Vatia as aedile [56]

Very neat, is it not? Aemilius personally trained Florus and Fructus on the craft of character-forming. But not a message Vatia would be too enthused about, you'd probably agree. Just along the street you'll find another one proclaiming that 'The petty thieves ask you to elect Vatia as aedile.' And across there you will see the name of another of the aedileship candidates who opposes Epidius's man. He is Isidorus Nummianus. Aemilius Celer has saved his crudest invective for this man, having written: 'Vote Isidorus fo aedile; he is best at licking cunt!' And you'll find many such painted messages all over town. Poor Vatia will awake tomorrow and discover that he enjoys the support of the whores, the boy-fuckers, the swindlers and the wankers. Within a week he will have lost all credibility, clearing the way for Epidius's man to take one of the aedileships.

Fructus scrambles down, takes a torch from Florus and holds it up to admire his work.

Aemilius Celer chuckles. – Perfect. Right, let's get out of here before someone sees us.

Aemilius is a contented man. He will do well out of tonight's work. And all this cost Marcus Epidius Sabinus was a small bag of sesterces. Epidius does enjoy playing dirty, no matter what the game.

Let's go see what other business he's got his hand in tonight.

SCAENA 21

I beg you to elect Epidius Sabinus duumvir with judicial power. He is worthy, and is a protector of the colony in the opinion of the worshipful judge Suedius Clemens, and by agreement of the whole council, on account of his merits and his honesty, worthy of public office [57]

Publius may believe that he occupies Epidius's mind for a considerable proportion of each day. A number of others in the town also believe the same – that they are the principal focus of Epidius's nefarious scheming. But all would be in error, as each of these men or women are to the ambitious, ruthless politician and businessman, as a single tessera is to a large mosaic.

Which is why I've brought you here, close to the centre of that colourful mosaic. We stand on the Via Dell'Abbondanza, just a stone's throw from the Stabian Baths, and that rather anonymous doorway before us is the entrance to the home of the said Epidius, which is almost as large as that of Gnaeus Alleius Maius. Let's go inside.

Impressive room, is it not? Look at that fine fresco depicting Hercules and Orpheus. He chose the subjects personally, you know? Hercules' achievements on earth have been rewarded in the afterlife by a place of equal among the gods. Perhaps Epidius has similar hopes? And as for Orpheus, well, he could enchant all things in this world with his music, even the trees and the rocks. Our Epidius isn't musical at all, however, but employs his manipulative skills and deviousness with, he believes, equal effect.

He's come a long way since that day on the mountainside when he crushed the skull of his former employer, Lucius Jucundus. He'd found four hundred aurei in the sacks tied to the mule, or forty thousand sesterces, and what a leg-up that proved to be for his business ambitions.

Caecelius's property was inherited by his two sons, Caecilius, the eldest, and Quintus. Caecilius junior died almost seven years ago, before he'd sired any children, and so according to Roman law, all his worldly goods passed to Quintus. Unfortunately neither Caecilius junior nor Quintus had their father's famed business acumen, and were both happy to let his trusted employee, Epidius, take over the reins. Within a couple of years, Epidius had gotten hold of the entire business and left the brothers with a paltry stipend. And since then, by means legal and illegal, Epidius has built a minor financial empire of his own, well, at least in the context of Pompeii and its greater locality. He leases thirty-eight properties, he provides loans at exorbitant interest rates, he runs a slave-trading business, and he has interests in a fullery, a garum manufactory and a wine exporting concern. Quite the entrepeneur, is Marcus Epidius Sabinus. And of course his election as duumvir would greatly underpin his success.

Epidius's principal competitor during his rise was Gnaeus Alleius Maius and, rich as he is, Epidius has yet to scale the financial or political heights of his more senior rival, which is something that has long stuck in his craw. He has never missed an opportunity to outbid or out-manoeuvre Gnaeus in their property dealings, or to out-bribe someone to gain valuable state contracts. Sometimes he was successful, others not, but the battle the pair have waged has driven both to new heights businesswise, and to new lows in terms of their methods. At this point it has become a deeply personal little war for both men.

Apelles the chamberlain,
ex-slave of Caesar, ate here most agreeably
and had a fuck as well 58

But now we have business at hand. And there sits the business at that table, Epidius, his chief slave and chamberlain, Apelles, standing at his side, a collection of documents before them. Apelles has a weakness for older whores with large breasts, by the way. It's a mother thing.

The young slave by the doorway is Felix.

– It is impossible to hide the trail, Apelles. I'll have to find another way. Leave me to think.

– But Dominus, I'm sure in time I can re-work the figures to conceal any illegality.

– Accounting skills might do that, but I'll still lose the fucking properties, you Greek imbecile.

Apelles's slight frame quivers and he bows his prematurely balding head.

– Forgive me, Dominus.

Epidius has a rare moment of regret. He waves a hand.

– Consider yourself forgiven. But this is a matter not of accounts, but of artful manipulation. I won't need you for the remainder of the day. Go. Fuck that fat slave from the kitchen that you like.

– Damoeta.

– By Vulcan's balls, I don't care who she is. Go! And leave the boy here.

Apelles departs and Epidius rises and seats himsef on the couch. He signals for wine and the boy hastens across with a goblet and a jug, he retreats and tries to become invisible.

Epidius sits for some time in silence, sipping a goblet of wine in the flickering lamplight. Pensive, isn't he, as he stares absently at that fresco opposite of a nude youth embracing an eagle in flight. His eyes drift briefly across the room to the young slave, Felix , who is fifteen next week. He has been here in attendance to his master for almost two hours. He is a handsome lad, isn't he?

Epidius has a big problem, you see, and its name is Titus Suedius Clemens. Epidius has been working hard to secure his elevation to the position of duumvir. And he is almost certain to be elected alongside another of the town's leading citizens, Marcus Lucretius Fronto. He has bribed, threatened and black-mailed enough people to ensure their collective votes go in his favour. And he has no concerns about sharing power with Fronto, who is reputed to be an honourable man, because in his experience, honourable men have the softest underbellies. And besides, he believes Fronto to be an ageing, withering fool, and he considers it possible that the old bastard might even die before his year as duumvir is up. So he believes the election a mere formality at this stage. Or at least he did until a couple of months ago when Titus Suedius Clemens showed up.

Titus used to be a soldier, a reluctant one. He was given the post through the influence of his father, who was a supporter of Emperor Vespasian before he came to power. Titus is an intelligent man, but he hadn't the first notion of how to command a Roman army and he allowed his subordinates to make most of the decisions for him. Unfortunately they decided to plunder and rape their own fellow citizens during the brief civil war that brought Vespasian to power. Afterwards it was decided that

Titus's talents lay elsewhere. Don't misunderstand me though. He's a fine man; honest, trustworthy and honourable. He's just a little weak in certain aspects, as you shall observe. Yet he has a considerable amount of power, and as if keen to make amends for his military failings, he uses his power now purely for the betterment of the Empire.

You see, when Emperor Vespasian came to power three years ago he realised that the finances of the state were in dire peril. I won't go into all of the tax reforms he instituted and so on in an effort to get things in order, but among the measures he introduced was one to reclaim lands and properties that private citizens had somehow swindled from the state. And nowhere had this been more practiced than in the region of Campania, where many had taken advantage of the destruction and death caused by the earthquake to lay their greedy little fingers on unclaimed property. The practice had been rampant in Pompeii and many of the town's council and leading citizens had profited to one degree or other, including Gnaeus Alleius Nigidus Maius. But even Gnaeus is put in the shadow by his hated rival, Epidius, who falsified documents, re-drew boundaries, bribed officials and in a couple of cases openly stole properties in the town and neighbouring countryside.

> *He got his profit by fraud...*
> *and he holds it through mighty turmoil* [59]

He has been clever, however, in concealing his tracks, and thus far Titus Suedius Clemens has failed to unearth any of his illegal acquisitions. But the man is persistent and has at this point seized numerous properties, expelled their occupiers and threatened them with prosecution. Epidius had a close call just a week previously, when Titus reclaimed a palatial house Epidius had built illegally on public grounds near the Marine

Gate, but not before Epidius had hastily destroyed the paper trail that identified him as the owner. But by the gods he had been furious. The loss had cost him dearly, and he didn't intend for it to happen again, especially as any major revelation of financial impropriety would immediately put paid to his political dreams. In fact, the only thing that stands between him and the duumvirship is Titus Suedius Clemens. And that's an obstacle he intends to remove, without upsetting any of Titus's powerful friends back in Rome.

But now inspiration has struck.

– Felix.

The boy snaps to attention and hurries across to refill his master's cup. As he does Epidius allows his eyes to fall upon his face first, and then his well-shaped arms.

– Felix?

See how the boy snaps upright, a hint of fear in his eyes? In the tone of that solitary utterance of his name he has detected something that disturbs him. He stands there mute for a moment, the wine jug clutched in his two hands.

– Yes, Dominus?

Epidius is silent and pensive as he studies the boy, allowing his eyes to wander from head to toe. – Put the jug down on the table, Felix, and then remove your tunic.

– Dominus?

Epidius doesn't repeat commands to slaves. His eyes bore into the young lad's and after a moment he begins to comply. Now there is real fear in his eyes. He is relatively new to the household and is nervous that he is about to discover his master's sexual preferences. He stands there wearing only a subigaculum, unsure where to put his hands, or his eyes. He stares at the floor.

– The subigaculum too.

Now poor Felix is certain he is to be buggered. Slaves come

to accept much adversity and humiliation as simply part of their lot. But of course some things are worse than others. His hesitant undoing of the ties at the side of his loincloth can probably tell you as much. But eventually it falls away to the floor and he stands there naked under his master's gaze.

Epidius smiles. But if you look closely you can see his smile is not in anticipation of any sexual gratification. Nor is it intended to put the boy at ease. His eyes at that moment seem to look through the boy rather than at him. He is seeing something that lies elsewhere. Perhaps in the future.

There is a brief knock on the door before it opens. Epidius is snapped from his reverie and turns to see Faustilla enter. You might recall her, the slave that Jucundus gifted to Epidius so long ago on the slopes of Vesuvius. She is now, and has been since that day, his willing slave, one who worships him as a dog does its master. She turned out to be quite the prize for Epidius and fitted his needs with the comfort of a silk tunic. She is loyal, smart, deferential only to him, tough as Roman nails and quite ruthless. And he has rewarded her with some degree of power, allowing her to command a few of his enterprizes, such as his money-lending business. He has fucked her every once in a while, although I might have equally said that she fucked him. But such events are rare and there is no notion of a romantic aspect to their relationship. Yet Epidius does put quite a value on the woman, one that cannot be measured in denarii.

She pauses at the sight of the naked youth, her lips part, startled. And believe me, it takes much to startle this one.

– Forgive me, Dominus. I thought you were…

Epidius waves her worries away. – Come in, Faustilla. I was just going to summon you anyway.

Felix has reacted to her arrival by clamping his hands over his genitals, which amuses Epidius. – The poor lad is shy.

Faustilla is unsure how to react to this statement.

– A fine boy, is he not, my little flower?

You can tell from his tone that the use of the term 'flower' is ironic, for Faustilla is no beauty. Her face is quite angular, and some of her features so sharp one might fear to cut oneself upon them. Her eyes are an unusual amber with a central halo of deep red, as though we are glimpsing a fire that constantly blazes within her. She keeps her black hair shoulder length although permanently tied behind. To her credit she has a fine athletic figure and is quite capable of taking care of herself, armed or otherwise.

– He is, Dominus. He was an excellent purchase.

Epidius makes a circling motion with his hand. – Turn around, Felix, arms up, and let us see you in your entirety.

The slave does as commanded, shuffling in a complete circle. Epidius gestures at Faustilla with his head and she takes the cue and walks across to Felix, then begins to stroke his chest with her finger.

– Yes, he's very pretty, Dominus.

Felix's penis stiffens and he reacts with fear, clasping his hands over himself.

– Forgive me, Dominus, I could not help...

But Epidius is laughing with joy as he watches Faustilla pull the boy's hands away.

– Oh, truly excellent! He can get it up with the slightest provocation!

Felix stands there naked, a look of bewilderment on his face, secretly praying to Isis to deliver him from this scene. She is the Egyptian goddess that the Roman world has taken to in a big way, especially the slaves.

Felix made a vow to the household gods 60

Epidius now addresses Felix as Faustilla returns to his side.

– You know, Felix, sometimes it falls on me to command my slaves to do things that are distasteful to them.

Felix nods hesitantly as fear swells and his erection does the opposite.

– Faustilla here could tell you of many such things from personal experience, couldn't you?

She smiles conspiratorially. – I could, Dominus.

– However, sometimes Felix, I am troubled by the commands I must give, and feel I must make some compensation. So, tell me, Felix, have you ever had a woman?

– A woman, Dominus?

Epidius reaches behind Faustilla and slaps her on the backside. – Yes, you know, a woman, like Faustilla here. Or perhaps you'd prefer a younger one, perhaps your own age, or younger even. Would you like that?

He stutters. You would have to pity him. Of course he would like a woman, given that his entire physical being is at his age directed towards that precise achievement. But he knows this offer is tainted. And darkly so.

Epidius chuckles. Faustilla joins him.

– You are a lucky boy, Felix. Not every master makes such a kind gift. I shall of course require you to do something for me before that happens. But don't let it concern you, Felix. Now, put on your clothes and leave us.

The youth scampers out, relief glinting through the sweat that coats his face.

He turns now to Faustilla and grins.

– You know, Faustilla, I was just sitting here mulling over what I should do about Titus Suedius Clemens, when I realised the answer was right before my eyes.

His gaze returns to the fresco depicting a beautiful naked youth being born skywards by an eagle. Faustilla looks at it but is bemused. Epidius seeks to enlighten her.

– That's Ganymede. Abducted by Zeus who took the form of an eagle and flew him to Olympus to serve as a cup bearer and lover. You know, when Titus Suedius Clemens and his lovely, charming wife were here to dine last week, I couldn't help notice how taken he was with the work. In fact his eyes frequently drifted to it as we ate. And on some reflection, I don't believe it was the skill of the artist he was admiring.

He grins at her.

Understanding dawns and she laughs aloud.

– My dear, I believe I believe its time we invited Titus back again.

– I'll have Apelles arrange it at once.

Epidius inclines his head and looks up at Faustilla. – What was it you wanted earlier?

– To inform you that I have heard from Albanus that he has successfully taken care of that business. Vatia's bodyguard.

PRISCUS. LIVED TWENTY-FIVE YEARS ₆₁

– Oh yes. His right hand man. Priscus.

She grins. – He is neither his right or left hand man now, Dominus, as he possesses neither.

Epidius chuckles. – Yes. Very good. Priscus was a shit gladiator anyway. And hopefully Vatia will finally get the message, opening the way for the election of my cousin Gnaeus Helvius Sabinus to the aedileship.

– And you to the duumvirship, Dominus.

– Indeed. The only thing standing in my way is Titus Suedius Clemens.

– Soon, Dominus, he will not be standing, but kneeling with Felix's cock up his arse.

Epidius chuckles heartily at the prospect.

SCAENA 22

Atimetus got me pregnant ₆₂

I've taken you somewhere else as you can tell. It is not sometime else, mind you, as this is the precise moment when Epidius is discussing Titus Suedius Clemens with Faustilla. You are lucky, as not many mortals get to be literally two places at the one time.

But as is evident, no longer do we stand amid the luxury of Epidius's oecus but in a much simpler room, decorated only by red painted walls, which still show the cracks in places left by the earthquake. But I notice your attention has been drawn to the man sitting hunched over the table. He lifts his head. Ah yes, Publius. We are in his home, in his tablinum, which if you remember, adjoins his bakery. He is writing furiously, is he not? His stylus almost breaks the papyrus in places, such is his enthusiasm. Of course Publius's dreams of being a great playwright may have been crushed under the collapsing walls of the theatre stage many years ago, but he has not been completely idle in his writing endeavours. Down the years he occasionally found time to write a simple farce or two, but only ones suitable for staging to small audiences on a wooden stage in the forum. The colourful Saenecio Fortunatus, the theatre director who offered the young Publius a job, has now been reduced to scraping a living staging such productions and has kindly produced a number of Publius's efforts, although the monetary reward was a mere pittance. You should see poor Saenecio now, the tragic drama of life has wrung him almost dry. But we shall have an opportunity to meet him again before our tale is done.

But judging by the look on Publius's face when he cranes his head in thought, that is no farce to titillate the masses. He seems he has found inspiration once more. Let's see if we can read what he's writing over his shoulder.

The oracle speaks:

A great plague shall sweep the city and the poorest shall perish first. But in time it will consume all who dwell there. The plague glitters golden like the sun on the sea.

Marcus: You speak in riddles woman. How can a plague glitter?

Oracle: It is all around you. Spreading even now. Its fingers creep and crawl like a thousand spiders. And soon there will be millions.

Marcus: Speak sense. How can I stop it? A sacrifice?

Oracle: A sacrifice? Yes, yes, a sacrifice.

Marcus: A goat? A sheep? A bull? What?

Oracle: You must sacrifice your greed.

Hmm. It is interesting, don't you think? It doesn't give you too many clues. But I think even you can tell that this is no empty farce with farting rich men and fat over-sexed daughters. He is an admirer of Horace, you see, who used gently mocking humour to satirise the world around him. Publius seeks to do the same, his focus generally being on the daily political corruption he sees and more specifically on Epidius.

But really, no writer likes his work read when incomplete,

and we should let him finish before we make our judgements. Besides, our own drama continues elsewhere in the house.

Here we are in the upstairs cubiculum of Cornelia. A simple space, isn't it? As is typical of the Roman bedroom. They're often small, windowless and cramped like this, even in the large houses. Here, plain green walls are brightened only by a couple of birds in flight.

Cornelia sits there perched on the edge of her bed, sniffling quietly to herself. The poor girl's thoughts whirl around her mind as though caught in a tempest. She looks down at her belly and places her hand there, worried her condition is evident, but also fascinated despite her fraught state at the notion that she carries a living thing inside her. What on earth will she do, though?

Atimetus evades her on the street, ignores the messages she has paid young boys to deliver. She has heard on the grapevine that he denies that he is the father. She thought him more honourable than that. It was one of the things that attracted her to him in the first place. Well, that and the fact that he comes from a wealthy home. And so her plan to lure Atimetus into her sticky web has come to nothing.

You are cruel! Why do you not love me?[63]

If Publius or her mother finds out, well, a year in the realm of Hades seems a better option to her. She feels sick each day and has to work despite her nausea.

She has heard that the woman Gavia Severa will get rid of the baby for her, but it costs so much, and besides, she has learned that Gavia so damaged some girls inside that they could never bear children again and that some even died. Besides, despite all the misery her pregnancy has brought upon heself, she wants this child to live.

She is about to extinguish the lamps and resign herself to troubled sleep for another night. But she stalls at the sound of footsteps. Her door opens and her brother, Restitutus, stands in the doorframe staring down at her. The oil lamp he clutches before him throws flickering shadows about his face in a way that unnerves her. And then it dawns why. He knows. Somehow he knows. He says nothing. She tries to ready herself for the flood of misery that is about to engulf her, but her body responds by releasing its own flood of tears.

Restitutus whispers. – Shhhhh.

He steps into the room and closes the door. You can probably guess that he has calmed a little since he departed the bar of Verecundus. He would not confess this of course, but as he hurried home he filled his head with rage about Cornelia's plight and the slight on his family's honour, and deceived himself that his motives were pure. But the idea also took root at the back of his mind that this was once again all the fault of Publius who he believes, as paterfamilias, should have married his sister off years before. Restitutus can certainly exploit it as such to demean his brother, and prove to the world just how honourable and courageous a man he has become. He doesn't even realise that by the time he'd reached their home he had been hoping the rumour he'd heard in the bar was true, otherwise he'd have been quite disappointed. And now, in her tears, he sees it confirmed with his own eyes.

But Restitutus can be a kind soul when the notion takes him. See how he sits beside her on the bed, puts a comforting arm about her shoulders and draws her shaking body against his.

– Shhh. Be quiet, sister. You don't want to draw Publius up here.

– Do you...know...?

He nods.

– How did you find out? Is it so obvious?

He ducks the question. – You are a foolish one. You always were.

– What am I to do, Restitutus?

He draws her wet face around towards his and looks in her eyes. – Tell me. Who is the father? And when did you fuck him?

– His name is Tiberius Atimetus Verus, but he goes by the name Atimetus. It happened in early May, on the tombstones near...

– I don't want to know the details. I know him. His father is well off, lives on the Via Nola. I think he has an importing business. Atimetus spends half his life drinking in whorehouses. He's hardly Apollo, Cornelia. How could you do it with an idler like that? Does he know you're carrying his child?

Cornelia manages a brief chuckle through her sniffles. – Restitutus, you spend half your life drinking in whorehouses.

He is affronted and pulls away a little. He is about to respond but stalls himself. It is a minor shock to him that he is seen in the same light as the man he castigates. Look. He is searching desperately for a point of differentiation.

– I...I spend only the time I have free. When I am not working. This man, this man, has never known hard work. He is a spoiled brat without any honour. Does he know you are pregnant?

She begins to sob again. – I have tried to see him, and I have sent messages telling him. But he ignores them. I have heard he is denying it. But I swear I've never been with another man, Restitutus. What am I to do, brother?

– He won't ignore me. Leave it to me. Tomorrow we will go to see this man and his father when he is conducting his morning affairs.

– And what about Publius? And Mother?

– Publius carries his own share of the blame for this. He should have found you a husband years ago.

– Publius is so distracted most of the time he couldn't find his own dick.

Restitutus laughs.

– Besides, who would marry a fat lump like me? And I wish you two would put your differences behind you. You're more alike that you pretend.

He scoffs. – We are no more alike than...than a fox and an owl.

– And which are you, brother?

He looks at her but doesn't reply.

– He loves you, Restitutus. And me. And I love the grumpy bastard in return.

– Loves me? Don't make me laugh. Sometimes I despise him.

She squeezes his hand. – Don't say that.

– Anyway, to the matter at hand. We will deal with Publius and Mother in good time. Where is Mother by the way? She was not in her room.

– She is with Gnaeus Alleius. He took her to the theatre in Herculaneum.

– Again? That's the second time this month.

– He is courting her, I think.

Restitutus grunts.

– Would it bother you? Were they to marry? I mean, he taking the place of father?

– He would not be taking the place of father. No man could do that. But I would be happy for our mother to have a companion. And he is rich and I think he is honourable, from what I can tell. At least one of the women in this house can choose her lovers wisely.

He smiles as he says this and she produces an ironic chuckle.

– Now, go to sleep. I will find a means of getting this business sorted in the coming days. And by the way, you're not fat. Don't put yourself down. Many a man would embrace you.

She raises a smile. – Only if he had very long arms.

He laughs, kisses his sister gently on the head and leaves. His mind buzzes now with plots enough to rival his brother.

A copper pot is missing from this shop.
65 sesterces reward if anybody brings it back,
20 sesterces if he reveals the thief so we can get our property back 64

What a pretty garden. Tall, flowering shrubs line two of the walls and the three rectangular ponds in the centre are occupied by a variety of colourful fish. Beyond that colonnade on the left is a broad corridor lined with numerous rooms, and at the top of the garden towards the house, you can see the rear walls of two private bath suites. Across the garden and behind that far wall is a pretty peristyle, somewhat smaller than this, which is mostly used by guests of Cominia's inn to relax and enjoy a cup of wine under the shade of its fig, apple and olive trees, at least when the weather permits.

Staphylus, Publius's slave lad approaches now from the rear of the garden, two sacks bulging with loaves slung over his shoulder and a wax tablet in his free hand. He was granted entry by Methe, a fifteen-year old slave, who then left by the back alley to pursue her own chores. Staphylus likes the look of Methe, as she has a pretty face and larger breasts than his current girlfriend, Quieta. He has tried to engage her in frivolous conversation, to flirt, despite his attachment of sorts with Quieta, but he doesn't appeal to Methe. She thinks there's something shifty about him. He followed her with his eyes as she walked off down the alley, admiring the shape of her backside beneath her tunic, but she turned suddenly and caught him, and he felt a flush of blood rising through his neck, which explains the rather red cheeks he sports as he passes us on the way to the kitchen. Let us follow.

He goes under the colonnade and calls into the kitchen, but no one replies. He looks about. There is no one to be seen. He has found that the Inn of Cominia Lucilla is often quiet at this time of the morning, when no meals await immediate preparation and the other slaves and servants are busy cleaning the guests' rooms. He glances over towards the rear walls of the bathhouse and smiles faintly. He turns and enters the kitchen and empties the sack of loaves into a large basket on the floor. He then looks about the many shelves, holding pots and pans, cups and plates, urns and small, delicate bottles. He picks up a round dish about the size of his hand and lifts the lid. He can barely believe his eyes, as it is filled with saffron, a highly prized seasoning among the wealthier Roman classes, and extremely expensive. He looks about and sees an old linen rag lying on the table, used for wiping, and he tears a piece off, then gathers a small clump of the precious strands between his fingers and wraps it in the cloth. This he deposits in a pocket of his tunic. He then fluffs up the remainder to make it appear as though untouched. As he returns the dish to the shelf he spots a number of olive oil dispensers on another shelf. They are small and could almost be concealed in a fist. They are made of a variety of materials, some of potter's clay, one carved from wood, and several more of bronze. He quickly grasps one of bronze and adds it to his pocket. It should fetch a decent price if he can find a buyer, not as much as the saffron, but he is pleased with his little haul.

The thief is not done yet. He leaves the kitchen and looks about. No one to be seen. From beyond the wall across the garden he can hear voices, probably those of guests lazing under the peristyle portico while unfortunate slaves like him pamper them with drinks and snacks and fan them with peacock feathers. This is his means of justifying his thievery to himself. He is just balancing the scales a little. He hurries across the grass now and leaps across the ponds, holding his arms to protect his face as he moves between the shrubs that line the wall. He looks up at the tiny vent that allows steam to escape from the caldarium then begins to climb using the roughly projecting blocks as footholds. This time he intends not to steal any object, but a glance at a naked woman as she indulges in her bath. He has ventured here several times and been rewarded once for his efforts with the sight of a woman of about thirty years, her back to him, having her hair washed by a slave. He considered her very old, yet her body was not without its attractions, and he masturbated to the vision of her that night.

As he approaches the vent he can hear splashing and his hopes rise, along with his penis. His eyes come level and he looks through to see a wrinkled old man reclining on the steps of the bath, half in and half out of the water, his flaccid member bobbing up and down. He curses silently as his own excitement dies, and scrambles the few steps down to the ground. He emerges from between the shrubs and pauses. The tepidarium is the next room along, but it offers no cover behind foliage. Yet his disappointment spurs him to take the risk and after a cursory glance about, he scrambles up. He expected moist, warm air to meet his face, but instead there is only a cool draught and when he looks inside he is again disappointed to see that the room is not in use, is in fact undergoing redecoration. Shelves are in the process of being erected, presumably for holding towels and oils and so on, and hammers and saws and other tools lie scattered about the floor beside a large marble basin, which is empty of water. The door opens and he quickly moves his face to one side in case he is spotted. He is about to drop to the ground and flee but there are voices now and their urgency stills him, and he stands there clinging precariously to the wall.

He risks a peek in and sees Cominia Lucilla, the inn's owner, and that large African who runs the carpenter's shop in the next street. The woman appears anxious. The black man closes the door behind them.

I'm sure you remember Chrestus, who saved Cygnia's life during the earthquake. Convinced that his family were long dead in Africa, or exported as slaves, he elected to remain at her side. He is a man who can sense the innate goodness, or otherwise, in people and in Cygnia, as she was then called, he found a soul mate. Secretly he was always been a little in love with her. At first he posed as her slave, but in name only, until she had established herself sufficiently to grant his freedom. Now he lives close at hand, a partner in a furniture and carpentry shop. Their friendship, and trust in each other, has never once wavered.

But let us listen.

– I'm sure she knew me. The way she stared at me.

– You are imagining it, Cygnia.

– Chrestus, don't ever call me that. I've told you.

– Forgive me. But how could anyone know you? You spent just a few weeks here ten years ago, and most of that was confined in Mariona's inn.

– She wasn't from here, at least I don't think so. She looked familiar. She may have been a woman my Domina, Severina, knew in Rome.

– And where did you see her?

– In the forum.

– Not here then? Not at the inn?

– No.

He exhales. – Then you have nothing to fear. She does not know who you are. She does not know you go by the name of Cominia Lucilla. For all she knows you are a freed slave who has done well in life. And even if she did know, what can she prove? She would have to dig very deeply to discover anything about you. She is not going to do that. People see others they think they know all the time. I say she has forgotten about you already. And she is probably already on her way back to Rome by now.

She seems comforted by his words. – Do you think so?

Chrestus smiles. He places a hand on her shoulder. – You have had such encounters before and they came to nothing. Forget the woman. No one shall ever know. Unless you choose to tell them.

She smiles now. – Not likely.

Staphylus hears a door open nearby. He quickly clambers down and drops softly on to the dusty soil. He hurries across the garden and under the portico, where he is stalled by the sight of Daphnicus approaching. His heart lurches. Has he been spotted?

Thief, beware of trouble 65

– You! What are you doing there?

– Forgive me. I was looking for you. I delivered the bread and need the tablet stamped.

Daphnicus regards him with suspicion for a moment. He recognises there is an uneasiness about the boy. He grabs him by the shoulder and pushes him into the kitchen.

– Where is the tablet?

– There. On the table. I've brought twenty loaves. You should mark here on the wax.

Daphnicus barks. – I know that, you fool.

A ring of keys and other small implements dangle from his tunic's belt. He lifts one and stamps the tablet. He then glances about the kitchen, sees nothing amiss and hands the tablet to the boy, who he clips lightly on the ear.

– Go on. Be off with you. In future you will wait at the rear entrance until I am available. I don't want you skulking about here alone.

– Yes, sir.

Staphylus backs out of the room with head bowed as though leaving an audience with the emperor. As he moves towards the exit he feels his nerves begin to settle and a vapour of satisfaction spread about his body. The conversation he overheard might be of value, he thinks. And he would much rather have seen a naked girl than a black man and a woman old enough to be his mother. But he has his saffron and his bronze and his mind already wanders in search of a buyer. Perhaps he might even be able to afford a whore or two with the profits, he is thinking. His first whore. Now there is a thought that makes him smile. A thought that banishes from his head any further curiosity he may have felt about Cominia and her secret.

Fortuna smiled on her today.

SCAENA 24

15 July. Earrings deposited with Faustilla
Per 2 denarii she took as usury
1 copper as from a total 30 [66]

We remain in the Inn of Cominia, but a day has passed since we last set foot here. We stand in the atrium once more, and Satura, the freed slave, waits anxiously outside that room off to the left, which Daphnicus uses as his tablinum, and from where can be heard the weeping of a girl. A peek over Satura's shoulder reveals Daphnicus seated behind a table and the young slave, Methe, standing facing him, head drooping.

Daphnicus yells. – You stupid girl!

He stands and raises his hand to strike her on the side of the head, then stalls himself as she flinches away.

– Look at me!

She lifts her head.

– How much did you borrow?

Through sniffles she manages a reply.

– Fifteen sesterces, master.

He raises his eyes to the heavens, picks up a piece of papyrus, looks at it, shakes his head.

– Fift.... Jupiter's balls! You stupid little cow.

But look. Cominia approaches across the atrium, attracted by the commotion. Let us squeeze inside the small room and observe from a better vantage point.

Cominia glances at Satura who avoids her eyes, and enters the room.

– What's going on?

Daphnicus stands. – I'm sorry, Domina, I did not intend to bother you with this matter.

– What has happened?

He sighs. – This stupid girl has gotten herself into debt with a moneylender and cannot pay it back. Look at this.

He brandishes the document.

– She borrowed fifteen sesterces, which would be hard enough for her to pay back with her allowance of one sesterce a week. But this Faustilla is charging her almost fifty percent interest. Fifty percent! Compound. Per month! She cannot meet the payments and the woman has threatened to bring her before a magistrate.

– Is this true, Methe?

She nods. Looks at the floor.

– Why did you want the money?

The girl doesn't answer. She sniffles.

Daphnicus barks. – Answer your Domina at once!

Cominia shakes her head at him. – Stop yelling, Daphnicus. Methe, have you gotten yourself in trouble with a boy?

She shakes her head.

– What then?

Satura's voice is heard from the atrium.

– Domina. Please. I know. She bought a new stola and some

make-up. She wished to impress a boy at the Vulcanalia celebrations.

Daphnicus scowls out at the older girl. – You should have more sense, Satura, allowing her to do this.

– Please, Domina. I only just leaned of this.

Finally Methe finds her voice. – Satura made me tell Daphnicus, Domina.

– Daphnicus is right, Methe. You are a stupid girl. If you paid more attention during your tutoring you would have seen that you could never meet the repayments with your allowance. This woman has taken advantage of your ignorance. Who is this Faustilla?

– If I may, Domina. She is bad news. She is employed by Marcus Epidius Sabinus. Runs a moneylending and pawnbroker service for him. A real witch, from what I know.

– A witch, is she? Well, let's see if I can cast a few spells of my own.

8 February Vettia, 20 denarii,
usury 12 as. 5 February, from Faustilla,
15 denarii: usury 8 as [67]

We've hastened to the Via del Fortuna and if you look east along the street you can see Cominia approaching with a determined step, garbed in a pale blue stola, her head covered by a light palla against the warmth of sun. Young Methe scuttles along by her side, hurrying to keep up, dressed in a simple white tunic that reaches her ankles. Cominia turns into the narrow Vicolo del Laberinto, Methe trailing in her wake. Come. Let us do the same.

This is little more than an alley, as you can see, high walls on either side are painted the colour of rust, but the paint is neglected and crumbles in places. The monotony of the wall on the left, that bounding a palatial house, is broken only by an occasional window high above us. A similarly high wall on the right features a few doorways, all shut against us, which lead to accommodations above, most of which are of the single room variety. It is a matter of some curiosity to foreign travellers that in this town the poor live in such close proximity to the rich, and that the sewer worker and dough maker and prostitute live just paces from Pompeii's élite, but in one sense dwell in another world.

Cominia reaches the end of the alley, where it crosses the Vicolo di Mercurio and pauses outside the last door on the right, this one open. The door is painted a garish yellow. She waits for Methe to catch up.

– Just keep quiet, girl.

– Yes, Domina.

Poor Methe is yet frightened to face Faustilla, who operates her money lending and pawn brokerage from this small office. She fully expects a beating when she returns to Cominia's Inn, as was the norm for a transgression with her previous Domina.

As we enter. a man emerges clutching a small purse, its contents, which amount to a handful of sesterces and a few as, spread across his palm. He has just pawned his wife's wedding ring, earning him just five sesterces. But that will keep his family fed for a while.

A stairs leads off the short corridor ahead of us, and there is an open doorway to the left. Cominia leads Methe into the small room. Bare, unpainted walls are lined with shelves upon which are many of the trinkets left here by the poor in desperation. Small statues of Venus, bracelets, bronze knives and spoons, a bronze candelabra, a phallus-shaped oil lamp, a child's rattle made of bone. The shelves are weighed down with misery.

Numerous wax tablets are piled on the floor, along with several drums of papyrus scrolls, each detailing the transactions that have taken place. A large table spans almost the width of the room, covered with documents and tablets, and behind it sits Faustilla, garbed in a bright yellow stola, her wrists and fingers and ears adorned with jewellery, her hair tied in a bun upon her head.

She looks up briefly at Cominia and Methe's entrance, then returns her gaze to a tablet in her hands.

– Loan or pawn?

– What?

– Do you want to pawn something or do you want an unsecured loan, which will cost you more?

– I have no need of your money.

That response has gotten her attention, as you can see. She looks up, lowers the tablet and sits back in chair, her hands on the table. Her burning amber eyes fix Cominia with a rigid stare.

Cominia takes a step forward, pulls her palla down and glances at Methe, standing just behind her to one side. She lays the papyrus scroll detailing the transaction before Faustilla, who ignores it.

– You made a loan to this girl, Methe, of the Inn of Cominia Lucilla. Fifteen sesterces. You are charging her over fifty percent interest. Fifty!

Faustilla shrugs. Says nothing.

– It is robbery. An outrage.

Faustilla smiles, but without humour. – She didn't have to take the money. Those were the terms.

– She didn't understand how much it would cost her each month. And you knew it.

– It is not my problem if your daughter is ignorant of simple arithmetic.

– She is not my daughter. She is a slave. But nonetheless, she cannot repay it. She won't repay it.

– Then as your slave it becomes your responsibility. You

shall repay me or I'll go before the magistrates. She may not have to pay it then. They may take it out of her in flesh. Deliberate non-payment of a debt can earn you twelve lashes in the forum. Her back would make a pretty sight then.

Faustilla grins, and this time there is humour in her smile. Methe utters a stifled cry at the notion that her punishment might be even worse than she had imagined. Cominia shushes her, returns her gaze to Faustilla, places her own hands on the table.

– Listen to me. If you go before the magistrate I will contest it. I will even hire a jurist to defend her. And everyone in the basilica, in Pompeii, will see you exposed as a bloodsucker. What will that do for your business?

Faustilla is unfazed. – Hire a jurist? Over a matter of fifteen sesterces? Don't make me laugh. It would cost you ten times that.

– And yet I would do it. Besides, I know a few jurists who owe me favours. They'd be glad to do it pro bono publico.

– What? Did you suck their cocks?

This is meant to shock Cominia, throw her off guard. It achieves neither. She now smiles.

– Your tongue is as twisted as your business dealings. Go ahead. Bring the matter before the magistrates. I look forward to it.

Cominia turns to leave, taking Methe by the arm.

– Wait. Don't be so hasty. I don't have such time to waste on something this trivial.

Cominia turns towards her. She waits for something further.

Faustilla picks up the scroll of papyrus and unrolls it, peruses it. – I will lower the rate to two as a month.

– No. I have another proposal. I will pay the full debt now, with interest of one as per each of the three months since the loan was made.

– You must be joking.

– That's more than the other moneylenders charge. It's the best you'll get.

– The other moneylenders wouldn't lend money to a little cunt like her.

– Take it or leave it. Or we'll see if the magistrates agree if my offer is fair.

Faustilla's mouth tightens. She sits forward.

– Pay sixteen sesterces in total and I'll agree.

It is a minor increase on Cominia's offer, and one she is willing to pay. She recognises that Faustilla needed to have a final puny victory in their dealings before she could agree. Cominia produces a purse and begins to count out the coins.

I paid the debt on March 15 [68]

– Mark the debt as paid on the documents.

Faustilla has recovered her composure fully. She titters as she fishes for the relevant tablet on the table. – What is it? Don't you trust me?

Cominia doesn't respond. She wishes to be gone from this woman's company. Faustilla records the transaction on a scroll. She rolls it up and holds it out to Cominia, but then pulls it away as Cominia reaches. She grins.

– I'm sure we'll have future dealings.

Cominia shakes her head in exasperation.

– Give it to me you fucking bitch.

Faustilla's grin weakens. Her stare grows more intense. Cominia believes for a moment that the woman might strike her. But Faustilla has no such intentions. She is in a different place, although she cannot tell where it is. A memory has intruded so sharply it is like a stick driven into the spokes of a turning wheel. But she cannot place it. The face. The voice. They are there in her mind. Somewhere in the past.

Cominia is disturbed by her expression.

– What?

But then the feeling weakens and Faustilla wonders if it was her mind playing tricks. She looks at the scroll in her hand. Holds it up.

Cominia snatches it, turns and leaves with Methe in tow.

Faustilla sits there for a time, staring into space, trying to dredge her mind for the fleeting memory she had briefly grasped. But it will not surface again. She swears under her breath in frustration.

A woman enters the room. She is clutching a folded red woolen stola, the one in which she was married. She lays it slowly on the table. Faustilla's thoughts revert to her day's business. She lifts the garment up briefly by the shoulders, then looks above it at the woman.

– You expect money for this rag?

But let us rejoin Cominia and Methe as they walk home along the Via della Fortuna. It is mid-morning and feels intensely hot already. People clutter the narrow path to the right of the street as it offers a small degree of shade. Tradesmen pass them pushing handcarts. Shopkeepers call out to them, each offering goods at the best prices in town. One or two loiter beneath the awnings of the thermopolia, spooning bowls of spiced chickpeas into their mouths, or dipping chunks of bread into honeyed wine. A woman above hangs a sheet from a balcony. A man holds a ladder for another while he paints the walls of a house a startling yellow.

But Cominia sees little of this. She is disturbed by her encounter with Faustilla. The way the woman had stared at her. It is the second time in a few days she has feared recognition. But she has no memory of the woman at all. And the sharp-edged Faustilla is not one she would easily forget. Perhaps it was nothing. And as Chrestus says, how could anyone uncover the truth now? Why would they even trouble themselves to undertake such an onerous task when it might prove completely fruitless? Was she a fool ever to undertake this enterprise? Perhaps she and Chrestus should simply have purchased passage on a ship to a far away land.

Whimpering, low and constant, eventually intrudes on her thoughts. She looks over her shoulder at Methe, shoulders drooping, face wet with sniffles. She is irritated by the girl at this point. So much trouble has she caused.

She snaps. – In the name of Mars what's wrong? Stop that damn snivelling!

– I'm sorry, Domina.

– The debt is paid. Why are you still crying?

She lifts her head, dares a glance a Cominia's eyes. – Am I to be beaten, Domina?

– Beaten?

– Yes, Domina.

– No. You will pay me two as each week from your allowance until the debt is paid. That is your punishment. But if you ever do such a thing again, I will not be so forgiving.

The girl appears startled. – That is all?

– Yes.

Methe leaps forward and embraces Cominia, burying her head against the sleeve of her stola.

– Thank you, Domina, thank you.

Passers-by stare, amused, curious about the scene. Cominia gently pulls the girl from her embrace. She is a little amused herself at her seeming overreaction. Then a new thought occurs. She recalls purchasing Methe at an auction in Herculaneum. The seller was a brutish man who smelled of wine and had a foul temperament.

...that this girl is healthy, not charged with theft or injurious conduct, is not a runaway truant, is being handed over...as is customary, which in this year with regard to buying and selling slaves has been prescribed and provided for, that this is thus being correctly done.
Gaius Iulius Phoebus witnessed.
Transacted at Herculaneum.[69]

– Your former master in Neapolis... he beat you a great deal, didn't he, Methe?

She looks to the ground. – Mostly the Domina Calatoria. For the smallest thing. But sometimes he did too, Petronius, the Dominus, I mean. And often he would take me afterwards. He was a brutal man.

– You mean...?

She nods. Cominia sighs. Her memories of her own youth are not so different, although with hindsight, mild compared with Methe's. She takes the girl's hand and begins to walk. She feels a brief glow of satisfaction at the thing she has done with her life. She has rescued a few from such misery, a handful of pebbles on the beach perhaps, but a handful nonetheless.

– So, Methe, what colour is the stola you bought for Vulcanalia? Is it pretty?

SCAENA 25

Staphylus was here with Quieta [70]

Another laneway with not a soul stirring, only a sprinkling of
moonlight to guide your step. I can sense you are wondering
why we're lurking here in yet another dismal, grim alleyway, but
it is in such places that men like Epidius conduct much of their
business, or rather, pay someone to conduct it for them. It's
quiet. You can hear a peal of distant laughter from the bar of
Salvius a few blocks away, and somewhere else a dog barks, and
if you listen carefully you can hear the occasional rat scam-
pering about our feet, feeding on the waste that Pompeiians
frequently dump on their streets. But those sounds are hardly
comforting, are they? In fact, they only serve to make this alley
of inky black shadows all the more threatening.

But listen. Those approaching footsteps do most definitely
not belong to a rat. Here he comes from the Via di Nola, his
movements furtive, trying to keep his step light. It is too dark for
you to recognise him, I think, even though he passes within an
arm's length. Come on. Let us follow.

Watch. The small figure will pause at a wall on the left towards the far end of the alley. He catches his breath then walks tentatively to the point where the rear wall of that building is partially damaged. That happened in the earthquake and the owner of this property still hasn't gotten around to effecting repairs. See how our prey peers over? Listen, he's calling out to someone in a whisper.

– Quieta? Quieta?

Shhh. A second whisper replies.

– Here.

Now he clambers up and over the breach in the wall. You can tell he is young from the agility he displays. Let us join him. Oh don't worry. I don't expect you to clamber over any walls.

You see. Here we are. A nice flower garden bounded on three sides by an elegant portico. Even in the moonlight it is pretty, don't you agree? The house there once belonged to Lucius Caecilius Jucundus, the employer of our Marcus Epidius Sabinus and now belongs to his son Quintus. But this is incidental to the reason I brought you here and Epidius's involvement with Quintus is a mere coincidence, and bears no relation to what will occur in the next minutes.

Look over there, under the peristyle portico. To your left. No, not at the fresco of a naked couple making love, but beyond that, in the corner.

Now you recognise him. Yes, that's Staphylus, Publius's young slave lad. Just fourteen and not too bright. And not too honest either, as you've seen. He's sneaked out of the bakery to make this little rendezvous, which is strictly forbidden, especially after dark. Should Publius's mother, Prima, discover he is gone, she will take a stick to his behind when he returns. But that is a risk he is prepared to take. The same holds for the young girl he is currently embracing. Her name is Quieta, slave and maidservant to Fabia, the Domina of this house. Quieta, who is thirteen, risks a similar punishment from her mistress, but she is confident she will not be discovered as Quintus and Fabia drank themselves into a stupor an hour ago and the last she saw them they were snoring their heads off in their cubiculum upstairs.

As you can see, Staphylus's tongue is inserted deeply into his little girlfriend's mouth and he is desperately trying to work his right hand beneath the folds of her tunic so that he can grasp her budding breasts. She seizes his hand and pulls it away. Let's listen to their breathless whispers:

– What's wrong?

– You're not doing that!

– Why?

– Because I'm not that sort of girl. I don't want to end up pregnant.

Staphylus chuckles. – You can't get pregnant if I squeeze your tit.

Quieta pulls his hair.

– Ow!

– Don't talk to me like I'm a whore.

– I'm sorry. I love you. I didn't mean to upset you.

Quieta softens. She gives him a peck on the lips. – Do you think your master will grant your freedom if you told him we wished to marry?

My boss isn't worth a rat's anus ₇₁

Staphylus shakes his head sadly. – Not now. His bakery's in shit and he's always in a foul mood these days. I hate the cunt.

– No you don't.

– I do. I'm just his fucking mule. But wait. Look. I brought you a gift.

– What is it?

He fumbles inside his tunic and draws out a simple bronze bracelet, the metal twisted into a pretty spiral along its length. It isn't worth much, perhaps five sesterces, but it would be the finest single item in Quieta's possession. He slips it on to her wrist.

– Hold it up to the moonlight.

She does as instructed.

– It looks beautiful. Oh Staphylus, thank you!

She smiles and kisses him. He responds by sticking his tongue inside her mouth once more, pressing his body tightly against her and settling for squeezing her backside, seeing as all other vital areas are off limits. She pulls away, almost breathless.

– Wait. Where did you get it?

– I bought it.

She is silent for a time, staring at the dim shape of his face. He feels her eyes upon him and he tries to break her stare by kissing her again, but she quickly turns her head away.

– What's wrong?

– You don't have any money. You stole it, didn't you?

– No.

– You did!

– Shhh!

– Answer me.

– Fine. It was Cornelia's, my Dominus's sister. The stupid cunt has ten more like it. I took it a week ago and she hasn't even noticed. It's yours now.

She pulls it from her wrist. – I don't want it. Take it back.

– No. Why?

– Take it. I might be a slave, but I'm not a thief.

He takes it back with a grunt.

– I'm sorry. I thought you'd like it. Please forgive me.

– I do, if you promise not to steal again. Ever.

He nods.

– Say it!

– I promise never to steal again.

Hm. Let's see how long he keeps that vow.

She pecks him on the lips. He slides his arms around her waist again. A noise from the house stalls their embrace and their heads turn with startled expressions. Their whispers have a desperate edge.

– Someone's up. Oh no! You must go! Quickly!

– Curse it! When will I see you again?

– I don't know. I'll find you when you're doing your deliveries. But you must go! Now!

Staphylus hurries on tiptoes from the peristyle, looking comical with the bulge still very evident beneath his tunic. Sorry for laughing. I may as well, as the next moments will be anything but funny.

We are back in the darkness of the alley. Here comes young Staphylus clambering backward over the wall, his tunic riding up as it snags on the top. He looks toward a niche in the far wall and hurries across into its deep blackness, where he begins to masturbate, images behind his tightly closed eyelids depicting Quieta willingly performing a variety of sexual acts at his behest. He is thus engaged when two dark figures suddenly appear in the street before him, lay rough hands on his arms and shoulders and yank him to the ground. A hand is clasped over his mouth to stifle any scream. He is terrified, his pleasant fantasies blown away like a pile of leaves in a gale.

He hears a titter. – Little fucker was having a wank.

Another voice from a black shape above him. – There'll be no more of that for a while.

The two men pull him along the alley, his arms flailing, and into the ruin of a shop that half-collapsed in the earthquake.

Even in the moonlight you can tell that they are giants compared to the boy, especially the one standing in front of Staphylus. His name is Albanus Octavus, a famed ex-gladiator. He was also the only man ever to defeat Celadus, but you shall hear more of that later. Epidius purchased him two years ago, but his battles now are not done before the adoring thousands, but in dim back alleys such as this. Not that you could call this a battle. The man holding Staphylus is Ampliatus Pedania. He's a petty thief who, when not employed by Epidius, picks the purses of his fellow Pompeiians in bars and market places. He considers this particular job easy money.

Ampliatus Pedania is a thief ₇₂

He releases his hand from Staphylus's mouth and the terrified boy starts to blurt out something, when Albanus abruptly smashes a fist into his face.

– Shut up you little cunt.

– What will we do with the bastard?

Albanus smirks as he addresses Staphylus.

– Was she good? Did the little whore suck your cock?

Staphylus's head is spinning, his lip pumps blood like a spout. Yet he is misguidedly driven to respond to what he sees as a slur on his Quieta's character.

– She's not a who...

Another fist. Staphylus's head snaps back and then lolls forward.

– He's passing out. Hold him up.

The thief hoists the boy back on his feet and Albanus slaps his cheeks lightly to revive him. Staphylus's eyes open a fraction.

– Listen to me you piece of shit. That slave girl is the property of a respectable family and they don't want filthy little pigs like you sticking your cock in her. If you ever come back here again or even look crooked at her again, I'm going to burn that fucking bakery you work in to the ground. You got that?

Staphylus moans. Albanus grips his cheeks in a pincer lock with his fingers.

– I asked if you got that?

A barely perceptible 'yes' confirms that Staphylus got the message.

This is all what you would call misdirection. Albanus, Ampliatus and Epidius have no interest in Quieta, other than the fact that she served as a convenient scapegoat for their attacking Staphylus. Their real target is Publius, who, even if he approaches the incumbent duumviri seeking justice, will have no grounds to blame Epidius. But Publius will know who was behind it. And soon he will be deprived of another pair of hands to run his struggling business.

Albanus grunts. – Give him to me.

You probably can't see it, but there is a wide grin on his face. He delights in his work.

Albanus, left-hander, of free status,
victorious 19 times, victor 73

Ampliatus pushes the barely standing boy at his colleague, who shoves him face-first against one of the remaining walls of the ruin, twists his arm behind his back and forces it well beyond its natural arc. As the muscle begins to tear the pain is so great that it brings poor Staphylus back to alertness and panic. A moment later there is a sharp cracking sound as his arm breaks. He screams. It is louder than any scream he has contrived in his short life, but nobody hears it as it is swallowed by the clasping hand of Albanus. Nobody, that is, but I. The boy passes beyond sense and collapses in an unnatural heap.

– You want to do the other arm?

Ampliatus Pedania shakes his head, displaying the one speck of decency that remains within him.

– Albanus, the little fucker's had enough.

But it is in vain.

– Suit yourself. I'll do it myself.

No such speck exists in Albanus.

SCAENA 26

All who are in love are at war [74]

We are here again in the tablinum of Publius, but he is absent. The curtain is drawn back and there stands Restitutus, lamp in hand. He is about to turn away when he sees the manuscript on the table. He looks over his shoulder and seeing the house quiet, sits in his brother's chair.

Oh Restitutus, Publius will not like this.

He begins to read, his interest growing. Notice how an occasional chuckle passes his lips. After a short while he is so absorbed that he fails to hear footsteps approaching.

Listen to the sound. You can tell a lot from a man or woman's footsteps. Light and so is their heart. Fast and they have urgent business. Heavy and they are angered by some matter. Clearly Publius's feet stomp as he returns, as his baker Narcissus, has just brought Staphylus's absence to his attention. And his anger will be heightened considerably when he pulls back the curtain.

Let us watch.

– What in Jupiter's cock are you doing?

He rushes to the desk and seizes the papyrus scroll from his younger brother, tearing it in the process. Restitutus remains calm as Publius gathers the other scrolls and pushes them into a box. Restitutus rises and moves away.

– What's wrong? I didn't think you'd mind.

– You bastard. You knew well I'd mind. I told you never to touch my work.

– I am not a bastard, Publius, but the son of Publius Comicius Restitutus, Centurion in the Roman Army.

– I know who he was. And if you'd disturbed his papers he would have flogged you.

– But you're not him, are you? Not by half. You're still dreaming of being the great playwright.

Publius rolls his eyes skywards in pleading to the gods. – What do you want, Restitutus?

– I think it's very good, by the way.

He gestures at the box containing the papyrus scrolls. Publius looks at him to see if he is being mocked, but Restitutus appears serious.

– It is incomplete. And private. And what do you know of the theatre anyway?

– I'm not stupid. And I know enough to recognise Pompeii in your play. And also Epidius. It would make him a laughing stock.

Publius stares at him in silent anger. The secrets of his work have been spilled.

– Is that how you plan to deal with him? With a play? Do you think he'll see it and suddenly fall to his knees, applaud your genius and forgive all your debt? More likely he'll run you through.

Publius speaks though clenched teeth. – I'll deal with Epidius in my own....

Restitutus suddenly shouts. – Father would have had his

head by now! And he would never have let his whole family fall into shame.

– How has our family fallen into shame? Speak!

Publius has moved closer to his brother now, his voice risen in anger.

Restitutus is about to blurt out about Cornelia, defying his own advice, but he bites his tongue and turns away. Publius grasps his shoulder. His brother whirls about and thrusts Publius's hand away. They are moments from exchanging blows. But not this night, as they are abruptly interrupted by the sound of loud hammering on the front door.

Publius pushes past his brother. – What in the name of...? Is it Mother? Is something wrong with Mother?

Both brothers run through the house to the door and almost battle to unlock it. Before them stands a youth they have never seen before, a torch held aloft.

– Is this the house of Publius the baker?

– It is. Who are you?

– I am Aufidius, slave of Cosmus. You have a boy who delivers bread?

– Yes. Staphylus. He's not here. I'll beat him when I lay my hands on him. He should have...

– I found him. Not far from here. In a ruin off the Via di Nola. He's....

The boy hesitiates. Restitutus pushes past his brother. – What is it?

– He was attacked. You better come.

SCAENA 27

Blessed is this house [76]

That woman bending over Staphylus bathing his forehead is called Epidia. His shattered arms are fixed by his sides in splints as he lies there on the couch. Should he live, he will require the arms of others to cater to his every need in the coming months, from eating to bathing to wiping his behind. Humiliating for the poor lad, is it not? Still, it could be worse, that is, if he survives. And his face is a swollen mess. The only compensation at this moment is that he is unconscious to the cruelties of this world. But that will not last.

Aufidius, who is fifteen and who you've already met when he brought the message to Publius, stands beside his master, Cosmus, a retired ship's captain. And this room? This is the oecus of Cosmus and Epidia, owners of this spacious yet modestly decorated home.

For once Publius and Restitutus have something in common, as you can probably guess from their faces. They are both filled with rage.

– Tell them what happened, Aufidius.

– I was returning from the Vesuvian Gate. I had been on an errand to my Dominus's daughter's hou...

– Never mind your errand, Aufidius.

– Sorry, Dominus. I took a short cut along an alley and heard someone moaning in the ruin of a house. At first I thought it was just a drunk from one of the bars or a man with a whore using the ruin...

Cosmus shakes his head in exasperation.

– Give me the patience of Hercules. He saw it was a young slave. He came and told me and we returned with another slave and brought him back here. Then Aufidius recognised him.

– I see him all the time with his bread cart when I'm running errands. So the master sent me to get the physician, Gnaeus Domiti, and then to your home.

GNAEUS DOMITI, HEALER 77

Epidia appears amidst them. – Who would do such a monstrous thing to a boy? I'd have their faces branded as animals.

Publius and Restitutus exchange a glance.

Despite Epidia's rather gory suggestion, she shares a kind soul with her husband of thirty years. Cosmus has seen many broken limbs while sailing the seas. But never has he seen man or boy with both arms broken at once. Neither had the physician who set the shattered bones.

– Domiti said that the biggest danger is poison in his blood.

Restitutus is startled. – He was poisoned also?

Cosmus shakes his head, almost smiles.

– No, no. From within. When a bone is broken the body may react badly to the shock. Even though the flesh was unbroken. But your slave is young and healthy. We can only wait and see he is comfortable.

As if in answer the unconscious Staphylus groans. Epidia bathes his forehead with renewed vigour. – Shhhh.

Publius speaks now. He has been almost silent since he saw Staphylus's condition. – We cannot burden you with this, Cosmus. I will come to some arrangement to have him brought to my home tomorrow.

Epidia interjects. – You will do no such thing. The boy cannot be moved for a long time.

– She's right, Publius. He may stay here as long as is necessary, Cosmus adds.

– You are both very kind. I will try to pay you for...

Cosmos sighs. – Please. I have no need of money. And beside, I believe my darling Epidia here has found a new project to occupy her.

Epidia feigns indignation. – If you think I'll be the only one wiping his behind and emptying his piss pot you can think again, Cosmus.

He smiles as she returns to attend to Staphylus.

– Aufidius. Fetch some wine for our guests.

– Cosmus, we will forego the wine. We must return home and let our mother and sister know what has happened. We're grateful again for your help. I will return in the morning to see how he progresses.

– As you wish, Publius.

Publius shakes his hand. – It is good to know that men such as you exist, Cosmus.

Cosmus modestly looks to the floor as the two brothers make their exit bearing a torch. Yet for Publius, all paths ahead seem to remain in complete darkness. In truth, he is at a loss and despairing of the future. He feels impotent and weak, and suspects that Restitutus's portrayal of him is not so far from the truth. Not that he is prepared to concede such a thing.

– What do we do now?

They are striding along the Via Nola, the light opening a short tunnel through the blackness of the street. Publius doesn't bother turning his head to answer.

– Tomorrow, go to the forum and hire another delivery lad. There are always boys hanging about the basilica looking for work.

– Fuck the forum! What do we do about Epidius?

– We have no proof he was behind this.

Restitutus grasps his brother's arm and pulls him to a halt. – We have no proof? Who gives a fuck? We both know this is his doing.

– Without proof we cannot seek justice from the magistrates. So we carry on running the bakery as normal. We show Epidius that we will not be beaten.

Restitutus's anger rises further. – You're a fool! Hire another lad? You can barely afford to pay the men we have, me included, or even put food on the table. We barely made the rent last month.

Since 14 days before the Kalends of April
our wages have been overdue 78

Publius angrily shrugs off his brother's hand. – Perhaps the bakery wouldn't be so close to ruin if you spent less time whoring in bars.

– Don't try to blame this on me. You waste hours each night poring over your precious plays. Do you think they're going to save you?

Restitutus emits a howl of bitter laughter.

The light from the torch isn't sufficient to completely relay the new rage in Publius's face. His frustration and helplessness are only heightened by his brother's mocking, as he suspects that Restitutus once more is right. His writing is a waste of time.

– I know what Father would have done. He'd have met fire with greater fire. He would have held a knife to Epidius's throat and put the fear of Jupiter into him. And if need be, he would have used the knife.

Publius steps so closely to his brother that they can feel each other's breath on their faces.

– You call *me* a fool? Epidius has powerful friends. You touch him and you'll end up having your head on a spike. Stay out of this, I warn you for your own good. Let me handle it.

Restitutus laughs in his face. – Let you handle it? At least you have a sense of humour, brother. That's probably handy when you write your plays. That's all you're good for after all.

Publius's clenched fist rises by his side. Clasped within it is the potential to destroy forever whatever love remains for Restitutus. But he lowers it again as quickly, then whirls away and hurries off into the night.

Restitutus stands there on the Via Nola in the dwindling light. Then his attention is drawn to the entrance to a house to his right. It is pure chance he and Publius paused on this spot, but poor, naive Restitutus believes the hand of Fortuna guided him here.

After a few moments, he hurries after the fading light of Publius's torch.

SCAENA 28

For the well-being of Nero Caesar Augustus Germanicus, at
Pompeii, there will be a hunt, athletics, and sprinklings by Tiberius
Claudius Verus on the twenty-fifth of February.
Good fortune to Claudius Verus [79]

We are precisely on the spot where Restitutus left us last night, outside the house that took his interest. Sorry if the sudden, early morning light blinded you.

You see those two men sitting on the stone bench? They wait to be summoned by the house's occupier, Tiberius Claudius Verus, who is their patron. Tiberius is in the importing business nowadays, mainly wine from other parts of Italy and even from Spain. But he also brings in linens and silks from Egypt, and some spices from the north of Africa. As a younger man he held political office but that was back during Nero's reign. He is very comfortable now, but not rich, and the house he occupies, although quite grand, is not his own but leased, it being the property of Gnaeus Alleius Maius, with whom you're acquainted.

IANUARIUS, LIVED TWO YEARS [80]
VALENTINUS, LIVED FIVE YEARS [81]
VIBIA PELAGIA, LIVED FORTY YEARS [82]

Tiberius is a tough businessman but isn't a bad sort. He has experienced much great misfortune in his life. His wife, Vibia, provided him with two sons, Valentinus and Ianuarius. Sadly, both perished in the earthquake when they were mere tots and Vibia also departed this earth five years later, choking to death on a fishbone. So Tiberius was left childless and wifeless. But before Vibia passed on, they decided to adopt the slave who had been part of their household since he was a small boy. You've met him. His name is Atimetus, and his is the young rascal that impregnated Cornelia atop a tomb. Which is what brings us to this place. And trouble will also be along soon.

Look. One of the men rises from the bench. He has been summoned into the atrium. He is the owner of a bar who purchases his more expensive wines from Tiberius, and he has fallen behind in his payments. Let us follow him in and meet Tiberius while we await our story's continuance.

Fine mosaic flooring, isn't it? It portrays a sea serpent pursuing a fish, as you can see. Tiberius had that put in himself as he believed it's symbolism would let his clients know that he would pursue them for their debts and swallow them whole if need be. Unfortunately too many of his clients aren't that bright and it goes over their heads, or under their feet, as it happens. Still, it looks nice. The walls are red-pannelled, each rectangle decorated with a small fresco: a semi-nude, flying female figure, a curious one of a panther with a rhyton or drinking horn and a tambourine, an image of Diana, goddess of nature, the moon and the hunt, and one of a cupid bearing an incense burner. Tiberius has eclectic tastes.

He sits in a high-backed chair beyond the impluvium giving

him a slightly regal appearance, dressed in a simple whitish toga. He is a man in his late forties, his hair prematurely bleached white with grief. He is plump but not fat. Slightly wrinkled face. Appulei, who is a slave officially, but in reality his master's trusted right hand man, stands at his shoulder with a wax tablet and stylus at the ready.

Appulei, assistant [83]

Countless scenes like this are taking place across the entire Roman world. They call it the 'salutatio'. Those with money and influence rise early to greet their clients one by one, each of whom seek some favour from their patron. And naturally, their patrons seek something in return. Let us listen.

To the innkeeper Euxinus
At Pompeii, near the Amphitheatre [84]

– Euxinus. What can I do for you?

The bar-owner is hunched over as he walks around the impluvium. A sign of deference.

– Tiberius, sir. A fine day and you are looking very well. each day you seem younger.

Tiberius rolls his eyes, then glances up at Appulei, who reads from his tablet.

– Euxinus, Innkeeper. Purchased twenty casks of fine Spanish Italica wine. Outstanding payment of ninety-four sesterces due on the Kalends of June.

Tiberius shrugs at Euxinus.

– Forgive the late payment. But after the last games some Nucerians started a fight and there was much damage...and there is one other matter that has contributed to my tardiness....

He coughs, looks down at the floor.

– Am I supposed to guess, Euxinus?

The bar owner looks up. – It is payment I myself am due from a customer who insisted on credit. It is for a substantial sum. Sixty sesterces.

– You gave a customer that much credit?

He coughs again. – Your son, Atimetus, sir.

Ah. The plot thickens. This will be amusing.

Tiberius's voice lifts. – Sixty sesterces? Are you telling me my son drank sixty sesterces of wine?

Another cough. Euxinus rummages in the folds of his tunic and extracts a grubby scroll of papyrus. He hands this to Tiberius tentatively.

– Some was for wine, sir. But most for...

Tiberius unrolls the document, which details the produce and services provided by Euxinus's bar. Haha. Look at his eyes lifting to the heavens. He passes the document to Appulei .

– By Mercury's balls, I'm amazed his dick hasn't fallen off. I have spoiled that boy, I know it. If Vibia were alive she'd beat me for allowing it and then beat him all the way to Gaul. Fetch him for me, would you Appulei?

My lusty son,
how many women have you fucked? 85

– Yes, Dominus.

Tiberius turns to Euxinus again. He sighs heavily.

– You may deduct sixty sesterces for Atimetus's bills. And next month a number of Greek gentlemen, traders, will visit me on business. They will have been on a ship for weeks and will undoubtedly be uncomfortable and weary. I will send them to your inn Euxinus. See to their every need. You may also deduct any costs they incur from your bill plus ten percent. But I will indulge your late payment no longer than the Kalends two months hence. Is that clear?

The man nods profuse thanks and departs as Appulei returns in the company of Atimetus.

Tiberius is about to bark at his adopted son when Appulei's voice lifts in surprise and annoyance and he hurries forward to block the approaching figure of Restitutus.

– Who are you? If you wish to see Tiberius Verus you must make an appointment.

Restitutus pushes him roughly aside.

– I don't need an appointment.

Well, this transaction should be different to those normally conducted during salutatio.

Tiberius rises from his chair. – Who are you?

– My business concerns your son.

Atimetus is startled. – Me?

Restitutus stares at him with furious eyes.

– What business have you with Atimetus?

Restitutus turns his head and shouts back towards the open doorway.

– Cornelia!

She enters, walking slowly, eyes to the ground, hands fiddling at the front of her tunic. Restitutus turns and points an accusing finger at Atimetus.

– My sister is pregnant. And he impregnated her and then abandoned her when he'd had his fun.

Tiberius closes his eyes briefly then looks at Atimetus. – Is this true?

– I know her, Father. I've met her. And maybe I've flirted with her at the basilica. But I've never fucked her. I swear it.

Cornelia yells a tearful reply. – That's a lie!

– Really, Father. Do you think I'd screw a fat cow like that?

Restitutus lunges forward and grabs a handful of Atimetus's

tunic. – Don't add to your treachery by insulting my sister, you little maggot!

You can hear Cornelia now sobbing openly behind us. Restitutus pushes Atimetus away and the youth almost stumbles and falls on his behind.

Tiberius stands. – Who are you? What is your name?

– I am Vibius Comicius Restitutus, son of Publius. My family owns a bakery not far from here.

– I swear, Father. Restitutus. She is mistaking me for someone else.

Restitutus lunges again. He grasps Atimetus in a head lock and pulls his father's knife from the folds of his tunic. He presses this to the young man's throat. – You fucking liar. My sister doesn't fuck around like a whore. You took advantage of her. Admit it or I swear to Apollo I'll slit your throat!

Tiberius takes several steps towards them, his hand outstretched in pleading. – No! Please. He's my only son! Don't hurt him!

Appulei runs from the atrium. Restitutus presses the blade into the flesh and the skin is broken. A tiny rivulet of blood runs down Atimetus's neck.

– Admit it or I swear you'll die on this spot.

Atimetus waves his arm about. – Alright! It was me. Don't kill me. Please!

– Where did you do it?

– What?

– Where did you do it with her?

– Why does...?

– I have written down what Cornelia told me. Where you did it. Say the place or I swear I'll kill you right now!

– Alright! On a tomb outside the Nucerian Gate. Release me!

Restitutus lets the boy up, who whirls away to safety clutching at the minor scratch on his neck. He then pulls a piece of papyrus from his tunic and pushes it into Tiberius's hands. The man glances at it, then looks up at his son.

He screams. – You idiot!

Appulei returns at that moment in the company of two burly slaves, both armed with swords in hand. They take their master's sides and point the weapons at Restitutus.

– Well, Tiberius Verus?

If Atimetus thought he was safe with the arrival of the slaves, he was mistaken. His father strides towards him and begins to beat him about the head with his hands. Atimetus bends and dodges to evade the blows, but his father pursues him as he speaks.

– Is it not enough that I waste money letting you indulge your lusts that you have to fuck a baker's daughter and a citizen? Could you not stick with whores? You've had enough of them for ten men! You selfish little fool! What am I to do with you? If only your mother was here…

As he says the last his breath is taken and he has to stumble back to his chair. Atimetus, sitting against the atrium wall, weeps like a little girl. When Tiberius has recovered sufficiently from his exertions he looks up and considers Cornelia, also sniffling away beside the impluvium. After a time he turns to Restitutus.

– I am a man of honour. But you have brought violence to my house and threatened the life of my only son. No man has drawn a knife in my presence before and not suffered greatly for it.

– Don't threaten me.

Tiberius holds up his hand. – Had you not done this, I would have consented to my son doing his duty by your sister. I will take no further action against you, Restitutus, but because of what you have done I refuse to force my son to marry her.

– Man of honour? You don't know what honour means!

– I will make a compensation to her, to you. It will be generous, towards the raising of the child. Or if she wishes, she may have one of the abortionists get rid of it and keep the money anyway. That is my offer. And it is final. Now leave my home and don't return.

Restitutus goes to make a step towards Tiberius only to be halted by the swords of the two slaves.

– You haven't heard the last of this.

– I think I have, young man. Now take your sister and go before you force me to bring worse violence into my home.

Restitutus grunts angrily, turns and takes Cornelia by the arm. He leads her stumbling from the house.

Dear, dear. And they still have Publius to face.

SCAENA 29

It took 640 paces to walk back and forth between here and there ten times [86]

– Stop pacing, Publius. You're making me dizzy. I'm sure there's a perfectly good explanation.

Yes, we're back in Publius's home.

Prima has just completed a late breakfast served in the shade of the peristyle. Vivia is clearing away its remnants. Prima rises from the small table and places a hand on Publius's arm to stall his endless stomping to and fro.

– Perhaps they went to see how Staphylus was.

– Both of them? I've had to put Hermeros on the counter, but now there's no one to lead the mule and Narcissus is going to run out of flour by noon. And there's nobody to make deliveries. Is Restitutus deliberately trying to ruin me? And Cornelia is as bad. You were too soft with her when she was a child. I have to go. I'll have to do the deliveries myself.

He stomps away. Prima follows him into the tablinum with a weary sigh. She is tired after the exertions of the previous night.

It is a short journey from Herculaneum and it may have been undertaken in a horse-drawn carriage, but it was very late when Gnaeus and his bodyguards left her to her doorway. And then she had to hear the shocking news about Staphylus. To compound this she woke late to hear from a furious Publius that Restitutus and Cornelia were nowhere to be found.

As they walk into the tablinum the missing pair enter from the far side. Hmmm. I believe this room is about to become a great deal hotter than the bakery next door.

– Where in the name of the gods have you two been? We're behind schedule with everything and we've nobody to....

Restitutus squares up to Publius. – I was out doing a task that you're too weak to do.

He says this, but not with quite the same conviction and confidence he previously had in encounters with his brother. The failure of his mission with Tiberius has deflated him somewhat.

Publius throws his hands in the air.

– Restitutus. I haven't time for whatever nonsense you're talking about. Cornelia. Where have you been?

The girl is silent, fearful. She looks at Restitutus, who for once, is also hesitant. – We've been to the house of Tiberius Verus and his son Atimetus.

Publius is bewildered. He shakes his head.

– What? The merchant? What's going on for the love of Jupiter?

Prima now steps forward. She's had her suspicions about her daughter's behaviour for a while. They are now confirmed. Or at least they will be shortly.

– I think I know, Publius.

She says this and no more. Her eyes rest on her daughter. Publius waits, his hands spread as though inviting further illumination.

– Cornelia's pregnant.

The word is spoken. Cornelia is further startled by her mother's knowledge. All four stand in momentary silence. Publius turns to his sister.

– You're *what*?

– I'm pregnant.

– Pregnant? And you knew of this, Mother?

– I wasn't sure until this moment.

He addresses Cornelia again. – By whom?

– A man called Atimetus.

Restitutus interrupts. – We went to see his father, Tiberius Verus.

– You *what*?

You can hear his anger rising, even though he speaks in a whisper.

– To make him do his duty by Cornelia.

– You went to speak as the head of this household?

– She would not be in this situation if you'd found her a husband. But you're always walking around with your head in the clouds. You can't even...

Restitutus's words are cut short as Publius rushes at him and sends him crashing to the ground over a stool. Now Publius turns to face his sister.

Prima screams. – Publius! Stop it!

She darts forward and tries to restrain her son, but he shrugs her off.

Publius looks about him. A pile of bamboo rods are stacked in the corner and he seizes one.

– You stupid little whore!

Publius brings the rod down hard against her arm and Cornelia screams and turns to run. Prima seizes her son and tries to stop his assault, but his blood is coursing through his veins, his mind has abandoned reason. He takes off after his sister and chases her along the fauces and out into the bright sunlight of the street. Let us follow and see what transpires from this ugliness.

Cornelia turns to her right and then right again into the Via Del Venditores, hoping to lose her pursuer amid the busy shopping street. But he sees her and bounds after her, quickly gaining on his sister's somewhat rotund form. Pompeiians making early morning purchases and shopkeepers laugh at the spectacle of the plump girl being pursued by the angry man waving a stick. Publius dodges around them, bumps them aside, clips and almost upends a display of spices, the only thing his eyes see is the lumbering girl ahead of him, and the only thing his mind sees is retribution for her shaming herself and his family.

Cornelia stumbles, gasping for breath, clutching at her chest, and a moment later he is upon her. He swings the stick and strikes her across the back. Cornelia screams and tries to crawl away on hands and knees. He swings again and it connects with her side and the arm. He raises it again. But now he is conscious of a shape on the edge of his vision and feels a powerful grip on his upraised arm. He is twisted away and a hand plants itself on his chest and shoves, sending him sprawling on to the hard paving stones. He looks up and sees the huge frame of an African towering over him.

Chrestus looks over his shoulder at the girl on the street, by now enveloped in the protective arms of Cominia Lucilla, who helps her to her feet.

Publius rises sharply. – How dare you, slave! I'll have your head for attacking a Roman!

– I am no slave. I am a free man.

Before Publius can speak another word he is thrown to the ground again by his brother, who proceeds to wrestle with him amid the scattering shoppers. Prima too has arrived and is screaming for them to stop. Chrestus reaches down and pulls the two men apart with great ease. They come to their feet and are separated by the grip and strength of the African.

Cominia has passed Cornelia to the temporary care of Felicia and Satura. The commotion it seems has drawn everyone in the vicinity to the street. It is not often they are granted such early morning entertainment and drama. Cominia forces herself in front of Publius.

> *Even if he is a savage Scythian,*
> *he shall never be such a barbarian*
> *as to strike a woman* [87]

– What sort of a man are you, that you would beat a helpless girl like that? Are you an animal?

– This is none of your business! It is a matter of family.

Publius struggles to wrest Chrestus's grip free from his tunic, but it is futile.

– Family? Is this how you treat your family? You're a beast!

– Get this man off me. I will take my sister and go.

– Your sister? I thought she was your dog. Although I would not treat even a dog with such cruelty. You may leave. Your sister will remain with me for her safety. Go, now, before you shame yourself further in front of the whole town!

Publius allows his gaze to widen now, to look about at the attention he has drawn. He lowers his eyes from those of the spectators and his shoulders slump. His breathing subsides and he tries again to release himself from Chrestus's grip. This time the African lets him go, as he does Restitutus. Prima hurries up and takes her two sons by the arms, leading them away like two naughty boys. Publius looks over his shoulder as he departs.

Cornelia is clutching at her side, but her dripping eyes are locked on his, and he is suddenly overwhelmed with guilt. His gaze then flicks to Cominia Lucilla who is leading his sister towards the entrance to her inn.

There he sees only contempt.

SCAENA 30

Celadus makes the girls moan 88

From the narrow Via del Veditores to the wide expanse of the Campanian countryside. I have taken you two miles from town as the crow flies, although the winding track on which we stand has almost doubled that journey for the man you can see approach on horseback. The horse he is riding was rented from a stable near the Vesuvian gate, paid for by Gnaeus, who is generous with expenses. But the money that rattles in his pouch often seems less like good fortune than a burden to bear.

Glory. Respect. Fame. Admiration. Dignity. Honour. The words bounce around his head. But none will be still, and these days he finds it hard to grasp any of them in his hand and claim it as his own. They are things of the past now, and they slip further away from his reach with each new dawn.

This day promises to be no different, although he is glad for once to be out of the town, which lately seemed to be suffocating him. A year ago when he walked about Pompeii's streets men would call his name and shout their support for him in the next games. Pretty women would often flock to him the way geese do around a man spreading food from a basket. They would ask him to write his name on their arms with charcoal, or sometimes even on more intimate places. Some of them would have sex with him without his barely having to grant them a smile and a few flattering words. Young boys played gladiators in the streets with wooden swords, and they would argue over who would have the role of Celadus the Thracian.

But now things are different. The men rarely call his name. Mostly now they see him and whisper among themselves. 'He works for Gnaeus Alleius Maius now. I've heard bad stories.' 'There's Celadus. The only fights he has now are with poor fuckers who can't defend themselves.' 'Look, there's Celadus. Getting old, isn't he? Too much good living, if you ask me.'

And the women. The women no longer surround him when he walks across the forum or goes to the market. There is the occasional smile from a passing pretty face, but mostly now they shy away as though he might harm them.

Come. Let us follow close behind. It should be easy for you to match the horse's lazy stroll.

You can see Vesuvius ahead, shimmering in the early morning summer haze. Celadus looks up at its rocky summit, above the point where no greenery can survive. He has never been there. He doesn't want to go. He has heard stories – there were many told in the gladiator barracks when they grew tired of talking about girls – of ghostly vapours rising from its centre, of men climbing the mountain and never returning, of animals wandering too high and simply dropping dead, as though Vulcan had reached inside them and plucked the life from their bodies. He thinks it must be a supernatural place, and he is a very superstitious man, and he doesn't even like being this close to the mountain.

But there is little to fear here on the gentle lower slopes. Below us lies a field of wheat, half of it harvested. Two men hack at it with curved blades. Probably slaves, he thinks. On the left stretches out another field, this one of onions, for which Pompeii has a minor reputation. Above that, some distance away, where the land deteriorates, is a broad plantation of olive trees. And there ahead, as we round the bend you can see a farmhouse. But no grand palatial structure is this. It is obvious there is little money here for ornamentation. A dull block of stone and cement with several similar smaller structures scattered nearby, holding olive presses, implements, winter storage.

Celadus enters the wide space in front of the almost windowless house. There is a small patch of cabbages on one side, looking limp in the dusty soil. It hasn't rained in three weeks. Chickens and geese scatter at his arrival, and their clamour brings a woman to the open doorway. He doesn't dismount.

– Is this the farm of Caecilius Felix?

– What do you want?

The woman wears a badly stained long tunic of coarse material. She is young, uncombed dark hair, not so attractive, he is thinking. A small child, a few years old, appears at her hip and clings to her tunic, its thumb in its mouth. He can't tell whether it is a boy or a girl.

– Where is he?

She flicks her head towards the fields behind the house. – He's working in the olive groves. What do you want with my husband?

– I have a message from your landlord.

– What message?

– Do you think I'm going to tell you? Go and fetch your husband. Bring him here. But fetch me some water first.

She disappears into the hut and returns a moment later with a cup.

Celadus dismounts and as his feet touch the ground he

hears the patter of running footsteps interspersed with heavy breaths. He swings about and draws his sword in a single fluid movement.

Caecilius Felix stands there a little breathless. He is holding a farm implement with a long handle that Celadus doesn't recognise. He grew up in Nola, his father owned a hardware shop. Doesn't know one thing about farming.

A young boy, perhaps eight or nine catches up with Caecilius and stands by his side. They both stare in silence at the threatening-looking intruder. Celadus returns his sword to its sheath.

– Caecilius Felix?

Helvia Marcia, daughter, wife, sacred person [90]

His wife, her name is Helvia, tries to explain why the man is here, as though it might give him some warning.

– He's been sent by Alleius M…

Celadus cuts across. – Shut up, woman.

He walks up to Caecilius. Eyeballs him. He doesn't want to use the threat of violence unless he has to. Perhaps his presence will be enough to secure what he needs. He stands almost a hand higher than the farmer. He removes a scroll of papyrus from within his tunic, holds it out.

– This details the amount of payment in rent and loans due to Gnaeus Alleius Maius Nigidius.

The farmer unrolls the scroll. Studies it. Looks up at the man who seems composed entirely of muscle. A glint of recognition appears in his eye. – Don't I know you? Are you the gladiator? Celadus?

Celadus doesn't reply. There was a time he would have grasped the recognition like a trophy, paraded it, relished it. But he no longer has a claim on such things.

– I saw you last year. You won four bouts in two days.

– Don't try to flatter me, farmer. Where's the payment?

– I spoke to Alleius Maius in April. I told him I'd pay as soon as I could.

– You were already overdue then. The ides of May and June have since passed and he still hasn't been paid. Alleius Maius has been very patient with you so far. But you owe him almost a thousand sesterces. His generosity is at an end.

– I will pay when the harvest is in. I swear it.

Receipt for the sale of a mule, sold by Caecilius Felix. [89]

Celadus looks back along the track he has travelled. – There is a wheat field down there that is almost harvested. Where's the money from that? And you must have gotten a handsome price for that mule you sold just last week.

The farmer stammers a little before managing to get a word out. – I had to pay for the seed with the money from the mule and I had to hire men to do the harvest. I have only two old slaves here. When all the harvest is in I'll pay the rest. I swear. It will leave us barely enough to live on. But I'll pay it. We've only had the farm two years. Alleius Maius knows that it takes some years before a farm starts to make any money.

Celadus heaves a breath, as though impatient. He looks about the place.

– If I don't return with the money, I am ordered to return with something that ensures you won't forget your promise.

He turns and walks towards the house. He stops next to Helvia, glances down at the child clinging to her.

– Perhaps I'll take him. Or her. Whatever it is. And if you don't pay Alleius Maius can sell it in the slave market.

The woman instinctively pushes the child behind her, a look of terror on her face. – Keep away from my child!

Celadus laughs. But his smile disappears as quickly as it formed. The remark was said only in jest. But his humour is lost on these people. He is only an object of fear to them.

Come. Let us follow him into the dim interior of the building.

One large room, three doors lead off it. It is sparsely furnished, the table and stools are homemade. A metal urn hangs over a burning fire. A few amphorae, cups, plates. Celadus can see nothing of value. The man has entered behind him and his wife is at his back.

Helvia speaks. – You see. We have nothing except a few sesterces to buy flour from the miller.

A sliver of light catches his eye. He glances down at the woman's hands. There is a ring on her finger. He walks across and seizes her arm. She gasps. The ring appears to be gold, and a tiny dolphin leaps from its surface. Clasped in its jaws is a speck of a jewel, red in colour. Fine workmanship, he gauges. Definitely worth something. Nothing near enough to pay the debt, but he guesses that Caecilius and the woman attach more value to it than you would get in the market place. He goes to remove it. She struggles. He tightens his grip on her wrist.

– Give it to me you bitch or I'll hack off your hand and take it.

She pounds at him with her free hand, thumping the side of his head.

– It was my grandmother's. Let me go, you bastard!

– Let her go or I'll kill you.

And now another flash of brightness jumps into the corner of his eye. But with this one, he is much more familiar. He pushes the woman aside and she falls to the floor. He turns on one foot and takes a step back. Caecilius stands there with a short sword in his hand. He is quivering. The blade is old. Specks of rust mar its surface. The farmer's feet are planted square, not a good starting point if you want to move quickly. Celadus guesses that he's never been in sword fight before. Perhaps never been in any sort of a fight before. This will be easy.

Caecilius voice quivers as he speaks. – Leave us in peace, I beg you. I'm a man of my word. I'll pay what's due when I have it. I swear to all the gods!

Celadus draws his blade. He approaches slowly and the man backs away out through the door into the sunlight. As the sobbing woman tries to rise he shoves her back to the floor.

They emerge from the gloom of the house and the man dances his way backwards across the dusty ground.

The boy cries out. – Father!

Bawling, the small child scuttles to her older brother.

Celadus feints. The man stabs at him. Misses by two hands' length. Celadus thrusts. Draws blood from the farmer's shoulder. He hears the wife scream. Caecilius takes a wild swing. Celadus draws back his body, but just then a rock hits the side of his head, thrown by the boy. It stuns him and the old blade cuts a small gash through his tunic, drawing blood. He is enraged. Suddenly the sand beneath his feet is that of the arena and the man before him is a deadly enemy. He launches at him with a series of swings and thrusts and Caecilius desperately backs away, deflecting them as best he can. But the clash of metal is heard no more than five times before the sword is knocked from the farmer's grasp and he stumbles and lies flat on his back. Celadus leaps on top of him and knocks the last of the wind from his body. He grasps the man's hair with his left hand and draws back the sword, ready to plunge it into the throat of Caecilius Secundus.

There is a scream in his ear.

– No! He's only a farmer! A farmer! Spare him, I beg you!

Celadus sees the man he was ordered to slay that day in the arena. Lying there helpless. Expecting mercy. He could not give it that day. But at least on this morning the choice is his. He looks at the pathetic figure beneath him, covered in sweat, blood and dirt. Is this what Celadus the Thracian, the girls' idol, champion of Pompeii, has become? Who will recall his name for cutting the throat of a helpless farmer?

There is a hand in front of his face. It is Helvia's, and it holds the ring.

– Take it! Take it! Let him go, please.

He looks at the small shiny thing. Was he about to take an innocent man's life for such a trinket? He clambers off Caecilius. His wife and the crying children descend on him, smother him in their care and concern. Celadus stands there watching them for a few moments. He picks up the ring.

– It will be returned when you make the payment. The ides of July.

He returns to his horse. Mounts. Rides away at a trot, faster than his arrival. He feels shame. And envy.

How can he feel such a thing for a man as poor as Caecilius Felix?

SCAENA 31

Weep, you girls, my cock has given you up
Now it penetrates men's behinds
Goodbye, wondrous femininity! [91]

– Yes, very convincing. You've done well, Faustilla, yet again.

You know that voice coming from the peristyle, don't you? It has a quality that makes even kindly words seem cold. We have returned to the home of Epidius. That's the young slave Felix standing with his back to us, waiting to be summoned outside by his master. Even from behind you can tell he is nervous. See how his right hand clutches and unclutches the fabric of his tunic.

Several days have passed since we were last here. Cornelia, for your interest, remains in the sanctuary of Cominia Lucilla's home and Publius has slumped to an even lower trough. Restitutus has announced he will soon join the army. Their mother tries to build bridges, so far unsuccessfully. Like Epidius, she is not averse to scheming, albeit scheming of a more altruistic nature. But altruism is not our concern this fine afternoon, but duplicity. Epidius is a master of such, no less a master indeed than the artist who painted that fine fresco over there depicting Hermaphrodite and Silenus. It is simply that Epidius's medium is not paint or marble or ink, but human frailty. Actually, that fresco is strangely appropriate to the business at hand, Hermaphrodite being the boy who was transformed into a creature who was half-man and half-woman. In a sense, the same will be demanded of young Felix.

Someone's coming. Ah. Two wealthy looking individuals by the look of them, their meeting with Epidius concluded. Look. They both cast glances at Felix and exchange a smirk. The one on the right wears the toga praetexta, bearing the purple stripe along its hem. Very nice. Expensive material. Fine stitching. He must be the senator of Rome, Helvidius Marcus Priscus. Hails from Capua. The other wears the toga virilis, less decorative, but expensive. He's Cornelius Lentulus Marcellinus, an advocate from Ostia who is rumoured to have an admirer in Vespasian.

Anteros wrote this [92]
Circinaeus lives here [93]

Actually, neither of them are anything of the sort. They are actors called Circinaeus and Anteros, hired for a small role by Epidius, but a role that will earn them more than they've earned in the last six months. The characters they play are very real though, and Anteros even has a passing resemblance to Helvidius. We shall witness their small but vital performance later this evening. But for now, let us join Felix, who has just been summoned to the peristyle by Faustilla.

Epidius sits beside a small table that has been set between the two pretty ponds. Lavish ornamentation surrounds us and the last of the evening's light illuminates the ocean scenes along the rear wall. But we're not here to admire the great art that ill-gotten wealth can purchase.

Felix stands facing Epidius, who sips wine from a goblet. Faustilla stands at his shoulder.

– You know what you must do, Felix?

The boy nods. Looks to the ground.

– Felix! Look at me!

He snaps his head up.

– Don't slump like that. And don't wear that face. You look like you are about to be tortured with hot irons.

At this moment, that seems a better alternative to the young slave.

What the master orders is not shameful [94]

– Brighten up, lad. I want you relaxed. Smiling. Faustilla, give him some wine. Don't water it.

She fills a goblet and holds it up to Felix's face. He takes it tentatively. Sips.

– Thank you, Dominus.

– Drink it back, boy.

He does as commanded. Coughs. A dribble of red runs down his chin, which he wipes away with the back of his arm.

– Remember what I told you. At some point you must convince him to let you play the man. Use the words Faustilla taught you. And try to be convincing. This is very important.

– It is just that....

– What? Stop mumbling.

– It is just that I am afraid that I will not be able to....

He looks briefly down at his groin and then lifts his head.

– Yes you will. At your age you can get it up at the sight of a hole in a sack. Anyway. All you have to do is close your eyes and imagine it is that slave girl from the kitchen I have promised you. Think of her sucking your cock this time tomorrow. That will get you as hard as Vulcan's dick.

– Yes, Dominus.

– Don't worry, Felix. He's a nice chap, Titus. Extremely kind to slaves. Ply him with wine. And he has an eye for fine art. Engage him in conversation. Ask him to tell you about the frescoes in the oecus. He will be keen to expound on the stories behind them. Especially the one of Ganymede. His dear wife Fabia had to return to Rome and he is a lonely man. Here in a strange town alone. Be his friend. And you can be sure he'll want to be yours. Won't he Faustilla?

– His closest friend, Dominus.

– There. Listen to an expert. Faustilla has seen it all and fucked it all. And Felix...

– Yes, Dominus?

His smile remains, but his words fall like shattering pottery.

– Don't fail me.

SCAENA 32

*Good fortune to Gnaeus Alleius Maius,
the leader of the colony* (of Pompeii) 95

As Felix exits, we too shall make ours. But we shall return later, do not fear. Another small event occurs on this very evening, in a house close to the forum, and one you have visited long ago. Do you recall this street? No? Of course it was shaking when you last saw it and people were screaming and things were falling all around. Well, no matter. Let me enlighten you once more.

Everyone loves a showman. Isn't that one of your sayings? Well Gnaeus fits that bill perfectly. Remember him? The wealthy politician who gave Celadus his freedom. The giver of games. He who couldn't help but smile when he saw the destruction that the earthquake had wrought upon the town. Destruction that would have to be repaired.

And repaired much of it he has, and reaped the rewards. If he was wealthy then, he is wealthy beyond reason now. And yet he persists in the quest for more.

Come on. Let us get off the street. Through this door. Look at the atrium. It is almost as though it was untouched by that terrible day ten years ago. The exotic birds in the frescoes appear not to have stirred from their perches, the twenty gold-painted nymphs once again decorate the compluvium above our heads and the impluvium before us is filled with crystal clear water, beneath which naked mosaic children frolic on the mosaic seashore. The statues of his ancestors also once again stand guard either side of the room. But there are a couple of additions you may have noticed. The last statue on the right is that of Traebia, Gnaeus's wife when last we visited. A terrible sickness took her and she shrank and shrivelled before his eyes, at the last resembling a withered flower stalk, and in terrible pain. Her passing in the end was a blessing. She was just thirty-three. He didn't re-marry, although he wasn't short of offers. One father had offered him his daughter of thirteen. You see, for these past seven years he has been occupied with his one true mistress: business. Yet that also is changing as his years accumulate. But we will return to that matter.

Now look to the line of statues on the left. The final one is a lady, but one of larger girth and with more aged features. That's one thing I like about the Romans – they rarely seek to falsely glorify themselves in marble. Big noses in flesh become big noses in stone. Dumpy in flesh, dumpy in stone. Bald as an egg in flesh...well, you get the picture. That lady was Pomponia, his mother. Once a slave, now a statue. Who would have thought? She lived to be sixty-seven, which is old by the standard of this age. She died a year ago, her passing more of a wrench for Gnaeus than that of his wife.

POMPONIA DECHARIS,
MOTHER OF ALLEIUS MAIUS
BURIED IN THE TOMB OF EUMACHIA [96]

So now he is almost alone. But not quite completely alone

yet. He had a daughter, remember? Alleia. And she will momentarily enter the atrium from that side room, which is the family's shrine. She has been praying, not to me I hasten to add, but to Venus and Cupid. Yet she has no lover, this girl of sixteen, at least as yet. Her prayers are, quite selflessly, for her beloved father. Look, the door opens. She is a delightful little thing, is she not? Her silk stola accentuates her sweetly curving figure, and fair hair surrounds a delicate face. She walks with confidence, this girl, whose father's money has bought her a fine education. She will do well for herself, will Alleia, in the years that remain to this place. We shall follow her momentarily, but do glance into the room from which she emerged. All Roman homes have such a shrine, you know? Although few are as elaborate as this one. The mosaic is very beautiful, is it not? The figure in the centre is Gnaeus, paterfamilias, and the four ladies in short tunics either side are the lares, the household spirits, who watch over all who dwell under this roof. The small statue on the altar is Venus. I wonder was Venus listening to young Alleia's prayers?

May Pompeiian Venus
be favourable to your offerings 97

But come, we must not idle here any longer. Follow me.

There is Alleia seated in the shade of the portico, the slave Lucia serving her a cup of fig juice as she admires the roses, marigolds and honeysuckle in the garden. The soft trickle of the fountain that springs from the central pool complete this pleasant little summer's evening scene.

Ah, the paterfamilias himself makes his appearance.

– Make sure they arrange the flowers on both sides of the triclinium, Primus. And tell them only to serve the Falernian from the two-year-old casks.

– Yes, Dominus.

– And stop that stupid grinning, Primus.

Primus's grin grows wider. – Yes, Dominus.

– Be off with you, you impudent slave.

Primus trots away. He has become Gnaeus's right hand man these past years and his master regards him as much as a friend as a slave.

Look how Alleia springs to her feet and hurries to greet him. He is adorned, as you see, in his finest white tunic, with gold-laced borders, and his dark hair has been oiled into perfect alignment.

– Father, you look wonderful.

She has to rise on her toes to kiss his cheek. He towers over most people as he towers over the town of Pompeii. He's not in bad shape for a man of forty-nine, is he? But why all the fuss – the fancy tunic, the flowers, his most treasured wine?

– I feel as nervous as if I was about to greet the emperor.

She giggles. – I have prayed for your happiness, father. And I'm sure Venus heard me.

We shall see.

– Your guest has arrived, Dominus.

Primus is back. Alleia links his arm and guides him through the atrium and out into the brightness of the summer's evening. A curtained litter sits on the Via del Terme, two perspiring, muscled slaves at either end. Gnaeus pulls back the curtain and smiles at the lady within.

– Prima, my dear. You look as beautiful as you ever did.

It is a little surprising to see the mother of Publius the baker arriving in such regal fashion at the home of the wealthiest man in town, is it not? Let us learn more.

– Really Gnaeus. Beautiful? I'm almost an old woman. And I'm so embarrassed to be travelling the streets of Pompeii in this thing. I was afraid my friends would see me and think I've gone mad. It's an unnessary extravagance.

Gnaeus helps her alight. She greets Alleia with an embrace and a smile.

– Prima, I couldn't let you walk the filthy streets. Allow me to indulge you every now and again.

Back in the atrium. Prima stops and finally rewards her host with a soft smile, albeit with a hint of suspicion in it. – I appreciate your gesture, Gnaeus. But what are you up to?

– Up to? Nothing.

Prima grunts. – Hmm.

The finest garum, from the shop of Scaurus 98

Gnaeus guides her towards the triclinium with Alleia in their wake. He begins to rattle on about the meal they are about to enjoy; stuffed dormice rolled in honey and poppyseed, Lucanian sausages, lamb cooked in the best garum from the workshop of Aulus Umbricius Scaurus, and so on and so forth. He does go on a bit when talking about the quality of his food. But we will allow them indulge in their excess of eating for a time. We will rejoin them when the eating is done and the small talk dispensed with. For now let me show you something else. Follow me, just through here, and let us enter Gnaeus's tablinum.

There is a cupboard here that holds a handful of mementos from more than two decades ago. Look, you know what this papyrus scroll is? Read it.

My darling Prima, each day I awake my thoughts fly to you. And each moment of every day sees my eyes filled with a vision of your beauty. You are a mere mile from my doorstep, yet until you grant me your heart I will feel as though you are in the remotest part of the empire. And how I wish to hold you close until the end of my days. Please say you will be mine. Please fill my heart with the presence of your beauty and the joy of your lightness. Your devoted servant, Gnaeus Alleius Maius.

Mushy, isn't it? Youth does bring out the worst of your emotional excesses, you humans. But here's another, and it will tell us a little more.

My darling Prima, my heart is broken at your hesitation. I carry a weight so great around with me each day that it feels like I bear the burden of Atlas on my shoulders. Your face is like the first flower of....

Yes, yes, but skip down to the last part.

My father's objections do not concern me. He will come around when he sees my love for you is so sincere. No matter, my love is above all such concerns. If it meant rejection by my own family and expulsion I would still pursue this course, as my heart demands it.

And there are lots more like these. Look at them. He wrote to her every day. Oh he was besotted with the beautiful Prima. And she was, you know. An earthly Venus. It is hard to conceive that her body produced the plain Cornelia. No wonder poor Gnaeus fell so hard. She returned all these letters to him when their relationship ended. Well, to be honest, it ended before it really ever started. His adoptive father, along with his ex-slave mother, threatened to disown him if he married below his class. They had him lined up to marry the unfortunate Traebia, who came from a wealthy Herculaneum family, their marriage securing a business agreement that would add considerably to the coffers of the Alleius clan. But he was young and besotted and prepared to forsake his family and his future fortune in exchange for the lovely Prima's hand. And when Prima learned of this she broke Gnaeus's heart, to save him from himself. She didn't love him anyway, although she did like him, and found him charming beyond measure. Her means of finally putting an end to Gnaeus's attentions, by the way, was to accept the courtship of another man, one Publius Comicius Restitutus, ex-soldier turned bakery owner. The news of their marriage sent poor Gnaeus scurrying under a blanket of self-pity for a month.

So we come to this day. Far into their futures. So much water has flowed along the Sarnus since then, so many clouds have drifted by above. Gnaeus finds himself alone again, his wife dead, and his mother and father. And he is the richest man in town, and among the most powerful. Prima too is a widow, her children grown although all unwed as yet. They are still worlds apart in terms of wealth, but Gnaeus would pride himself on making such a match, simply because it gives him the feeling that he can do as he pleases. Besides, he thinks, it would look good with the public, whose adoration he dearly craves.

There is a small wooden box missing from that cupboard. You see its shape in the dust on the shelf? I think I can guess where that is at this precise moment. Let us rejoin the diners now and observe what transpires.

Come along, we don't want to miss anything. Out here, through the peristyle. The triclinium is just along at the end. Just follow the music.

Here we are. What a pretty, familial scene. The citharista, hired at great expense by Gnaeus, tickles out a soft air that evokes the ripples on a pond. Flower baskets hang from the ceiling and vases explode with the colour of summer blossoms. The scent is almost overpowering. Bacchus watches all from the walls, clutching a cornucopia of fruits and more flowers, his other hand lifting an overflowing jug of wine. And two slaves fuss over the stone table in the centre, removing the remnants of so many delicacies; milk-fattened snails in garlic, mussels in garum with leek, cumin and wine, dates stuffed with nuts and black pepper, fried flamingo tongue, salted pheasant brains, and Gnaeus's favourite, roasted dormice stuffed with pork and nuts and dipped in honey. Of course no three mortals could possibly consume so much, so the lucky slaves will feast on the leftovers this evening.

The main couch at the far end is naturally occupied by the reclining Gnaeus. See how he barely sips his wine? He is fearful of over indulging, at least at this juncture. He needs to be in control. But despite his smiles and easy conversation you can probably tell he is nervous. This woman has broken his heart once before, remember. He shifts on his couch and adjusts the cushion under his arm so he can more directly address Prima. Her blue stola is pretty, the finest she possesses, but it is clearly inferior to that of Alleia, who reclines opposite her, and whose tunic and stola cost the same as a centurion earns in a year. But that matters little to Gnaeus. In fact he has barely noticed Prima's clothes or the effort she put into her hair. Typical. Yet the trouble she took suggests she has her own reasons for impressing her suitor this evening. Perhaps she senses what is coming? Do you think?

– And then Infantio leaned over too far to see the garum pits and fell in head first.

The ladies explode with laughter. Gnaeus is pleased with himself. He struggles to complete his tale through gulps of his own merriment.

– Scaurus had the slaves pull him out and wash him. But by the gods, after six baths he still stank of rotten fish.

Alleia guffaws. – Father had Primus cover him in my perfume when they brought him home.

The laughter resumes at a higher pitch, almost enough to

drown the citharista. Finally it recedes and Prima gently nudges the conversation towards more serious matters.

– How is Aulus Umbricius Scaurus these days, Gnaeus? The whole town was shocked when his son passed away so young.

– He's as well as can be expected. A fine statue of young Aulus he erected in the forum, is it not? I have the impression that he lost himself in his commerce to banish his grief.

– I suspect you are not so different yourself, Gnaeus.

Clever isn't she? She manipulated the conversation from things trivial to matters of life and death. She knows which direction the words will flow from here, and she is anxious to get to the business at hand.

There is a brief, awkward silence. Gnaeus reaches out to grasp his goblet to fill it. Alleia senses that her presence is suddenly like that of a stone in a shoe. She heaves herself up and swings her legs from the couch.

– Father, I have a pattern I've been weaving these past weeks. May I be excused while the light holds?

– Of course, my dear.

She walks around to Prima's side. Kind parting words and kisses are exchanged, and then the girl leaves, taking the attending slaves with her. Prima and Gnaeus are alone, except for the citharista.

– Did you enjoy the stuffed dates, Prima? I had them brought from Herculaneum. There's a man there....

– Gnaeus. Why have you lavished me with such riches?

– I merely wanted you to enjoy...

– Oh come, Gnaeus. I'm sure you don't meander in this fashion when it comes to doing business.

He sits up straight now, plants his feet on the floor and looks down on her. From beneath the cushions of his couch he pulls the small wooden box and holds it towards Prima.

– Forgive me. My business dealings are simplicity itself

compared to this. Prima, I offered you this once before and you rejected it. I offer it again in the hope that you will grant me the comfort of your company for the rest of my days. You know I love you. I always have.

If you know what strength love has, if you know yourself to be human, pity me, and give me leave to come (to you) [99]

He opens the little hinged box and sitting inside it, on a small bed of silk, is a simple gold ring. Prima sits up now and faces him, their knees touching.

But she doesn't take the box. She doesn't love Gnaeus. She's never loved any man. Fate determined that. Well, not counting her two sons. But you know what I mean. She didn't love Gnaeus back all those years ago, and his courting of her in the recent months has revealed to her that her heart has not shifted on this matter.

Nor did she love Publius, her husband. He seemed a fine man, and he was just that to her, with the exception of a solitary night in their lives, when he betrayed her. But he'd come along at the right time and the match was a good one. But now he was dead and Gnaeus still pines for her.

And love is no longer so great a consideration. The poets write odes to treasured loves, the singers sing songs of love, the artists craft mosaics of love scenes and plays hinge their action on the quest for love. But Prima has never felt the intensity that moves people to create such things, or even on a more basic level, to scratch their declarations of love on to so many of the walls of this town. She wonders sometimes if such a thing really exists at all, or is it like the giant in the great cave to the north who creates the wind with his breath? A nonsensical figment of imagination. Anyway, she has long given up on the quest to find it. So Gnaeus, she knows, will never offer her those answers, but he has other things to offer. And she is not thinking of his money.

– You know Gnaeus, when you approached me in March and invited me to join you for the display in the forum, I suspected then that this day was coming. And as the months went by I knew it with a greater certainty. And I tried to think of what I'd say to you. What answer I'd give you.

– And have you decided?

– I know it doesn't bother you that I am merely the widow of a baker...

– I myself am the son of a slave, Prima.

– The very rich son of a slave. And I confess I am uncomfortable often in the company of some of your friends. They look down on me. They are sometimes condescending. I imagine them joking behind my back.

He waves this away. – They are not my friends and I don't care about them. And you've never let such pretentious nonsense bother you. You're well able for any of those idiots. What matters is that I love you, as does my daughter. Beyond that, who cares what the world thinks?

– To be honest, those people don't trouble me too greatly. But there are other considerations. Serious ones.

Gnaeus frowns. See how the small box he holds suddenly seems to carry weight of a boulder? His arm drops to knee.

– My family is in turmoil at the moment. I feel I would be betraying them should I leave. Restitutus spends much of his time in bars and with the wrong kind of women, whores, to be frank. And now he is talking of joining the army like his father. I shiver at the thought. I may never see him again. And what a waste! He is a bright boy, a bright young man. And I saw to it that he was educated, I saw that they all were. But the loss of my husband was more than his shoulders could carry. And Publius has never been able to fill that void.

Gnaeus suddenly finds himself irritated by the music, especially when he notices that the citharista's concentration on her craft has been interrupted by the entertainment of Gnaeus's proposal.

– Come, let us talk in the garden.

He leads Prima to the peristyle and they wander slowly among the roses and the marigolds.

– As I was saying, Publius and he quarrel endlessly. Sometimes I fear it will come to blows. And then there's Cornelia. That foolish girl. She's gotten herself pregnant to the son of Tiberius Verus, a young philanderer who has no interest in her. It is unlikely his father will do the honourable thing and force him to marry a baker's daughter. And now Publius has driven her from the house and is filled with remorse and shame at what he did.

Prima gives an exasperated sigh.

– Publius is as grumpy as ever, then?

– Grumpy is not the word. Perhaps if Curtia had given him a child before she died, things would be different. He spends most of his days fighting to keep the bakery alive, cursing Fortuna, cursing his brother, cursing Epidius. Much as I despise the man, I wish he'd taken Epidius's offer and was done with the bakery. But his pride won't let him. Or his loyalty to his father's memory, not to mention the baker Narcissus and the others.

Did you notice Gnaeus flinch ever so slightly at the mention of Epidius's name? The man has become a greater rival in business these past years. And as Gnaeus's influence with the council has waned, Epidius's has grown. First he was elected aedile and now runs for duumvir, and it is clear to Gnaeus that bribery and intimidation are the principle currency with which he purchases his success. Not that Pompeii's leading citizen is above a little bribery and intimidation himself, as you saw when Celadus visited the farmer. Gnaeus is fearful that Epidius has even greater political ambitions. But for now he puts such thoughts to one side.

– And you feel that to leave them now would make matters worse?

– Perhaps.

– You've done your duty by them, Prima. They are grown adults.

She chuckles. – Are they?

– So, once more I'm left clutching this.

He holds up the ring.

Here love will be shrewd 100

Notice the hint of a grin on Prima's face. She turns away to conceal it. She sighs. The sound is almost theatrical. – As I said, Gnaeus. If only my family matters were somehow settled. It would certainly leave me open to consider other things. I wish one of the gods would appear and make some of these worries vanish.

Forgive my laughter. But the look on Gnaeus's face. He has suddenly realised that he is not dealing with a matter of love, but one of business. If he wants this contract, he must make a healthy offer. But he is good in matters of business and his thinking is quick.

– Perhaps I can help in some way.

Prima swings about to face him. – What can you do?

– Well, it seems to me that Restitutus just needs some focus. And as you say he is a bright, educated lad. He's wasted in the bakery. I've been looking for just such a young man to assist Primus in my business. It would mean him having to learn a great deal about accounting and legal matters. And he would have to start at the bottom, of course. See every aspect of my business. But I'm sure he'd thrive.

– Oh Gnaeus, that would be wonderful. I'm sure I can persuade him to accept such an offer.

– And as for Cornelia, well, I believe that difficulty could resolve itself relatively simply.

– How?

– Well. Tiberius Verus's interest lies in making a good match for his son, one that will assist his business interests. Should his son marry the stepdaughter of the wealthiest man in Pompeii, and the man who provides him with so much business, surely he would see it as a beneficial match. Of course, for Cornelia to become my stepdaughter would require...

– ...me to accept.

– I'm not so sure how I might help Publius. I would gladly purchase the bakery and get Epidius off his back. It could be a fine business venture. But Epidius would never sell to me as long as the gods exist.

– Publius wouldn't accept any help anyway, Gnaeus. He's a stubborn beast. But I think he'd be forced to move on should such a torrent of changes hit him all at once. I would speak to him and try to persuade him to take a different course.

Silence descends between them. Prima is smiling now. He knows he has been manipulated, and she knows he knows. He admires her for it. He looks down at the box in his hand.

He lifts it and opens it again. Prima gazes at the ring.

– Do you love me, Gnaeus?

– You know I do.

– There is one other matter I must discuss with you before I can accept.

– You drive a hard bargain.

Prima's face now grows suddenly grim.

– I don't require anything else of you. Except your acceptance of something. And your silence. But knowing who you are, your position in this town, you must be told before you take me as your wife.

– What is it?

Prima sits on a stone bench. Gnaeus joins her.

The citharista plays in the background. The fountain trickles away and the bees buzz. In a room off the atrium, Alleia weaves a colourful pattern on her loom.

And here in this world, the gods weave theirs.

SCAENA 33

Suedius Clemens, most venerable judge [101]

We leave Prima and Gnaeus to their private discussions and hasten across to the west of the forum to witness the arrival of Titus Suedius Clemens in Epidius's home. Epidius proffered an invitation to him to dine, you see, and to provide his services in helping Titus identify properties that have been illegally appropriated from the state, of which Epidius of course is the principal offender. He has no intention of helping Titus, quite the opposite in fact.

He greets Titus at the door and leads him along the long dark fauces into the spacious atrium. Quite an ordinary-looking soul, I think you'll agree. He is thirty-four and an expert in the legalities of property ownership. Although his tunic is of a reasonable quality, it is oversized and hangs awkwardly about his shoulders. And the nice patterned leather belt about his waist is too loose, appearing as if it might fall about his ankles at any moment. He has rather a prominent bulbous nose, a rosy complexion and his hair recedes before its time. He is short also, half a hand below Epidius, who, even with his own hook nose and gaunt frame seems like Apollo by comparison. But none of these things trouble Titus too greatly, for his gifts lie within rather than without. He is a gentle man, and a very bright one. He is dedicated too, and honest, and his character is almost without blemish. His marriage to Fabia has been reasonably happy and she has provided him with a daughter and a son, but beyond those and a handful of other occasions during their five year marriage, their sexual congress has been almost non-existent. And that is due to the fact that Titus has a weakness, correctly identified by Epidius, for young men. Fabia suspects this, naturally, what woman wouldn't? But she endures it, as she is happy that her marriage brings her into close social contact with influential families in Rome.

Epidius takes Titus gently by the arm and leads him around the impluvium. Apelles follows them.

– This is most embarrassing, Titus, my dear friend.

– What is, Epidius?

– I had no time to cancel our meeting, as I have been summoned to Herculaneum on important business.

Titus stops and faces Epidius. – Oh, well, don't trouble yourself. I can eat at the inn. Cominia Lucilla provides excellent fare and....

– Yes, I have heard she does.

There is a tinge of bitterness in his words. He still has not forgiven Cominia for snatching that property from under his nose.

– Yet, I will not hear of it.

Epidius slaps Titus on the shoulder, as though they are old friends. Titus responds with a brief, uncertain chuckle. Epidius leads Titus towards a small door out into the peristyle, and all the time you will notice that his hand never leaves Titus's shoulder.

– I will be gone for several hours, but I should return soon after dark. In the meantime I have arranged food and also provided all the necessary documentation I was going to review with you. I was hoping that you might go through it in my absence and that we could discuss it when I return. I am anxious that all of this business about property ownership is done with before the election next month. It is upsetting many members of the town council and may affect decisions that I might have to make regarding appointments and so on.

– That's assuming you are elected, Epidius.

Epidius turns his head to take a measure of Titus's intent, sees him smiling and realises it was an attempt at humour. He bursts into a howl of laughter, puts his arm fully around the man's shoulder and pulls him closer.

– Yes, my friend. But I pray for the benefit of Pompeii that I am successful.

They leave the peristyle and enter the largest room in the house, the oecus, which you will recall is decorated with fine frescoes depicting Hercules and Orpheus and the one of the naked Ganymede embracing the eagle in flight. The nude statue of Apollo is new, however, and very prominent. Epidius had it moved here from another room just this morning. Titus's attention is drawn to it, but then, it is hard to miss.

– I see you've noticed Apollo. Just been finished. Magnificent, isn't it?

He glides his fingers along Apollo's smooth marble hip. – A sculptor from Rome called Secundus Servulus. Perhaps you've heard of him. One of the greatest in the empire.

Titus shakes his head. He seems overly keen to turn away, as though allowing his gaze to linger might betray his secret. He spots the collection of document cases on the table. – Will your slave there assist me with this material?

– Apelles? Oh, apologies, no. He must accompany me. I wouldn't ask this if my business not so pressing. I have a meeting with a senator, Helvidius Marcus Priscus, who has travelled especially from Rome. However I assure you that the documents are quite straightforward for a man of your knowledge.

Epidius turns and claps his hands sharply in the direction of the door. Faustilla, accompanied by the young Felix, enters the room, right on cue. Faustilla has had him dressed in a tight tunic that takes the shape of his fine figure and is so short it barely conceals the boy's modesty.

– Faustilla. You will provide our guest with a meal and then you are to see he is undisturbed for the evening. He has much important work to carry out.

She bows her head. – Yes, Dominus.

– Felix. Come here.

It is obvious the boy is struggling to maintain an untroubled countenance. Titus doesn't recognise this, distracted as he is by the beauty of the youth.

– This is Titus Seudius Clemens. You will be his personal assistant for the evening. You will see to his every need, however small or large. Is that clear?

– Yes, Dominus.

– Titus is your Dominus for tonight, Felix. If he is displeased in any way you will be punished severely.

Felix lowers his gaze to his feet. Titus holds up a hand. – Please, Epidius, I am sure there will be no need for that.

– I hope so, my friend. Felix here may be of use to you in your work. He can read and write and understands arithmetic.

– Thank you, Epidius. You've gone to so much trouble. Now I don't wish to delay you further from your business.

They make their farewells and Faustilla closes the oecus door, enclosing Titus and Felix in the room's embrace.

Epidius does not travel to Heculaneum. In fact he travels no further than another small oecus concealed behind the western wall of the peristyle, where he sits and reads. Faustilla walks around to the kitchen and latrine, which share a wall with the main oecus, climbs on a stone bench and there she fixes her eyes against a small opening that Epidius had made, which gives a clear view of almost the entire room. And there she stands, watching and listening.

The evening will pass slowly for the faithful Faustilla and for Epidius. But, come, we shall sit for a time in Epidius's fine peristyle where, if you will permit, I will take that opportunity to tell you a little more about the man. We have some time to kill, after all.

You may be wondering, with all of his sexual scheming, where his own urges lie in this regard. And why, at the age of thirty-five, does Epidius not have a wife and children? Well, he does actually. Her name is Stephania, daughter of a man who owns the largest fullery in the town, Numerius Stephanus. She is a pretty girl ten years his junior and he married her when she was sixteen in a deal which saw him secure a substantial interest in Stephanus's business. It is a completely loveless union, and she serves only to give him the respectability a politician and businessman requires, and also as an instrument to provide him with children, which she has done four times. The first three times produced daughters and the only reason he continued to have sex with Stephania is that he wished for a son, which she provided at the fourth attempt. Does that not all sound terribly cold? Well, sadly, that describes their relationship precisely. She discovered this on their wedding night when he took her to his bed, took her virginity with barely a word exchanged, and then left her to rejoin some of the important guests at the festivities. She has grown used to the situation by now, and devotes herself to the raising of their children. At least she has the comfort of his wealth in which to pass the rest of her days. Currently she and the children are in a summer villa Epidius purchased just down the road in Stabiae. At least she has good company there as most of the other villas are occupied by the elite of Rome during the summer months.

Does Epidius despise her? Not in the least. But she is to him no more or less than any other mortal with whom he must do business. When she is in her Pompeii home in the winter months they share the occasional polite conversation, but not a bed. Most of the time she simply stays out of his way. But when formal occasions demand it, she dresses in finery and does her duty as the perfect hostess or by sitting at his right hand with a rigid smile when they attend games, religious ceremonies in the temples and the like. She is a devotee of Isis, the Egyptian goddess that the Romans adore. Stephania prays frequently to her and makes generous offerings in the hope that the goddess will grant her eternal happiness. She even persuaded her husband to make a large donation towards the rebuilding of her temple after the earthquake, which is almost complete now. Epidius had no trouble with this benefaction, as it is a popular way to win votes here. And Stephania will one day soon be elevated to priestess of Isis. This also pleases Epidius as he gains more respect by a marriage to one held in high regard by the devotees of Isis, of which there are many here. That, in a nutshell, is the life of Stephania.

So does Epidius have a mistress who provides sexual fulfilment? Well, he has had several dalliances down the years, one even with the son of a business associate, but he decided that men were not really to his taste. He is a strange beast in this regard. He lacks the hunger for sex and sexual experimentation that most male humans possess. The urge does occasionally take him of course, and he has once in a while had sex with Faustilla or another slave. His sex drive is often fuelled by his successes, when hot blood courses rapidly through his veins, such as that moment he'd murdered his employer, Caecilius

Jucundus, and then taken Faustilla immediately after, the thrill of bloody violence still fresh in his heart.

But in terms of longer-term affairs with Romans, were you to look back at his few partners down the years, you would soon define a pattern: most were a challenge to bed. Other men's wives, girls half his age who were reluctant due to his married state, the boy I mentioned, which was an exercise in curiosity for him, nothing more. Epidius's whole character can be discerned from this behaviour. He lives to possess what is difficult to obtain, or even seemingly impossible. And no barrier to his progress is insurmountable, he believes. It just requires the abandonment of conscience. Epidius cast aside the last remnants of his into the earth of Vesuvius, when he stained it with the blood of Jucundus.

So a little game like this is merely that. And the game is about to re-commence. Look, the sun has almost disappeared below the rooftop. Yes, almost two hours have passed, and here comes Faustilla, trotting with pace towards the room where Epidius waits, now in the company of his two actors, Circinaeus and Anteros, and Apelles, his slave.

No need to stir, they shall all return this way very shortly. Ah, I hear their footsteps. Yes, Epidius strides with purpose, the toga-clad 'senator' and 'renowned advocate' at his shoulders, trailed by Apelles and Faustilla. Do you wish to witness this ugly little charade, or will imagination suffice to complete the picture? No? Oh very well, we shall have the briefest of glimpses, but I take no pleasure in witnessing the humiliation of a good man like Titus Suedius Clemens, nor of the young Felix.

Epidius stands silently at the door to the main oecus, he turns and nods to the actors, Anteros and Circinaeus, and then laughs as he makes casual conversation. – No Helvidius, I don't think the Emperor would appreciate...

The words die falsely on his lips. He has burst through the

door and his face contorts in feigned shock at the sight of Titus naked, on hands and knees, and Felix kneeling behind him, also naked. There are gasps from the actors as they advance into the room.

I want to bugger a boy ₁₀₂

Epidius gasps. – Titus!

Poor Titus leaps towards his discarded tunic and tries desperately to cover himself. Felix also, the unwilling player, stands and pulls his tunic from the back of a chair, hastily re-robing and standing with his head bowed in shame.

By now Apelles and Faustilla are also witnesses to the scene. The more the merrier, were Epidius's precise words. He gathers his wits and turns to his actors, ushering them out.

– Forgive this unfortunate incident, gentlemen. Please, let the slaves bring you some wine elsewhere. I shall speak to you shortly.

'Helvidius' speaks the couple of lines required of him. – Is this the man you spoke so highly of, Epidius? A man who likes to be buggered by children? I am shocked beyond reason!

Not bad, Circinaeus, for a second-rate actor.

– I assure you there must be an explanation. But please, please, take some wine to calm yourselves. Faustilla! Fetch the finest vintage we have and see my good friends are catered for. Apelles, ensure our guests are comfortable.

– Yes, Dominus, at once.

Epidius closes the door and turns to face Titus, who now sits on the couch, thankfully dressed, his head lowered, his hand covering his eyes. He vents his wrath first on Felix.

– You! I'll have you flogged before the sun sets! When I told you to see to his needs, I didn't mean to fuck him!

The anger is pretence, yet Felix is very fearful. See how he sobs and shakes. His is no act.

– Forgive me, Dominus. I thought...

– Get out of my sight! I'll deal with you later!

Felix scampers from the room. Epidius stands in front of Titus, hands on hips, like an angry parent looking down on a naughty child.

– What have you done, Titus?

He looks up. His face, normally high in colour, now resembles beetroot. His eyes glisten.

– Forgive me, Epidius. Please do not punish the slave. It is I who... persuaded him to...

Even now his first thought is not for himself, but young Felix. His graciousness is lost on Epidius, who shakes his head slowly.

– What am I to do, Titus? Were it simply me, I would forget and forgive such an indiscretion. I am a man of the world. I understand that we all have our needs. But my friends....

He sighs and sits at the other end of the couch, cranes his head back and covers his eyes.

– You were not supposed to be back until after nightfall. I would....

He lets the thought perish. The world knows of his secret weakness now, and getting away with it would not have made him any less guilty.

– Who are they, those men? he asks despondently.

– One was Helvidius Marcus Priscus from Capua. He's been serving in Judea for several years with great distinction, putting down the Jewish rebellion. He has just been elected to the senate. His father is also a veteran senator, and is a keen supporter of Emperor Vespasian's reforms.

Titus lifts his head now as the name triggers a memory. His lips part in horror. Epidius nods sympathetically.

– And the other is Cornelius Lentulus Marcellinus, a renowned advocate from Ostia. Titus, you know how Vespasian feels about these things. The whole empire came to know his views when those rumours about Licinius Mucianus started flying in Rome. He despises arse-fuckers. And especially those who take it. I personally know that young Helvidius out there feels the same.

Epidius's use of crudity is deliberate, the words casually dropped in to remind Titus of the public scorn he will face.

– What am I to do, Epidius?

Another shake of the head. – When word of this gets out, I fear your position here will be at an end. I'd say you may count your career ended. And the public scandal. You will not be able to show your face in the street. I pity your dear Fabia most. Such shame and humiliation will be heaped upon the dear woman.

Titus begins to weep openly now. Epidius allows this to continue for a time, then rises and pours a goblet of wine. He pats the man gently on his shoulder and holds the drink to his face.

– Take this, my friend, and calm yourself. Perhaps there is a way out of it.

A light blinks on in Titus's eyes. – How? What can I do?

Epidius walks about the room, apparently pensive. – You don't have to do anything, Titus. Yes, I think it can be done.

– What?

– I will speak to Helvidius and Cornelius tonight. I don't want a word of this leaving my home. They are both in debt to me to some considerable degree, favours I have done them. You understand. We go back many years. I believe I can persuade them to forget they ever witnessed this...unfortunate scene. Of course, it will be at considerable loss to myself, but that is neither here nor there.

He throws a dismissive wave with his arm. Titus finds the

strength to stand, although his legs still tremble. – Epidius. How in the name of all the gods could I repay you for such a favour?

– Think nothing of it. A gesture of friendship.

Titus, the unfortunate naïve man, takes three steps forward and clutches Epidius's hand, which he pumps heartily. Epidius retrieves his hand and not too subtly wipes it clean on his tunic.

– But you know, on reflection, perhaps there are one or two small favours you could do for me.

– Anything, Epidius. *Anything.*

Epidius turns away and observes the fresco of Ganymede and the eagle. Soon, he thinks, *he* will ascend as the great bird, although he won't clutch the baggage of a naked man in his arms. He turns back to Titus and smiles.

He who buggers a fire burns his cock [103]

In the course of the next handful of minutes, he lays out the small favours he seeks. He requests Titus's public support in the forthcoming election: to have the name of the respected agent of Vespasian behind him will be the final weapon he requires to ensure success. Titus agrees willingly. He also reassures Titus that certain properties in his possession are legally his and suggests that no investigation into them is required. Titus is given pause, not because he will not consent to this, but because he now realises that Epidius is not the blemish-free loyal citizen of Rome that he'd been led to believe. Yet after a moment's hesitation, he nods. He hardly has a choice. Epidius also wishes his name mentioned favourably in senatorial circles when Titus returns to Rome. He has ambitions beyond this small town council, and Titus can help him scatter a few early seeds. Titus nods his enthusiastic consent. And finally, Epidius offers him a favour in return: he will assist the man in identifying other properties around the area taken illegally by other individuals, they being business or political rivals of Epidius. Top of that list is the name of Gnaeus Alleius Nigidus Maius.

When it is done he spirits the man out of his house, promising to see him tomorrow, when they will make their first joint public appearance in the forum in support of Epidius's election bid. He wastes little time, does he? He grins as Titus hastens away towards the sanctuary of the Inn of Cominia Lucilla.

– He is gone, Dominus?

Epidius grins broadly. – I do believe that Fortuna smiled sweetly upon our plan tonight.

– I have paid the actors, Dominus, and they departed by the rear entrance.

Epidius releases a howl of laughter. Faustilla looks at him in puzzlement.

– The rear entrance has served us well in many ways tonight.

She joins him in his joke. – Dominus, are you not fearful that Circinaeus and Anteros may be revealed for who they are? If Clemens saw them around...

– Don't worry. In two days they'll be in Ostia, sworn not to return for a year at least. If they do they'll have their throats cut. Besides, once Titus has done what I asked, it will make no difference. Anyway, he's not going to kick up a fuss about this night one way or the other, is he?

– You are a wise man, Dominus.

He regards her in silence for a short time.

– Faustilla, when was the last time I fucked you?

She is a little surprised, but ponders this and replies with a smile.

– Saturnalia, Dominus.

– So long? I feel like celebrating tonight. Come here to me, my little thorny flower.

Faustilla takes his embrace on the couch and he begins to

loosen the strings of her tunic. But he pauses as she pulls back when a thought strikes her.

– Dominus. You know where my loyalty lies, and that of Apelles. What of Felix? If Titus Clemens ever suspects the events of tonight were arranged, he may even seek out the boy and persuade him to speak.

Epidius weighs the matter in his mind. He nods.

– It is too late to do anything tonight. Tomorrow, give him the kitchen slave as I promised. Let him enjoy himself. Then just before nightfall send him on an errand.

– To where, Dominus?

– Anywhere beyond the walls. Just tell Albanus to make sure he never comes back.

SCAENA 34

Mustius the fuller 104

The girl at the counter is attractive, Celadus is thinking. Maybe eighteen, nineteen. Heart-shaped face, smooth skin, small nose, hazel eyes, chestnut brown hair tied back, slim body, but with nice curves, reasonably well-endowed in the breast area. Shame about the sour expression.

He stands there waiting his turn while she neatly folds another elderly customer's clothes and pushes them into a sack. Behind her are shelves stacked with hundreds of garments and he wonders how she can tell which tunic belongs to which customer. It occurs to him that this would be a good way to strike up a conversation. In days past this would not have been a consideration. The girl would have seized the opportunity of his presence to engage with him in vaguely smutty talk so that she could boast to her friends afterwards about having met the great Celadus. He still gets the occasional compliment, mostly from former male fans, but new gladiators have arisen. New heroes. And yet, he finds he cares less and less about such things. His perspectives on the meaning of success in life have changed.

The elderly woman leaves with a grunt of thanks and he steps to the counter. The sour expression on her face will make sense soon enough.

– I left a tunic four days ago, and two subigaculi.

– Name?

– Celadus.

And then after a beat. – The Thracian.

She consults a wax tablet then turns away and inspects the shelves.

– How do you know what belongs to each customer? There are hundreds...

She answers with her back to him. Sharply so, as though in defence.

– You'll get the right clothes. Don't worry.

– I didn't mean that...

A man appears through the doorway at the back.

– You're Celadus The Thracian!

Celadus has no interest in the recognition. He would have preferred a few moments alone with the girl, who now returns to the counter with the subigaculi.

– Your tunic isn't ready.

The man behind the counter is Barca, brother of Mustius, who is the owner of this small fullery. He is middle-aged, short beard, fat, high hair-line. He steps up to the girl's side and slaps her on the backside. It is meant to be playful, but his hand lingers. Her expression turns from sharp to acrid. But she endures his paw. Celadus takes this in. It annoys him, even if she is a slave.

Barca picks up one of the subigaculi and holds it before her eyes.

– Hey Idaia! This belongs to the great Celadus! Once champion gladiator of Campania. Just think of what he keeps in here! That's something to dream about in your bed!

He roars laughing at his own joke. Celadus ends Barca's guffawing by snatching his underwear from Barca's grasp. He has taken an instant dislike to the man.

– What of my tunic? My name is on it.

Barca is taken aback. He glances at Celadus then snatches the tablet from the girl. – Four days ago? It's probably still in the pile beside the rinsing room you stupid bitch. Go and look.

Barca, may you rot ₁₀₅

She casts a malice-filled eye at him then disappears through the door. The man eyes Celadus with curiosity, notices the way his head turned to watch her departure.

– Don't bother with that slut, Celadus. Anyway, you can probably have half of the girls in town with a snap of your fingers. Hey, will you do me a favour? Will you write that you were here on the wall? Write it big so I can show my customers.

Celadus ignores him. – Is she your slave?

Barca takes a moment to realise his request has been scorned. His smile disappears.

– Idaia? No. She works here. But forget about her, like I said. She's disgraced. Shamed. *Fucked* a slave. She's from Herculaneum. Her father gutted the slave and threw her out and she has to walk here every day because nobody there will give her work. We only employ the stupid cunt because Mustius doesn't want to spend thousands of sesterces on another slave. She works cheap.

Idaia returns with the tunic. She places it on the counter and begins to fold the subigaculi inside it. Celadus interrupts her, deliberately taking her hand away. This is calculated on two fronts. He gets to touch her hand for a moment and he also has contrived a reason to confront Barca, his dislike of the man having swelled. He lifts the tunic and smells it.

– You're lucky. Last time I left a tunic here it hadn't been rinsed properly and still smelled of piss.

– Not from this fullery, friend.

– Are you calling me a liar?

The man, so confident behind his counter with just the young girl to intimidate, suddenly appears like a rabbit confronted by a lion.

– No, but perhaps...

Celadus reaches across and grasps Barca's tunic with two hands. – Just as well, for your sake. And you see the girl there? Idaia?

Confused, his eyes glance momentarily to the side. – Yes?

– When you said her name I remembered. Idaia. From Herculaneum. She's my cousin.

You can see the shock that registers in Barca's face, not to mention that of Idaia.

– And if put your hands on her again, I'll remove them. Permanently. Got that?

Barca nods fervently. Celadus pushes him and he stumbles back against the shelves of folded tunics, sheets, cloaks and togas. A couple of them tumble about his head. He makes a quick exit through the back door.

Idaia stares at him. Her sourness remains and has been supplemented with suspicion.

– Why did you say that?

He shrugs.

– Don't think I'm available for a fuck in payment.

He shakes his head. Starts to bundle his tunic.

A few moments pass before she reaches and takes it from him, folding it properly with the underwear inside, so that it wont come open in the street. She hands it to him.

He begins to leave. He pauses.

– Perhaps we could...perhaps I could take you...

She stares silently at him. But the sharpness is gone. There is the tiniest sliver of an opening between her lips.

Celadus looks at her. She is too good for a brute like him. Too genteel. She inhabits a different world. They are ill-matched.

– Forget it, he mutters.

He gives a vague shake of his head and walks out into the mid-summer sunshine.

He has yet to admit to himself the truth. He has fearlessly faced down formibable oppontents in the Spectacula, yet when confronted with the challenge of courting a pretty girl, found himself deserted by his courage.

SCAENA 35

Venus is a weaver of webs; from the moment that she sets out to attack my dearest son, she will lay temptations along his way: He must hope for a good voyage 106

– You're what?

   – I'm getting married.

   – To Gnaeus?

Prima smiles, rolls her eyes. – No, Publius, to Emperor Vespasian. Of course, Gnaeus!

I have brought you back to the peristyle of the House of Publius for a brief visit, to witness this little interchange. Publius rises from his chair and walks out from under the shade of the portico into the evening sunlight. He stands there with his back to his mother, his fingers touching his forehead, as though he has been beset by a sudden headache. Vivia, who is pouring water into their goblets, exchanges an apprehensive look with her Domina, Prima nods for her to leave and the slave hurries away as quick as her ageing legs will carry her.

Publius turns back sharply. – And Gnaeus simply ignores ordinary civil conduct when it suits him?

– What are you talking about?

– The last time I checked, I was the paterfamilias of this household.

Prima shakes her head in exasperation. – Oh for Jupiter's sake, Publius, I'm not going to have Gnaeus ask my son, whose backside I wiped when he was a baby, for permission to marry.

– It seems this entire household regards me as something they can ignore. You, Restitutus, Cornelia. What next? Will Hermeros start giving me orders? Or will I have to ask Staphylus for permission to....

Prima raises her voice now. – Publius! Be quiet and sit down!

He falls silent. Stares at her. After a few moments he complies. In the end, no Roman legionnaire is as obedient of his centurion as a man is of his mother. Publius's face is red with frustration. Prima hands him a cup of wine.

– Now calm down and listen. I have more to tell you.

He pauses mid-slurp. – What more?

Prima spends some time explaining the position Gnaeus is to offer Restitutus and the fact that he can arrange for Tiberius Verus's son, Atimetus, to marry Cornelia. Publius listens with rising irritation. He of course has no quarrel with any of what his mother is telling him, indeed, it solves many problems. But he is ashamed that he was not the one who had provided the solution. At the same time, he cannot but admire what his mother has brought about.

– And one other thing. I'm taking Vivia with me. She's too old to work here for an entire family. I'm going to find her some small task in Gnaeus's home.

– Mother, please tell me how am I supposed to pay for not one, but two weddings?

She shakes her head. – Gnaeus suggested that a double

wedding would be the simplest solution. And he insists on paying for everything. Especially as the honour for Tiberius Verus of being involved in such a family celebration with Gnaeus was what clinched his agreeing to Atimetus marrying Cornelia.

– It seems you and Gnaeus have sorted out everything.

He says Gnaeus's name with some hostility. Prima sits back in her chair and regards her son.

– You don't really like Gnaeus, do you?

– Can you really trust this man, Mother?

She laughs. – In what way? Do you mean would he cheat on me?

– I don't know. There's something about him I don't like.

– Firstly, Publius, he's been in love with me since I was sixteen. And I know he is not the saint that half the town believes. But I'm well able for him. And you don't like or trust anyone with money, Publius.

– And with justification. Besides, look at the position you're leaving me in, as if things aren't bad enough. Restitutus gone, Cornelia gone, you gone, Vivia gone. How am I supposed to run the bakery now? It was supposed to be our family's business.

Prima is becoming impatient with his stubbornness. That face she has contrived is the same one she had when her children were small and behaving naughtily. Although this time she slaps the table, and not his bare legs.

– Stop it, Publius! You pay Restitutus and Cornelia and even have to provide me with an allowance. It will simply be a matter of hiring new staff. And really, you should be jumping for joy that Restitutus will be gone from this house before you try to cut each other's throats. And you will have fewer mouths to feed. Must you always look on everything in the worst light?

He looks away. He is chastened by the truths his mother has set before him. But see how he tries to maintain the anger in his expression? He wishes to be stubbornly displeased, against his own deeper instinct. Prima recognises this and reaches across to place a hand on her son's forearm.

– Publius, will you not simply wish me good fortune? Would you deny me the chance of some comfort and companionship in old age?

He grunts. Breathes deeply. But finally his expression takes on a tinge of warmth. He reaches across and embraces her.

– I am happy for you, Mother. Very happy. It is just that this has all happened so suddenly. It is hard to take in. When will the wedding be?

– The Kalends of Augustus.

His face drops. – What? That soon? Why?

She shrugs, laughs a little. – At our age, Publius, you want to waste as few days as you can.

He sighs. – I'll have to start looking for staff...

– Publius.

There is a gravity to the solitary word that interrupts him

– What?

– The bakery. Why are you so dedicated to it? Why are you punishing yourself by working like a galley slave to keep it going?

– What are you saying? That I should submit to Epidius? Take his offer.

– You know I despise the man. But his offer is a good one. Take his money. You've earned it. Move on. Get him off your back once and for all.

– But what would I do? And what about the men? This has been our home forever. And my father's business. And your husband's. How can you suggest that I abandon it?

Prima makes a dismissive sound.

– These are only walls. As we found out too well during the earthquake. Your father would have sold up long ago if he'd been in your place. Despite what Restitutus says he wasn't the fearless warrior he thinks. He was much more pragmatic. As you should be. And the men? I don't know, but there are answers to every problem, Publius. It's just a question of finding them. Why are you so stubbornly hanging on?

He doesn't reply, but stares out into the fading light of the peristyle. He is thinking that his father despised Epidius almost as much as he, that to submit would be a betrayal of his memory. Beneath that thought lies another. It is that Restitutus is right. And that he didn't do enough to save his father's life. And that his first thought when the world collapsed around them that day was not of the death of his father, but of the demise of the career he'd always dreamed of. And he has been doing penance for those moments ever since.

He who does not know to look after himself
does not know how to live 107

Prima snaps him back from his reverie. – We all have to move on in life. Perhaps it is time you did also. I'll say no more on the subject.

He turns to her slowly. – I'll consider what you've said, Mother.

– You'll have to do something else also.

– What?

– You'll have to apologise to Cornelia.

– What? But I wasn't the...

Prima holds up her hand. – You know you must, Publius. Need I remind you what you did to her? And in public. I suggest you be the one to bring her the news about her forthcoming wedding. It can be your peace offering.

He sighs wearily. – Bring her home and I'll tell her....

– Uh, uh. You'll have to go to her.

– What do you mean? Go around to that woman's inn and apologise in front of strangers?

Prima merely shrugs. Her scheming isn't yet complete.

Publius snaps up his drink and downs the remainder in a single, long swallow.

– Balls of Jupiter!

– And that woman, as you call her, Cominia Lucilla. She's very nice, you know? I've visited Cornelia numerous times and gotten to know her. She's been so kind to your sister.

Publius eyes her suspiciously. – You two haven't been discussing me?

– You? Not at all. Female things, you know. Weaving, dresses, gardens, the paintings on the walls. She's really pretty, I think, even with that scar. Did you know she adores the theatre? Oh, she's very bright. I'm sure you two would have plenty to talk about. Not that you ever really came up in conversation. Not really.

– Mother...?

He wishes to project vexation, but is smiling despite himself.

– Do you know something, Publius?

– What?

– I haven't seen you smile like that in a long time.

SCAENA 36

By virtue of authority conferred upon him by the Emperor
Vespasian Caesar Augustus,
Titus Suedius Clemens, tribune, having investigated the facts and
taken measurements, restored to the citizens of Pompeii public places
illegally appropriated by private persons 108

What's that noise, you're wondering? And what is this room?
No, it's not like any of the houses you've visited. A little dull, is
it not? Exceptionally dull, in fact. But it is large and has a high
ceiling. Look behind you, the tall door is a little ajar and
through it you can see the columns that surround the forum
accompanied by the buzzing of a hundred voices going about
their business. Actually, when that fat man steps out of the way
you will be able to catch a glimpse of the corner of the Temple
of Jupiter at the other end of the forum. There. See it? I know
you can't see very much from here, but we will visit again in
daylight, I promise. Besides, you really don't want to go out
there now as it is almost noon, and very hot. Most Pompeiians
will drift away to the coolness of their rooms for the next
couple of hours. And we too shall not linger long in this drab,

stuffy building. Just long enough to observe a little interchange.

CRESCENS, ARCHITECT [109]

Actually, I'm being unfair to the architect of this place, one Herennius Crescens. It is brand new in divine terms. They've been building it for seven years. It replaced a similar structure that stood here until that day the earth trembled and revealed to the people here the inconsequentiality of all their works. There are two more similar structures next door, but only one of them is completed as yet. You see these are the offices of public administration in Pompeii. Money has been in short supply for the council, and the fine decoration intended for this place is simply not there. So poor Crescens believes he will be an old man before his creation here is complete. If the truth be told, the buildings will never be complete.

But I digress. This structure is currently being used by a number of civic office holders, including the serving aediles. They are not present today, but some of their senior attendants carry on their work. That's them on the left. Each one is partially secluded by a thin wooden partition, which is supposed to grant them some privacy. But come down here to the rear. There. Another low partition. And sitting behind it at a table you'll recognise the face of the hapless Titus Suedius Clemens.

Looks worried, I'd say. Nervous. He sweats even more than usual. And here comes the cause of his disquiet. Gnaes Alleius Maius Nigidus. See how the others present bow their heads in greeting as he passes. But they all withdraw quickly, as his face is not presently that of a man in the humour for exchanging banalities. He strides towards Titus, who stands and extends his hand in greeting. Gnaues shakes it. Fleetingly.

– Titus Suedius Clemens. I am not used to being summoned

to the forum in such a manner. I am a former quinquennial duumvir and am a priest of Caesar Augustus, in case you are unaware, not some stall-keeper.

– I apologise, Alleius Maius. But I have so much work to complete here on behalf of the divine Emperor…

Titus gestures to the table, which is littered with scrolls and wax tablets. – …that the council kindly granted me this space and suggested I conduct my business from here, rather than trying to personally track down all of the owners of properties across half of Campania.

Did you notice his mention of 'the divine Emperor' in his explanation? He wants to leave Gnaeus in no doubt that he has the authority to summon whoever he pleases. Not that he was pleased to summon Gnaeus, who he most certainly does not want as an enemy.

– I wonder was it just the council who suggested you summon me?

Titus slowly sits. – What do you mean?

Gnaeus seats himself on a stool, then waves an arm in the general direction of the forum.

– Everywhere I go I see notices announcing your support for Marcus Epidius Sabinus. I'm curious. Do Roman tribunes normally interfere in local politics? What interest does Rome have with a little backwater like this?

– None, I assure you, other than the business of its finances. And I also assure you my support for Epidius Sabinus is purely a personal matter and carries no subversive political motives.

Gnaeus stares coldly at him without replying. Titus drops his gaze to the table, where he commences fishing for a document amid the jumble.

– But t-t-to the matter at hand.

– Yes.

– You are registered as the owner and landlord of a property on the Via Mucianus, currently occupied by Lucius Ceius Luci, the banker, with exterior rooms sublet?

– What of it?

Titus continues to stare at the scroll in his hands.

– I'm afraid that property is owned by the Roman Empire and you will have to relinquish any claim to it immediately.

The building is large, although not exceptionally grand, yet its loss would not be insubstantial to Gnaeus. However, it is not the potential monetary blow that enrages him, but the fact that he has been accused of such a thing.

He slams down a fist, which turns the heads of everyone about the room.

– How dare you accuse me of theft from the state! I purchased that property in good faith from Marcus Casellius Marcellus, a former aedile, after it had been damaged during the earthquake.

– Please don't raise your voice. I am merely doing my duty by Rome.

– Then do it fucking properly. I can produce documents to prove that I am the rightful owner.

Titus finally has the courage to meet his eye, he was once a soldier of sorts, after all. Mind you, he never saw the whites of an enemy's eyes as he is seeing those of Gnaeus.

– I'm afraid Casellius Marcellus had no right to sell it to you in the first place. The building was one of the first structures when the colony was established in ancient times. It was built with state money as a home for the early administrators of the region, and it has remained in state ownership ever since. I do not accuse you of theft, as you stated, Alleius Maius. However I must tell you that you have been the victim of a swindle. I personally regret Casellius Marcellus is long dead, so you have no recourse to reclaim your money from him.

Gnaeus restrains himself from grasping Titus by the throat and throttling him. He suspects that another hand is behind this matter, because he was never swindled by Casellius Marcellus. The fact is that he and Marcellus cooked up this little deal between them and Gnaeus paid a relative pittance for the property. The earthquake was responsible for shifting a great deal of property, but many of the boundaries of those properties were also shifted by human hand. And so much documentation was destroyed in the catastrophe. I mean, who could prove what belonged to whom amid so much death and destruction? Unless of course someone informed Suedius Clemens about certain property records. Casellius Marcellus had many dealings with Lucius Caecilius Jucundus, the dead banker, and Epidius took control of his business when the man died. And now Gnaeus sees Suedius Clemens supporting Epidius in the election. He has been dealing with figures all his life. And he can certainly add one and one together.

He tries to calm himself. – I invested a great deal of money in rebuilding the place. It was a ruin when I purchased it.

Titus again looks at his papers. He rubs his forehead and his fingers come away dripping with moisture. You can tell he is about to deliver more bad news.

A cough before he speaks. – Of course, I am prepared to refund your investment money from the proceeds you have accumulated in rents since you purchased the property.

It takes a moment for this to sink in. Then Gnaeus stands and plants his hands on the table. – Are you suggesting that money I earned from rental must also be paid to the state? That's almost nine years earnings!

Titus is feeling quite, quite unjust, and embarrassed. But

these are secondary to the terror rumbling in his gut. He holds a rolled scroll out to Gnaeus without looking up.

– It's all detailed in here. Thirty-nine thousand five hundred and seventy-four sesterces.

Gnaeus doesn't accept the document. He kicks the stool behind him away and it clatters across the floor, its echoes silencing everyone present. With all ears pricked, Gnaeus leans as close as he can to Titus and speaks in a whisper. Or perhaps you would describe it as a hiss.

– I'll check your document against my own. You can expect a legal challenge. And if the law decides I must pay, then I'll pay, tribune. But I guarantee you, there will be a much higher price for others to pay.

Titus manages a handful of chattering words. – I am the Emperor's r-r-representative. It would be w-wise not to threaten me, Alleius Maius.

Gnaeus snatches the scroll. He turns away and strides towards the door. He is thinking that Titus Suedius Clemens is correct. It would be unwise to make threats against the tribune. But before things get any worse, it would be very wise to make some threats against Marcus Epidius Sabinus.

Anyone could as well stop the winds from blowing and the waters from flowing as stop lovers from loving 111

He spots the tall, dark-skinned African as he approaches the doorway.

Publius has cut through the Via del Venditores countless times but never before noticed the little store on the corner of the laneway at the side of the Inn of Cominia Lucilla. The shop seems to open out into a larger workshop at the rear, where he catches a glimpse of piles of wood stacked against a wall. From within he can hear a saw hacking through a piece of timber. He remembers that day when he chased Cornelia and the sudden appearance of the African. There is a low counter at the front upon which sits a finely crafted chair with an ornate back support and arms, and the African appears to be showing it to a couple of ladies. He now runs a small furniture shop with a skilled wood engraver called Priscus Vecilius. The shop has become very popular with Pompeii's wealthier citizens.

Priscus the engraver wishes good fortune

But now Publius's approach catches the corner of Chrestus's eye and he excuses himself from his customers, swings back a flap in the counter and steps into the baker's path.

Publius is bothered that his nerves have begun to dance. He wonders if he is so weak that he can tremble merely at the sight of a threat. He is also a little embarrassed to be clutching a bunch of roses that his mother has picked from their garden, their thorny stems wrapped in an old piece of sackcloth. See how he holds them heads down at his side, trying to conceal them behind the folds of his tunic?

Publius manages to keep his voice even.

– What is it? What do you want?

Chrestus stares down at him. The smile he had for the customers has been replaced by a snarl. – Where are you going?

Publius is irked by the man's impudence. He takes his courage in his hands. – That's my business. Get out of my way.

He attempts to go around the African, but Chrestus shifts on his feet a little and his bulk is too great to easily circumnavigate. Publius gasps in exasperation.

– Let me pass!

Chrestus angles his eyes towards the building behind him. – Are you going to the inn?

– That's none of your business.

– I've seen how you treat women. And the women in that house are my business.

Pubius closes his eyes and sighs. The phrase 'how you treat women' has jarred immensely. What he would give to take back the shame of that day.

– Look, friend. I'm not the sort of man who...

Publius is exasperated. He realises he is still holding the

roses and lifts them up to display them to the African. – Do I look like I mean to harm anyone?

Chrestus studies him a moment longer, then glances back towards his shop where the two ladies are growing impatient.

– The first Romans who came to my village bore gifts. It was just a means of discovering our strength. They next time they came they bore only death.

Publius is at a loss.

– You cause any trouble for Cominia Lucilla and you will have to deal with me, baker.

He turns away and returns to his shop. Publius exhales in relief. He walks the final few steps to the inn and enters.

The richly decorated atrium is empty of souls, but voices and laughter drift in from the rear of the property and he can spy several people seated around a table through the columns of the large peristyle at the back, a slave serving them wine. He is about to explore further when a voice stops him in his tracks.

– What do *you* want?

Daphnicus sits in a dim alcove to the side. It is not the tone he would normally use to greet guests.

– I am here to see my sister, Cornelia. Where is she?

– Elsewhere.

Daphnicus stands and walks to him. He doesn't behave in the normal deferential manner of a slave. Publius decides to grin and bear the impudence.

– Is she out there?

He points towards the peristyle.

– They are guests.

– Well then tell me where she is, curse you.

– Or what? Will you take a stick to Daphnicus?

Despite the words it carries, the new voice behind him has a pleasing cadence and he greets it with relief. He turns to see

Cominia Lucilla striding across the atrium. His mind can't deny the pleasure he feels upon seeing the woman.

– Please spare me. I've already had your African friend threatening me with all sorts of violence.

Cominia stands in front of him and smiles. Coldly so. – Chrestus, yes. He is very protective of us. You should see what he can do with a sharp knife.

Publius doesn't reply.

– I mean as a carpenter.

– I'd like to see Cornelia.

Cominia glances briefly down at the roses.

– It will take more than those to win her trust again.

– Where is she?

– She's very loyal, you know. She actually defended you the very day you thrashed her in the street. Said she probably deserved it, and that you had a lot of troubles. Personally I don't think you deserve her as a sister.

It is unfortunate for Publius that they are standing almost directly beneath the compluvium and the light that spills through it from the summer sky above, as there is no hiding the redness of his face. He glances away.

– Listen, I regret what happened. I would take the moment back if I could. But I cannot.

Cominia turns to Daphnicus. – Tell Cornelia her brother is here and see if she is willing to meet him.

Daphnicus departs. They stand in silence. Cominia continues to stare at his face. Publius looks about he atrium, pretending to study the fine frescoes and decorative plaster.

– It's a very fine establishme...

– I would have kept her here as my guest, you know, considering her condition. But she insisted on earning her stay. She's been working in the kitchen these past weeks. She's a good girl.

She makes us all laugh. A little naive. But weren't we all at that age? And you know what brutes men can be.

He coughs. His mind is torn. He hates this woman. Yet he admires her. And he cannot help but find her attractive.

Daphnicus returns with Cornelia trailing behind him, her head bowed. Cominia gestures to him to leave them and he returns to his little alcove.

– Cornelia.

His sister doesn't lift her head. Publius turns to Cominia. – Could you leave us alone, please?

– No.

The woman is infuriating, he thinks.

– I have news of a private nature, family matters, that I wish to discuss.

– Discuss them, then.

He shakes his head, sighs and takes a step closer to Cornelia. He proffers the flowers.

– I brought you these, sister. I am so sorry for striking you. Please forgive me and come home.

Cornelia gingerly lifts her eyes to the flowers and accepts them, but her gaze seems unable to quite rise to Publius's level. Cominia watches this with an implacable face. He continues.

– I let you down. If I had paid more attention to your needs this might not have happened. But I had so much...no, I'm not making excuses. It was all my fault and I'm sorry. Again. Will you not forgive me?

Now she looks at him and she is smiling. She suddenly steps forward and embraces him. Cominia cannot quite conceal a grin.

– I love you, brother, even though you are as cranky as a bear with piles.

He laughs. – You cheeky... I have good news for you.

She pulls back but stays in his embrace.

– Tiberius Verus has agreed that Atimetus should marry you. Gnaeus's influence was what changed his mind.

Cornelia's jaw drops. She pulls free of him and begins to jump up and down on the spot, hooting like a crazed animal. The commotion brings Daphnicus running back into the atrium. Cominia rushes to her and tries to calm her.

– Cornelia! Consider the child inside you!

– But I'm to be married! Married! To a wealthy man!

The pinnacle of her life's ambitions is within her grasp. Perhaps she is better off in such innocence. Publius smiles at her joyful reaction. But his feelings are tempered by the less than ideal circumstances.

– Cornelia. I don't want you to get your hopes up too much about what to expect. This Atimetus isn't a very honourable man, from what I've heard. But his father is, and his influence may force Atimetus to treat you well. But we must be cautious. And there is more. Concerning mother. But that can wait. Come with me now and we shall all eat together and discuss the weeks ahead.

Cornelia, her cheeks rounded like eggs and rosy with happiness, looks to Cominia. It is as though she seeks her permission.

– Go on girl. Get your things. Time to go home.

Uncomfortable moments follow as Cominia and Publius are left alone. He attempts some small talk about the frescoes. She replies with indifferent bluntness. He shuffles on his feet. In his desperation he even considers for a moment inquiring how she came by the scar on her face. But then realises insensitivity of such an inquiry. He has little or no skills in conversing with women. Finally he comes up with something.

– You'll ...you'll still take our bread, I hope?

– I considered changing baker. But that would only have hurt Cornelia and your mother more. No, we shall continue to buy your fine bread. It seems you are good for something at least, Publius Comicius Restitutus.

He rankles at this last statement. His anger rises again, but the sight of Cornelia returning with a bag overflowing with clothes offers him the opportunity of escape from the woman's presence.

They exit into the Via del Venditores, the fresh air a blessed relief to Publius, who cannot wait to be back in the sanctuary of his home.

But look, he is stopping. What is he up to? He seems to be standing perfectly still looking at the ground. Cornelia pauses beside him.

– What is wrong, Publius?

– Nothing. Go on ahead. I forgot something.

She does as requested, almost skipping away like a small girl.

He walks back to the house. Through the open door he can see Cominia Lucilla standing with her back to him, staring into the almost dry impluvium.

Cominia sees her reflection in the thin layer of rainwater. And she herself reflects on how she has acted with the baker. She wonders if she was too harsh. If her past experiences have clouded her views too greatly, and left her with a lingering bitterness. A gentle knock causes her to turn before she has time to restore the face she maintains for public inspection – the face that conveys poise, confidence, dispassion. In that small fragment of time, Publius is granted a glimpse of this woman's real beauty, one without scars. He is barely conscious of it, but it registers somewhere. Cominia quickly restores her normal façade.

– You again.

– Forgive me, I meant to ask you something.

She stares silently at him.

– As a means of thanks for helping Cornelia, my mother wished me to invite you to dinner tomorrow evening.

– Your mother did?

– Yes.

– And what about you? Would you be able to endure my presence for an evening?

He shakes his head. She seems determined not to relinquish her view of him and she has defensive walls that seem impenetrable. But something makes him persist.

– Well, only if they keep the wine flowing.

Her laughter startles him. As does the manner in which it alters her face. He was unsure what brought him back. It seemed to defy logic. How many short moments since he felt he despised this woman? And now, seeing her cheeks swell and her lips curl up with mirth, he understands his own motivations.

Seek you joyfully and willingly, and you will be glad for ever, because of what shall be given [113]

– Tell your mother then, that I would be happy to attend.

– I will. And thank you for caring for Cornelia.

He hesitates a moment longer, then turns to depart.

– Of course, if you really wish to thank me, you could escort me to the performance of Andromache in Herculaneum that is starting in three days. Unless of course, such a play would be too 'high brow' for a baker.

Now Publius's eyes light up. 'You like Euripides?'

She shrugs. 'I prefer Sophocles. But there's something about Andromache that appeals to me. Well?'

He beams. He cannot help himself. – I'd be hon...I would like to escort you.'

– Well, let us discuss the matter more when I visit. Now, I

have a lot of work to do. I'm expecting several new guests from a ship before nightfall.

– Yes, of course. Goodbye.

Cominia smiles as he backs away almost like a deferential slave. She is unsure about the course she has committed to. But she has taken many risks before and is prepared to deal with the consequences. Or reap the rewards.

Let us leave her there with her thoughts and briefly flit out to the street.

Look there, beyond the spice seller. You can still see Publius as he makes his way home. And even from this distance, you can see that his walk is now little different from when he arrived at this house just a short time ago.

SCAENA 38

May you always be in good health
my girl, and may Pompeiian Venus
be well disposed to you ₁₁₄

Why have I brought you here, to stand in the middle of this ruin, you are likely asking. Columns that once would have towered far above your head now lie scattered across the weed-choked paving that covers a plot larger than the battleground in the amphitheatre. Piles of rubble sit where marble-encased walls once rose. Most of the statues fell during the earthquake. Except that one over there. The one of the almost naked Venus. Vulcan thought it would please her if he spared that. She is the patron goddess of the town after all. The council can't afford to fix this yet, but they have plans and have asked some wealthy benefactors in Rome for help. But these things take time, and sadly, it will take more time than is available. Hardly anyone comes to the Temple of Venus now, except the occasional visitor who wants to pray to the statue. Most think it bad luck to pray at a ruined temple, but some still visit and try to grasp a sense of

Venus's presence, so that it might inspire love in the hearts of those they desire.

Come up here, onto the wall where you can see the couple sitting with their backs to us. You know what's on the other side?

There. Is there any sight more beautiful that the summer sun glistening on the sea? Look. It laps at the base of the wall below as though knocking on it, trying to gain entry into the town. Mind you, before the earthquake the water used to come half way up the wall. And in time, the vast ocean will be swept completely away from the walls and dry land will stretch from this point for two miles to the east. Do I make you feel small? Inconsequential?

No matter. I will tell you this. We do not measure you by the scale of your influence on the world. Yes, the Romans would be shocked to hear a goddess tell them that Augustus, Caesar, Alexander even, are weighed with the same scales as Cominia the Innkeeper, Urbana the whore or Celadus the gladiator.

And speaking of Celadus. Look to the left. Do you recognise the girl that sits by his side. Yes, it is Idaia, the girl from the fullery. Celadus had considered asking her to keep him company, then decided in a moment that the thought of him with a girlfriend, perhaps even a wife at some time in the future, was laughable. But the notion preyed on him. And no whore could make it vanish. Neither could any amount of wine. And so, let me tell you this, it is amusing: he deliberately spilled wine on a tunic of his so that he would have an excuse to return. He learned that she walked alone home to Herculaneum each night where she slept in a tiny windowless room. He expressed his fear that it was dangerous for a girl to travel alone on the road as night approached and insisted on accompanying her when his duties permitted. The fact that she didn't protest too greatly emboldened him. He has done this four times.

Today she finishes her work early as the fullery is closed

tomorrow and Celadus asked her to accompany him here. To this beautiful spot. It is funny to see them sitting there with their legs dangling over the water, hers swinging a little. In some ways they look like two children, friends imagining sea monsters battling with Neptune far beneath the waves. Happy in their innocence.

Who knows? Perhaps the spirit of Venus flits about somewhere nearby. Perhaps she will alight between them. Perhaps not.

Let us move closer along the wall.

– More wine? Bread?

Celadus offers her the canteen. She smiles and declines.

– Are you trying to get me drunk?

Idaia has had little cause to smile this past two years. She is so different from the women he is used to and he is trying desperately to be honourable. She thinks he is trying too hard.

The girls' idol,
Celadus the Thracian gladiator 115

He protests. – No, I'm not. I swear.

– It's alright Celadus. I was joking.

– Sorry. Barca isn't bothering you anymore?

– No. He's terrified of me. And the others. I thought Mustius might dismiss me, but I think he's afraid you'll come back and disembowel him or something.

Celadus laughs, throwing his head back. As he does a flock of gulls pass overhead and his eyes follow their progress out to sea. Idaia watches his face, wondering what he is thinking. She speaks softly then, her words almost washed away by a wave striking the sea wall.

– Doesn't it bother you, Celadus, about what happened to me? I mean, what I did?

He turns to look at her. – What was his name? The slave you...?

– Fucked? Aemilius. He was from Pompeii. His master used to sell spices in Herculaneum. They'd travel there every week. That's how I met him.

– And is it true your father killed him?

– Beat him to death with a club.

– I'm sorry.

– It has been two years now.

– Did you love him?

She considers the question for a time.

– I used to believe I did, but now I'm not sure. Anyway, I'll never know. All that matters now is that I'm spoiled property. Thank Venus I didn't get pregnant.

– It doesn't bother me. That you were with a slave. I was almost as good as a slave when I was a gladiator. I was paying off debts. But even free citizens are treated the same as slaves when it comes to the arena. Many of the men I fought alongside and against were good men.

She looks down at the water. Folds her hands in her lap.

– It's just that...

– What?

– I just wondered if that was why you hadn't...because I'd been with a slave.

His head turns sharply towards her. He is terrified of having offended her. He is terrified of everything when it comes to this girl. It is as though his life balances on this very wall and if he shifts the wrong way to either side he might plunge to his end.

– No! I just didn't want to dishonour you.

She gives a half smile then reaches out and takes his hand.

– You'd be doing the opposite.

Their kiss is our cue to depart.

*Restitutus slept here alone
and missed his darling Urbana* [116]

There is little light here. The tiny window high above admits
only a small haze of brightness. Soon the night will steal even
that away and the people here will seek to replace it with the
flickering flames of lamps. But the oil in those will burn away
and the flame will die.

I thought you should see this place, Pompeii, warts and all. It
is not all bakers, shopkeepers, innkeepers, councillors and palatial homes. There is a much sadder side.

This is not a brothel, although there is one of those in town.
But there are lots of prostitutes. Most of them work for bar
owners or innkeepers – they provide a little extra cash and keep
certain customers happy. That pretty woman on top is one such
prostitute. Her name is Urbana. Do you recall you glimpsed her
briefly outside the Spectacula? Oh and yes, the man beneath her
on his back is Restitutus, brother of Publius.

Previously I took you to the Tavern of Verecundus, and this is
another establishment of his, much nearer the forum. Actually,

were you to climb up to that window, you would be able to see the rear walls of the Macellum, or the provisions market.

But you can't take your eyes off them, can you? Naked, writhing, groaning, in the full passionate flow of a sweaty coupling. You can actually smell the lust.

There is a voyeuristic streak in all of us. We like to watch others. For pleasure, curiosity, entertainment, mischief. And knowledge of others also gives you an advantage, a little power over them.

But look. They are almost finished. Urbana rises and falls with increasing rapidity. Her high-pitched groans suggest she is in paroxysms of pleasure. Restitutus is less vocal, although you can tell from his face that he is transported with sensual joy. They cry out each others' names.

– Restitutus! Oh Restitutus! Oh Restitutus!

– Urbana! Urbana! Don't stop!

Comical, is it not?

The end is greeted with howls loud enough to fly to the window above and drop to the street below, where a man and his wife are passing on their way home from the baths. They laugh and move along.

Here I fucked many girls ₁₁₇

Urbana collapses on top of him, her generous breasts flatten against his chest and she throws her head upon his shoulder, turning away from his face. See how her expression changes? It is as though the joy she felt has evaporated as quickly as a droplet of water cast onto a hot iron. Suddenly she is impassive. The little play she performed for Restitutus is complete. Although the poor young man often finds it hard to distinguish reality from the fiction he has created for himself of life. His breathing subsides.

– Urbana. You're the best. The very best.

Her face lights up again as she turns to him. Act two. It is called 'keep them coming back for more'.

– No, Restitutus. You are. You're a lion. A bull. You fuck like Apollo himself.

He smiles at the flattery. He chooses to believe it.

– I missed you two nights ago. Where were you?

– Yes, I heard. You had to settle for Myrtis. She said you were so drunk that she had to leave you to sleep it off here.

– Myrtis is no Urbana. If only I could have you to myself every night for the rest of my days, then I'd never want for another girl in the whole empire.

Myrtis, you do great blow jobs [118]

She laughs. – Ha. Sure.

– No, really. But where were you?

The girl turns her face away from him. She stares at the graffiti-covered wall. Stares somewhere *beyond* it. Her smile vanishes once more.

– Verecundus may work us to the bone, but he does have some small pity. He allows us some time off to visit the temple and pray. He says no one should be denied that. Not even a slave.

– Which temple did you visit?

– Isis, of course. Do you think your Roman gods give a damn about slaves? She is the only mother I have ever known.

Restitutus has heard something in her voice. Some lonely sound that is new to him. He looks at the back of her head.

– You didn't know your mother?

– Nor my father. Or if I have a brother or a sister. I was taken as a baby in Germania. Sold four times before I ended up here, fourteen years after I was stolen.

Restitutus feels a little guilt now. For it is men like him who deprived her of her family. Romans. He is at a loss for a few moments.

– And did Isis answer your prayers?

– For a short time.

– What does that mean?

– Oh nothing.

She wrests herself from her melancholy and lifts her head, folding her arms on his chest and resting her chin there so that she is looking down on him. Her smile has reappeared.

– So, Alleius Maius is to marry your mother? The whole town is talking about it. She is a lucky woman. He is so rich. Does it bother you that he'll be fucking your mother?

He slaps her playfully on the backside.

– Don't speak about my mother like that.

– Oh, I see. That talk is only fit for whores like me.

– I didn't mean that. She's my *mother*.

– Well? How do you feel about it?

– Alleius Maius? He may be rich, but he's not the man my father was. He can't replace him. My mother knows that. And so does Alleius Maius. They are simply looking to have someone to share their old age. I don't begrudge my mother that. She had a struggle to raise us.

– But how did she snare him? The widow of a baker?

– She didn't snare him. He came begging her. It goes back to when they were young. I think he's always been in love with her.

– That's romantic.

– Anyway. I probably won't have to think about it much.

– Why?

– I'm thinking of joining the army.

– What? Leaving Pompeii? Why?

– Would you miss me? I'd miss you.

– Yes. You know I would. But why?

He closes his eyes. Heaves a sigh.

– Alleius Maius has offered me a job. But I'm not sure I want it. I would have to spend my life bookkeeping. Adding this sum to that. Keeping records of rents, purchases. Numbers and figures. Meeting other boring clients. Hardly ever seeing the light of day. I think I'd go insane. If I don't take that I'd probably have to stay in the bakery, with my fucking brother breathing down my back all day long. My father was a soldier. A centurion. A great man. All I want in life is to honour his memory and join him in the afterlife in glory when my time comes. I want him to be able to look on me with pride. I can't do that stuck in an office.

– So you think the only honour you can achieve in life is in war.

This is said with a critical tone. He opens his eyes and looks into hers.

– No, I just don't...

He sees sadness in her face. She lays her cheek on her arms and looks away.

– What's wrong with you?

– Nothing. I should be getting back downstairs. There may be other customers.

– I've paid. Who knows how long our business will last? Don't worry about them downstairs.

They are both silent for a time. He wraps his arms around her bare back. He strokes her hair. He stares at the ceiling.

– You know. We should both flee. Run away together. I will find a job somewhere and support us. And I can protect you. I'm good with a sword. My father taught me. I'd love to be rid of this town. We could go north. They say the land up there is rich. Perhaps I could get some land and grow grapes. A vineyard. Or we could open a....

Urbana suddenly rolls off and sits on the edge of the cot, her back to him.

– What's wrong?

– What fantasy are you talking about? A moment ago you were going to join the army. Now you're talking about owning a vineyard. Do you know anything about wine? Besides drinking it? Have you any money to buy land?

– I was just....I thought you'd like to get away from this, as I do.

She stands and takes two steps to the tiny table in the corner. She pours some wine. There is only one cup. For the customer. She is not permitted wine while she works. She hands it to him. He is confused at her abrupt antagonism.

– Here. Get drunk and forget this nonsense, Restitutus.

He sits up, takes the cup, but doesn't drink from it.

– Why are you angry, Urbana?

She stands there barely aware of her nakedness. The life she has been forced to lead has made her thus. And even in this dim light you can see that her body still sports the scars of that life. The rumpled flesh below her stomach the result of countless aborted babies. Three short scars; on her ribs, above her left breast, on her right thigh, these are the marks of blades left by dissatisfied customers. Were she to turn you would see the remnants of welts from the times she was beaten with a stick by unkind masters.

– You say you would be bored in that job. Doing numbers and figures from sunrise to sunset.

– Yes, but what's...

– When I came here first, to Verecundus, I couldn't read or write or add. He had a Greek slave woman teach me the basics. I thought it was wonderful. I thought this master has a better intention for me that the others. But then I learned that the reason I had to understand these things was so that I would know the difference between an as and a dupondius. So that the customers couldn't swindle me. So that I could tend the bar when I wasn't fucking someone. So I could calculate how much I earned in a day if I fucked twelve men.

– Why are you...

– You know, once, when I'd finished work for the day I used my new knowledge to add up something else. Fifteen years a whore. Five men a day. Sometimes ten when the games are on. You see what we just did? The way we fucked? I've had to do that thirty thousand times with thousands of men.

Restitutus is startled at the thought. He looks down into the cup he still has not touched.

– That's right. Sometimes I go on the top like we just did. Other times I'm on my back. Or maybe on my knees. Or sideways. Or I use my mouth. Or my hand. Whatever they want. And every time I have to pretend I'm enjoying it. Like I'm having the best time of my life.

She commences a mimicry of her own passion.

– Oh Restitutus. You're a bull! You're a tiger! Fuck me! Oh yeahhhh. You're a God. Fuck me! Oooooohhhhh Ressssstittutuus....

He can bear her mocking no more. He suddenly stands and slaps her face.

– Stop it!

Her head is thrown sideways by the blow, but she doesn't move from the spot. She turns back to look at him. – I've taken worse blows than that.

– I'm sorry.

He goes to touch her face where he struck her, but she turns away and sits again on the edge of the bed. He holds the cup of wine down to her.

– Take a drink.

She takes the cup. She drinks. Looks at the floor.

– You want to run away with me? I'm a whore. A filthy whore. I've got nothing. Thirty thousand fucks and nothing to show for it except a broken body that can't even bear a child any more. And besides. I don't even like....

- What?

- Do you know that I met my friend at the Temple of Isis. We prayed together. Then we lay in each other's arms for an hour before we had to part.

– You have a lover? I didn't....

– My lover is called Eutychia.

He is standing beside her. She lifts her head and sees that his limp penis is inches from her face. She laughs mirthlessly.

– You look ridiculous standing there. Put your clothes on. Give me mine.

He continues to stand there looking down on her with his mouth open.

– A woman?

– You know so little of things, Restitutus. I never even liked having sex with men.

He turns slowly away, gathers up the clothes from the floor. They dress in silence. They sit beside each other on the bed. Restitutus's mind still reels from what she has told him.

– Listen to me, Restitutus. You're a good lad.

– I'm not a lad.

– A good young man. And I do like you. But you're young and reckless and stupid. Don't interrupt me. I may be only a whore, but I know what I'm talking about. You have the chance of a good life. A decent job. A home. You know what I dream of? Besides my Eutychia, that is?

He shakes his head.

– I dream of one day I don't have to fuck someone. Just one day. Rising at dawn in a clean bed. Eating some porridge. Filling my belly. Visiting the baths. That would be so nice. To feel clean. Just once. Wearing some soft clothes. Just once. Walking by the sea with my Eutychia's hand in mine. Then drifting off to sleep, and lying there undisturbed until morning. Just once. Just one day in my life. Haven't I earned that? But I know I'll never have it. I know I'll probably never be able to share my life with Eutychia. In a couple of years, Verecundus will decide I'm too old and nobody wants to buy an old whore to work in their house. He'll probably just throw me out on the streets. And the only way I can survive will be to keep doing this, but in laneways and under bridges and for just the price of a day's bread to keep me alive.

– If I could help you...

– I'm not asking for your help. But when I hear you complain about your life, I laugh. Because I would give anything to enjoy just one day of the life you are talking about throwing away. Go home, Restitutus. Take the job you've been offered. Find yourself a girl. A nice one. Have a family. Stop whoring and drinking. Live a good life the best you can. Your father will look down on you with pride, as much as if you were fighting on some battlefield.

She plants a kiss on his cheek.

He has had sex with her countless times. Yet he realises now that it is the only true moment of affection they have shared.

– Come on. I have to get back downstairs.

She pulls at the sleeve of his tunic and he rises. They go out into the narrow corridor. Grunts and moans sound from behind the closed door of another room. Suddenly Restitutus is desperate to be gone. They descend the stairs into the small bar.

Euplia was here with two
thousand handsome men 119

Another girl, Euplia, serves behind a counter. There are six customers. Verecundus, a barrel-shaped man with heavy stubble and thinning hair, sits with them, a mug of wine pressed against his face. He turns as they enter. He laughs.

– Hey! Restitutus! I thought you'd stolen my slave! You've been so long I ought to charge you double! Had a good time with my Urbana? Eh?

He tries to force a smile, but this man he'd often shared jokes with, he wants to be rid of his company forever.

– Goodbye, Urbana.

– Go on.

He leaves the bar, pauses. Looks back in through the open doorway. Urbana is smiling broadly. One of the customers has his arm about her waist. He slaps some coins on the table in front of Verecundus and rises, leading Urbana back across the floor towards the stairs.

– Come on my darling. You're my favourite whore in Pompeii! I thought you'd never finish with that fucker.

They disappear up the stairway.

SCAENA 40

Whoever loves, let him flourish
Let him perish who knows not love
Let him perish twice over
whoever forbids love [120]

There is Celadus, strolling along the Via del Terme, breaking pieces off a quarter loaf he has purchased and chewing as he goes. The frown he has been wearing most of these past months has vanished, or at least it hides itself for the moment. He walks from the apartment Gnaeus provided with his employment. It is in an alleyway just of the Via di Nola and consists of a window-less cubiculum and a small room with a table and two stools with a tiny window overlooking the alley. There is a shared latrine in the house below it. It is not much but it is better than the tiny cell he shared in the gladiator barracks. Yet it seemed like a palace to him during the night just passed, for its space was illuminated by the presence of Idaia, the first time she has made love with him. I use the term deliberately, for it was not the casual sex that he has become accustomed to, and the night before revealed that fact to him.

They've been talking a great deal this past month. She accepts what he is and does not resent it. But she does not like it. He countered that it paid very well, but this was said without commitment. She spoke of her desire to be done with the fullery. But it was hard to find other work. He tentatively suggested that she make her life easier by moving to Pompeii. He would ask his employer to provide her with a room and he was confident that Gnaeus would be generous with the cost. He even mooted the possibility that Idaia move in with him, then withdrew the suggestion as quickly when he saw her an instinctive distrust in her eyes, a legacy of her past with men. Yet at some point during all of this conversation it dawned on Celadus what they were talking about. The future. Such a thing has never been a subject to dwell on. Especially for a gladiator. And ever since he's been done with that business, his life as a bodyguard cum enforcer for Gnaeus has merely been a collection of days, one leading into the next, strung flimsily together by shallow pleasures. Rarely a thought for what lies ahead. But now for the first time since his youth a potential future has appeared before him and he stares into it with dreamy eyes.

But Janus has clearly been watching, the god of two faces, one of which observes the future, and one the past, as a reminder of his past awaits him not ten paces distant.

The street is quite busy. Mostly with people coming and going through the nearby Porta Stabiana. Traders, farmers, a few women shoppers heading for the Via dell'Abbondanza. He passes the Bar of Verecundus and sees a woman standing in the open doorway. A whore. He spent many a night in the tavern and shared many a coital embrace with the woman. He remembers her well. Urbana. He liked her, and not just her body. She had something about her. A spirit. Intelligence. A sense of honour. It sounds stupid now to say that about a whore and a slave. She has clearly been ordered to try and tempt some early morning customers inside. She catches his eye and recognises him. He averts his gaze. Then he feels ashamed of himself. He won't deny her. Or deny his own past.

He looks across and sees she has turned her head, clearly trying to spare him any embarrassment.

– Good morning, Urbana.

She looks back at him and smiles softly.

– Hello, Celadus. I hope life is treating you well.

A passing woman gives him a dirty look. He cares not. Fuck her, he thinks.

– And you, Urbana, he replies.

She smiles again. But it is ironic. As if the notion of life treating her well was a joke.

– Well, I hope Fortuna smiles on you, Urbana.

She nods in acknowledgement of his sincerity. He passes on.

The brief encounter stirs a memory and causes a grimace to cross his features. When Idaia had risen to leave this morning to return to the fullery he had been so filled with warmth towards her that he sought to ease the day ahead for her by offering her some money. It was the only moment during the past hours that he saw anger in her. He realised his mistake and sought to explain his motives, cursed his own stupidity before her eyes and begged her forgiveness. Her anger subsided and she had made a joke of it, saying that if she could earn that much as a whore perhaps she should consider it as a profession.

But now pleasant thoughts have returned. He is wondering how long he must do this job to make enough to get out. He's already accumulated more money than he's ever held at any moment in his life before, a couple of thousand sesterces. But not enough to start anew. And as what, he wonders? What becomes of old gladiators, those who survive the years inside the arena? Perhaps he could open a bar? But he rejects this idea immediately. Drunks and whores do not feature prominently on the landscape of his imagined future. Perhaps he can learn a new trade. Carpenter? Housepainter? Blacksmith? This last one widens his eyes as he realises he already has some knowledge of that skill from working with the blacksmith responsible for the animals in the arena. He juggles with this happy thought until his daydream is interrupted by the sight of a cart outside the home of Gnaeus Alleius Maius that is laden with piles of colourful bunting and fancy decorations in the shapes of spirals and diamonds and circles.

A man and woman are carting bundles of these things in through the front door.

The wedding, he thinks. Or rather the weddings. They are just a few days away.

Perhaps one day he and Idaia...? One thing at a time. And for now, he has other business to attend to.

He enters, emerging from the long vestibulum into the brightness of the atrium and a flurry of activity. Slaves clamber up ladders to attach bunting to the walls, streamers of colourful cloth are draped across every structure, with the exception of the statues of the family's ancestors – Gnaeus wouldn't permit such a disrespect. Tall elaborate candelabra stand like guards along each wall, an indication that the celebrations will extend well into the night. And there towards the back on the left you can see the ladies, Prima, Cornelia and Alleia, an effeminate man displaying an array of bottles on a table. Cornelia seems dazzled by the finery surrounding her. She never believed she would set foot in such a palace, let alone celebrate her wedding here. Her thoughts are so bright that they blind her utterly to the potential pitfalls of the marriage that awaits her to Atimetus. How will that turn out, you may speculate? I can detect your scepticism. But the road ahead holds many turns.

She accepts a bottle from the man and spills a droplet on to the back of her writst. She sniffs.

– Oh I like that one.

Her mother sniffs it and she grimaces.

– Cornelia, that smells like a something a whore would wear. You are absolutely not wearing that on your wedding day.

Cornelia is embarrassed in front of Alleia. But as usual she uses her quick tongue to extract herself from the situation.

– Mother, I wasn't thinking about my wedding day, but my wedding *night*.

Alleia giggles and her mother even manages a smile.

Prima turns to the man. – Epaphroditus, only the finest perfume, you hear?

He nods enthusiastically and proffers another bottle.

'I collected this in Alexandria, made from jasmine blossoms...'

Epaphroditus,
slave of Novius, perfumer
from the Via Sacra, was here 121

Celadus is a little amused by all of this. To a man used to a bare existence in the gladiatorial barracks, such opulence seems a little preposterous. But who he is to question the behaviour of those who put money in his pocket? He looks towards the tablinum and sees that the folding doors at each end have been drawn back, affording him a view right through to the peristyle, where numerous others are engaged in similar decorative practices. It is obvious that Gnaeus is absent from his office.

A voice beckons from one of the cubicula off the atrium and he turns to see Primus standing at the door, gesturing for him to approach.

– Primus. I'm looking for Alleius Maius.

– He's in the oecus. Trying to escape this.

Celadus smiles.

– Come in here for a moment. I want you to meet someone.

They enter the room, which is illuminated only by light from the doorway. A young man sits at a document-covered table. He rises. Celadus knows his face. He has seen him about town, mostly in bars.

– Celadus, this is Restitutus. Vibius Comicius Restitutus.

Restitutus's head inclines a fraction. Celadus recognises the recognition.

– And this is Celad...

– Celadus the Thracian. Champion of Campania.

– It seems your fame has followed you beyond the arena, Celadus.

Primus says this a little enviously. He is a trifle vexed that Restitutus displayed no obvious thrill at meeting *him*, who is regarded as the finest accountant in Pompeii.

Celadus for his part has moved far beyond the point of treasuring such things as balms to soothe his ego. A different world beckons.

– I am no longer champion.

He says this more coldly than he meant. A brief silence falls, broken by Primus.

– Anyway, Restitutus here has been employed by our dominus as my assistant in financial and legal matters. I'll be training him over the coming months. I thought you should know in case you mistakenly thought him an assassin and beheaded him or something.

Primus produces a burst of laughter. Restitutus makes a half-hearted effort to share it.

Celadus forces a smile. – Good to meet you. I must be about my business with Alleius Maius.

He leaves. It takes but a handful of seconds to walk to the closed door of the oecus, but in that time he is bombarded by a confusion of thoughts. If only he could keep hold of some parts of his old life and discard others. Fame he now understands as fleeting, its currency worth only a quick fuck and a night's drinking. But it gave him pride in who he was. But as what? As a brute who hacked at fellow beings for sport, occasionally taking their lives. No, there was more. There was honour. And courage. Does he retain those? He desperately wishes that he could pluck some things from the past and take them with him, leaving the rest behind, as though he were simply selecting fruits he liked from a market stall.

He knocks on the oecus door and an irritated voice bids him enter.

– Oh it's you. Come in and close the door.

Poor Gnaeus. Three baskets of scrolls are lined up on the table. A number of other scrolls are unwound before him, held flat by a weight in a poor likeness of Jupiter and another of his brother, Neptune. Gnaeus's hair is ruffled, almost wild, and his tunic hangs untidily to one side.

He gestures to a stool. – Sit, Celadus. I thought you were another of those fucking tailors or some other fool. I've never seen such fuss over a simple wedding garment. And listen to the noise!

He waves a hand above his head. Thirty or more voices murmur from beyond the door and from behind the shuttered window at Gnaeus's back.

– I'll never get this complete in time.

– May I ask what is the problem, Dominus?

– That bastard Epidius is the problem. He had Suedius Clemens dig around in some of my property deals. I have to get a legal challenge underway before the wedding, as I'll be gone for a month after that. I'm taking Prima to Rome.

– Can I help, Dominus?

Abruptly Gnaeus stops moving the documents about and

looks up at Celadus, as though it just occurred to him why the man is here.

– Yes, you can. You can help me with a matter related to all this shit. I've been too soft on that cunt Epidius for too long. It's time I began to deal with the problem. But before that, I just remembered, I have something for you.

He reaches behind him towards a shelf and passes a pouch across the table. Celadus is surprised by its weight. Through the fabric, he recognises the feel of coins sliding against each other. He lifts his eyes in puzzlement.

– The farmer, Caecilius Felix paid up. That's a bonus for you. Two hundred sesterces. You've earned it these past months. Have yourself a good time.

Why, Celadus wonders, does the bag suddenly feel heavier? Something comes to mind. – Dominus.

– Yes?

He hesitates. It occurs to him that his question might make him appear weak. But he gave his word to the farmer's wife. Celadus values his own word far more than the bag of coins in his hand. – Did you...was their ring returned to them?

– What ring?

– The farmer's. I told them it would only be held until he paid.

Gnaeus recalls it after a moment. He laughs. – Oh yes. He asked for it. I'd forgotten it. It wasn't worth that much, but the man was very anxious to get it back. A moment...

He turns and removes a box from the shelf. He fishes about in it.

– Ah. Here it is. Here, you have it. You might get fifty sesterces for it.

Celadus takes the ring. He recalls the dolphin emerging from the surface of the metal, and the tiny jewel clasped in its jaws and how he almost took the farmer's life. He looks away, stares at the wall.

– What's wrong?

He shifts on his chair.

– Forgive me, Dominus, I am very grateful for all you have given me, but... protecting you when you walk the streets with money is one thing, but there is no hono...I take no pleasure in threatening or beating farmers or simple householders.

He expected a sharp rebuke. He is surprised at the evenness of Gnaeus's reply.

– Hmm. The gladiatorial code of honour. I can understand why you are troubled. Unfortunately these things are sometimes necessary. Some of the men in my debt are little more than ruffians and thieves. But I am lenient, Celadus, in comparison to some. Were you employed by Epidius, to name but one, you would be required to draw much more blood. But you may be surprised to learn that one of the reasons I chose to hire you, Celadus, was precisely because you are a man of honour. I want to be paid, but I don't want my tenants and business partners living in terror. That would be counter-productive. But a little fear can be useful. I hired you Celadus, because of the man you are.

Celadus's eyes brighten a little. The weight of his conscience lightens. Gnaeus's speech is a fabrication, of course. You were probably even taken in by it yourself. He is good at that sort of thing. He knows which strings on the puppet to tug. He has always been a master of manipulation.

– Which brings me to the reason I summoned you. I have another task suitable to your skills. Unfortunately it also requires violence. Personally I abhor bloodshed. But occasionally it just becomes a necessary evil.

Celadus looks uncomfortable again. He in not afraid of potential bloodshed, but what new dishonour will be demanded of him. Gnaeus recognises his disquiet and holds up a calming hand.

– I think you'll find this task more to your liking. Do you remember the only fight you lost?

His interest is piqued. He sits up.

– Two years ago, in Puteoli. I was cheated.

– I remember. I was there. Do you recall that the sharper eyed among the crowd saw what had happened and began demanding the fight be stopped?

He nods. – Albanus. He had a dagger concealed beneath his shield. The rules forbid that. You must only fight with the weapons you are allotted. When we grappled he stabbed me in my right side. Had he not I would have defeated him. But he was a good fighter. I see him still about. He mocks me with boasts of his victory. Sometimes I have been tempted to respond, but the pig isn't worth it.

– He's worth something to me, Celadus. He's Epidius's principle enforcer. I've heard tales of some of the things he's done. Murder, rape, torture. A complete thug. I'm giving you the chance to settle the score, Celadus. And there will be a handsome bonus in it for you. I want his head. I've been letting Epidius away with too much for too long and he's grown bolder and bolder because of it. It's been niggling at me and it's long past time I sent him a message he won't forget. I want it done quickly, quietly, tonight. Tomorrow at the latest.

A small problem gets larger
if you ignore it 122

As much as Celadus despises Albanus, the notion of cold-blooded murder is repulsive to him. – You simply want me to kill him? To cut his throat?

Gnaeus shrugs. – I'll leave the details to you. But I want this business done with as soon as possible. I'm to be married in a few days. I have to turn my thoughts to that. Let me know when the deed is done. Any questions, Celadus?

Celadus shakes his head. He departs. He walks though the gaiety of the atrium, bedecked with colour and filled with happy voices.

Celadus sees none of it. He enters the street and turns towards his home. He is making plans of his own.

SCAENA 41

If you want an excuse for delay,
scatter millet and pick it up again [123]

It is a black day for Pompeii. But don't be concerned, nothing of great moment has happened or is about to for that matter. It is what the Romans call a *dies ater*, a day when it is considered unlucky to do a great many things. No council sits, no legal matters are resolved, many businesses close. This particular day is so designated because of a defeat the Romans suffered at the hands of the Gauls four centuries ago. It led to the sack of Rome itself, which is about the worst happening a Roman citizen can possibly contemplate, as they believe such a thing would mean an end to all civilisation.

Some are not so fearful of superstition as others. And there is no law against romance on such a day. Not that either party below would admit that there is a romantic motivation to their presence there, outside the ruined theatre of Pompeii. But come, let us go down and accompany them as they subtly probe each other's shield and try to glimpse the feelings of the other, without leaving their own open to injury. I find it amusing that mortals do battle in this way when it comes to affairs of the heart. It is not so different from when Celadus would fight an opponent in the arena. Each seeks to disarm the other, find a vulnerable spot, and then make their move in the hope that their opponent will submit. It is simply that here words are the choice of weapon.

Now. Here we are. Publius and Cominia will emerge through that archway into the orchestra, directly in front of what remains of the stage. The man high up there on the seating is a public slave called Servulus. The council use him occasionally to take care of what is left of the place, in the vain hope that some day they will have sufficient funds to re-open it. He has been clearing small amounts of debris, pulling weeds, preventing the theft of marble and so on for years now. He sees Publius and Cominia. He calls out, not very loudly, and the sound is funnelled to their ears by the theatre's shape.

Servulus, slave of the colony of Pompeii [124]

– Hey. What are you doing in here? It is not allowed to...

He stops. He has recognised Publius, who he knows is a friend of Saenecio Fortunatus, the former theatre director. Publius has made many melancholic visits here. He would describe them as searches for inspiration. But really he comes here to wallow in self-pity and regret.

– Hello, Servulus.

He waves. It is returned, and then Servulus resumes his thankless labours.

– You see how my voice carried? The design of this theatre is the finest outside Rome.

– What a pity there is no money to rebuild it.

Cominia turns full circle, taking in the seating and then the stage, topped with a scaenae frons that is missing much of its top half. Most of it lies about her feet. Publius steps up on to a large chunk of concrete that lies in his path, jumps down the other side. Cominia lifts her long tunic to follow and you'll notice his eyes drop for a moment to capture a glimpse of her bare leg. He lifts them before she notices, then offers his hand. She takes it and jumps down on to the dusty ground again. His grip on her fingers lingers a little longer than necessary. Cominia is tempted to allow it, to see what might progress from that simple touch, but instinct prevents her and she withdraws her hand sharply. Publius is a little abashed. He quickly looks up at the stage. He struggles for something to say. Now Cominia feels regret that her action was too reproachful and decides to soften the blow by speaking.

– So you might have spent the past ten years here instead of as a baker.

He continues to stare at the scaenae frons.

– The gods decided otherwise.

– Do you honestly believe that? That it was the will of the gods?

He shrugs. – Who knows? Perhaps it is arrogant to think I'm even be in the gods' thoughts.

Cominia wipes sweat from her brow. It is late afternoon and the sun still illuminates a small pool of space where they stand.

– Come on. Let's sit in the shade.

They walk across the orchestra to the tiers of seats. They climb to the third tier, which is in the shade, and sit facing the stage.

– These are the bisellia. I've never been so honoured.

Publius bows and waves his hand theatrically. – Only the finest seats for my girl...for my guest.

His attempt at humour has brought him to another awkward pass. He blushes, coughs. Cominia once more tries to move things along. She slaps the hard concrete.

– Yes, but I'm sure the duumviri and aediles don't have to sit on hard stone. Where is my cushion? I wouldn't want to sit here for three hours.

– Even if it were Sophocles 'Lemniai'?

– Well, perhaps then.

This is Cominia and Publius's third outing, not including the time that Prima invited Cominia over to dinner. Publius had found the entire evening excruciating as his mother had continually made less than subtle attempts to play Cupid between them. Cominia had also been a little embarrassed, but amused at Publius's discomfiture. Both other evenings had been trips to the theatre at Herculaneum, a regular pilgrimage for Pompeians these past years. Yet the theatre rules, more strictly enforced than those in the amphitheatre, forced them to be separated and their journeys to and from the town had been filled only with discussions of long dead Greek playwrights, the performances of Paris the actor, the merits of the staging and so on. Neither dared to venture a personal inquiry, or to share the touch of each other's bodies in even the most minimal way. Both want to delve deeper into the other. Both are afraid of the same for different reasons. Cominia is wary of most men, a legacy of her past. Publius is fearful of failure and humiliation.

– I wonder what it would have been like, sometimes.

– Is this why you come? To dream of what might have been?

– I don't know. Perhaps.

– What is the point of that?

He briefly glances sideways at her. Her gaze doesn't meet his, but is fixed on the stage. He is a little irked at her apparent criticism. His tone becomes defensive. – With the struggle to keep the bakery going, I don't have much else.

– I don't believe in considering what might have been. Only in shaping my own future as best I can.

– Fortuna has been kind to you.

Now it is her turn to raise her shield. She turns her body towards him.

– Hard work has been kinder. I earned everything I have.

– Are you saying *I* haven't worked hard?

– No, of course not! I'm saying that...oh this is pointless.

Both fall quiet. They stare ahead. The theatre seems to amplify their silence. Eventually Publius speaks.

– I will be glad when these weddings are done with.

Cominia is pleased with the change of subject. – It is the talk of Pompeii. I've heard rumours that Alleius Maius has spent ten thousand sesterces on the preparations.

Publius makes a sound of disgust.

– What is it? Don't you like weddings?

– Such excess irritates me.

– But surely you must be pleased for your mother and your sister? They both seem very happy about it.

He shrugs. – I suppose I am pleased for them. Although I have my doubts about Cornelia's husband-to-be. Not to mention my mother's. Gnaeus Alleius Maius. There's something about the man I don't like. Mind you, I am grateful to him for taking Restitutus off my hands before I killed him.

– Perhaps you're simply jealous of Alleius Maius.

– Of his wealth? I don't begrudge anyone their wealth.

– I didn't mean that. I meant the fact that he's found a woman he loves to spend the rest of his days with.

He stares at her. Again she doesn't meet his gaze. Cominia has granted him an opportunity, a small lowering of her shield. He must strike before her defences are fully restored. He laughs, ridiculing the notion, but there is no heart in the sound. – That's complete nonsense.

She remains silent. Publius turns his head away for a moment and fills his chest with air. He returns his gaze to her. He is looking at the side of her face that is unscarred. He is suddenly taken with its beauty. Its perfection. He knows there is a side to her that has been scarred by the past, and he wonders what secrets that beautiful head holds. He wants to know more. And he suddenly wants her. Physically. It is a desire so intense and unexpected that he cannot explain. He is shocked to realise that he has an erection. Its intensity makes it almost painful. He drops his hands over his crotch. Attempts to make the gesture appear casual.

She turns abruptly towards him. – Why are you staring at me?

He coughs. – I'm sorry. I wanted to ask, as we were discussing the wedding, if you would do me the honour of accompanying me. To the celebrations, I mean. In three days. If you have the time. If you wouldn't mind.

She seems to ponder. – I've never been to a rich man's wedding. It will probably be gaudy and excessive. And then there's the cost of new dress...

She laughs at the sight of his wilting expression. – But I'd like to. It should be interesting.

– Thank you.

He says this as though she has handed him a fabulous gift. She grins – You're welcome.

The allure of her smile only makes his penis grow harder. He is desperate to conceal it beneath the folds of his tunic. He contrives to divert his own attention. He searches for small talk, although he is fearful of losing the openness they shared fleetingly.

– So. How goes business at the inn?

To his surprise she responds with enthusiasm. – Very well. Better than I could have dreamed. Even when there are no games or festivals I am usually full. Most of the guests are wealthy merchants or traders who come in through the port. It is strange, but Pompeii has been booming since the earthquake. I have heard stories about other places where similar catastrophes have happened. Property is suddenly cheap and many new people with money arrive to take advantage. There is much rebuilding. The port thrives, bringing in supplies to support it. And the government in Rome provided a fortune towards reconstruction. Ten years on and the place is almost back on its feet, but there is still lots to be done. Like the work here in the theatre. I am already thinking of expanding the Inn of Cominia Lucilla. There is a small vacant premises adjoining mine and when I have the capital I hope to buy it. It would provide me with six more rooms and there may even be space enough for another bath suite. That is what really brings in the wealthy customers, I think.

Publius laughs at the fervour of her response. – You have other passions besides the theatre, obviously.

– Yes, many.

She says this in a way that was unintended. It is vaguely suggestive. Although some of her passions are unfulfilled. Now she begins to feel a blush rise and hurries on to conceal it.

– But I must be cautious. I used most of my capital in establishing the inn and it is paying well, but I need an investor now.

– Perhaps you should ask my future father-in-law.

Publius says this in jest.

She responds as though it were a serious suggestion. – I considered that. But he would soon gobble up the entire thing. Men like him are driven to own more and more. I'm sure he'd want to push me out sooner or later and I want to keep control for myself.

Publius, who is relieved that his erection is finally fading, makes another attempt at humour. – There's always Epidius.

She touches her fingers to her lips and stares at the ground, deep in thought. Publius, a little startled that she might be considering such a thing, raises hand towards her as though to awaken her from her musings.

– Cominia. I was joking. Epidius is the last....

She looks at him. – What about you?

He is completely shocked. He stands. – Me? Where do you imagine I might get the money to invest in your inn?

She shrugs. – You've told me how much you hate the bakery.

– But I don't own it! I don't own the building, I mean. Epidius does.

– And has he no interest in getting the lease back? I'm sure it is worth a lot.

Understanding dawns. Then anger crosses his face. – Cornelia! What else has she told you? That is private family business. I'll kill her!

The look on Cominia's face makes him retract. – I mean, that's only an expression. But I'm very angry with her.

– Actually, it was your mother who mentioned the possibility.

– Wait a moment. Have you two cooked this little scheme up between you?

Cominia stands and faces him, suddenly furious. – No! I put your business from my mind moments after I heard it. It simply occurred to me now to propose it. I thought it might serve both our purposes.

He starts to turn away. She grasps his arm.

– And understand this. What I am proposing is merely a business arrangement. Nothing more. Don't be so arrogant as to think anything else!

He who hates, loves 125

It seems Cupid has departed again. Perhaps Mars is sticking his nose into this little encounter.

– You're the arrogant one! Assuming to tell me that I have failed in the bakery business and that I would be better off as a partner in your business!

– Perhaps it was a mistake to suggest it. People as stubborn as you rarely make good business partners.

– *I'm* stubborn? Look who's talking!

– You *are* stubborn. I didn't say you failed in the bakery business. But Epidius is making it impossible to succeed. Why do you keep putting off the inevitable? Why do you keep fighting him? Is it something personal? He's made a good offer for the lease, or so your mother told me. Why are you so desperate to make yourself miserable?

– I'm not miserable!

– Don't make me laugh!

Publius brings his face close to hers. In his dreams when they stand like this, a passionate kiss is what follows, and then much more. But now his lips spout anger.

– You don't know the first thing about me.

He whirls away and stands with his back to her. Cominia's fists are clenched by her sides. He mouth is closed tightly as though attempting to contain further words of rage. She is about to leave.

Applause startles them. A single pair of hands clap with enthusiasm. Both spin on their soles to stare up at the seats high in the theatre. A lone, bearded man sits there. Servulus the slave is nowhere to be seen.

– The finest drama I have witnessed here in ten years. Mind you, it is the only drama I have witnessed here in ten years. But it was very illuminating nonetheless.

Publius recognises the man immediately.

– Saenecio. Do you always eavesdrop private conversations?

Saenecio, begins to descend, tier by tier. He spreads his arms wide. He bears a large scroll in one hand. – This is my theatre.

Well, it belongs to Rome, but it is still in my care. If you have private business to conduct, why do you do it here? It is my right to know everything that goes on here.

Cominia looks at the ground. Publius turns his head this way and that. Both are acutely embarrassed. They wait in silence until he has descended to their level. He heaves a few breaths.

– Age is starting to take its toll.

He is correct. Yet he still retains some of the air of charisma from the day when Publius first encountered him a decade ago.

He looks at Cominia, then turns to Publius.

– Well, are you going to introduce me?

Publius sighs. – This is Cominia Lucilla. And this is Saenecio Fortunatus, theatre director.

Saenecio Fortunatus, salutations,
wherever you may go 126

He leans towards Publius, claps a hand on his shoulder, and whispers loud enough for Cominia to hear. – You have chosen well, lad. A walking Venus.

Publius is horrified. He starts to explain.

– No, you're mistak....

But Saenecio has cut him off. He pushes between them and bends over the seats, unrolling the large scroll he carries.

– Listen. I'm glad I met you. I want to show you something. It's very exciting. I've been working on this for months with Herennius Crescens, the architect. He's just left. He's passionate about theatre and is doing this without payment.

He has spread the scroll wide now. He secures it open with a couple of loose bits of concrete, then stands back to afford them a better view. Their conflict is briefly forgotten. They both bend over and inspect it. They are staring at what appears to be a reconstructed scaenae frons, but parts of it are shaded darker than the rest, as though made of a different material. Publius looks back at Saenecio in hopeful anticipation.

– Have you found the funds to re-construct the theatre?

He shakes his head. – Sadly no. Well, not exactly. It's a proposal. But let me show you both.

He leans between them with such eagerness they are both pushed aside. Cominia stares at the strange man then shakes her head and smiles. Saenecio begins to point out different aspect of the drawing.

– You see these darker areas. They are the original parts of the theatre. Herennius Crescens says they are as solid as when they were built. Not even Vulcan could shift them. There lighter parts are constructed of wood.

– Wood?

– Yes, yes, listen. We remove any unstable material and rebuild around the solid parts. The entire structure of the scaenae frons can be rebuilt and supported at the back with these large struts anchored in this space between the rear of the stage and the gladiator barracks. It can be done for a fraction of the cost of rebuilding entirely. Then all we would have to do is clear away the rest of the large rubble, put supports in a couple of archways and the theatre could be open again in just three months.

– It would still cost a lot of money, Saenecio.

– Yes, but nothing compared to the cost of re-building, as I said. I am very hopeful that if the council doesn't support it, some benefactor might. Perhaps your new father-in-law. He again slaps Publius on the shoulder.

Publius stares at the plans again, then turns and gazes up above the stage. Cominia watches him. Her anger is receding. It has been overwhelmed by Saenecio's eagerness. At least for the moment.

Saenecio sits and contemplates Publius's back.

– You have given me little in the way of new work this past year, Publius.

Cominia also sits, her interest aroused. Publius turns and realises he is the focus of their attentions.

– With the bakery to run it has always been difficult, Saenecio, you know that. And besides, I am tired of writing stupid comedies to appeal to the rabble that are performed in the forum in front of one hundred people.

Cominia rolls her eyes. She puts on a stupid voice. – Oh, you dirty unwashed plebeians. Keep away. Who's the arrogant one?

Publius frowns at her but doesn't respond. He addresses Saenecio. – You know what I mean Saenecio.

– Well, I am personally grateful to the vulgus for keeping me from starving these past years. And to people such as Alleius Maius for their support. But If you mean you would prefer to challenge the greats with your skills, Publius, this could be your chance.

Publius holds up his hands, palms flat. – I didn't say I could challenge the greats. I couldn't. And besides, even if I could, I still have the bakery.

Saenecio stands and pushes past him. He steps down into the orchestra and strides to its centre.

– Bakery, bakery! It's the only word in your head these days.

– It is easy to mock me, Saenecio. You don't have to deal with the problems I've had.

– I haven't? Are you mad? Who do you think pays those actors in the forum plays? Who do you think begs and crawls to everyone within twenty miles for money to stage productions? Don't tell me about your problems. But do you know what I think your real problem is, Publius?

Cominia crosses her arms. She is enjoying this little discussion.

– What? Tell me?

Saenecio doesn't appear angry. He actually has a satisfied grin on his face. It is as though he knows the solution to a puzzle.

– You've been putting off applying yourself to playwriting for years not because you haven't time, but because you are afraid of failure.

– Afraid? You have no idea what you're talking about!

– Its true. You are terrified that I will think your work unworthy. Or that even if I like it that the audience will not. That they'll mock you. Laugh at your efforts in the streets. Point you out. Snigger. There's that stupid baker who thought he could write. That's it, isn't it?

Publius turns his head from both of them.

– That's nonsense.

Cominia and Saenecio exchange a subtle smile.

– You know Publius, immortality is a big prize, and a man can achieve it in many ways. As a general, an emperor, a politician, a gladiator or as a playwright. But each carries dangers and if you're not prepared to face them, then you've no right to aspire to the prize.

Publius looks to the heavens. – You don't understand. If you knew what I...

Cominia sighs, rises. – I must go.

She steps down into the orchestra and gestures a farewell to Saenecio. – It was good to meet you. I hope you are successful with your plans. I'll go now while it is still bright.

Publius is taken aback at her decision to depart so suddenly. The visions he entertained earlier of accompanying her back to her inn and being invited inside for a more intimate farewell have rapidly vanished like steam in the breeze.

– But I'll take you, Cominia.

She waves him away. – No, stay here. Talk with Saenecio. You have much to discuss.

She begins to walk towards the exit tunnel, clambering over a couple of pieces of rubble. Publius wonders if this is a rejection of him. A final one, perhaps. He curses himself. He should never have started that stupid argument about business. He suddenly recalls the invitation he made to the wedding. – Cominia. What about the wedding? Are you still coming?

She stops and looks at him as though puzzled. – Why? Have you withdrawn the invitation?

– Of course not.

– I assume you'll collect me?

– Of course.

– Then I'll look forward to defeating you in another argument.

Publius doesn't know whether to be relieved, joyous or furious.

Cominia exits stage left, knowing precisely how she has left him, and wearing the mask that smiles.

SCAENA 42

Learn this: while I am alive, you,
hateful death, are coming ₁₂₇

It's difficult to see Celadus lurking there in the deep recess of
that doorway. That is his intention. But even without my help, if
you look hard enough the moonlight proves just sufficient to
distinguish his vague outline.

He has had a long day. And that following from a similar one
yesterday, when he met with Gnaeus. He has spent all that time
wandering the bars and brothels of this town. One end to the
other. The bar of Athicus, Verecundus, Salvius. And twenty
others. You might imagine that he has been spending freely
from the bonus provided by his master, enjoying the intoxi-
cating diversions of wine and the company of whores, trying to
divert his troubled mind, but you would be wrong. Not a drop of
wine has passed his lips and the only company he's had is his
own. He's been in search of Albanus, the only gladiator to defeat
him. Of course he has put that life behind him now, so does the
defeat really matter any more? There are but a handful of souls
in this world who even remember the battle. Were it not for the

task he has been given, he probably would have pushed the matter from his memory. New challenges await. The prospect of a different life. Idaia.

And yet, he considers that Fortuna surely had a hand in this. Perhaps the gods were unhappy to be denied the prayers he would have offered to them in thanks had he claimed victory that day. And now they are giving him the opportunity to set matters straight. But why did the gods allow him to be defeated if that is the case, only to later present him this chance? He cannot reconcile the celestial manoeuvrings in his mind. But who is he to question their ways? All that matters is that he is here now.

A girl passes. She gets no sense of his presence. His breathing is low and even. He feels calm. He watches as she strolls along the Via di Mercurio, moving towards the dim light escaping through the shutters of the Bar of Mola, perhaps hoping to pick up a customer who has been given to melancholy by the effects of wine and seeks solace in the arms of a woman. The girl knows it is a common occurrence. She is fifty paces away, across the street from the bar, watching its door. Celadus curses under his breath.

Time moves on. He sees the moon drift across the sky to a backdrop of countless stars. Voices grasp his attention. The door to the bar has opened and two men stagger out.

Mola the Fucktress ₁₂₈

He sees the bar's owner, Mola, framed in the orange glow from the lamps within. She shouts something after the men. She's an ex-whore herself. Left a tidy sum in a will by a devoted customer. Opened her own bar. Mola watches as the girl opposite approaches the men, offer herself to them, but they are too drunk and irritable. When the girl persists one of them pushes her to the ground. She curses after them and then returns to her spot. Mola shakes her head and thanks the gods that that life is done with. The door closes.

Celadus is becoming restless now. Two hours have passed since he watched Albanus enter the place. He doesn't want the man drunk. But he has a huge frame and can consume large quantities of wine before it has any noticeable effect.

The door opens again.

– I'm closing up, Albanus. Go home, Mola cries.

Celadus hears the man protest. Then he sees him. Albanus steps backwards into the street but paws at Mola. He is fully double her bodyweight. She pushes him away.

– I thought you preferred boys, Albanus. And I'm not a whore anymore! But look, there, you're in luck.

Albanus is a sodomite 129

Mola points at the girl across the street. Albanus turns his head and Mola seizes the opportunity to close and bolt the door. The ex-gladiator's curses follow her into the room. But now he turns again and the girl approaches. Celadus watches as Albanus walks the few paces to meet her in the middle of the street. He is steady on his feet. Celadus listens.

– Are you looking for love, big man?

Love is the last thing she offers, but it brings a grin to his face. The girl briefly pulls apart her clothing and reveals generous breasts, white in the moonlight. But the glimpse Albanus has been granted is but an inducement.

– How much do you cost, bitch?

– Only four sesterces, and my name's Attice.

He laughs aloud.

– What? Are you a whore of noble birth? I'll give you one. And I don't give a fuck what your name is.

Attice turns away. – You must be joking.

He catches her arm. – Hold on. Two then.

– Three.

– Two and two as.

– Agreed.

Her bargaining face disappears and a smile replaces it. In the dark Albanus doesn't notice that she is missing several front teeth. She takes his arm.

– There's a place up here. Just outside the gate.

Albanus laughs. – The dead can watch us and have some fun.

Celadus is pleased that Albanus's voice is even, not slurred.

If anyone sits here, let him read
this first of all: if anyone wants a fuck,
he should look for Attice; she costs 4 sestertii 130

Attice leads Albanus away. Finally Celadus moves. He carries a small bundle made of sacking. Years of training for the arena have given him the skill to move with stealth. He does so now, following the pair along the almost silent streets, their shapes often disappearing amid the blackness, but their footsteps guide him. They exit through the Herculaneum gate. They are never closed unless the threat of war hangs in the air and it has been so long since that happened here that Celadus wonders if the hinges have rusted solid. Huge tombs line the road, much more elaborate than those you saw on that night we visited Cornelia and Atimetus outside the Nucerian Gate. The noble families have lined the way with great monuments to their dead. This is good, thinks Celadus. A fitting place to visit death on a man. And a quiet one. But now, as the act draws near he begins to feel the first real tinglings of fear in his gut. It was always this way in the moments before he entered the arena. He recalls that when he faced the farmer on the mountainside that he felt no such sensation, and realises that this was because that deed demanded no courage. He finds it strange that he welcomes the fear. It has been absent too long from his life.

This is a favoured spot for the girls. And Attice has a liking for the tomb of Mamia, once a priestess of Isis, the favoured goddess of prostitutes, among others. She believes, she hopes, that here the spirit of Mamia will protect her from potential violence.

The tomb is impressive, is it not? Oh, you find it difficult to see in the moonlight. It takes the shape of a large semi-circular stone seat, the design chosen by the priestess herself so that those still living could sit here and contemplate their lives with her guiding spirit nearby. She was beloved of the whole town, a great benefactor, and the council rewarded her in death with this expensive monument. The inscription reads:

MAMIA, DAUGHTER OF PUBLIUS, PUBLIC PRIESTESS. THE PLACE OF BURIAL WAS GIVEN BY DECREE OF THE DECURIONES [131]

Albanus naturally has no interest in this. He pushes the girl towards the stone seat.

Celadus hears the rattle of coins as fees are paid. He creeps closer. He has no prurient desires to witness the act, simply to gauge the area for what is to come. He ventures a glance around another tomb and sees them; two dark shapes against the sky. The girl sits and Albanus kneels, fumbling with his clothes. Celadus draws back out of sight and listens to their grunts and Attice's feigned moans of pleasure. He is concerned at her presence. He does not want any witnesses. But he is not prepared to kill her.

He doesn't have to wait long. He hears Albanus's final outburst and his voice collapsing in heaving breaths. He listens as silence settles. After a while there is the rustling of clothing.

– You were a lousy fuck. You weren't worth a quadran.

– Fuck you, you bastard.

Celadus hears a slap and a startled yelp. By now his nerves are on fire. He grits his teeth.

A moment later Attice hurries past clutching at her face. A movement draws her attention to her left. She looks. Sees him there. Gasps. Celadus flicks his head, indicating she should be gone. She needs no further encouragement. He reaches into the sack he carries and withdraws two swords, something he could not carry in plain sight as he toured the bars earlier. And yes, I said *two* swords.

He walks out into the road and stands facing Albanus, who now sits where the girl had moments before. It occurs to Celadus that the flat space surrounded by the stone seat resembles a tiny arena, or at least a half an arena. He smiles at the appropriateness.

Albanus sees the shape standing there. He stands sharply.

Albanus, left hander, free, nineteen victories [132]

There is a loud clang of metal as a short sword lands at Albanus's feet.

This will not be the quick murderous thrust from behind expected by Gnaeus. He betrayed his own honour once when commanded to kill his opponent by Alleius Maius in the arena. Not this time, he thinks. And besides, his master had said that he would leave the details to him. The details will involve one final battle in the arena. Celadus steps up from the road on to the tomb space.

– Albanus.

– Who the fuck are you?

– Celadus the Thracian.

Albanus recognises him now. Recognises also his stance. Knees bent, arms wide, sword in hand, circling slowly to his left. He hesitates no longer. He seizes the sword from the ground and readies himself.

– I've no quarrel with you.

You can hear the fear in his voice.

– You robbed me of victory at Puteoli. Don't you recall?

They continue to circle.

– And now you've come for revenge? Are you mad?

– Perhaps.

Celadus swings and Albanus deflects the blow. Another comes. And another. Without shields they must keep their distance. They dance about the space. Albanus aims a swipe at Celadus's head, but he pushes it high with his sword and delivers a punch to his opponent's stomach. The man staggers away quickly before Celadus can bring down his sword.

– You've waited two years for this? We're done with the fucking arena, for Jupiter's sake!

This is spoken through heaving breaths. It sounds to Celadus like a plea for mercy. He isn't feeling merciful. He launches forward again. Five blows are deflected but Albanus retreats constantly. He takes a wild swing and misses Celadus completely. The Thracian uses the moment to aim a thrust at Albanus's face, but the man tilts his head in time and the blade merely cuts across his ear. He screams and stumbles back off the raised area into the road. He sprawls on his back. Celadus follows him. He plants his sandal on Albanus's arm as he goes to lift his sword then allows himself to fall so his other knee lands squarely on his opponent's chest. The wind is squeezed out of Abanus's lungs with a grunt.

He is beaten. Celadus holds the tip of the sword to his heart.

– As it should have been at Puteoli. Had you not cheated me, you cowardly shit.

– Don't Celadus. You're right. You're the better man. Spare me!

Celadus is thinking now of that final day in the arena, when he was ordered to kill a man he had at his mercy and whom he should have spared. Events have repeated themselves. He wonders if this was Fortuna's real intent. To give him the chance to redeem that act by sparing this man. But what of his orders? What can he tell his master? Will it be the end of his position?

While his thoughts occupied him, Albanus has withdrawn a blade from within his tunic. He thrusts it into Celadus's side.

Celadus responds with an enraged thrust. There is a brief, shocked grunt as Albanus's heart is cloven in two. He is no more.

Such violence.

Celadus staggers to his feet, clutching his left side. He curses. He has been fooled again by precisely the same ploy. But this time Albanus paid with his life. Pain courses through his side and blood seeps through his fingers. Yet his work is not yet done.

We will leave him to it for a while.

Come back here, towards the gate. There is but one other small drama to witness, one of no real consequence, except that it serves to enlighten a little.

You can see her there, hiding behind a tomb. Attice has been watching with fascinated horror. She watches still as Celadus drags Albanus's body out of sight. It will not be discovered for days.

Now the man approaches. He clutches at his side. She wonders if she should flee or try to remain out of sight. He carries no swords now, just the sack dangling from his right arm.

Celadus found a pouch about Albanus's neck. He didn't count the money, but experience told him there were maybe fifty sesterces inside. Fifty sesterces, yet he argued with the whore over a matter of a couple of as. But Celadus is no thief. Even if the victim has no more use for currency. As he passes the spot where Attice cowers his eyes flit ever so briefly in her direction. He tosses the money pouch towards her into the shadows and continues on his way.

SCAENA 43

Hail, profit! [134]

Faustilla sits opposite her master in the small oecus off the tablinum. It is a windowless room and having just stepped in from the atrium, her eyes struggle to adapt to the dim lamplight. Epidius is seated sideways to her on the other side of a table. He doesn't appear to be doing anything besides staring into space.

– Publius Comicius Restitutus is here, Dominus.

Epidius stares at her for a moment. Then he becomes alert and smiles.

– Ah Publius. I'd almost forgotten. Perhaps our efforts have been successful. Gavius Rufus will be most pleased if that is the case.

– Will I show him into the tablinum, Dominus?

– No, no. Here will be fine.

Epidius sometimes prefers to conduct business in this small, dark room. It makes his guest uneasy, he believes, and eager to be gone, which works to his advantage.

Faustilla returns with Publius. She doesn't bother announcing him.

– Leave us.

Faustilla fixes Publius with a hostile glance as she exits and closes the door behind her.

– Please sit, Publius.

He gestures to a chair. Epidius looks like a black shadow to him, having just come in from the morning sunlight. He has to fumble to find the stool. He sits. He is uncomfortable on many levels. He despises himself for submitting to Epidius's intimidation. He feels he has been a failure at business. He believes he has let his dead father down. And yet, he knows the others are probably right. He recalled his suspicion that Epidius might have somehow been involved in the death of his first wife, Curtia, but ultimately convinced himself that the suspicion was guided by how own paranoia, and his willingness to ascribe any evil event to Epidius.

He will be better off done with this man. Although he will always despise him. Yet he hasn't come here to bow and plead. He intends to salvage at least some of his pride.

– Well, what can I do for you?

– The message I sent was clear. You know well why I'm here, Epidius.

– Oh yes. You wish to reconsider the offer I made to you.

– You want my lease returned. I am willing to hear any reasonable offer.

Epidius sits forward, leans his arms on the table.

– But I've already made a very generous offer. And since then I've had cause to consider withdrawing it. Another suitable property may soon become available. I may have no further need of yours.

Publius laughs. – The price of property in Pompeii has been rising for years. I seriously doubt you'll be able to find another as large as mine for so little cost. And why bother when you already own my bakery building?

– You display a limited knowledge of the world of real estate. But that aside, by any measure my offer was more than generous.

– By your measure, perhaps. But I could easily find an advocate that could plead my case before an aedile, and let him make the judgement. That's my right.

Epidius throws his hands up. – Oh by Vulcan's dick, do you really want to get into advocates arguing before the courts? Why not settle this...

– My father negotiated a thirty-year lease. Eleven years still outstanding, as I said. Were this any normal bakery, one not subject to intimidation, it is reasonable to expect an annual profit of five thousand sesterces. Any aedile looking at the figure would agree. That puts me at a loss of fifty-five thousand sesterces if I hand back the lease. You offered ten, plus the write-off of my loan, worth another four and a half. I also have to consider that I have four paid employees, friends, who would be left without income. Generous? I think not.

Epidius is a little surprised at Publius's spunk. He expected this to be a simple matter of signing documents. He is irritated, but grudgingly admiring nonetheless. – That is based on the premise that your business would be a success. You have shown little ability to make it so. It might well go broke next year or the year after.

– People will always need bread. And ours is the best. The business was fine until y...until someone started interfering in our dealings. I can make an aedile aware of all of these matters if you wish.

Epidius slams a fist on the table. – Stop threatening me with a public hearing. I assure you it would be a mistake. Don't fucking forget who you're dealing with here, baker.

Publius feels the threat in his gut. He knows this man would have him killed as easily as he might drink a cup of wine. But that would be awkward and messy. And could be dangerous now that – and he is loath to concede it – he is about to be an honorary member Alleius Maius's family. He holds his nerve. His voice doesn't waver.

– Are you prepared to make a better offer?

Epidius seems to grow calm. He sits back in his chair. Stares at Publius.

– Twelve thousand, plus the debt written off.

Publius starts to rise and turn. – We're wasting our time.

– You're making a mistake!

– Goodbye, Epidius.

– Thirteen, that's it.

– Fifteen.

– Fourteen.

Publius sits again. – Fourteen plus the debt. Agreed?

A sigh. – Agreed.

Epidius reaches a hand across the table. Publius stares down at it as though it were a venomous snake. He is thinking that this man has had a hand in much of his family's misfortune. He meets Epidius's eye.

– Let's just draw up the papers and be done, Epidius.

Epidius withdraws his hand. – You don't want me as an enemy.

– But you've already chosen to make yourself mine.

Epidius considers him. A smug grin appears. He leans his head back as though looking at the ceiling and suddenly yells. – Faustilla! Apelles!

A moment later the two enter the room.

– Faustilla. Send a slave to that idiot notary down the street, what's his name...?

– Stronnius, Dominus?

Stronnius knows nothing 135

– Yes, that's him. The little fat bastard. Tell him Epidius Sabinus requires his presence immediately.

– It is mid-morning business, master, what if he's…

– I don't care if he's having a shit or fucking his slave. Tell him I require him now.

– Yes, Dominus.

Epidius is given to these little displays of power, especially before the eyes of those outside his household. He wears them with pride like a woman wears a new silk dress.

– Apelles. Prepare the documents we discussed earlier. We shall sign them in the tablinum.

– Yes, Dominus.

They both depart. Publius and Epidius sit staring at each other in an uncomfortable silence. Yet Publius is pleased with himself. Or at least less dissatisfied. He has negotiated a further four thousand sesterces, and while his topmost thoughts are that he can release his staff with a decent pay-off, beneath these the satisfaction derives mostly from having extracted it from Epidius. It is a small victory of sorts.

– Some wine, perhaps, to seal the agreement?

– No. Thank you.

Publius's eyes drift to the fresco on the wall to his right depicting a bearded god holding a golden sword on an anvil with a tongs, while he fashions its shape with a hammer. The tip of the sword glows red.

Epidius offers enlightenment. – Hephaestus.

– Son of Zeus and Hera. God of blacksmiths, craftsmen, sculptors and the like.

– You are well read. A theatre lover, of course. Perhaps a writer even, some day. I hope your plays are better than your attempts at business.

Publius ignores the jibe. – I wonder, why would you have an image of a god worshipped by people engaged in honest work?

Epidius does not rise to the insult. He grins.

– But Hephaestus is also the one who forges all of the weapons for the other gods in Olympus. I like to think I have a large arsenal of weapons at my disposal, purely for my own defence, of course.

– Perhaps that is your plan for my bakery? The manufacture of weapons.

He laughs. – Swords? Spears? No. But weapons come in many forms. Some are made of steel, some of paper. And money is the greatest weapon of all. And I hope the building your bakery occupies will be turned into an enterprise that makes a lot of it.

– What is it?

He shrugs. – No reason I can't tell you. An acquaintance of mine, Gavius Rufus, wishes to make an investment. I am a co-investor. It will be only modestly profitable initially, but wait a few years and it will be worth more than you can dream of.

Gavius Rufus, a good man 136

Epidius waits for Publius to inquire further. He doesn't. He actually has no real interest. He simply wishes to fill the silence until he can be gone. But Epidius cannot help himself.

– There are more than twenty rooms in your bakery. Gavius Rufus plans to convert it into a first class brothel. The best in Pompeii. It's very convenient too. Located near the Spectacula and the market they hold on the Palaestra. Will do a roaring trade.

Publius doesn't know whether he is amused or revolted by the idea of his home being rented out for sex.

– A brothel? You hounded me out so that you could open a fucking *brothel*?

– Hounded you out? I have no idea what you mean. But there's more to it than that. Are you aware that there's a huge shortage of slaves in the empire? There hasn't been any real expansion since Britain was conquered over thirty years ago. Of course there are the privateer raids that bring in a trickle of slaves, but not enough to cope with the demand. Just recently I had to purchase a boy of twelve to replace a slave of mine, Felix, who, who unfortunately died. It cost me over seven thousand sesterces.

Publius is intrigued by where this is going.

– What does all that have to do with a brothel?

Epidius lifts his eyes to the heavens as though Publius is too stupid to see the opportunity.

– When whores get pregnant they usually abort the child. Ours won't. They'll be kept and raised by a few older whores who are past fucking. They'll be fed, kept healthy, educated even. As the demand grows the prices will become even greater. Have you any idea how much a healthy boy or girl of five or six will fetch? I'd estimate ten thousand. Fuck, you'd even sell a four year old for seven or eight. Oh I know it will put the whores out of commission for several months each year, but even then the place will still turn a tidy profit.

Epidius leans back with pride. – In six or seven years, allowing for some of the little bastards dying, we'll have twenty or thirty boys or girls to sell each year. Even being pessimistic, that's two hundred thousand sesterces every year. Compare that to the pathetic five thousand you earlier boasted you could make. It's a long-term investment, as I said. But I'm still young. I can afford to wait.

Publius looks bewildered. He doesn't know what to make of the scheme. He has no moral objection to the concept of slavery – every society in this time accepts it as a fact of life – but he is disturbed by the notion of breeding children like animals for sale.

As am I. I am the goddess of childbirth, as you know. Perhaps it would be better, and a great deal kinder, if I left those little mites to smother in their mother's womb. Maybe I will.

Publius shakes his head. – You're right. It is more money that I could ever imagine possessing. What do you plan to do with it all?

Epidius looks confused by the question.

– What do you mean?

– Do with it. How do you plan to spend it?

Epidius gestures vaguely with both hands. His reply is less impassioned than his prideful explanation of his scheme. It is even a little deflated.

– I have no idea. Who cares?

There is a knock on the door. Apelles enters.

– The notary is here, Dominus. And a delivery.

Publius is relieved. As he rises he considers that the motivations of men like Epidius and Gnaeus, whose sole ambition in life is to acquire more with no discernible goal other than that, is as bewildering to him as ever.

They emerge into the tablinum, which adjoins the small oecus. The curtains have been drawn at either end and light spills in from the atrium and the peristyle. A short, rotund man in a good-quality tunic (donned hurriedly for this meeting) stands at the far side of the table, inspecting the documents. He seems nervous. Faustilla stands behind him. A large box wrapped in sacking also sits to one side of the table.

– Stronnius. Thank you for coming on such short notice.

Epidius thanks are laden with sarcasm. He knows that poor Stronnius wouldn't dare refuse. He sits. Epidius completes the various contracts and shows them to Publius, who nods. Stronnius witnesses the dealings and all sign. Epidius completes the legalities by stamping each document with the ring on his middle finger.

– That's it then. Your money will be paid in two sums, one tomorrow, the other when you vacate the premises on the Kalends of Augustus.

– That's it then.

– What is this?

Epidius is pointing to the box by the edge of the table.

Apelles replies. – It arrived at the same moment as Stronnius. It was delivered by a slave boy. There was no message with it. I assumed it was related to this business, Dominus.

Epidus shrugs. He lifts it. It is heavy. Not documents. He takes a small papyrus knife from the table and cuts away the sacking. A wooden box. Sealed with wax. He is mystified. A small latch fastens the lid. He flicks it open. The top swings back on a hinge.

Epidius emits a short, horrified yelp and leaps to his feet, pushing himself back from the table. In it lies the severed head of Albanus, whose purple lips sit partially open as though he too is in shock, although his is permanent.

Publius turns his head away. He feels he is going to be sick. Stronnius throws up the hearty breakfast he ate, luckily away from the table. Faustilla walks casually around and stares into Albanus's eyes as though seeking some clue to his death, or perhaps into the afterlife. The waxy white skin on Albanus's face is enough to send Apelles fleeing.

Epidius regains his composure. His mind quickly connects Albanus and the baker's slave boy whose arms he broke. He looks at Publius.

– Have you a hand in this?

Publius is incredulous. – *Me?* I've never seen such a horror? Why do you think that I...but this is madness!

Faustilla speaks. – Dominus. Look. There's something at the side. Papyrus. I will have to lift it to get it out.

She grasps Albanus wild black hair and lifts. As the head emerges from the box Stronnius inches towards the exit.

– I have clients to attend to, Epidius Sabinus. I must be gone.

– Go then. But keep your fucking mouth shut about this!

The man nods fervently and runs across the atrium.

Publius is revolted by the sight of the head dangling not an arm's length from his eyes. He tries to push past Epidius, who blocks his path.

– Linger a moment.

Faustilla lifts the piece of papyrus with her free hand. She reads it.

– 'Former property of Marcus Epidius Sabinus, rightfully returned to the ownership of the state and the care of Titus Suedius Clemens.'

Epidius audibly snarls. – Alleius Maius.

He turns and stares at Publius.

– I have no idea what this is about. I'm leaving.

Epidius stops him with a hand on his chest.

– Coincidence that it arrived at the same moment the deal was completed. You and your new father-in-law make a pretty couple yourselves.

– Get your hands off me! I have no dealings with the man.

Faustilla drops the head back into the box. It lands with a thud, startling the two men. Publius uses the distraction to move around Epidius, who calls after him as he strides across the atrium.

– Publius. Pray to the gods you never receive a box like this yourself.

But Publius doesn't break his stride. He disappears out into the street.

Epidius steps up to the table. He addresses Albanus's unhearing ears.

– You useless cunt.

Faustilla looks at him. – What will I do with it?

– Throw it in the sewer. Where it belongs.

Let one bad thing
be carried off by another 137

SCAENA 44

Nuptiae

Iulius XXX

Lovers, like bees, live a honeyed life
(Then in different handwriting): *I wish* 138

Oh. Where are we now? Who are all these fine people?

There is gay music, laughter abounds, juices and wines are flowing and there is so much merry chatter it sounds like a plague of bees.

We're back in the peristyle of Gnaeus's home, and yes, the big day, or should I say days, have arrived. Two weddings for the price of one. Not that money was a consideration, of course, a fact attested by the awnings above our heads that Gnaeus had erected to protect his guests from the hot summer sun. It is the thirtieth day of Iulius, a day during which Romans honour Fortuna Huiusce Diei, or The Fortune of this Day, and Gnaeus and Prima chose this in the hope that the goddess would smile benignly upon them and upon Cornelia and Atimetus.

Come, let us wander among the guests and see if there is anyone we know.

There is Saenecio Fortunatus, the theatre director, standing near the small fountain in the centre. He has never been officially married, although he's been living with that pretty, flame-haired girl, Noete, an ex-slave, for six years now, which is itself a sort of marriage. He is indulging too heavily in the wine, especially as the day is so young.

And over there under the portico, snacking on honeyed bread is Marcus Lucretius Fronto, the duumvir you met briefly in the tent the day we visited the Spectacula. Notice how happy he appears? He has reason to be as he has just been re-elected to the post of duumvir two days ago, his fourth term, although it shall be his final one. His fellow duumvir also celebrates today, although he will most certainly not be a guest here at the wedding. Marcus Epidius Sabinus. As we speak he hatches plans to exploit his post to the fullest. But let us not talk politics on this day of celebration.

> *If integrity in life is thought to be of any use,*
> *this man Lucretius Fronto is worthy of office* [139]

Peer through the crowd down towards the rear. Standing just inside the exedra beneath the statue of Venus you'll see Cosmus and Epidia, the kind couple who have been helping Staphylus back to health these past months. And there is the lad himself. The swelling on his face has disappeared, but his right arm is still in a sling. The other arm wasn't broken as first feared, although it was badly strained and he has partial use of it again. But something about his face has changed, I think. The bright, youthful optimism and energy has faded. Now he appears wary of everyone. And more envious than ever.

But where are the happy couples and their families, you ask?

We shall meet them very shortly as the first part of this ceremony is about to commence. These things can go on for days. And the richer the groom, the longer it drags.

Come. Let us go inside. The brides are about to arrive. I shall endeavour to explain some of the more important wedding customs.

In the atrium, Gnaeus waits towards the front, with Alleia by his side. He looks nervous. Do you think he might be getting cold feet? No, not a chance. The man has his flaws, and many of them, but he does adore Prima. Always has. The toga he wears is the toga praetexta, brand new, bearing the ruby red trim along its edges. He must be hot in that, you would think. No wonder he has hired all those slaves on either side to fan the guests from one end of the day to the other. But Gnaeus' toga clearly defines him as the man of highest standing present. As has been a practice for centuries, he wears a wreath of flowers in his hair.

And there is Atimetus standing with his father, Tiberius Claudius Verus. Both he and his father wear the plain white toga virilis, the normal dress of choice for formal occasions. Atimetus is trying his best to appear happy, assisted by repeated prods from his father. He is hardly getting a bride to rival Venus in beauty, as he'd always imagined. But he has made his own bed and he must lie in it, alongside Cornelia.

Caius Cuspius Pansa, son of Caius, the son, priest, duumvir with judicial powers [140]

The man with the red cloak over his toga, and with that funny-looking pointed leather skull cap is the priest or flamen. His name is Caius Cuspius Pansa and he's actually of a similar standing to Gnaeus in this town. He's been duumvir several times and he is another beloved of the people as he and his father paid for the restoration of the Spectacula after the earthquake. They'll both be honoured with statues in the forum in the coming years. He doubles as a priest when his business of making money permits. Before we arrived he cut a goat's throat and then gutted it and examined the entrails for bad portents. He saw none and declared that the marriages could proceed, much to everyone's relief. To be honest, even if the poor goat had been filled with maggots he would have declared that things could go ahead, as he wasn't going to be the one to spoil the big day. Priests have to be flexible in interpreting the signs of the gods.

Ah, at last. Something is happening. The men come alert and stand almost to attention. The crowd flock in from the peristyle. Honestly, even Gnaeus's massive atrium is starting to feel crowded. They all fall silent as the citharista and flautists by the impluvium strike up a gentle wedding melody.

If you look along the fauces you can just see a litter, and from it alights Prima, looking quite splendid in her white tunica recta overlaid with a white stola. The knot about her waist is called a Hercules knot, worn so that the spirit of the great legend will guard over their married life. Her face is covered with a thin veil and her hair tied into six braids. A wreath of flowers frames her forehead and besides these, the only colour in her outfit is the flame-red veil about her head and shoulders. Last night she and Cornelia donned the iron rings provided by their prospective husbands, placing them on the finger next to the little finger of the left hand, the nerve of which the Romans believe is connected directly to the heart. They then dedicated small tokens of their past to the household lares. Prima gave up her bulla – a small metal locket containing locks of her parents' hair. Cornelia handed over a cloth doll from her childhood – a symbol that childish things are behind her. But as we know she'd already put childish things behind her by the time she'd climbed on to that tomb with Atimetus.

Prima enters accompanied by a matronly lady called Fortunata, a friend of hers, whose husband Balbus owns a pottery business. She is the pronuba, or what you might call the maid of honour, her qualifications being that she must have been married only once and that her husband is still alive and kicking. She is a living symbol of what they hope Prima's marriage will reflect – a lifetime of wedded bliss. Actually her husband is a bit of a drunk who cheats on her regularly and she has threatened to throttle him in his sleep numerous times, the fact of which Prima is aware. But Prima isn't overly superstitious, and Fortunata is her closest friend, so insisted she play the role.

Behind them approaches Cornelia, with her pronuba, Matrona, with whom she's been friends since they were children. She's considerably prettier, and thinner, than the bride, but that never bothered Cornelia as Matrona would attract the boys and Cornelia was happy to take her cast offs, so to speak.

Matrona has a nice bottom 142

Following closely upon the ladies' heels come the men. Publius and Restitutus enter wearing the toga virilis. They smile, but their efforts at communication, even on this happy day, are strained. They will both be glad to be rid of the other's company. In their wake come a procession of slaves, helper boys and girls who spread rose petals, and various other participants who each have a symbolic function of some fashion. The Romans do love their symbolism.

Cominia Lucilla arrives in a beautiful yellow dress, although not overly ostentatious like some of those we can see. She also wears simple earrings of gold with a solitary pearl dangling from the end. Very tasteful. The innkeeper was an honoured guest of Prima and Cornelia at all of the pre-wedding doings. Indeed, Prima would be very happy for Cominia to end up as a member of the family. But more of that later.

Oh, and there's Vivia, the ageing slave from Publius's house. I point her out only because she is part of the dowry that Prima brought to the marriage. Not much of a dowry, you'd think. I mean, you'd barely fetch fifty sesterces for the poor old dear at the market. But Prima also brought a few thousand sesterces that she'd secreted away over the years, from the times when business was good, and she contributed a couple of thousand to Cornelia's dowry. Publius provided three thousand sesterces, so his sister could leave with a respectable sum and he could continue to hold his head high. Roman law has provided that the ladies will keep ownership of their dowries even if the marriage ends up with the couple throwing household items at each other followed by the divorce courts. But enough of this. It's starting to get interesting.

The flamen approaches, spreads his hands wide and welcomes the brides. He gestures to Gnaeus and Atimetus to stand by their sides. He then proceeds around the impluvium towards the peristyle. The crowds silently part, bowing their heads. The couples and entourage follow, one taking either side of the impluvium and everyone makes their way to the large exedra right at the back of the property. It is going to be almost impossible for everyone to see the proceedings, but I'll take us right to the front.

A statue of Juno stands in the centre of the rear wall. She's the Roman goddess of marriage. Gnaeus purchased her especially for the wedding. Romantic sort, isn't he? Two more statues, Venus and Apollo stand to either side, and a table sits in the centre bearing a large, ornate ceramic bowl. A knife sits to one side and two jars of scented oils.

The flamen turns. The two couples face him, their families

in close attendance. He lifts his eyes to the heavens and begins to chant, the language is Latin, but of an era three centuries in the past and so archaic that only a couple of the very educated guests present have any clue what he is singing about. They catch snatches of words like 'infinite', 'powerful' and 'merciful', along with the names of the gods in Latin and Greek, so they gather the gist of it. Our divine blessings invoked, he reaches and takes Gnaeus's and Prima's right hands and brings them together. He repeats the action with Atimetus and Cornelia. More chanting begins. His eyes and hands are raised skywards. He then summons a group of six young girls bearing candles to surround the couples and himself with their flickering light. He takes the oils from the table and dips his thumb in, then gently rubs a drop from each on all four foreheads. He then finally says something everyone can understand.

– Prima Restituta. Speak the words.

Prima turns her head towards the man she declined in favour of Publius senior twenty years before. Her dead husband's face comes to her now. She has been unable to summon it for many, many years. She is thinking that he was a good man, but a flawed one. She wonders if he is watching her now, thinking this a betrayal. She hopes not. But she has reason to vex him anyway. Good reason. In the moments these thoughts take, Gnaeus and the hundred waiting guests hold their breath. Gnaeus feels a cold drop of perspiration trickle from his under-arm. But then Prima smiles beneath her veil and speaks.

– As you are Gaius, I am Gaia.

The flamen exhales silently in relief and looks to Gnaeus.

– Gnaeus Alleius Nigidus Maius?

There is no hesitation. – As you are Gaia, I am Gaius.

That's the traditional wedding vow, by the way. Gaius has been so common a name in the empire that it now has come to be a generic term for a man, and Gaia a woman, and they are also considered lucky names, luck the couple hope will follow then through life.

Now the priest turns to Atimetus and Cornelia and the rite is repeated. Any possible hesitation on Atimetus's part is banished by a prod in the back from his father. The priest nods to the men and they lift the ladies' veils. Gnaeus is met with a broad smile. He leans forward and kisses Prima gently on the lips.

Atimetus knows there is no going back now. He does battle with his instinct to flee. He knows it would be pointless anyway and would probably only result in his banishment and disinheritance. In that moment, he decides to make the best of the fate he has wrought for himself. He forces himself to be happy. How long it will last is another matter, for he is weak of will. But who knows what the gods have in store for him? He lifts Cornelia's veil and gazes at her plump face. Tears run down her cheeks, which are puffed with joy. He leans forward and kisses her, lingering as long as is decently permitted so that she will believe in his commitment. What he is actually thinking is that at least Cornelia is a good fuck, and that she'll save him money on whores.

All then turn to the crowd who burst into applause. Hands are clasped in congratulation, hugs and kisses exchanged, laughter abounds once more. Smiling, Publius gently pulls Atimetus to one side and leans in to whisper in his ear.

– Brother. Atimetus. If you are in any way unkind to my sister I'll have your balls. Have you got that?

Atimetus looks shocked. – I...I'll treat her well, I swear.

– Good. Welcome to the family.

A squealing is heard and all turn to the right where two slaves approach, each carrying a piglet. The first is handed to the priest who stands behind the table. He holds the wriggling creature over the ceramic bowl. Gnaeus and Prima lift the knife as one and draw the blade across the animal's throat. Blood pours from the gash as though from a fountain. The piglet wriggles and squeals no more. The lifeless body is returned to the slave and the process is repeated with Cornelia and Atimetus. There is more applause. The gods have been appeased. Life has been sacrificed so that they may enjoy more of it, and more of its joys.

There will be a procession now. The groom must return to his home and await the arrival of his bride. Of course as Gnaeus is already home, Prima will leave by the back gate, walk around the block and then be carried over the threshold by two slaves, a peculiar custom you may be interested to hear has rather unsavoury origins. After the founding of Rome by Romulus, his men found they had a shortage of women so they attacked the people who lived in the surrounding lands who were known as the Sabines and simply took theirs, carrying them away in their arms to be their wives and bear their children. It became known as the Abduction of the Sabine Women. When the Sabines attacked the Romans years later the Sabine women coura-geously threw themselves between their fathers and their new husbands and forced them to abandon the battle, after which they united. And so now Gnaeus symbolically is carrying his bride over the threshold so they they, and their families will also be forever united.

But watch now as Atimetus makes his way through the crowd towards the atrium. He is interrupted by Restitutus and drawn to one side.

– Atimetus. I don't care who your father is. If you fail to honour Cornelia you fail to honour me – and my father. And I will have your balls if that happens.

Atimetus shivers. His testicles twice threatened with removal in as many moments, he replies in a trembling voice. – I promise I will.

Restitutus nods. Smiles. Turns away and collects a drink from a tray.

Atimetus turns. He spots Prima making her way directly towards him. She is smiling, and yet there is something in her eyes that acts as a warning. He is suddenly desperate to be gone. They exchange kisses on the cheek. Prima seems as happy as a bride should be.

– I'm glad I caught you before you departed.

– Yes. As am I. I am so pleased for you and Alleius Maius and grateful for this wonderful ceremony.

– You're welcome. And I hope you and Cornelia share a long and happy life. But take care that you play your part.

– I shall. I promise.

– Otherwise you'll have me to deal with.

She doesn't make any threats, but the smile vanishes and she fixes him with a cold stare. A moment later she is her happy self again.

Poor Atimetus. He has been denied any sexual release these past weeks. Banned from the bars and the brothels by his father. He had actually been looking forward to the wedding bed, even though it was just to be shared with Cornelia and not his favourite whore.

> *My life, my sweetheart, let's play for a moment,*
> *let's imagine that this bed is a field*
> *and that I am your horse* 143

But now all thoughts of sexual gratification have vanished. But don't worry for Cornelia's sake. Atimetus being who he is, the carnal thoughts will have reappeared within a week.

He leaves with his attendants. Cornelia follows soon after with hers and the crowds along the streets will by tradition shower her with small nuts and bawdy suggestions.

A young man cries out – Hey! You look like a girl who's hot for it, honey!'

Cornelia glances at him. 'That's funny, so do you.'

The crowd laugh and the young man reddens.

A wrinkled old woman calls out. – I hope he has the cock of Vulcan darling!

– I don't. I don't want to burn my lips.

The woman cackles loudly.

Another young man risks a jibe. – I hope your husband has what it takes to satisfy you, baby!'

– I was just going to say the same to you.

There are howls of laughter. The crowd adore her wit, and Publius and Restitutus watch her departure with pride, laughter and sadness. Their gazes drift briefly together in a rare shared moment.

Back within, Prima prepares to leave with Fortunata and raises her eyes to heaven. She whispers. – What nonsense, Fortunata. Out the back door, down a couple of streets and then back in the front door.

– The priest says it would be a bad beginning should you not enter the home of your husband in the proper fashion.

– Oh for Jupiter's sake. It's not like I'm a virgin of sixteen.

Fortunata laughs. – Hardly. But just think, when you return you may discover that your husband's dick is as large as his fortune.

Both women explode with laughter. Prima collects herself and heaves a sigh. – Let's get this stupid procession done with then.

We shall take our leave now. The ceremony is done.

The feast and celebrations will mostly take place tomorrow and the following day and possibly the day after that. You see, they cannot really celebrate in earnest until the consummation is complete. Which it shall be when the ladies reach their respective new homes. And we shall leave them to it. Not even I care to intrude on the intimacies of the wedding night.

SCAENA 45

Another cup of Setinan (wine) ₁₄₄

Here we are again. Consummations complete. The place brims over with happiness like an overfilled cup of wine. And there are many of those to be seen. People wander the house as though it was their own, in an out of all but a few bolted rooms, in search of merriment, or sometimes privacy. As you can see the atrium has been filled with benches and chairs, and here mostly you will find the 'lesser' guests. Not that they are bothered or insulted. Just to be invited to the wedding of this small town's richest man they regard as a great honour. And besides, they are very happy indeed to indulge in his generosity, not to mention his fine foods and wines. And from the look of things even Pompeii's finest citizens are prepared to throw their inhibitions to the winds. A man and woman wander past us, both unsteady on their feet. They are young, laughing, exchanging intimate gestures. A fat man at the far bench bellows at a slave to bring more meat. His plate overflows already, but gluttony is common at wealthy celebrations such as these. A woman in a gaudy green dress watches her husband as he slaps the backside of a passing slave girl. She twists his ear and he yelps. Then she laughs and they share a drink. It is all positively bacchanalian.

Let us move outside, where things might be a little calmer.

Well, it is a little quieter here at least, relatively speaking. Gnaeus had to dispense with the normal triclinium dining of course, due to the number of guests, so instead has had cushions arranged around the ground in the centre of the peristyle. He even had the fountain removed and the pond covered to create more space. And under the portico surrounding us you can see more guests seated at tables. Wine flows freely from jugs, served by thirty-two hired slaves. Where the pond usually sits is a life-sized bronze pig with metal bowls projecting from a saddle on its back. The trays are piled high with olives, stuffed dormice, sausages, eggs hard-boiled in red wine, stewed snails. The guests help themselves liberally from these, and also from the endless tray-bearing slaves that wander the garden with innumerable other delicacies, all cooked especially in a nearby thermopolium. Most of the guests lie prone upon the cushions, others wander about, inter-mingling, searching for company and conversation. Gnaeus and Prima of course lie at the topmost cushion, towards the rear of the peristyle. Atimetus and Cornelia are absent of course, as a similar gluttonous scene currently proceeds in the house of Tiberius Verus. To Gnaeus's right we can see his pretty daughter, Alleia, who looks a little bored, stuck as she is talking to Porcia, the ageing wife of Marcus Lucretius Fronto, who lies next along the line of cushions. You might recall he is the ageing, newly elected co-duumvir, the other co-duumvir being Marcus Epidius Sabinus. Poor Alleia cannot wait for the dining to conclude, which will allow her a little more freedom to wander and mix with the guests, one in particular, I should say. Fronto also doesn't look too comfortable, as he is trying to make idle chatter with Saenecio Fortunatus and his mistress, Noete. Poor

Saenecio is becoming very drunk and insists on trying to explain every detail of his plan to re-open the theatre, with the vague hope in his drunken mind that the wealthy duumvir might offer to foot the bill. Saenecio considers himself greatly honoured to have been invited to dine with the host, and to recline next to the duumvir. But in reality Gnaeus has no close family beyond his daughter, and Saenecio and Fronto are the nearest thing he could call friends. His business dealings have seen to that.

Health, as we drink skins of wine! [145]

On Gnaeus's left we have Prima's family, Publius and Restitutus. Their conversation is minimal, although there was an unspoken agreement to put their mutual antagonism aside for the duration of the wedding. It hasn't been a particularly enjoyable dining experience for them. They can agree on one thing: that they loathe eating like this because they've been used to dining at a table since they were children. Publius finds that lying interferes with the digestion and Restitutus continually spills his wine on to the cushion. Publius is further irritated that beside Restitutus, lies Prima's pronuba, Fortunata, and then Cominia Lucilla, making conversation with her impossible. He too cannot wait for the meal to end and the entertainment to commence.

– Publius, you've hardly touched anything. Are you feeling alright?

It is his mother. He believes that she has been watching his intake of food like a hawk since the day he was born.

– Oh, I'm fine, mother. Don't fuss.

Cheer up brother, you bear a look of misery [146]

Restitutus belches. Publius looks at him. He wonders if it is possible on this day to begin to build bridges.

– So, Restitutus, how goes the new work? Are you enjoying it?

Restitutus regards him a moment. – Nothing could be worse than working for you, brother. So in that respect, yes.

Publius sees that the wine has started to take effect on his brother. If he persists, he fears an argument will develop. He sighs and starts to rise.

– I'm going to the latrine.

He is gone before a reply can be offered. Restitutus follows him with his eyes, which now have a tinge of regret. He seeks to drown his minor attack of guilt with a gulp of wine, which he manages to spill down the front of his tunic.

– Really Restitutus, you're like a baby.

He is about to retort sharply when he realises it is Alleia opposite who has spoken. His face lights up.

Prima catches this. Gnaeus does not. She watches as her son begins an animated conversation with her stepdaughter. Prima turns to her husband, lowering her voice. – How is Restitutus progressing?

– You mean in his work? Well enough. He is a bright young man, good with numbers. Although he has trouble keeping his mind on things, so says Primus at least. A daydreamer. He should take a wife, if you ask me. Give him some responsibility. That will help focus him mind.

Prima glances at her son to her left and stepdaughter to her right. Restitutus mouths something silently and makes a gesture with his fingers. The girl explodes with laughter. Prima is bewildered sometimes by the interactions of the young. It is as though they speak a different language. Although this time she is certain that the exchange was of a bawdy nature.

– Gnaeus. What of Alleia? What plans do you have for her?

– Oh she is to become a priestess of Ceres in the spring and wishes to use some of the money her mother bequeathed her to help restore the Macellum.

Let me explain to you that Ceres is the goddess of agriculture and crops and so on. She's also a good friend of mine. And the Macellum is where many of those crops end up, it being the enclosed market place in the forum. It makes sense that a priestess of Ceres would undertake such a task.

– That's very admirable. You must be so proud. She is a wonderful girl. But what of a husband? Have you chosen anyone? I mean, she's seventeen now. She's long since reached the marrying age.

– I was considering Caius Lollius Fuscus. He plans to run for aedile. It would be a very beneficial alliance. They are an influential family on the council and I need all the help I can get now that Epidius is one of the duumviri.

> *Make Caius Lollius Fuscus aedile for looking*
> *after the roads and the sacred public buildings.*
> *Aselina's girls (prostitutes) ask this* 147

– Caius Lollius? That horrid little spotty man?

– You know him?

– I've seen him about the forum. He is a loud mouth and I've seen signs supporting his election written by whores.

Gnaeus smiles and shakes his head. – An old trick, probably done by Epidius. It serves to discredit the man. He's not so bad, Lollius, and it is the duty of a Roman girl to marry for her family's best interests.

– But really, Gnaeus! How could you subject your only daughter, your only child, to that?

Gnaeus considers what she has said. Prima nibbles on an olive, but her eyes continue to observe the exchange of banter between Restitutus and Alleia. Gnaeus is oblivious to this. Prima is scheming yet again. She wonders should she broach the possibility now. No. Best to wait. Subtlety will provide the best approach.

– I'll dwell on what you said. But for now, let us just enjoy ourselves.

Prima is sick from enjoying herself. She too is overawed by the extravagance and does not favour dining prone, but has decided to bear it. She has little choice. But she thanks Venus that her troubles are but paltry ones.

What has become of Publius, she wonders? He has disappeared. He doesn't seem to be enjoying himself very much. She sighs. The story of his life.

SCAENA 46

*What use to have Venus
if she is made of marble?* [148]

Watch as Publius is stopped by at least three other guests on his way to the latrine. He is sick of shaking hands and being congratulated on 'becoming a part of Alleius Maius's family.' He hates the sycophantic manner in which so many of the guests behave towards the man, as though he were a god. At least that's what he tells himself. In reality he is begrudging of Gnaeus's celebrity. He has the talents to merit greater fame, he believes, but has been denied the opportunity. Well, at least until now.

He walks to the corner of the peristyle, dodging tray-laden slaves emerging from the kitchen, which adjoins the latrine. The smells of a myriad of hot foods blending with the stench coming from the latrine makes him feel queasy. He hurries past the harried slaves.

There are two latrine holes cut into the white marble, and despite it being one of the few private houses connected to the town sewer, the stink does not seem to have been alleviated by any great measure. A young woman of about sixteen or seventeen occupies one of the latrines, dress hitched up, revealing thighs that appear plump when pressed against the cold marble. Publius can hear the sound of her pee hissing into the blackness below. She smiles at him. He tries to smile back, but he is reluctant to urinate in full view of her.

– Hello. You look nice.

She sounds intoxicated. He is about to return the compliment when he realises that telling her she looks nice while sitting on the latrine might not be the best idea.

She giggles. – Don't wait for me. I've drunk so much wine I'll be ages. What's your name?

He sighs. He wants to be gone. But he is badly in need of relief. – Publius.

Her face lights up as though Jupiter himself has appeared. – Publius! That's my husband's name! Well, sort of... Lucius Statius Publius Receptus.

– The ex-duumvir?

– That's him. I'm Sab...Sabina.

Her voice is slurred.

– He forbade me to drink. But I keep slipping away and sipping some.

– You've been doing a lot of sipping.

She giggles again. He can't wait any longer. He undoes the tangle of his toga and pees long and hard. She glances down.

– Not bad. Not bad at all. Better than the short little one my fat Lucius has. You know he fucks the slaves? Lucius. Thinks I don't know. Says I'm no good in bed. That I give a lousy blow-job. *Me!* And everyone thinks he's this great, honourable politician! The fat prick.

Publius reddens. – Really I don't think I...

Sabina, you're not very
good at blow jobs 149

She finishes, finally, he thinks. She climbs down and fixes her clothing. He is just about finished when he feels her hands on his back, then sliding around his sides. He hastily sorts himself and turns around. She begins to paw at his face.

– If only I could have a real man just once, instead of a fat pig.

Publius tries to pull her hands away. She persists, pressing her body against his. At that moment, Saenecio Fortunatus staggers in. He has to use the wall for support. He sees them. Smiles broadly.

– Your secret...is safe with me...my friend.

His voice is terribly slurred. Is anyone left here that is sober, Publius thinks. – It's not what you think.

Saenecio waves away his protests. – Do you think, do you think, think...that I might get the money from Gnaeus for the tea-tea-theatre? I think I'll ask him. What do you...think?

Saenecio has commenced his business as he says this. He sways to and fro, repeatedly missing the hole. Publius has still not shaken off the girl's attentions.

– Not today, Saenecio. It's his wedding feast. And you're drunk. Go home!

Publius turns to leave. Sabina follows at his heels, a hand clutching at the back of his toga. He emerges into the peristyle. He turns at the incessant tugging and the girl puts her arms around his neck and goes to kiss him. He is horrified. He pulls her hands away and steps back.

– Are you mad? Go back to your husband, you stupid child.

He turns and walks across the rear of the peristyle, almost clashing with Cominia as he rounds a column.

– Cominia. I'm so glad to see you!

She smiles. – Really? Nice little thing. What's her name?

– Who?

She smiles again. He looks over his shoulder, then back at her.

– That girl? She was drunk.

– All the easier for you then.

He is frustrated. Flustered. He takes her by the arm and leads her under the portico. There is an empty table. He sits. She sits also, after a moment's hesitation. – You can't think I was...

She shrugs.

– She was a stupid drunken girl. I didn't...

– You're a free agent.

He sighs. – Cominia...

– Yes?

He hesitates. – I don't want to be.

– What do you mean?

– A free agent. I mean I...I like you. I'd like if we could...

– We could what?

– Vulcan's balls! Why are you making this so difficult?

In the name of the sacred Lares,
I implore you to love me! 150

She stares at him. She is wondering the same thing herself. Many times in the past decade she has been to object of men's attentions, and she has rebuffed them one and all. Despite even liking a couple of them. Is she to do the same here? And she knows she more than likes this man.

Publius looks left. Looks right. Looks at her.

– Fine. I'd like if we could be more than friends. I really like you.

She remains silent. Her deepest fear is her deepest secret. She knows that the reason she has never let a man into her heart is that one day he may discover the truth there. And that could be her ruination. But must the fine life she has wrought for herself be one of loneliness?

– What is it? That you come from a noble family in Rome and that I was reared in a bakery in this little backwater? Is that the problem? Is that why you can be as cold as marble to me...to people?

– Who told you where I came from? And who says I'm cold?

He is relieved at least to extract a few words from her.

– Everyone that does business with you. And that was the rumour when you arrived here. Inherited money in Rome. A wealthy noble family. Were caught in the earthquake in Herculaneum.

– I don't wish to speak of my family.

– But did you...?

– Are you deaf?

She almost shouts this. A group of revellers nearby fall momentarily silent.

– I'm sorry.

Her voice softens. – I have reason to act as I do in business. But I did not think that you considered me cold.

He relaxes a little. He forces a smile. – Well, perhaps not cold. But a little chilly sometimes.

– How chilly?

He considers his response briefly. – Like when the icy winds cut down from Vesuvius in the dead of winter.

After a moment she laughs. He joins her.

He reaches across the table and takes her hand. His heart leaps when she allows it.

– Definitely not cold.

– Publius.

– What?

– If we are to be...together...you must promise never to ask me about the past. I am sure we all have memories we'd like to forget.

Publius thinks of his father's death. He recalls the guilt that accompanied the loss of his future being as great, if not greater than the loss of his father.

He nods. – I give you my word.

Cominia glances towards the now empty central space of the peristyle. Dark-skinned men in strange clothing are arranging elaborate decorations constructed of tree branches and feathers.

– The entertainment is about to commence.

Publius regards the large troupe for a moment. – Would you like to see it?

– Not really.

– Nor me.

– Then why don't we leave?

And they are gone.

SCAENA 47

Postpone your tiresome quarrels if you can,
or leave and take them home with you 151

The light begins to fade as a troupe of black-skinned African dancers take to the centre of the peristyle. There are twelve of them and they have been brought all the way from Rome at the cost of a centurion's annual wage. They have set up arches of wood bedecked with feathers and ribbons and a large tiger skin has been spread on the ground in the centre of the grass. The men's modesty is saved only by loincloths and the women wear only skirts of grass, their upper bodies unclothed. All wear colourful headdresses of dangling beads and more feathers. Small drums are beaten by rapid hands as the dancers writhe about, passing through the arches and chanting to the skies. The guests crowd into the portico all about to witness the spectacle.

I am sure it will be fascinating, but now that Publius and Cominia have made their excuses and departed, I wish to eavesdrop on some other guests, who I am sure will provide even greater entertainment.

Shall we seek out another blossoming romance? Look.

Towards the top of the peristyle, where the ceremony took place yesterday. A large table has been set and at it sit Gnaeus, Prima, Restitutus, Alleia and a few other notables, like the duumvir, Fronto, and the very rotund ex-duumvir, Lucius Statius Receptus, whose little wife Sabina made approaches to Publius in the latrine earlier. Lucius rises as we approach and walks towards the house, in search of his wife, perhaps? Restitutus is pleased to see him go. He was having difficulty enjoying a meaningful conversation with the fair Alleia.

The dancers continue to writhe before them, the drums beat, the chants echo about the building and beyond. The men have produced large wooden phalluses, the size of a forearm, and now they mime the pursuit of the women through the arches. The women leap across the tiger fur as though their feet are not permitted to touch it. Eventually a woman feigns capture by a man and he thrusts her on her back upon the skin, waving the phallus back and forth above her face. She grasps it, a sign of submission, and he pretends to fall upon her and mimic the act of sex.

Prima grimaces. – Gnaeus. It's very bawdy. I'm sure it cost a great deal, but I don't think I like it during our wedding celebration.

He shrugs. – My dear, it is the dance they do especially for weddings.

He then lowers his voice and brings his lips to her ear. – It is said to bring fertility and joy into the marital bed.

– I'm afraid I'm long past the fertility bit, Gnaeus.

– You never know.

Prima turns to her right – What do you think of it, Alleia?

The girl smiles. – I have seen such rites before, Mother. They do not shock me. Especially as these are African savages. But it is amusing.

Prima frowns. – I can't keep up with the opinions of young people.

Just then one of the female dancers bounds to their table in a crouch and waves a phallus before the faces of the bride and groom, before passing along the table and doing the same before Restitutus and Alleia. They laugh as the dancer turns away. Prima tuts.

Marcus Lucretius Fronto chips in. – In Augustus's day you might have been banished for having such a spectacle, Gnaeus. Not that I am criticising it. It is most entertaining. My dear Porcia here thinks it is wonderful. But I will side with Prima on this occasion.

Restitutus leans closer to Alleia. – Perhaps old Porcia will try the same dance with Marcus when they get home.

Alleia giggles. – Then I think his duumvirate shall be rather short.

The pair look at each other unspeaking, but smiling. Restitutus clearly believes her beautiful. And she is. A ripe peach waiting to be plucked. She considers him handsome and honourable, but given to stargazing, his mind always elsewhere, as though there is always some other place he would rather be.

Restitutus breaks the moment. – So, I hear you are to become a priestess of Ceres?

She becomes animated. – Yes, I shall have my studies completed and be initiated in the spring, should all go as planned.

– And does that really mean you can never ride a horse again, or leave the town for more than three nights or even touch metal?

She laughs. – I am not to be the pontifex maximus! I may do all those things, although I am restricted in some matters. I have to swear...

There is a crash that is heard even above the sound of the

drums. A metal tray has been knocked to the ground beneath the portico. Restitutus and Alleia look across to see Lucius Statius Receptus arguing loudly with his Sabina.

> *His neighbours beg you to elect*
> *Lucius Statius Receptus duumvir*
> *with judicial power, a worthy man.* ₁₅₂

He glances at Gnaeus, whose line of sight of the drama is blocked by a stone column. But the voices grow louder. Sabina is clearly very drunk, Lucius not far behind. He has taken her by the shoulders now and shakes her. Other guests move away from them, whispering to each other. Restitutus decides he cannot let the scene continue. He excuses himself and walks across.

He sees the ill-matched pair, one fat and middle-aged, the other drunk, but in the full flush of youthful beauty. What a waste, he is thinking.

– Lucius. This is my mother's wedding. Please lower your voices.

The man is red-faced, sweating profusely.

– My little whore wife has been flirting all day. She...

– Let us continue this elsewhere.

Restitutus takes each by the arm and gently encourages them towards the house, dodging around the guests. They reach the atrium, which is all but deserted. A male and female slave are busy striving to keep some level of tidiness, collecting empty cups, scraping the remains of food from plates.

Restitutus directs the couple to one of the side rooms off the atrium.

Let us follow.

Lucius is breathing heavily. Sabina weaves as she walks. As

they enter the room Lucius immediately faces her and begins to yell.

– You little bitch! I saw you acting like a whore with that garum trader!

Sabina finds some resistance amid the depths of her drunkenness.

– Me! You're only angry because I caught you fucking a slave.

– I was not!

– I saw her running from that room over there with her tunic hanging off. And then you emerged with your face the colour of cherries! Do you think I'm stupid?

– No! I think you're a drunken little tart!

Lucius abruptly swings his hand and catches her full in the face. She crumples to the ground bawling. Restitutus, who to this moment was an embarrassed observer, leaps between them, restraining the fat politician.

– Sir! Do not strike a woman like that! Have you no honour?

As he says this the memory of him doing precisely the same to Urbana comes to him. He pushes the thought away.

– She is my wife, and I'll strike her as I see fit! It is none of your business.

He goes to move around Restitutus to get at Sabina, who by now has struggled to her feet and clings to the back of his toga. He is too fat and slow to get past the younger man, who holds a hand against his chest.

– Have you no honour? Leave the girl be.

– Don't talk to me of honour. I am Lucius Statius Receptus, esteemed duumvir and...

His voice vanishes like water into the soil. His eyes grow wide as though he is witnessing some shocking event. *He is.* His hand reaches and clutches at his chest. It is the final willed move of a muscle his body will ever make. He crumples to the ground.

Restitutus stands there unmoving for a moment. Sabina peeks out from behind him. She is sobbing heavily.

– What happened?

– I don't know.

Restitutus kneels. Feels Lucius's pulse. Nothing. He turns his head and looks up at the man's seventeen-year-old wife. There is shock in his voice.

– He...he's dead.

Now Sabina's eyes roll. Her knees buckle. Restitutus makes an attempt to catch her. She knocks over a stool as she falls unconscious to the floor.

He stands there. His mouth is open. He wonders for a moment if this is a dream, the result of too much wine. But that is a denial of what he sees at his feet. He is frozen. His mind doesn't seem capable of decision.

A noise outside grasps his attention. A slave clattering a tray on a table. A slave, he thinks. Should he call for help? Alert all the guests to the death of one of their esteemed party? He imagines the chaos. No, but a slave can help. One in particular. He opens the door a fraction. A girl stands there bearing a tray piled high with waste food.

– You!

– Yes, Dominus?

– Do you know Primus? The head slave of this household?

– Of course, Dominus.

– Fetch him! Quickly! Go, now!

The girl drops the tray on the table and skitters off. He waits. The minutes pass slowly. He sits on the stool and looks at the two people at his feet. The girl breathes gently. The man lies there, mouth open, dead eyes staring at the ceiling, a small trickle of spittle on his chin. In the flickering lamp light Restitutus imagines he sees his lips quiver. Or perhaps it is his spirit departing his body. He shivers.

The door opens and Primus stands there. The balding slave takes in the scene, his lips parted. He quickly steps inside and closes the door.

– What happened? Did you kill them?

Restututus is startled from his immobility by the accusation. His personal honour is affronted, which of course he holds above all, or likes to pretend he does.

– No! Of course not! He was arguing with his wife and he suddenly dropped dead. It as though the gods reached inside him and plucked the life force from his body. She fainted.

Primus exhales in relief. He squats and examines the man's face.

– His heart probably gave out.

He glances at the girl. He half-chuckles.

– Surprised the fat fool lasted this long considering he took that little Venus to bed each night.

– How can you joke? We must inform Alleius Maius at once. But I wasn't sure if I should fetch him here or what I should do.

Primus stands and regards him. – We must do no such thing. Do you wish to ruin the wedding celebration?

– Are you mad? We cannot leave him here like this!

Primus shrugs. – Fine. Then you be the one to go and inform him. I am sure he will not be troubled that the tens of thousands he has spent on this day shall be wasted and all his guests forced to depart.

Restititus is silent.

– Come, help me.

– What are you doing?

– We must get the girl to one of the bedrooms upstairs.

– But what if she wakes up?

He laughs. – From the stink of wine, I'll wager all my worth she won't wake up until Saturnalia.

So they lift her. An arm around each shoulder they carry her outside. The three slaves in the atrium stare.

Primus snaps at them. – Get back to work! Have you never seen anyone drunk before?

He struggles to find a ring of keys beneath his tunic and then locks the door behind him. They cross the atrium to another room that holds a wooden stairwell. The girl moans every now and then, but her eyes remain closed to the world. An empty bedroom is located and they lie the girl down. Primus takes a blanket from a shelf and throws it over her. Restitutus stands there staring at her.

– I can't believe this.

– What is that?

He looks at Primus. – This! This! And that downstairs.

– You did nothing wrong. You have helped rescue your mother's wedding day celebration.

– No, I mean, I mean, I was just talking to him. Minutes ago. He was standing there before my eyes. And now...he's gone. How old was he? I know he was fat but he was only what, forty? Forty-five?

Primus shakes his head. Smiles. – Pluto's drum.

In case you are unaware, Pluto is the god of the underworld and he who judges the dead. Forgive my interruption...

– Pluto's drum? What is that?

– You've never heard it?

– What is it?

– A song we learned as children. Forgive me if I don't sing it. It went...

> *A number marks us each and every one*
> *And Pluto keeps the numbers in a drum*

Which, each moment, he pulls a number from
And when yours is pulled, your time is done

He places a hand on Restitutus's shoulder. – None of us knows the moment of our end. But come young Dominus, let us return to the celebration and enjoy ourselves. Just in case Pluto pulls out our number this night.

He laughs.

Resitutus doesn't join him.

He has suddenly begun to wonder how deep his number lies within the drum.

SCAENA 48

Once a man drinks, thereafter,
everything is confusion [154]

We are almost done here. But we shall linger for one final, small drama. Let's return to the peristyle.

The dancing and drums have ended. Thankfully. It will make conversations easier to overhear, for you I mean. Two citharista players and another two flautists now entertain the guests with sounds a little more soothing to the soul.

But there is still a great deal of raucous laughter, bawdy banter and swilling of wine. Prima has departed for the present. Fled to her room for some rest. She has never been to a celebration so prolonged or exuberant, or should I say excessive. But Gnaeus remains. He must, as the host. And he likes to think he is capable yet of indulging in some youthful revelry. Alleia also remains. She has taken little wine and besides, her youth sustains her. She now engages in conversation with a girl of her age at another table.

Restitutus returns in the company of Primus. Gnaeus sees them and raises a goblet of wine to toast them.

– Restitutus! To my fine new step-son! And to Primus! The finest slave in the Empire!

The others at the table join in the toast. Primus takes a goblet of wine from a slave and cheerily returns the toast. Restitutus struggles to compose himself, so Primus guides him to an empty table under the portico. He takes a goblet of wine and pushes it into his hand.

A drunken male guest under the opposite portico stumbles and falls across a table, sending plates and goblets crashing. His friends try to help the man, who laughs uproariously, back to his feet.

Gnaeus frowns. He beckons to Primus who leaves Restitutus to his thoughts and hurries across.

– Yes, Dominus?

– Some of the guests are becoming a little too rowdy. Where is Celadus? I wanted him here so that the sight of him would make the drunker ones behave.

– He did not show up today, Dominus. Nor yesterday. I haven't seen him since he came to you two days ago.

Gnaeus recalls the meeting when Celadus informed him that the task concerning Albanus had been carried out. He remembers the man looked pale.

– Send a boy to his apartment. Find out what's wrong.

– Immediately, Dominus.

Primus scurries away.

Marcus Lucretius Fronto yawns and leans to exchange a whispered conversation with Gnaeus. – I'm afraid my age begins to tell, Alleius Maius, and it is telling me I must be home to bed. My thanks and congratulations.

– And congratulations to you, Marcus Lucretius, on your election victory. I wish you luck in curbing the excesses of your co-duumvir.

He leans closer to Gnaeus. – Don't worry my good friend. I

may be an old man but I won't let that arrogant little shit push me around.

Gnaeus laughs. He is desperate to retain some influence in the council now that Epidius occupies one of the most powerful positions.

Fronto's seat has barely a moment to grow cold when Saenecio Fortunatus sits without invitation. He is very drunk. He claps the groom on the shoulder in an attempted display of comradeship, but the blow is too strong and Gnaeus flinches.

– Congratulations, my old friend. You have been too...too long a single...a single man. Lonely. That's what it is without a wife. Lonely. A man...a man...is not a man...is not complete... you know what I mean, don't you? My lovely Noete, now, she warms my bed, not to mention my...my...

> *Noete, my light, Greetings, greetings!*
> *Forever greetings!* [155]

– I get the idea, my old friend.

Saenecio is slobbering, leaning too close to Gnaeus, who is uncomfortable. – Saenecio, I think you've overdone the wine. Perhaps you should let Noete take you home.

He waves a goblet in the air, spraying wine across the table. – I'm fine. Fine. Just wannned to talk. Wannned to congrat....did I congratulate you already?

– You did.

Gnaeus looks about for Noete. He is in need of rescuing.

– But also, I wish to disgust...to discuss a matter. Important matter.

– Perhaps we should wait until....

But Saenecio has pulled a scrap of papyrus from his tunic and is struggling to unfold it on the table before Gnaeus.

– Look. Look at this.

Gnaeus sighs. – What is it?

The papyrus is a badly scrawled version of his plan to rebuild the theatre.

– It is the theatre, of course.

– The theatre?

– Yes. Been working with Herennius for months.

– Who?

– The arc...acr...architect.

– Saenecio. I think we should discuss this matter anoth...

Saenecio's voice rises. Becomes insistent.

– No, no! Hear me! Can be done with wood. Very cheap. And think of the glory. The honour. For you. To give Pompeii back its thea...theatre.

Gnaeus spots Noete. His eyes inform her that assistance is required.

– You could be the one, Alleius Maius! The one to give Pompeii back its be...be...beloved theatre.

– Made of wood? It might easily burn down.

– No. Herennius says. No. Won't burn. Special liquid.

– What?

– There is a...

Noete is suddenly behind him. She places hands on his shoulders.

– Saenecio, my dear. We must leave now, you have had enough. Apologies, Alleius Maius.

– Ah, my sweetness, my beloved...but don't ap...ap...apologise for me, my treasure. We're fine here, are we not, my friend?

– Perhaps you should go with Noete. It is very late now and...

He resists Noete's attempts to move him.

– Listen. Consider it. Consider it please, Alleius Maius.

– I shall.

Even in his state of extreme drunkenness he can hear the insincerity in Gnaeus's voice. He is standing now, but only just.

He suddenly thrusts his head to within an inch of Gnaeus's and grasps the fabric of his toga.

– The means to destroy him. It could be. Laughing stock. Is that not your desire?

– What are you talking about?

– Epidius! Epidius, of course. There's the play. Very good. I think. Not Plautus but good. Nor Aeschylus. But...

XII AESCHYLUS IB
(*Pompeii theatre token*) ₁₅₆

Saenecio totters backwards as his drunken legs give way and despite Noete's best efforts he lands on his backside with a thud. Gnaeus stands, calls for a couple of slaves to get him to his feet.

Noete is blushing with embarrassment. – I'm so sorry, Alleius Maius!

– Just take him home.

Primus and the others hoist Saenecio upright and proceed to haul him towards the house, Noete in close pursuit.

Gnaeus sits, shaking his head. He sees the scrap of parchment on the table before him and lifts it.

– Wooden theatre. Destroy Epidius. Drunken fool.

He laughs and crumples the papyrus in a ball.

I think we shall depart, although the revelry shall continue until the dawn for some. All very lavish, was it not? The dancing troupe from Rome, poets reciting Sappho and Herodas, two troupes of musicians, then there's the free-flowing wine, the endless displays of food, the small army of slaves, bronze pigs, awnings, specially purchased statues, enough flowers to fill a field.

To what end? To impress Prima? I think not. But it was designed to create an impression. All of these things state but one thing. Treasure me in your memory forever.

SCAENA 49

I beg you, my lady, by Venus Fiscia
I beg you not to refuse me. Remember me 157

There is Idaia, Celadus's girlfriend, hurrying along the dark street. She has just completed fourteen hours work in the fullery of Mustius. A large consignment of tablecloths and napkins arrived from the double wedding and Mustius insisted she remain at work until they were all trampled and rinsed. And now she faces a choice of returning home to Herculaneum or staying the night with Celadus. She hopes he does not take her arrival as eagerness to make love, as she merely wishes to share his bed and not his body. She is deathly tired.

A man calls out to her from an alleyway. She hurries her pace. It is not normal for a respectable girl to be upon the streets after dark. Three times during her short journey here she has been mistaken for a prostitute. She reaches the block of homes. She enters a narrow, pitch black hallway and feels her way along to the stone steps, which take her up to the door to Celadus's rooms. She knocks. There is no reply. She knocks harder. She hears a groan. The thought occurs to her that he has a whore in the room, and that all his sweet words to her were mere invention. But then she dismisses the notion. Perhaps he is just drunk. She knocks and calls out. No response. What is she to do, she wonders?

She hears footsteps from within. But it more resembles a shuffling. She hears a bolt drawn back. Then there is a thud. Her heart races. Idaia pushes against the door. It opens a hand's length but meets resistance, spilling out lamplight. She shoves harder. It gives enough for her to squeeze through. She looks down.

Celadus lies at her feet. His eyes struggle to remain open. Her tiredness is forgotten. She yells. – Celadus!

Idaia falls to her knees and cradles his head in her lap. Her gaze drifts down his tunic to his left side, where it is stained with dried blood.

– You're bleeding.

He groans. His forehead is bathed with sweat.

– I must get the physician.

His hand clasps her wrist and his eyes struggle to open.

– No. No physician.

– But I...

– No! Fools. Butchers.

She looks about. The cot. She is thinking she must get him on to the cot.

– Come! You must get on the bed.

He shakes his head.

– You must!

She tries to lift his massive shoulders.

– Try!

He grunts and struggles on to his side. He pushes a hand against the floor and forces himself up, and with Idaia's help, rises sufficiently to tumble on to his back on the narrow bed.

His eyes close. His breathing becomes shallow. He has fallen from consciousness. Idaia looks about and finds a knife. It is the same one with which Albanus inflicted the wound. She cuts at his tunic and tears it piece by piece from his body. The wound horrifies her. It is small, no more than the length of her small finger, but it oozes pus and all about it is a garish purple.

Idaia uses pieces of the tunic to cleanse it as best she can, and to cool his brow. And then she sits with his hand in hers and watches his chest rise and fall. She wonders how many times since I, Lucina, brought Celadus into this world that breath has filled his lungs. And then she prays that it shall be many millions more before it finally ceases. Tears spring to her eyes and as they roll down her cheeks, she falls asleep.

Three hours have passed now. The first slivers of dawn's light begin to pierce the small window above them. Celadus stirs yet. He looks about, believing it a dream that his Idaia had come to his room and spoken to him. But there she sits by his side, her hand still clutching his, her eyes closed to the world. Celadus's head pounds and his breath wheezes. His wound sends sharp stings through his body. He has seen men in this condition before. He knows what awaits him. But with the sight of Idaia, he finds his voice.

– Idaia.

She stirs at the tug of his hand upon hers. Her eyes open and she is shocked anew at the sight of him.

– Celadus!

She throws her face against his and kisses him gently. He places his hands around the back of her head and stares at her.

– My Idaia.

– What happened to you? Why did you not get the physician?

His voice is weak. – It does not matter what happened. I did not realise it was so bad. I fell asleep. Almost a full day. When I awoke, I could barely move. And by then it was too late.

– Too late? No, we must...

He holds her fast as she goes to pull away. His voice is soft.

– Listen, Idaia. There are things I must say. Before I leave you.

Her tears fall on to his face.

He continues through laboured breaths.

– Our time together was so short. And yet it was the sweetest of my life.

– Celadus, we must get help. We can...

– Shhh, girl. I am beyond help in that way. But please help me to ease my passing.

She sobs as she speaks. – What do you want?

– Hear me first. You gave me, for the first time in my life, a reason to hope. A reason to live. The glory I once enjoyed, it was nothing. Nothing compared to what I felt when you were with me. I hear you call my name and it fills me with joy more than thirty thousand voices screaming it in the arena. I am glad I escaped the arena, not because I was afraid to die, but so that I could die here, in your arms.

Idaia sobs uncontrollably. He pulls her closer. Her face presses against his.

– In the corner, under the table there is a loose brick in the wall. Pull it out.

Idaia gets up, wipes her face with her sleeve.

– What is there?

– Do it. The brick. There is little time.

Idaia gets to her knees. She reaches in a finds the loose brick beneath the table. She pulls it out and fishes in the darkness of the hole with her hand. It clasps a large purse. It is heavy.

– Give it to me.

She sits on the edge of the cot. He takes it and upends its contents on the stool by his bedside. She is startled to see perhaps fifty gold aureii lying there, along with almost as many denarii. Some scatter around the floor. She also sees a small gold ring lying among the coins.

– Where did you get all this?

– I was granted the prize money in my last fight in the arena. And Alleius Maius has paid me well.

– And what is this?

She lifts the ring.

– I wish I could say it was mine and that I could make a gift of it to you. But it is not. Put ten aurei and the ring aside and return the rest to the purse.

Idaia does what he requests. She holds the purse to him, but he clasps his hands around hers.

– I want you to have this.

– Me? I can't.

– Please. You cannot refuse a man about to leave this world. Get out of that fucking fullery. Please make a life for yourself. Find a good man. Please promise me you will do this.

Idaia is sobbing again. She embraces him once more, kisses his lips.

He smiles. – Nothing in the afterlife could compare to your kiss.

She sits up, looks at the remaining coins on the stool.

– What of the rest?

– I must ask you to do a task.

– Anything.

A fit of coughing assaults him. His entire body shudders. The coughing subsides but he moans as a wave of pain passes through him. Idaia clutches at him. She bathes his faces, holds the water to his lips. Eventually, his body calms itself. She can see he is struggling to speak. He wheezes heavily.

– Idaia. Listen to me. Take the money and the ring and travel up the mountain to the farm of Caecilius Felix. Two miles beyond the Vesuvian Gate. Take the track to the right when the paved road ends. Give him the money and the ring. Tell him Celadus the Thracian returns the ring as promised and makes a gift for an injustice done. And that he is more honourable and courageous than most I have fought in the arena. Can you recall all of that?

– Caecilius Felix. Yes. But who is he?

– It doesn't matter. Will you do it?

He takes her hand. Her eyes are red. She lays her head on his chest.

– I promise. Oh Celadus.

He stokes the back of her head. – Don't cry, Idaia.

She whispers through her sobs. – I will erect such a monument to your memory. You will never be forgotten. Celadus the Thracian, the greatest gladiator in Pompeii.

– No. Fuck it! No monument. Don't waste money.

– But I wish...

He squeezes her hand. – I wish only to live on in your memory. No more. None of the rest matters. And I wish...

– What?

– That I could have given you a child.

He falls silent. She remains with her face pressed against his body. She can hear how his breath struggles to enter and leave his lungs. She can also hear his heart beat. After a time it grows irregular. Her sobs subside and her eyes close.

– Idaia.

She hears her name. She opens her eyes. His breathing has ceased. His heart is silent. She lifts her head and looks down upon him. He stares into emptiness. She closes his eyes and presses her lips against his. She sits there in silence until a knock on the door draws her attention.

She walks across and opens it. A young slave, a male youth, stands there. He stares at her red, tear-stained face for a moment before speaking.

– I am looking for Celadus. His Dominus Alleius Maius has been seeking his presence since last night.

– Tell him that Celadus the Thracian is no more.

SCAENA 50

Come in, o lovers! [159]

Publius and Cominia encounter a woman on the street as they pass the crossroads shrine at the junction of the Via di Nola and Via Stabiana. The torch Publius holds gives only a hint of her features, as her face is swallowed in the darkness of her hooded cloak. She glances their way but ignores them. They both assume her to be a prostitute, given the late hour, but her clothes are not the garish fabrics favoured by girls of the night. She hurries away in the direction they are going and eventually disappears ahead of them into the darkness.

That was Idaia, hurrying from her workplace to the home of Celadus and a night of brutal loss. Yes, I have taken you back a little in time. Perhaps to a less tragic scene.

They walk the near-empty streets mostly in silence, and their only other encounter is with a tramp, who begs some coins from the doorway in which he lies curled. They reach Publius's home. He pauses and looks at her.

– Will you come in?

– Yes. For a while, perhaps.

Publius takes a sliver of wood from the box mounted by the doorway and lights it from the torch, which he extinguishes and drops. He opens the door and proceeds to illuminate the way ahead with the help of a lamp, leading Cominia into his tablinum and then along the narrow passage that leads to the peristyle.

Cominia is struck by the silence. – Your home is empty now.

Publius stops beneath the colonnade. He looks at the upper floors and then back to her face.

– My mother, brother and sister all gone in a few short weeks of each other. Not to mention two of my slaves. And soon the bakery will be silenced too. Twenty days and I shall be without a home or a means of support. And instead of men baking bread this place will be filled with the sounds of whores moaning.

He sighs, as does Cominia.

– Epidius's plan disgusts me.

– I'm forgetting myself. Shall I fetch you some wine?

She shakes her head. – Some water perhaps.

– I'll be a moment.

He disappears into the shadows. Cominia sits at the table beneath the colonnade and stares at the dark peristyle garden. Her head turns at the sound of cups clattering in the house and she spots some words scratched upon the wall behind her. She lifts the lamp nearer, straining to read the tiny letters.

> *You're just like the sweet apple*
> *Reddening at the highest branch*
> *And missed by the apple pickers*
> *No they did not miss you!*
> *They just couldn't reach so high.*

Cominia smiles. She continues to hold the lamp to the poem

as Publius returns bearing a jug and two cups, which he sets on the table.

– Your work?

– Oh, that was scratched there long ago. Before my father's time.

– Looks more recent.

– No.

– Someone was in love.

– Someone borrowed it from Sappho.

– He made a good choice then.

He sits and pours the water. He looks about the peristyle.

– This has been my home all my life.

– Will you miss it?

He considers. – Only my home, not the bakery. But even then...

– It provided for you.

– And for others. And I will miss the company of the men. I have no idea how I will support myself. At least before Epidius started interfering, the business provided a good income. As for writing plays...

He shakes his head.

– What?

– I sometimes think I am on a fool's errand, me being the fool.

– Saenecio Fortunatus doesn't think so.

He laughs humourlessly. – Him and his mad schemes. He's turning into a drunken idiot. Did you see him today? Nobody takes him seriously anymore.

They return to silence. Cominia sips her water, watching him from the corner of her eye.

– What about my proposal?

– You mean investing in the inn?

She nods.

– Tell me, and answer honestly, did my mother tell you I had some money I could invest and suggest that scheme.

She is a little annoyed. – No. Absolutely not! The idea just occurred to me. It is purely a business arrangement. That's all I seek.

– Purely business.

– Yes.

– So I would treat you as any partner in business, with a cold financial eye.

– As I would you.

– And the aim is purely to make money.

– Isn't every investment?

– I'll think about it.

He regards her for a time, meeting her eye. Even in the dim light the sight of her makes his heart race. She lowers her gaze from his.

Publius cannot bear it any longer. He stands. He reaches and takes her hands, pulling her gently to her feet, their faces inches apart.

She whispers. – What?

– I would prefer a different arrangement.

– What do you mean?

– One not so cold.

Before she can respond he presses his lips against hers. She instinctively draws back, but only for a moment. They kiss as their arms lock about each other. Finally they break and Cominia rests her head against his shoulder.

Who is it that spends the night with you in happy sleep? Would that
it were me!
I would be many times happier 160

He whispers. – Cominia. I lied to you.

– When?

– I did write that poem on the wall. Not two days ago. That day we argued in the theatre, when we met Saenecio. I felt so angry with myself that I might have done anything to drive you away. I came back here, drank some wine and scratched that into the paint.

She smiles. – So you only did it when drunk?

He strokes her hair. – Only with love. Come.

He leads her into the house and up the stairs to his cubiculum. He closes the door. And we shall not pass beyond it. At least not for a while.

Now, the hours have passed. I have taken you within. Dawn approaches. Dim light creeps through the window that overlooks the Via del Venditores, where you will find the Inn of Cominia Lucilla. Your eyes will adjust soon.

And there lies the lady, awake, staring at the ceiling, the blanket pushed down to her waist. She glances at Publius, by her side, his back to her. He breathes gently in contented sleep.

A mere five hundred paces away, in a street just off the Via Nola, Celadus the Thracian has just breathed his last.

But let us talk not of endings.

Cominia allows a finger to trace the outline of the swan-shaped birthmark below her breast. And then she slides her hand across her belly and rests it there.

She wonders what might be happening within her and she wonders what twists and turns and obstacles lie on the road ahead.

She prays.

And I hear her heartfelt prayers.

END OF LIBER 1

PLEASE LEAVE A REVIEW

If you have enjoyed The Lost Voices, I would really appreciate it if you would leave a brief review.
Independent authors or those with small publishers simply do not have the resources to compete with the big publishing houses in terms of advertising or influencing reviewers in the press and other media. So we rely on you, dear reader, to help balance the scales a little.

Reviews help authors enormously in
bringing their work to a wider audience.

To leave a review simply visit your point of purchase on Amazon and scroll down to 'Customer Reviews'.
Thank you!

FREE BOOK

Sign up to my mailing list at
colincharlesmurphy.com
and receive your completely free copy of
'What Have the Romans Ever Done For Us?'

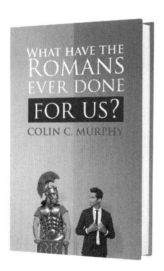

'What Have the Romans Ever Done For Us?' is a fascinating, informative and entertaining look at how our modern lives have been affected by the influence of ancient Rome. The Roman State existed for 1,000 years and encompassed a vast area spanning Europe, the Middle East and Africa. Their influence was so enormous that we can still feel their presence, although most of the time we aren't usually aware of the fact. This engaging book explores thirty different ways in which we can still sense the spirits of the ancients in today's world...and often in ways that many people will find very surprising!

Visit Colin C. Murphy's website at colincharlesmurphy.com where you can discover more of his critically acclaimed books including:

- The Lost Voices Trilogy
- Boycott
- The Priest Hunters
- Fierce History

It is completely free to sign up and you will never be spammed by me and you can opt out easily at any time.

ACKNOWLEDGEMENTS

A NOTE OF THANKS

I am indebted to my brilliant editor, Helen Falconer, for her invaluable input into the storylines and characters, not to mention her patience! My copy-editor Marian Broderick is also extremely deserving of my gratitude for correcting innumerable errors, both grammatical and narrative-wise. And my deepest thanks also to Donal O'Dea who patiently listened to my incoherent briefings on the cover yet still managed to produce what I regard as three wonderful designs. And lastly my gratitude to Brendan O'Reilly his skilful and speedy typesetting.

Researching this book was a very large labour of love and I gratefully acknowledge the following sources of information and inspiration. 'Pompeii: The life of a Roman Town' by Mary Beard is the first stop for anyone wishing to grasp the minutiae of daily life in Pompeii. 'Discovering Pompeii' by Natasha Sheldon also provided many valuable insights. For technical historical detail no book rivals 'Pompeii – A Sourcebook' by Alison E. Cooley and M. G. L. Cooley. Among the countless other works I employed were 'Pompeii: A Guide to the Ancient City' by Salvatore Nappo, 'Roman Life in Pliny's Time' by Maurice Pellison and 'Pompeis Difficile Est - studies in the political life of imperial Pompeii' by James L. Franklin, Jr.

My online research was assisted enormously by the extensively detailed pompeiiinpictures.com. Another great source of information was pompeionline.net, as was archive.org, which provided access to a myriad of older texts such as 'Pompeii – Its Life & Art by August Mau.' And lastly a mention for ancientvine.com for its technically brilliant digital recreations of the Roman world.

ABOUT THE AUTHOR

Colin C. Murphy is the author of the critically acclaimed historical novel **Boycott**, and has also penned numerous historical non-fiction books including his recent book about Roman influence on the modern world '**What Have The Romans Ever Done For Us?**'. Formerly a multi-award winning creative director of an advertising agency, he quit the business a decade ago for his first professional love, writing. He has had a fascination with the ancient Roman world since childhood, and has researched extensively in Rome, Pompeii, Ostia Antica, El-Jem in Tunisia, Arles in France and Italica in Spain. He also has a love of history in general, and is particularly interested in exploring the lives and stories of the past's lesser known, yet no less fascinating, men and women. When not writing or travelling he enjoys hill-walking, and has climbed every mountain in Ireland. He lives in Dublin with his family.

CAST OF CHARACTERS

AD62

Household of Publius

- Publius Comicius Restitutus: Baker, would-be playwright.
- Vibius Restitutus (Restitutus): Publius's brother, baker, teacher.
- Prima: Their mother.
- Cornelia Quieta (Cornelia): Their younger sister.
- Publius senior: Prima's first husband.
- Vivia: Slave woman.
- Narcissus: Head baker.
- Epaphroditus: Freedman.
- Servulus: Slave, mule-keeper.

Household of Gnaeus Alleius Nigidus Maius

- Gnaeus Alleius Nigidius Maius (Gnaeus/Alleius Maius): Wealthy businessman, former politician)

- Traebia Fortunata: His first wife.
- Pomponia Decharcis: His mother.
- Alleia: His daughter.
- Primus: His chief slave.
- Sarra: A slave.
- Euxinus: A bar owner and wine trader.

Others

- Lucius Caecilius Jucundus: Wealthy banker.
- Marcus Epidius Sabinus (Epidius): His assistant.
- Faustilla: His slave.
- Perari: A smuggler and thief.
- Saenecio Fortunatus: Theatre director.
- Rufus Caesennius Paetus: Formerly wealthy Roman exiled to Pompeii.
- Severina: Rufus's wife.
- Cygnia: Their beautiful young slave.
- Mariona: Elderly innkeeper
- Chrestus: Mariona's slave.
- Primigenius Gellianus: A Roman soldier in Herculaneum.

AD72

Household of Publius

- Publius: (Baker/would-be playwright)
- Restitutus: His brother.
- Cornelia: Their sister.
- Prima: Their mother.
- Vivia: Elderly slave.
- Staphylus: Teenage slave.

- Narcissus: Head baker.
- Hermeros: Slave of Publius.

Associated with household:

- Matrona: A friend and maid of honour of Cornelia.
- Fortunata: A friend and maid of honour of Prima.
- Balbus: Fortunata's husband.
- Quieta: A young girlfriend of Staphylus.
- Curtia: Publius's first wife (deceased)

Household of Gnaeus Alleius Nigidus Maius

- Gnaeus: Businessman.
- Alleia: His daughter, now a woman.
- Primus: His loyal slave and chamberlain.

Associated with household:

- Caius Cuspius Pansa: Ex-politician and flamen or priest.
- Lucius Statius Receptus. A middle-aged politician and philanderer.
- Sabina: His very young wife.
- Marcus Lucretius Fronto: A senior politician and friend of Gnaeus.
- Epaphroditus: A perfume seller.

Household/Inn of Cominia Lucilla

- Cominia: Owner.
- Daphnicus: Head slave.
- Felicia: Slave.

- Satura: Slave.
- Methe: Slave.

Associated with household:

- Chrestus: African freedman. Carpenter/wood carver, loyal friend of Cominia Lucilla.

Household of Marcus Epidius Sabinus

- Marcus Epidius Sabinus (Epidius): Politician/Wealthy businessman.
- Faustilla: His loyal slave, assistant. Also runs his money-lending enterprise.
- Apelles: His slave and chamberlain.
- Felix: A teenage slave.

Associated with household:

- Albanus: Ex-gladiator, Epidius's enforcer.
- Ampliatus Pedania: Albanus's sidekick.
- Titus Suedius Clemens: Accountant sent by Rome to investigate illegal property theft.
- Fabia: His wife.
- Aemilius Celer: A sign-painter.
- Fructus and Florus: His two assistants.
- Anteros: An actor hired by Epidius to impersonate a senator.
- Circinaeus: An actor hired by Epidius to impersonate a senator.
- Aulus Suettius Certus: Ex-politician and business partner of Epidius. Co-owner of brothel.
- Stronnius: A legal notary.

Household of Tiberius Claudius Verus

- Tiberius: Wealthy wine merchant and ex-politician.
- Atimetus: Adopted son of Tiberius.
- Vibia: His deceased wife.
- Ianuarius and Valentinus: His deceased children.
- Appulei: His slave and chamberlain.

Bar of Verecundus

- Verecundus: Bar owner.
- Urbana: A prostitute in the Bar of Verecundus.
- Eutychia: Urbana's lover and a slave in another household.
- Restituta: A prostitute and bar tender for Verecundus.
- Marcus Lucretius Fronto: A senior politician and friend of Gnaeus.

Household of Cosmus and Epidia

- Cosmus: A retired merchant.
- Epidia. His kindly wife.
- Aufidius: Their young slave.
- Aeneia: A slave and nurse.

Associated with theatre

- Saenecio Fortunatus: Theatre director.
- Noete: Saenecio's young wife.
- Servulus: A public slave who tends to the theatre.
- Herrennius Crescens: An architect.

Others

- Celadus: A former champion gladiator, employed as an enforcer by Gnaeus.
- Pomponius Faustinus: Owns gladiator school, former owner of Celadus.
- Pugnax: A defeated gladiator.
- Caecilius Felix: A farmer on the slopes of Vesuvius.
- Helvia Marcia: Caecilius's wife.
- Mustius: A fullery owner (unseen).
- Barca: Brother of Mustius. Works in fullery.
- Idaia: Fullery worker, girlfriend of Celadus the gladiator.
- Attice: A prostitute.
- Mola: Bar owner.
- Harpocras: A passing slave.

GLOSSARY OF ROMAN TERMS

- **Aedile:** One of two annually elected magistrates responsible for public buildings, streets, markets and so on.
- **Apodyterium:** Changing room in a bathhouse.
- **As:** Copper coin of little value; one quarter of a sesterce.
- **Atrium:** Foyer or reception room in a Roman house.
- **Aureus:** Valuable gold coin equal to 25 denarii.
- **Basilica:** Building where town business was carried out.
- **Barbarian:** Term used by the Romans referring to people who lived outside the Roman Empire.
- **Caldarium:** Hot room in a bathhouse.
- **Cannae:** Site in southern Italy of the greatest military defeat in Roman history, which occurred in 216 BC. There were between 70,000 and 80,000 Roman casualties at the hands of Carthaginian general Hannibal.
- **Censor:** Government official who took the census. He

also was responsible for public morality and some of the government finances.

- **Census:** Taken every five years, it provided a register of citizens and their property upon which taxes could be levied.
- **Cithara:** Multi-stringed musical instrument similar to a lyre. The most popular musical instrument of ancient Rome. It is also the source of the word 'guitar'.
- **Compluvium:** Square or rectangular opening in the roof of the atrium toward which the roof sloped and through which the rain fell into the impluvium.
- **Cornu:** Long, tubular, metal, musical wind instrument that curved around the musician's body.
- **Cubiculum:** Small bedroom.
- **Denarius:** Silver coin equal to four sesterces. To put this in context, an average legionary in the army earned about 250 denarii per annum.
- **Duumvir:** One of two annually elected senior magistrates and the leaders of local government, responsible for the administration of law and order, collecting taxes and awarding contracts for public buildings.
- **Duumvir Quinquennial:** The highest-ranked position of local government, elected every five years and in place of the duoviri. They had the responsibility over the census and could remove or add people to the Ordo Decurionum, award public contracts and make legal judgements.
- **Exedra:** Room in a house or temple used for conversation and formed by an open or columned recess and furnished with seats or benches.
- **Falernian:** Wine produced on the slopes of Mount

Falernus on the border of Latium and Campania. It
was the most renowned wine of ancient Rome.
- **Forum:** Large open space in the middle of a town.
- **Frigidarium:** Cold room in a bathhouse, normally a
  cold plunge pool.
- **Fullery:** Laundry.
- **Garum:** Fermented fish sauce.
- **Hypocaust:** Roman central heating system,
  comprising a heated hollow space under a building's
  floor, allowing warm air to circulate into the rooms
  above.
- **Impluvium:** Small pool in a house, usually in atrium
  floor for collecting rainwater, positioned directly
  beneath the compluvium (see above.)
- **Lararium:** Shrine to the household spirits.
- **Lares:** Household spirits.
- **Latrina:** Latrine.
- **Legionary:** Infantryman in Roman army.
- **Ludus:** Gladiator training school.
- **Lupanare:** Brothel.
- **Macellum:** Market area or building.
- **Odeon:** Theatre or building used for musical shows
  or poetry readings.
- **Ordo Decurionum:** The local legislative body
  consisting of one hundred members; in effect the
  local council.
- **Palaestra:** An area for wrestling or a gymnasium or
  athletic training ground.
- **Palla:** A loose outer garment worn outdoors by
  women, usually consisting of a large rectangle of
  fabric draped over the body, and often worn as a
  hooded cloak.
- **Peristyle:** Internal garden in a house, usually

colonnaded.

- **Praeco** (pl: praecones): A herald or 'shouter'.
- **Pronuba:** A Roman bride's matron of honour.
- **Scaenae frons:** Elaborately decorated permanent architectural background of a Roman stage, often two or three stories in height, with three entrances on to the stage.
- **Sesterce:** A large brass coin worth quarter of a denarius. A legionary in the army earned approximately 1000 sesterces per annum.
- **Setinan:** A local Campanian wine.
- **Spectacula:** Amphitheatre.
- **Stola:** Long, loose female tunic that extended to the feet.
- **Strigil:** Metal object used to scrape off sweat and dirt.
- **Stylus:** Metal pen for scratching words into wax on wooden tablets.
- **Subligaculum:** Underwear, usually in the form of a simple loin cloth.
- **Tablinum:** Office or living room for the head of a Roman household.
- **Tepidarium:** Warm room in a bathhouse.
- **Thermopolium:** Informal café.
- **Toga:** Loose flowing outer garment used on formal occasions, made from a single piece of cloth and covering most of the body but leaving the arms free. Its colour and design depicted a person's social status.
- **Triclinium:** Formal dining room of a Roman house.
- **Tunic:** Loose garment, typically sleeveless, belted at the waist and reaching the knees.
- **Venalicius:** A slave-seller.
- **Vestibulum:** Entrance hall of a Roman house.
- **Vulgus:** The common people.

LAYOUT OF A WEALTHY
ROMAN HOUSE

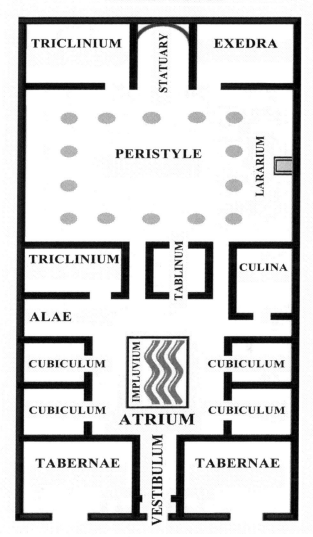

ROMAN HOME TERMINOLOGY

- **Alae:** Windowed alcove often used for the display of ancestral death masks.
- **Atrium:** Large, high-roofed central court where guests were greeted.
- **Cubiculum:** Bedroom.
- **Culina:** Kitchen.
- **Exedra:** Recess or room used for conversation, often containing a raised stone bench.
- **Impluvium:** Rectangular pool in the centre of the atrium directly beneath opening in the roof (compluvium) that admitted rainwater.
- **Lararium:** A shrine to the household spirits.
- **Oecus:** Hall or large room, usually with columns around the interior.
- **Peristyle:** A garden or courtyard usually surrounded by a roofed colonnade.
- **Tabernae:** Shops in rooms rented out by the house owner.

- **Tablinum:** The office of the paterfamilias usually opening on to the atrium and peristyle.
- **Triclinium:** A formal dining room with couches on three sides.
- **Vestibulum:** The narrow entrance hall to the house, also known as the fauces.

ROMAN CURRENCY AND COINAGE

Emperor Augustus (reigned 27BC–AD14) introduced a series of currency reforms that were largely still in use in AD79. Below are the currency terms referenced in this book.

- **Quadran:** Low-value bronze coin, the smallest unit of currency.
- **As:** Copper coin worth four quadrans. A loaf of bread cost 2–4 as.
- **Sesterius:** Large brass coin worth four as. A Roman legionnaire's annual pay was about 1000 sesterce.
- **Denarius:** Silver coin worth four sesterce.
- **Aureus:** Gold coin worth twenty-five denarii.

PRINCIPAL ROMAN DEITIES (GREEK EQUIVALENT IN BRACKETS)

Apollo (Apollo)
The Archer; son of Jupiter and Latona, twin of Diana; god of music, healing, light and truth.

Ceres (Demeter)
The Eternal Mother, goddess of agriculture, grain, women, motherhood and marriage.

Diana (Artemis)
Daughter of Jupiter and Latona, twin of Apollo; goddess of the hunt and the moon.

Fortuna (Tyche)
Goddess of luck and good fortune.

Isis
Originally an Egyptian goddess, worship of her spread throughout the entire Greco-Roman world. She was the goddess of marriage, fertility, motherhood, magic and medicine and she

was beloved by women in particular, but also widely
worshipped by slaves and freedmen.

Juno (Hera)
Goddess of women and childbirth. (Lucina is believed to be an
'aspect' of Juno.) She was the wife of the god Jupiter.

Jupiter (Zeus)
The chief Roman god.

Mars (Ares)
God of war, guardian of agriculture, embodiment of virility,
father of Romulus, the founder of Rome.

Mercury (Hermes)
God of profit, trade, travel, trickery and thieves, guide of dead
souls to the underworld.

Minerva (Athena)
Goddess of wisdom and war strategy.

Neptune (Poseidon)
God of the sea and freshwater.

Pluto (Hades)
God of the dead and ruler of the underworld.

Priapus
A minor fertility and horticulture god, he was popular in
Pompeii and multiple representations of him were discovered.
Depictions of him feature an enormous phallus.

Venus (Aphrodite)

Goddess of love, beauty, desire, sex, fertility and victory.

Vesta (Hestia)
The virgin goddess of the hearth, home and family.

Vulcan (Hephaestus)
God of fire, volcanoes, metal work and the forge, maker of the weapons of the gods.

GRAFFITI REFERENCES

Graffiti and Inscriptions in
The Lost Voices - Liber I

Unless otherwise stated, the graffiti is from Pompeii. Although all of the graffiti existed, much of it has been lost thanks to exposure to the elements and incompetence during early excavations. However a complete record was kept of each graffito and inscription, although some of the precise locations of such were in many cases not recorded. CIL refers to Corpus Inscriptionum Latinarum, which is a comprehensive collection of ancient Latin inscriptions begun in 1853 in Germany. AE refers to L'Année Épigraphique, which is a French collection of ancient Roman epigraphs, founded in 1888.

- 1) Graffito in the basilica.
- 2) Inscription on an amphora.
- 3) Pompeii Graffito. Ref. CIL 04 02386a.
- 4) Pompeii Graffito. Ref. CIL 04 01234. (4a Graffito on a column in the House of Pascius Hermes.)

- 5) Graffito on a wall in Ostia.
- 6) Graffito in the basilica.
- 7) Graffito on the Vico del Balcone Pensile.
- 8) Graffito in the House of Fabius Rufus.
- 9) Pompeii graffito. Ref. CIL 04 10246e.
- 10) Pompeii graffito. Ref. CIL 04 08241.
- 11) One of multiple entries in the wax tablets of Lucius Caecilius Jucundus, Pompeiian banker.
- 12) Pompeii graffito. Ref. CIL 04 4764.
- 13) Painted sign on the Via Consolare.
- 14) Pompeii tomb inscription, ref. CIL 0410.01078.
- 15) Tomb inscription in the Porta Nocera necropolis.
- 16) Graffito in the House of Neptune in Herculaneum.
- 17) Graffito in the House of Fabius Rufus.
- 18) Graffito on a wall in the small theatre (Odeon).
- 19) Graffito in the town of Trebula Mutuesca.
- 20) Pompeiian funerary inscriptions.
- 21) Graffito on a wall in the lupanare (brothel).
- 22) Pompeii graffito. Ref. AE 2000, 00300.
- 23) Graffito in the basilica.
- 24) Painted sign on the Via Dell'Abbondanza.
- 25) Inscription on a herm, or grave marker, east of the amphitheatre.
- 26) Graffito on the wall of the lupanare.
- 27) Inscription on a tomb outside the Stabian Gate.
- 28) Notice painted on the exterior wall of a house near the amphitheatre.
- 29) Inscription on a stone near the entrance to the amphitheatre.
- 30) Graffito in the triclinium of a house on the Vicolo dei Centenario.
- 31) Painted sign near the home of Epidius Sabinus.

- 32) Pompeii inscription. Ref. CIL 04 00998.
- 33) Painted sign on the Via Nola.
- 34) Inscription in the Herculaneum Gate necropolis.
- 35) Graffito on a column in the Julian-Claudian gladiator barracks.
- 36) Graffito on a column in the gladiatorial ludus.
- 37) Pompeii graffito on a tomb. Ref. CIL 04 02508.
- 38) Graffito in the Inn of the Muledrivers.
- 39) Graffito in a niche of a public shrine near the large palaestra.
- 40) Graffito on the Vicolo del Vettii.
- 41) Pompeii graffito. Ref. CIL 04 02218a.
- 42) Graffito on the Via Del Vesuvio.
- 43) Graffito in the Vicolo del Balcone Pensile.
- 44) Graffito in the House of the Mosaic Atrium, Herculaneum.
- 45) Graffito in the Grand Taberna, Herculaneum.
- 46) Graffito in the basilica.
- 47) Graffito outside a Pompeii bakery.
- 48) Graffito in the Inn of Gabinianus.
- 49) Pompeii graffito. Ref. CIL 04 02119.
- 50) Graffito in Pompeii bar. Ref. CIL 04 1830.
- 51) Graffito in the lupanare.
- 52) Pompeii bar graffito depicting a soldier holding up his cup to a barmaid.
- 53) Pompeii graffito. Ref. CIL 04 01383.
- 54) Graffito in the basilica.
- 55) Graffito on the Via di Nola.
- 56) Painted sign on a street near the forum. Ref CIL 04, 00575.
- 57) Painted sign by the crossroad junction beside the Stabian Baths.

- 58) Graffito in a Herculaneum bar.
- 59) Graffito in Forum Novum.
- 60) Graffito in a house on the Via Dell'Abbondanza.
- 61) Inscription in Porta Nocera necropolis.
- 62) Graffito on a tomb near the Porta Nocera.
- 63) Graffito on the Vico degli Scienziati.
- 64) Graffito in Via del Teatri.
- 65) Written on a dish recovered in Pompeii.
- 66) Graffito in the courtyard of a house on the Via di Castricio.
- 67) Graffito in a bar near the Vesuvian Gate.
- 68) Graffito on the Via Dell Abbondanza.
- 69) The remains of a legal document found in Herculaneum, detailing the sale of a young slave girl.
- 70) Graffito in the peristyle of the House of Caecilius Jucundus.
- 71) Graffito on a wall near the amphitheatre.
- 72) Graffito in the House of Curvius Marcellus.
- 73) Graffito in a house on the Vicolo del Menandro.
- 74) Graffito on a wall on the Vicolo di Balbo.
- 75) Graffito on the House of Cosmus and Epidia on the Vicolo di Lucrezia.
- 76) Graffito on the House of Cosmus and Epidia on the Vicolo di Lucrezia.
- 77) Pompeii graffito. Ref. CIL 10 08048,17.
- 78) Graffito in a Pompeii bakery.
- 79) Notice painted in the large palaestra.
- 80) Inscription in the Necropoli di Porta Nocera.
- 81) Inscription in the Necropoli di Porta Nocera.
- 82) Inscription in the Necropoli del Fondo Azzolini.
- 83) Pompeii graffito. Ref. CIL 04 Suppl. 2 3376.
- 84) On three amphorae found in the Bar of Euxinus on the Via di Castricio.

- 85) Graffito in the House of the Centenary.
- 86) Graffito in the peristyle of the House of Mars and Venus.
- 87) Graffito in the basilica.
- 88) Graffito on a column in the gladiator barracks.
- 89) One of multiple entries in the wax tablets of Lucius Caecilius Jucundus.
- 90) Inscription in the Porta Nocera necropolis.
- 91) Graffito in the bar of Innulus and Papilio on the Vicolo del Citarista.
- 92) Graffito on a wall in the Via della Fortuna.
- 93) Graffito in a house on the Vicolo di Cecilio Giocondo.
- 94) Graffito on Via dell'Abbondanza.
- 95) Graffito in the courtyard of the Forum Baths.
- 96) Inscription in the Porta Nocera necropolis.
- 97) Graffito on the tomb of Mamia near the Herculaneum Gate.
- 98) Painted labeling on an amphora.
- 99) Graffito in the Eumachia building.
- 100) Graffito in The Samnite House, Herculaneum.
- 101) Graffito on a wall on the Vicolo di Balbo.
- 102) Graffito in the lupanare.
- 103) Graffito in the basilica.
- 104) Painted sign on the Vicolo del Vettii.
- 105) Graffito in the amphitheatre.
- 106) Graffito in the House of Hercules.
- 107) Graffito in the House of the Telephus Relief, Herculaneum.
- 108) Inscription near the Herculaneum Gate.
- 109) Inscription in the peristyle wall of the House of Triptolemus.
- 110) Inscription in the Porta Nocera necropolis.

- III) Graffito on a wall near the Nolan Gate.
- II2) Graffito in the large palaestra.
- II3) Inscription in Forum Novum.
- II4) Graffito on the wall of a house near the Stabian Gate.
- II5) Graffito on a column in the gladiator barracks.
- II6) Graffito in a small room on the Vicolo di Eumachia.
- II7) Graffito in the lupanare.
- II8) Graffito in the lupanare.
- II9) Graffito in a bar.
- I20) Graffito in a room in the House of Caecilius Lucundus.
- I21) Graffito on a wall in Ithaca.
- I22) Graffito in the basilica.
- I23) Graffito in the House of Holconius.
- I24) One of multiple entries in the wax tablets of Lucius Caecilius Jucundus, Pompeiian banker.
- I25) Graffito on a wall near the Nolan Gate.
- I26) Graffito in an inn on the Vicolo di Eumachia.
- I27) Graffito in the House of Jason, just off the Via Stabiana.
- I28) Greek graffito in the lupanare.
- I29) Graffito in the Via Degli Augustali.
- I30) Graffito above a bench near the Marine gate.
- I31) Inscription on the tomb of Mamia in the Herculaneum necropolis.
- I32) Pompeii graffito. Ref. CIL 04 8056.
- I33) Pompeii graffito beneath a picture of two fighting gladiators. Ref. CIL 04 00538.
- I34) Mosaic on the vestibulum floor of a house on the Vicolo dei Lupanare.

- 135) Graffito on the wall of a neighbour of Marcus Epidius Sabinus.
- 136) Pompeii painted electoral sign. Ref. CIL 04 03516.
- 137) Graffito in the Grande Taberna, Herculaneum.
- 138) Graffito in the Bar of Astylus and Pardalus near the Palaestra.
- 139) Graffito outside the House of Marcus Lucretius Fronto.
- 140) Inscription on pedestal in the forum.
- 141) Graffito in the home of a pottery merchant on the Via dell'Abbondanza.
- 142) Pompeii graffito. Ref. CIL 04 8473.
- 143) Pompeii graffito. Ref. CIL 04 01781.
- 144) Graffito from a bar near the Herculanean gate, beside a drawing of a man holding out a cup to a slave.
- 145) Graffito in the Tavern of Aticto.
- 146) Pompeii graffito. Ref. CIL 04 03298.
- 147) 'Negative campaigning' on the exterior wall of the House of Marinaio.
- 148) Graffito in the basilica.
- 149) Graffito in the peristyle of the House of the Silver Wedding.
- 150) Graffito in the atrium of a house on the Via dell'Abbondanza.
- 151) Graffito in the House of the Moralist.
- 152) Painted electoral notice on the House of Primigenia.
- 153) Graffito in the basilica.
- 154) Graffito on the wall of the bar of Salvius.
- 155) Graffito in Eumachia building.
- 156) Inscription on bone theatre token, of which over

one hundred have been found. Aeschylus was a famed Greek playwright.

- 157) Graffito in a house just off the Via di Nola.
- 158) Graffito on a wall in Rome.
- 159) Graffito in the Via dell'Abbondanza.
- 160) Graffito in the House of Fabius Rufus.

Printed in Great Britain
by Amazon